BLOODLINES
OF
EDEN
BLUEPRINTS

M. BRYAN HAGGARD

Bloodlines of Eden: Blueprints

© 2025 M. Bryan Haggard

This is a work of fiction. Names, characters, organizations, places, and incidents are either products of the author's imagination or used fictitiously. Any resemblance to actual persons, living or dead, or to actual events is purely coincidental.

For information, contact:

mbryanhaggardauthor@gmail.com

ISBN (Paperback): 979-8-9936525-0-4
ISBN (eBook): 979-8-9936525-1-1

Cover art by Rica Graphics
Edited by Marni McRae

Printed in the United States of America
1st Edition

For everyone who has ever been told they were not enough. For the ones who carried scars instead of praise, yet still rose to face another dawn.

To my mother—whose quiet strength taught me to endure. To my daughter—my butterfly—whose faith in me never faltered. And to the friends who stood beside me when the night was long, reminding me that every story worth telling begins in the dark.

This book is for you.

Keep going. You are enough.

In loving memory of Brutus — forever the good boy.
The loyal companion who inspired a legend.

You may be gone, but your spirit lives on in these pages.

If Brutus dies... we riot.

Contents

CHAPTER ONE

The Man in the Purple Robe

O ne whisper. A voice so quiet, the world didn't notice. One whisper lit the spark of a prophecy, setting in motion events that would echo across the ages. It all began with a single boy. A shepherd standing alone in a valley, with nothing but faith and a stone.

David left Saul's camp, the rough linen of his shepherd's clothes clinging to sweat-damp skin, scratchy and worn like the burdens he carried. A tattered belt sagged at his hips; its pouches swollen with tools from a life he'd tried to forget but never left. His fingers found the familiar strap of his sling—the one weapon that had never failed him, the only one he still believed in.

He made his way to a brook nearby.

Kneeling at the water's edge, he plunged his hands into the icy stream. The cold bit through his skin while the current pulled like it wanted to keep a piece of him. He sifted through jagged stones, the gray rock catching the dim light, their rough edges scraping raw against his fingers. A low, gravelly sound filled his ears. Then he felt it. His hand stilled, a sudden chill running up his arm. Fingers curled around the smooth weight of a stone, and he lifted it into the morning light.

The stone was cool against his skin, smooth and perfect. Its polished surface shimmered, worn by centuries of patience and running water. He turned it, the familiar weight a comfort in his hand. It seemed to whisper of destiny amidst the chaos.

David scanned the water, his breath shallow, each stone a prayer answered. A perfect circle here and a glint of gray there. Unlike the rough gravel in the brook's bed, they felt chosen. The tightness in his chest eased with each collected stone. His heartbeat steadied by the fifth.

Cold water nipped at his ankles as he gripped the stones— every motion driven with quiet purpose. They were more than weapons; they were his answer. He stood in the stream, the chill rooting him, fingers curled around the stones, clinging to faith and destiny.

As he looked up, his eyes widened, and a chilling wave of paralysis washed over him.

On the far bank, a man stood as still as carved stone. A robe of deep purple fluttered at his sides, the gold trim catching the light with every faint ripple. The hood obscured his features, but the chilling aura surrounding him was unmistakable. A chill ran through David, but it wasn't fear that caused him to tremble. It was recognition of something holy.

The man in purple shifted, the deep fabric of his robe slipping back to reveal a pale hand. He extended a single finger across the valley. This wasn't a warning or a command. It was a declaration— quiet but undeniable, like a secret finally brought to light.

David's breath caught in his throat as he stared across the brook at the man in purple.

His grip on the stones tightened until his knuckles ached, the cold weight anchoring him to reality. He turned toward Saul's camp, heart racing, expecting to find someone else in the man's sights—a hidden warrior or an unseen hero. Instead, confusion filled the camp. Fear gripped the soldiers, who moved slowly with downcast eyes, caught in their own personal dilemmas.

He turned back around, half expecting to see nothing, like it had all been a dream.

But the man in purple still stood there, frozen in place. Cloaked in mystery, like a silent sentinel.

David stared, pulse thundering.

Who are you?

The question echoed inside him, louder than any war drum.

How could he have known what was coming?

With a slow, almost ceremonial gesture, the man in purple lowered his arm.

David inhaled deeply, the air filling his lungs as he fortified himself. The man in the purple robe had offered no words; his silence was enough. David knew the actual fight wasn't with the figure across the brook. It was with the giant who waited across the valley... and the fear that already ruled this camp like a second king.

He turned around and started walking toward the valley.

As David moved through the camp, the air turned foul, thick with the stench of urine, vomit, and something worse... despair. His nostrils flared, his stomach tightening at the smell of men whose courage had emptied from their bodies long before the battle began. A soldier sat slumped against a cart, muttering nonsense to no one, his voice paper-thin. Another gripped his sword like a drowning man clings to driftwood, knuckles bleached and breath coming in panicked bursts.

A low hymn drifted from somewhere deep in the ranks, heavy with surrender. It tolled like a funeral knell, rolling through the lines with a hollow weight. David kept walking. Each step was deliberate, heavy with the weight of the camp's fear. He could feel it pressing in on him, wrapping around his ankles, whispering to him through their stares. Eyes followed him—some pleading and some resentful, but most were hollow.

Amid the mournful hum of the hymn, a voice pierced the air.

"You there!" A soldier lurched forward from the huddled ranks. His rigid knees refusing to yield, locking him in place as fear coursed through him. His face, slick with cold sweat, trembled, a harsh canvas of fury and panic.

"What are you doing, boy?" he said, his voice cracking like something brittle under pressure. His hand shook as he pointed, the other clenched white-knuckled around his sword's hilt like a lifeline. "You're no warrior. You're not even grown! That giant will snap you in half and scatter your bones across this valley. You think this is bravery? You think this is salvation? All you're doing is marching us into slavery. You're signing our chains with your pride!"

The words didn't just land; they echoed like a spark in dry brush.

Around the camp, heads turned. A few muttered, the beginnings of agreement rumbling in their throats. One man spat into the dirt, scoffing loudly enough to be heard. Another man folded his arms across his chest, his eyes narrowed and his jaw grinding against words he didn't dare let loose.

Most said nothing. Their silence pressed in on David as dozens of faces turned toward him, some filled with doubt and some with anger but most with fear. He felt their expectations like a weight across his shoulders. Waiting to see if he would break.

David stood firm, the soldier's words striking him like lashes across the back—each syllable raw with doubt and each breath a wound. His fingers tensed, then curled into fists, nails biting into flesh until pain became his anchor. He said nothing.

Words couldn't reach the men drowning in their own despair. So, he gave them silence. He met the man's glare with something deeper—a quiet fire of conviction. When the soldier's eyes broke from his, dropping to the ground, David continued his march.

One slow step after the other. Each footfall cut through the rising tension like a blade through taut rope.

Around him, the camp turned hostile. Jeers cracked the air as curses spat from clenched jaws. Stones thudded near his feet and against his shins, sharp and stinging. Still, he didn't break stride. His steps remained measured and unhurried. He knew he was walking toward something greater than a battlefield.

The strap of his shepherd's bag bit into his palm, the leather slick with sweat. Beads rolled down his brow, stinging his eyes and pooling at the corners of his mouth. But his breath was steady, despite his chest tightening with the pressure of holding everything in.

An apple—half-eaten and bruised—struck his shoulder with a wet smack. It fell to the dirt, forgotten. David didn't flinch. He kept his eyes fixed forward, refusing to return the hatred and refusing to carry what wasn't his.

Their fear wasn't his burden.

He kept walking.

Each step became an act of defiance—not against them but against the fear that ruled them. His fingers tightened, the stones in his bag pressing like silent witnesses to his resolve. *Stay the course. Stay the course.* The mantra repeated in his mind.

After passing through the last stretch of the camp, David paused at the edge of the valley. He caught movement in his periphery—off to the right, half-shrouded by distance and sunlight.

It was the man from the brook.

Still cloaked in violet, the gold inlays of his robe catching in the breeze like dying embers. He extended his arm again. One finger still pointed toward the shadow that awaited David across the valley floor.

David's stomach churned.

How does he know? Has he always known?

He blinked, steadying his breath. The man in purple didn't speak or move. David felt the weight of his eyes—or perhaps the weight of the silence between them—and turned toward the battlefield once more.

As he descended, the valley appeared, a silent stretch of land where he could hear the echo of his breath. The tremor tore through the valley, as if a massive beast was stirring beneath the surface, and a giant emerged from the far ridge, his mass blotting out the horizon. Sunlight bent around him. Each step pounded the ground like a warning, the tremor humming up through David's bones. The giant's armor groaned with each step, a grinding clash of metal on metal.

Bronze scale armor draped from his shoulders, plates shimmering like molten fire in the midday sun. The coat alone could've buried a man. His gauntlets were massive and dented, marked by the weight of history and looked as if they could crush boulders, while greaves wrapped around legs like living pillars of ironwood.

The giant's face came into view. A bronze helm too large for any mortal, its edges etched with the scars of countless battles shadowing it. Beneath its rim, his eyes burned like dying coals, and his lips curled into a sneer of pure contempt. The helmet caught the sun, reflecting menace instead of brilliance. Every jagged line radiated violence.

David stopped for a breath. His hand brushed the stones in his pouch. They felt... small, but somehow, his heart didn't.

Upon seeing David step into the valley, the giant scoffed and bellowed across the distance. "Who is this... child that dares stand before Goliath? Do you not know who I am, little boy?" His voice thundered through the valley, loud enough to rattle the bones of the men in the camp behind David.

David didn't flinch. He took a breath, his voice steady and sure. "I am David, servant of the Creator. I accept your challenge— to decide this conflict not with armies but with one fight."

Goliath laughed, throwing his head back. "You?! You are the champion they send?" He pointed at David, grinning like a beast before the kill. "I've crushed animals larger than you beneath my heel. I'll end this fast—and let your bones feed the dogs."

Goliath turned his back to David, as if he wasn't worth facing.

Over the giant's massive shoulders, something shifted—and David's breath caught. A sword unlike anything he'd ever imagined came into view.

The blade rose almost as tall as a man but moved with the grace of light. It shimmered, carrying the glow of first dawn, a radiance profound enough to feel like breath before creation. Every edge shimmered with silver and soft white. Morning woven into metal. Along its length, etched patterns moved like they were shaped by some celestial force. They flowed like stardust, symbols too ancient to name, and carried the feeling of beginnings and

7

endings; of promises kept... or broken. The hilt gleamed with a warm, golden light, sunlight trapped in crystal, its glow calm and its design flawless—as if it had never known a hand unworthy. Where strength met grace, a perfect balance. The grip invited but did not beg. At the pommel, a sphere turned, its core a churning storm of light and shadow. It offered no warmth or comfort, only a gleam that whispered of power untouched by man. It didn't shine upon Goliath; instead, it made him appear darker, larger, and more terrible. A sword crafted by the Creator—capable of ending worlds or beginning them anew.

Goliath turned to face him, his armor creaking like the groan of an ancient gate as he approached, stopping not far from David, close enough to see the menace in his eyes.

"So," he said, "you want to know who I am, little man?" With a grunt, Goliath dropped to a seated position. The ground trembled beneath him, a quake of mass and menace. He motioned for David to step closer, and when he spoke again, his voice rolled low and thunderous, echoing off the stone walls of the valley. "I am Goliath, the first Nephilim—part angel, part man. Born of the old order. We were sent to oversee your kind, to lift you from the dust and teach you order. What have you done? You squandered it. You took beauty and turned it into ruin." He leaned forward, casting a long, suffocating shadow over David. "I serve no king or prophet. I serve the one who sees the truth of your failure. He is the Right Hand, and I am his judgment. His answer to the sickness of mankind." His eyes narrowed, voice tightening to a low growl. "Yet here you are... standing. Why? Why aren't you afraid? Do you not see what's coming? Do you not understand what I can do to you?"

David's heart thundered in his chest, but he didn't step back. Out of the corner of his eye, he caught a flicker of violet. The man in the purple robe stood still—arms crossed, eyes fixed on David. He nodded once, slow and deliberate.

David turned back to the giant. "I am not afraid," he said, his voice steady, "because my faith does not rest in what I see but in the One who sent me. He has already given me my answer." He raised his hand and pointed with conviction—toward the robed figure.

Goliath followed his gesture. When his eyes landed on the man, something shifted. A ripple of fury passed over his face. "Him?" Goliath roared. "His illusion is your hope?" He shot to his feet, the full force of his height blotting out the sun. His sword came down from his back in one seamless motion, the surrounding air shimmering as it moved.

"Enough of this! Let's end it."

With a roar, Goliath stormed forward, closing the distance in thunderous strides.

He swung with all his might.

David ducked, but the force of the blade's arc tore the air open. The shockwave slammed him to the ground, dust exploding around him. The sky spun as his thoughts scattered.

He blinked, and his vision cleared. Goliath was already recovering, stomping closer, sword raised again, his steps hitting the ground like earthquakes.

David glanced to his left, where he saw movement. The man in the purple robe. He stood still, untouched by the surrounding chaos. Without urgency, he raised his hand, first pointing at Goliath, then David. No words. A simple gesture, deliberate and final, like a prophecy spoken without breath.

Something cracked inside David. A roar escaped his throat, raw and unfiltered. It echoed off the cliffs like thunder ripped from flesh. His voice shredded, blood flecked his lips, but still he screamed. A cry of terror transmuted into resolve.

His hand plunged into the shepherd's bag, and panic consumed David as he found only one stone in his pouch. His fingers curled around it. It was heavier than it should've been. Pulling it out, the stone shimmered like black midnight, its polished surface absorbing the surrounding light. As he turned it over in his palm, he saw a distorted reflection of his own face.

This isn't what I brought with me.

This was no simple stone. It pulsed with a quiet gravity, as if it carried the weight of a thousand forgotten wars.

Goliath barreled toward him, each stride pounding closer, the giant's shadow stretching wider with every thunderous step.. The ground shuddered, and David's faith quivered. His hands trembled. For the first time... he doubted.

His breath rasped, a ragged sound in the heavy air. Sweat stung his eyes, blurring the world around him. His knees, weak and trembling, threatened to buckle.

The thought ran through his mind. *Am I enough?*

He squeezed the stone tighter, anchoring himself to its impossible weight. As he shut his eyes, a prayer escaped his mouth that only his heart could hear. When he opened them again, the world slowed down.

Goliath moved like a storm in slow motion. Every breath was a drumbeat, and every heartbeat was a countdown.

David slipped the stone into the sling. His arms shook, but the motion steadied him. The rhythm of the swing—around and around—became a mantra, a tether, and a lifeline.

Each revolution sped until the moment was perfect.

Then David released the missile with all the might he could muster. The black stone cut through the air with a sound like the tearing of the universe. The moment stretched, and time fractured.

After what felt like an eternity, he heard it.

CRACK.

The sound split the valley like lightning as the stone struck with finality. Goliath's helmet tore free, spinning through the air like a falling crown, before slamming into the earth with a metallic clang.

David stood frozen, chest heaving, the sling limp in his trembling hand. Goliath's frame rocked—a swaying tree before the fall. Then the giant crashed to the ground with a shuddering groan that shook the valley.

A cloud of dust exploded on impact, swallowing Goliath's body.

Silence followed. Pure, suffocating silence.

The jeers stopped. The hymns died, and the wind fell still.

David's legs wobbled beneath him.

He thought to himself. *Did I...?*

He took one step, then another, each one shaky, as though the ground might split beneath his feet. His heart thundered, each beat echoing with the terrible stillness of what followed.

He approached the body with caution, blood pulsing in his ears. The valley that had felt endless moments ago now felt like a tomb.

Three words repeated in his mind over and over. *Please be dead.*

He reached the giant, now a broken mass of flesh and armor. A single, ragged hole marked the center of Goliath's forehead—blackened at the edges with the stone embedded deep. Blood pooled around his head, the smell of iron filling David's nose.

Thoughts swirled in his mind. *One more breath from him, and I'm gone.*

He nudged the massive arm with his foot—nothing. No twitch or growl. No last curse. He let out a gasp that turned into a sob and fell to his knees beside the corpse.

It's over.

With trembling limbs, he climbed atop Goliath's chest and raised his arms—because he didn't know what else to do.

For a moment, there was only silence. Then the valley exploded into a roar behind him, building into a crescendo.

It began with one shout, then dozens. The camp behind him erupted in an avalanche of cheers and weeping. Some fell to their knees. While others ripped helmets from their heads and threw them into the air. Grown men screamed like children. The hymn returned, but this time it was wild, off-key, and out of rhythm yet full of life.

David tried to smile, but his eyes were still locked on the valley.

The man in purple. Where did he go?

He scanned the ridge, the hill, and the brook. The purple robe was gone.

Who was he? Why did he choose me? His stomach twisted. *Was I chosen?*

Shaking his head, David climbed down and approached Goliath's sword, laying half-buried in the dirt. He knelt beside it and reached for the pommel with both hands. The moment his skin contacted it, a sudden surge of energy coursed through him. He experienced a burst of memories that weren't his own—of battles fought before time began, stars being named, and of judgment and mercy intertwined like threads in a tapestry.

He gasped and staggered back, blinking hard.

The villagers—cheering, laughing, and crying—didn't notice. They saw only a boy reach for a weapon too great for him and wrap it in cloth handed by a trembling elder.

David's hands shook as he secured the wrapping, still reeling from the daze that had come over him. When he turned back to the crowd, something shifted in his voice. It was hoarse and raw yet strong.

"Tonight..." he shouted, raising the sword-wrapped bundle high, "we celebrate victory and our freedom!"

The crowd erupted again, a wave of joy crashing over disbelief.

Somewhere unseen, the man in the purple robe walked away from the valley—his work, for now, complete.

Later that night, David sat at the head of the banquet table, surrounded by the sounds of revelry. Laughter bounced off the timber walls, hymns rose like smoke to the rafters, and the scent of roasted lamb and spiced ale hung heavy in the air.

David raised his cup high, his voice booming with forced joy. The people cheered for their champion and for their freedom.

Inside him, something was already slipping.

The ale burned as it went down, but it didn't fill the hollow space inside his chest. He drank again, chasing silence where there should have been celebration. When he stood to refill his cup, the motion was unsteady. The ground beneath him felt crooked, and the surrounding faces warped like reflections on disturbed water.

A chill crept across the banquet hall.

At the far edge of the room, away from the firelight and praise, stood a lone figure cloaked in violet. The purple robe was unmistakable. David blinked.

Not here. Not now.

He moved toward the figure slowly, staggering slightly. Voices called to him, but they were muffled—like echoes in a dream. As he drew near, the sounds of celebration fell away, swallowed by a deepening silence.

When he reached the figure, David stopped.

The man didn't speak at first. He leaned in toward David, his face hidden in the shadows. When the words came, they weren't loud but more like an eerie whisper. "You've won the battle but not the war. Through your bloodline, the prophecy will rise—and so will those who seek to end it. Protect the sword and the stone until I come back for them."

David felt a chill run through him. The weight of those words pressed into him, heavy as Goliath's shadow.

The sword... the stone...

He didn't speak. All he could muster was a nod.

As the weight of the words settled on him, the man in the purple robe disappeared into the shadows.

David turned, as if waking from a dream. The music and laughter returned like a wave crashing in his ears, but the warmth was gone. All he felt was the tremble in his fingertips.

He set his mug down, the metal hitting the wood with a sharp clang. The room had not gone quiet, but something shifted. A hush settled beneath the noise. A ripple flowed beneath the joy.

David stared at the spot where the man in purple had stood, then turned to a nearby servant and spoke with a voice that came from a place deeper than fear. "Fetch me the giant's sword."

Several heads turned, and conversations paused. For a moment, even the fire seemed to flicker.

David's grip tightened on the table.

"This... is only the beginning."

CHAPTER TWO

Voyage into the Unknown

"This is only the beginning," the whisper echoed through time, through empires, and into glass halls lit by fluorescent suns.

Centuries had passed since the man in the purple robe last stood on soil soaked in blood. Now, he watched as a new battle loomed: one not fought with stones and slings but with questions that tore through the sky.

The halls of NASA bore the weight of a prophecy—one spoken in a forgotten tongue and recorded in no scripture. It hadn't promised war. It had promised reckoning.

From an age of swords to one of satellites, humanity had changed. But the fear was the same. It lived within the whitewashed walls, in the nervous energy of scientists, and in the ever-present hum of machines that never slept.

It was a calm, normal day outside, but inside, at the NASA Space Center, the atmosphere was tense. Scientists shuffled between rooms with papers clutched in their hands, their voices a mix of hurried conversations and exasperated sighs. Stained mugs crowded every desk, and the faint smell of burned coffee wafted through the air as an intern rushed out the door, clutching a list for yet another caffeine run.

The giants of this age wore no armor, but the questions they posed were no less daunting. Could humanity face what lay beyond the stars? Would they triumph—or would the spark of progress, born of a prophet in purple instead of a scientist, ignite something far more dangerous, waiting in the dark between stars?

The air outside the NASA briefing room hung heavy, a palpable tension that contrasted with the nervous hum of fluorescent lights overhead and the distant, rhythmic buzz of printers.

Hank stood like a condemned man waiting for the gallows. His tie twisted in his hands, damp with sweat, while his foot tapped out a jittery rhythm on the tile floor.

"I... I'm not sure I can go through with this," he said, voice trembling like a wire in the wind.

Jeff looked at him, and despite his steady posture, the slight tug at his cuff revealed a hidden nervousness. "Take a breath. Don't improvise. Stick to the script, and no one will even notice your nerves."

Hank pressed his fingers to his temples, blinking through the fog in his mind. "This is the biggest announcement in history, and I'm supposed to lie through my teeth to the entire world."

Jeff's tone sharpened. "We're not lying, Hank. This is a scientific voyage."

"Is it?" Hank shot back. "Because it feels like we're opening a door to something we don't understand. That man... the one in the robe—he said this would be the beginning."

Jeff didn't respond right away. He turned toward the hallway window, the outline of the launchpad a dim silhouette through the glare. "You have kids, Hank?"

"Yeah."

"So do I. Let's hope this buys them a future."

From down the hall, a low chime echoed. It buzzed in Hank's ears like a warning. He swallowed hard, his throat dry, and turned toward the briefing room. The soles of his shoes squeaked on the tile, each step too loud in the silence and each breath caught somewhere between his chest and his throat.

Behind him, Jeff remained frozen, eyes still locked on the horizon. "We've done our part. The rest is in the Creator's hands," he said. Jeff's eyes followed Hank into the briefing room, but his thoughts were elsewhere—drifting backward in time, to the moment everything changed.

It hadn't started from ambition or a new discovery. A mysterious visitor dressed in purple had arrived, and his words had convinced the President of the United States to set a plan in motion.

He'd arrived without credentials, only a bundle of parchment and the weight of prophecy behind his eyes. Security dismissed him as a madman. The president's advisors laughed at first. Until he spoke.

He told them of things buried beneath the Earth, Voyager's original trajectory, before they changed it, ancient texts lost to fire, and symbols etched into stone long before humanity stood upright. One phrase lingered like a splinter in Jeff's mind.

"Your golden record will not echo into silence. It will return—with a reply."

He'd revealed just enough to prove himself and infect them with doubt. The kind of doubt that metastasized in quiet meetings and redacted reports.

They had thought they were acting on science and evidence. They hadn't realized they were being led, step by step, toward destiny.

Only the man in purple understood what waited at the end of that road.

If there were indeed another universe out there, what would it mean for humanity? What secrets awaited them on the other side?

The sound of the briefing room door opening interrupted Jeff's thoughts. Hank emerged, his face pale but determined. He had rehearsed his lines countless times, knowing that the weight of the world rested on his shoulders. As the public relations officer, he was the voice that would deliver this monumental news to the public.

The conference room buzzed with energy—voices layered over one another, chairs screeching across the floor, and the hiss of overworked air vents pushing stale, recycled air into every corner. Young interns shuffled in and claimed seats like they were boarding a rocket themselves.

*   *   *

"Hey, save me a spot!" Jerry said, weaving his way toward Sadie with two steaming coffee cups balanced in one hand and a clipboard tucked under his arm.

Sadie rolled her eyes as he plopped down beside her. "Is that for me, or are you double-fisting your nerves again?"

Jerry passed her a cup. "Sixth coffee run today. If this internship doesn't land me a job, I'll at least have a caffeine addiction and third-degree burns."

Sadie offered a distracted smile as she flipped through her notebook. "You think today is the day they'll teach about in schools?"

Jerry gave a half-shrug. "Feels more like the kind of day that gets buried in blacked-out documents."

Sadie let out a nervous laugh.

Jerry leaned back, scanning the front of the room, where NASA officials shuffled paperwork behind the podium. "I still can't believe we're here for this. The launch of Voyager 2. Our names are on the intern log for history."

"You nervous?" Sadie asked.

"I'm not nervous," Jerry said. "Just... skeptical."

Sadie arched an eyebrow.

"I mean, think about it," he said. "We're launching a golden record into space—a cosmic mixtape—hoping some friendly alien civilization finds it, listens to whale sounds, and doesn't decide to vaporize us. Does that sound like a safe bet to you?"

She shook her head with a small grin. "We're explorers, Jerry. You discover nothing new by hiding in your own solar system."

The room hushed as Hank approached the podium.

Sadie straightened in her seat. "Here we go."

Jerry tightened his grip on the coffee cup, knuckles white against the cardboard sleeve. Something twisted in his gut. Whatever this was... it had already started.

*   *   *

19

Hank stepped up to the podium, gripping the edge as if it might anchor him to the moment. Cameras clicked and lights flashed around him. Every muscle in his face ached from trying to hold still.

He cleared his throat. "Good morning, ladies and gentlemen." His voice rang clear through the conference room speakers, steadier than he felt. "Yesterday, August 20th, 1977, NASA launched the Voyager 2 space probe into interstellar space. This historic launch marks the first phase of humanity's boldest journey yet—one that will take us beyond our solar system, beyond our known sky."

He glanced down at the index cards but didn't need them. He had etched the words into his memory.

"Voyager 2 carries with it a gold-plated audiovisual disc—a time capsule from Earth. On it are images of our planet, mathematical data, human greetings in fifty-five languages, and a collection of sounds that define our world. The voices of children, the breaking of waves, the music of Mozart, and the rhythm of rock and roll."

A ripple of emotion ran through the crowd—interns leaned forward, reporters scribbled notes as fast as they could, and scientists contemplated the weight of the moment.

"This is more than a scientific mission. It is a message in a bottle cast into a cosmic ocean, an offering of peace or a beacon of curiosity." Hank paused. He could feel the sweat collecting at the base of his neck, sliding beneath his collar. "This is a voyage into the unknown—not just for NASA but for all of us. Whatever awaits us out there... we will face it together, with open arms and open minds." His voice faltered just for a moment, but no one seemed to notice. "Thank you."

He stepped back from the podium, the weight of the moment pressing down on his shoulders as the room erupted into controlled applause. His hands trembled as he returned to the briefing room, the sound of clapping fading into static in his ears.

Behind him, the golden disc of Voyager 2 sailed farther from Earth with every passing second—carrying humanity's hope... and something humanity didn't yet understand.

*　*　*

The applause had ended, and the room buzzed again—chairs scraping, voices rising, and coffee sloshing in paper cups.

Sadie nudged Jerry. "See? We just witnessed history, Jerry. That was incredible!"

Jerry didn't respond right away. His eyes were still on the now-empty podium, his face pale.

Sadie leaned in. "Come on. Tell me that didn't give you chills."

Jerry blinked a few times, like waking from a bad dream. "It did," he said. "Just... not the good kind."

Sadie raised an eyebrow. "Oh no. Here it comes."

He lowered his voice. "What if we're not sending a greeting? What if we're sending a target?"

She scoffed. "Jerry..."

"I'm serious." He turned toward her now. "We're just assuming whoever finds that thing will be curious, kind, and enlightened. What if they're not? What if we're flashing a beacon at something that doesn't care what Mozart sounds like?"

Sadie folded her arms. "You think we should just do nothing? Crawl back into caves and stay there forever?"

"No," he said. "I think we should know what we're walking into before we go waving flags."

"NASA isn't just waving flags. We've got a plan. I'm sure of it."

Jerry glanced around at the crowd, now filing out, chatting about launch specs and applause lines like they'd just left a movie. "Plans won't matter if what's out there doesn't play by our rules."

Sadie looked at him, softer now. "You sound like you don't believe in this at all."

He hesitated, then said, "I believe in curiosity. I just don't believe it always ends well."

Sadie shook her head. "We've tackled the impossible before. This is who we are and what we do."

Jerry's eyes dropped to the floor. "This isn't the Moon. This isn't a flag and a footprint. It's David versus Goliath..." He looked up. "... only this time, Goliath has lasers. And David's still throwing stones."

As the interns filtered into the corridor, the argument between Jerry and Sadie didn't die down, it gained traction. Their voices echoed down the hallway, cutting through the hum of passing footsteps.

"NASA's job is to face the unknown," Sadie said, arms folded. "We can't just stop because we're afraid of shadows."

Jerry rubbed his temples. "This isn't just the unknown. This is opening the door to something we might not be able to close."

A few employees glanced over. One muttered agreement under his breath. Another rolled her eyes and kept walking.

"That's the job," Sadie said.

Jerry gestured down the corridor. "Then I hope whoever made the call to launch isn't playing with a slingshot thinking they're David."

Their words lingered long after they'd passed, picked up and passed along like static in a wire. Something had shifted. The further the probe traveled, the more that shift would grow.

*   *   *

22

Hank stepped out of the briefing room like a man leaving a battlefield. His shoes scuffed against the tile, his posture folded inward, like his own bones had betrayed him. The applause was over, and the cameras were off. Only the weight of his words remained.

Jeff didn't say a word as Hank passed by, just watched him disappear down the corridor like a man retreating from a disaster. He turned to the wall. The crimson phone gleamed beneath a flickering overhead light.

He hesitated for a brief second. Then reached for the receiver and lifted it, as if the act itself might trigger something unstoppable.

A quiet click followed by silence.

"Mr. President," Jeff said, clearing his throat. "It's done. We launched Voyager 2 as requested. The media received the official script. Everything stayed within parameters."

A long pause. Then the voice on the other end cut through. "He seemed... nervous."

Jeff's fingers gripped the cord tighter. "He did his job."

Another pause.

"Await further instructions."

The line went dead.

Jeff lowered the phone and stood there, hand still resting on it as if it might speak again.

* * *

Far above him, Voyager 2 sailed through the silence of space.

Somewhere much closer, the man in the purple robe was watching.

The president turned away from the phone, but he didn't stand. He kept his eyes locked on the figure across from him—still, silent, and out of place beneath the flags and framed oil portraits of democracy.

The man in the purple robe didn't speak. He didn't have to. He moved forward like a shadow sliding across marble. His robe whispered against the floor, the folds shimmering in the light.

The president inhaled a deep, cautious breath and took a moment to compose his thoughts before he addressed the man in purple. "It's done. Voyager 2 has launched. The world believes it's a scientific mission."

The figure stopped just short of the desk. From beneath the hood, his voice emerged—deep, and dry like wind in a tomb. "The seed is planted, and the prophecy begins."

The president swallowed hard. "If this works—"

"There is no if," the man replied. "Only when." He leaned in, the folds of his robe brushing against the edge of the desk. The lights seemed to dim as he did. "You are not the author of what comes next," he said. "Only its witness."

The president's knuckles whitened around the arms of his chair. Sweat beaded on his forehead. He opened his mouth to speak—then closed it again, looking down.

Silence pressed against the walls like rising water.

In the corner, one of the president's advisors shifted in his seat. Another wiped his brow with a trembling hand.

No one spoke. No one moved.

The only sound was the quiet rustle of silk as the man in the purple robe turned and walked away.

The president watched him go.

Outside, the late sun cast long shadows across the lawn.

The president remained still long after the robed figure had gone, as if motion might undo something he couldn't name.

He reached for the phone again—ignoring the crimson one and choosing the secure line just inches away, as if proximity offered safety.

"Jeff," he said, his voice flat but strained. "We cannot afford to underestimate the consequences of what we've done."

*   *   *

Jeff stood in a darkened corridor at NASA, the handset pressed to his ear. He didn't speak at first.

"Alert the agencies," the president continued. "I want every scenario and its contingencies mapped out. Leave no stone unturned."

Jeff exhaled, eyes fixed on nothing. "Understood."

The line went dead.

Jeff lowered the phone and stared at it for a long moment. His reflection flickered on the brushed metal surface—a man out of place, out of time, caught in the undertow of something far older than politics or science.

Down the hall, the hum of computers and fluorescent lights felt alien, like artifacts of a civilization already on borrowed time.

Outside, the sun was setting. Above, Voyager 2 sailed farther into the void—its golden disc glinting like a coin tossed into a wishing well.

Somewhere beyond the stars and silence, something stirred.

CHAPTER THREE

International Space Station

I t was never supposed to return.

Sadie had said that a hundred times over the years—to interns, reporters, and herself. They built Voyager 2 to leave humanity behind. A farewell to Earth, not a boomerang. It was a message in a bottle tossed into an ocean that no one expected a reply to.

But it was coming back home, and no one knew why.

The command center thrummed, a symphony of artificial light reflecting off the screens, the whisper of air vents a constant drone. Today, however, the usual sounds scraped like fingernails on a chalkboard. A prickle of sweat bloomed on Sadie's back as she focused on the bright glow of the telemetry feed.

"Jerry," she said, not turning around to look at him. "Look at this."

He rolled his chair over beside her. The data pulsed in lines and numbers as they both stared in silence.

"That's a live signal," he said.

Sadie nodded, her eyes fixed on the screen.

"It's ours. It's Voyager 2."

The spacecraft had transmitted nothing for years. Not like this; not from inside the solar system.

Jerry leaned in, his brow furrowed as he tried to make sense of what was being said. "That can't be right."

Sadie refreshed the screen, the cold light reflecting in her eyes. The feed stream was endless. Lines of green text, a dizzying cascade, kept appearing. Each update brought position data—stark and unforgiving. A high-pitched, insistent beep accompanied each new update. Static crackled as the low-band telemetry flooded her senses.

"It's not just broadcasting," she said. "It's navigating."

He stared at the velocity vector. "Is it... changing trajectory?"

"It's aligning with Earth," she said.

They both looked at the heading. The trajectory didn't curve. It turned, sharp and clean, like a ship turning into port.

Jerry pushed back in his chair, the color draining from his face. "No. No, no, no. It doesn't have the propulsion to do that."

"Then something else does."

A technician across the room called out. "We've lost contact with the ISS."

Sadie turned her head. "Comms down?"

"No data. It just dropped."

Alarms shrieked, a deafening sound that filled the air. Overhead, the lights blinked and whirred, catching everyone's attention. Red. White. Red. White.

Sadie's hands trembled as she opened a direct channel. Her voice cracked. "Station, this is Houston ground control. Please respond."

Nothing at first. Then, through the static, a voice emerged, choppy and distorted. "If any... can hear... this... Ma... zalez... station copy... is anyone—"

Jerry grabbed another headset. "We've had interference before. Could be solar."

Sadie wasn't listening. She kept her eyes locked on the Voyager data stream. A new feed had opened—one she hadn't seen before.

"Jerry..." she said. "What is that?" A waveform pulsed across her screen. "That's not telemetry," she said. "That's... something else."

In the silence of space, a metallic object reflected against the distant light of the sun. It moved with voracious grace— like a predator stalking prey—its smooth body cutting through the void with purpose. As it neared the International Space Station, tendrils unfurled like fingers. They extended with unnerving precision, probing the exposed communication tower, searching for a connection. One by one, the needle-thin filaments curled around ports and nodes, merging with the system in an almost organic clasp. A faint pulse of light rippled down the object's spine.

Then something else appeared—bigger, slower, and more threatening. It moved in a way that created no noise, yet the surrounding area seemed to vibrate with an undefined force. It expelled a silvery mist, a cloud of liquid and gas that shimmered and spun around the station like a living shroud. There was a strange, oily glimmer on the substance, as if it were alive.

The smaller object transmitted back to its origin, its signal faint but constant. In perfect choreography, the mist responded, opened, forming a narrow corridor, just wide enough for passage.

When Voyager 2 crossed through it, the mist closed behind it like a lid snapping shut. The larger object followed, vanishing into the swirling haze.

An otherworldly cocoon enveloped the station, blurring its silhouette and silencing signals.

Inside the mist, nothing moved. Outside, nothing could reach it.

* * *

At the International Space Station, seven astronauts worked in tense silence, following procedures, flipping through diagnostics, trying to make sense of a total comms blackout. In the command module, Marcus Gonzalez and Tammy Adams hunched over flickering consoles, surrounded by a soft hum of machines that on a normal day meant everything was fine—but this wasn't a normal day.

Tammy hovered near her keyboard, typing, as cascading error messages flooded the screen. Dark rings hollowed her eyes. Stray strands of hair drifted around her damp face.. She looked wrecked, but she wasn't stopping.

"Tammy," Marcus said, drifting behind her, "don't tell me you haven't tried resetting the breakers."

She froze mid-stroke and turned her head. Her voice was flat. "You want to check my knitting log next?"

Marcus raised his hands. "Hey, we're sealed off from Houston with zero feedback. I'm asking."

"I know what zero feedback means." She turned back to the console, eyes narrowing. "For the record, I've tried resets. Hard and soft. Nothing is working. The system keeps pushing back."

"So, what? You think it's external interference?"

"No." Her tone was sharp. "I think something's overriding us. Running a diagnostic causes it to reboot itself. I lock the controls, they unlock. I try to isolate the fault tree—"

"Let me guess," he said. "It overrides the override."

She paused, then said, "It's like the station doesn't belong to us anymore."

The words hit harder than she expected. Marcus stilled his drifting. His eyes lifted to the status indicators above them, flickering like nervous ticks. After a while, he said, "Okay. Let's not jump to conclusions. We'll go through every system again."

Tammy pushed back from her workstation, her body floating a few inches before she steadied herself against the console.. "Sure. Round three. Maybe the third time's the charm." She blinked and rubbed her eyes in disbelief, catching something out of the corner of her eye.

A flicker. Outside, just beyond the glass, something shimmered in her peripheral vision. She leaned forward, pressing her forehead to the window, breath fogging the surface.

"Marcus," she said, almost in a whisper. "Look at that."

He moved to her side, scanning the void. "What am I supposed to be seeing? It's just black out there."

"I swear I just saw something. It looked like... Voyager 2."

Marcus turned to her. "That probe? You're sure?" He leaned toward the window. His breath caught in his throat. "That's Voyager 2."

Tammy nodded, eyes wide. "It has a symbol on the side, a tree with thick branches and a snake wrapped around it. An 'E' in the middle, and below that the letter A."

Before he could reply, a hiss split the silence. Soft and steady— like air escaping a pressurized seal.

Marcus straightened, his whole body on alert. The sound deepened, building into a low rush that echoed through the walls.

"That's not a vent," he said.

"No," Tammy said, "it's not."

Marcus grabbed the handrail and backed toward the hatch.

"I'm going to check it out. Stay here. Keep working on comms."

"I'll call if anything changes," Tammy said, though her voice didn't rise above a whisper.

She kept staring out the window, eyes locked on the dark—watching for a probe that shouldn't be there.

With determined pulls along the handholds, Marcus left the control module, his boots brushing the metal as he propelled himself forward. The corridor stretched ahead, dim and flickering, the emergency lights casting long shadows that moved when he didn't.

The hissing grew louder. Instead of being erratic, the rhythm was steady and pulsing, similar to the sound of breath forced through clenched teeth.

As he rounded the corner into the environmental systems room, his breath caught. One oxygen tank had ruptured, releasing a hiss that faded into a chilling silence, broken only by the echo of expanding frost blooming in erratic patterns across the deck. The air stung with the acrid smell of burned metal as scorch marks marred the paneling. Walls, once pristine, now bore deliberate gashes, the raw edges a testament to precise, surgical violence.

"No way this is a system failure," Marcus whispered.

His training screamed at him to seal the room and alert the crew, but something primal told him; don't turn your back on this.

He moved closer, and as the frigid air nipped at his cheeks, he froze in place.

31

Outside the narrow window hovered a metallic drone. Its tendrils writhed with purpose, threading into the station's exposed communications panel. Sparks danced across its limbs with the crackling sound of static electricity. It didn't drift away. It was stuck, as if it had become one with the ship.

A cold knot formed in Marcus's belly.

He backed away, fumbling for his comm.

"Tammy! There's something—" The words caught in his throat.

Behind him, a shadow moved. He turned, and everything inside him recoiled.

A figure hovered at the far end of the hall. Towering and human-shaped, it looked wrong. Its skin shimmered with a sheen like polished graphite, pulsing from within. It radiated a pressure that Marcus felt more than saw, like gravity had thickened in its presence.

The creature moved forward, its shadow stretching long and distorted. "You know nothing of what lies ahead," it said, voice rich and resonant, vibrating in the air like struck metal.

Marcus backed against the wall, heart pounding against his ribs. "What are you—"

"Tremble... for you now stand in the presence of the Right Hand's will."

Before the world went dark, Marcus saw its hand, a blur of motion that was alien and swift.

A sharp, distant shriek sliced through the silence, reverberating through the station's corridors. Tammy froze, her hand hovering above the console.

"Marcus?" she said.

No answer. Just the mechanical hum of systems. A crackle of static boomed through the station. Marcus's voice broke through, distorted but urgent.

"Tammy—get to the escape pod now! We are under atta—"

Another burst of static.

"They said—" his voice faltered, strained. "I'm the first. A sacrifice... to the Right Hand of the—"

The transmission cut off like a blade.

Tammy drifted backward in alarm, her breath catching in her throat. "Marcus!" she cried, slamming her hand against the console. But only silence answered.

The alarms erupted, their screaming piercing the air as the red light pulsed. She spun toward the door, heart pounding so hard it made her dizzy.

"This can't be happening," she said, panic clawing at her throat. "We're the only people up here. Who the hell is attacking us?"

She grabbed the comm headset, switching frequencies. "John! Priya! Louis! Anyone—do you copy?"

Silence. Just the wail of sirens.

Her chest tightened. The control room was collapsing into chaos, with every warning light flashing.

Adrenaline surged, an icy fire in her veins. She pushed away from the console in a frantic burst, her body ricocheting off the corridors handholds as she shot forward.. Her vision swam as she took shallow, painful breaths, the world closing in on her.

"You can do this, Tammy. Get to the pod. Just get to the pod."

She reached the metallic door and spun around once inside, chest heaving. The air thickened, heavy as water in her lungs.

From the shadows, a colossal figure emerged. Its presence dominated the corridor, a suffocating force that seemed to pull the very light into itself.

"You cannot outrun what has already begun," it said, voice like stone dragged across metal. "When you reach your destination... tell them: He is coming."

Tammy's breath hitched. Slick with sweat, her fingers located the launch button. After missing once, she slammed it with a resounding bang.

The door hissed shut on its hydraulics, then the pod jolted, hurling her into the seat. Straps cut into her shoulders as the acceleration crushed her back.

Outside, the figure vanished into the dark as the pod rocketed away.

Through the window, the mist writhed—alive and shifting to let the pod slip through. As soon as it was on the other side, the mist closed again.

A heartbeat later, something inside the mist sparked.

A silent, blinding explosion lit up the void, and Tammy cried out, shielding her eyes.

The mist pulsed once more, then swallowed the fire.

As the pod drifted, Tammy blinked the image from her eyes. Then she saw it. A faint glint beyond the mist. It was Voyager 2.

It moved through the void untouched.

She shivered. The mist hadn't just allowed it through, it had cleared a path.

The comm crackled to life.

"Escape pod Icarus, do you copy? This is Ground Control."

Tammy blinked, still disoriented from the pod being jettisoned. She reached for the console with trembling fingers.

"Ground Control, this is Astronaut Tammy Adams," she said, voice raw. "The ISS is gone. It—" she swallowed. "Something destroyed it."

"Tammy, it's Jerry." His voice was flat. "What do you mean, gone? We're still getting telemetry."

Her blood turned to ice. "That's impossible."

Another voice broke in. "Be prepared for a full debrief upon landing."

Tammy stared out the window. "Copy that."

She looked down at the Earth growing larger below, unaware of the chaos she was about to bring with her.

Behind her, the stars held their silence, and something within them watched.

CHAPTER FOUR

The Island of Misfit Toys

It was a crisp June morning at Elmendorf Air Force Base in Anchorage, Alaska. The faint tang of jet fuel mingled with the earthy scent of distant pine. An occasional gust of wind swept across the flight line, carrying faint traces of dust and debris, blending with the low hum of maintenance equipment. Airmen representing thirty-five different countries stood in a straight line at the eastern end of the flight line. The sound of shuffling boots and distant murmurs from maintenance crews underscored the morning's quiet efficiency.

A burly Master Sergeant, his voice like gravel, barked a command that snapped the air like a whip.

"Airmen! Begin FOD Walk!"

In perfect unison, the airmen began their walk, heads down, eyes scanning every inch of the flight line for wayward screws, scraps of metal, or anything that could spell disaster for a jet engine. Among them, a British airman turned to his American counterpart, his eyes bright with mischief, breaking the disciplined silence.

"Hey, mate, what's the craziest thing you've ever found doing one of these?"

The question lingered in the air, adding a thread of camaraderie to the meticulous task. A smirk played on the lips of the American airman.

"One time, I found a set of dog tags from the Korean War. Made me wonder about the stories behind them. What about you?"

The Brit chuckled, his voice low yet vibrant with disbelief. "Aw, mate, you won't believe this, but I swear it's true. I found an entire assortment of sex toys one time. We work with some crazy blokes who love pranking the new recruits. I think they had too much fun and forgot to clean up."

Laughter rippled between them, a momentary break in the seriousness of their duty. Their shared humor, brief but contagious, lightened the atmosphere like sunlight breaking through a storm cloud.

The growl of an expediter truck shattered the moment. The blue box truck lumbered onto the flight line, its diesel engine belching a faint haze into the crisp air. A loudspeaker mounted on top crackled to life, the voice slicing through the stillness with commanding urgency.

"Attention, airmen! Airman First Class Roosevelt Washington, report to the Flight Chief's office!"

A ripple of murmurs broke the disciplined silence. Some airmen exchanged knowing glances; others smirked. Roosevelt caught the fleeting expressions out of the corner of his eye—a mix of relief it wasn't them and the subtle judgment he had grown used to. Shaking it off, he broke formation and jogged toward the hangar.

The British airman raised an eyebrow.

"What's that about, mate?"

The American shrugged. "Beats me."

Roosevelt passed them without a word, boots striking the flight line in a steady rhythm as the wind pushed at his back. Inside the hangar, he eased his pace. He took a moment outside the flight chief's office, his breathing steadying. From his pocket, he retrieved a faded photograph—his father in a sharp Air Force uniform, smiling alongside his squadron. He recalled sitting on his father's knee, listening to stories of powerful engines and far-off places.

"Always carry yourself with pride," his father had said. "Your name is your first salute. Protect it—and those who depend on it."

Those words weighed heavier now, tangled with the memory of Jefferson's laugh on that playground. Protecting had taken on a different meaning since then—a duty not just to others but a way to atone for what he couldn't undo. Jefferson's fall had left a scar no one else could see, shaping everything Roosevelt had done since.

His parents, both lovers of history, had named him Roosevelt—drawn to the symmetry of pairing a president's name with "Washington." His friends just called him Roo.

He tucked the photo away, adjusted his belt, and brushed his hands off. His jaw tightened as he looked up at the door.

According to Roo, he was an average—maybe below-average—crew chief. He still remembered the moment he got the assignment. While others celebrated, he'd stared at the paper as if it had betrayed him. The word "Crew Chief" felt more like a sentence than a purpose.

"Guess I'll have to prove them wrong," he'd muttered, stuffing the sheet into his pocket

Roo stepped into the office just as the flight chief entered behind him. He snapped to attention.

"Sir, Airman First Class Roosevelt Washington reporting as ordered."

The flight chief looked him up and down, eyes sweeping from Roo's wrinkled blouse to the dull scuff on his boots.

"I guess you didn't feel like ironing your uniform or shining your boots last night. You look like a pile of smashed ass. At ease, Airman."

As Roo shifted into position, the sting of humiliation settled in, causing a flush to creep up his neck. He said nothing. His hands curled, then relaxed at his sides.

The flight chief dropped into his chair, already reaching for a folder.

"I won't sugarcoat this. You're not part of the war games today. We need our best out there. You couldn't pour piss out of a boot with the instructions written on the heel." He flipped a page. "You'll be manning the snack bar where you belong."

"Yes, sir," Roo said. He turned on his heel, already moving for the door, when the flight chief spoke again.

"Oh—and before you head over, go help the new UK crew get situated. Give 'em the squadron tour." There was an awkward pause before the flight chief finished. "Now get out of my face, Airman."

"Yes, sir." Roo exited without another word. His shoulders dipped as the door clicked shut behind him while his hands slid into his pockets, fingers tightening into fists before easing open again.

He kept his eyes ahead.

Roo stepped outside the hangar doors and spotted the new UK crew clustered near the edge of the flight line.

He approached with a steady gait, voice clear and formal.

"Good morning. I'm here to show you around the flight line."

As the words left his mouth, his gaze caught on one of them—a young woman with wavy brunette hair that fell just past her shoulders. She stood about five-six, posture straight but uncertain, like someone trying to project confidence while still finding her footing.

Roo's breath hitched. For a moment, the world narrowed to the way the sunlight lit her profile—soft curves, calm eyes, and something poised yet vulnerable. He just stared, jaw slackened, struck by something he couldn't name.

She looked up, caught his gaze, and blinked.

"Do I have something on my face?" she asked, brushing a strand of hair behind her ear. "I knew I shouldn't have eaten that meatball sub before we left."

The tone of her voice was a charming mix of teasing and self-awareness.

Roo blinked, color rushing to his cheeks. "Oh—no, ma'am. I, uh... thought I saw something behind you. Must've been my imagination."

She smiled, disarming and kind. "I'm Pilot Officer Elizabeth Miles, but my friends call me Lizzie. You are?"

"Airman First Class Roosevelt Washington," he replied. "You can call me Roo." He straightened and regained his focus on the task at hand.

"It's nice to meet you, Lizzie. Let's get started. Follow me."

Roo led the group around the hangar and across the flight line, pointing out key areas and walking them through the squadron's standard protocols.

He stopped at a corner of the hangar marked by organized shelves and tool racks. A laminated checklist hung from a pegboard.

"This," he said with a faint grin, "is the toolshed—sacred ground, ruled by one man. Marvin's been running this setup for over twenty-five years. He's more protective of these tools than most folks are of their firstborns."

He turned toward the back. "Marvin, care to share your wisdom with the new crew?"

Marvin stared at Roo like he'd just been asked to give a TED Talk on patience. "I hate strangers, Roo. You know that. They never follow instructions. Last time, someone put a wrench in the wrong drawer and I looked for it for a week. Don't even get me started on the idiot who tried to clean a socket set. Clean it! Like a damn fork."

Roo chuckled. "Come on, Marvin. Give them a shot—they're from the UK. They're civilized."

Marvin let out an audible sigh before he responded. "Fine, but if they mess up my system, you owe me a twelve-pack of Dr. Pepper. That's the only thing keeping me sane in this madhouse. That and *Matlock* reruns on Thursday night."

Roo laughed. "You got it. I still remember when you wouldn't let anyone touch the sockets until I handed you a cold can. Man's got priorities. I respect that."

Marvin grumbled but stepped forward and started explaining his system to the UK crew.

Roo's smile softened, then a clatter echoed through the vast hangar, pulling his gaze. Shouts, harsh and strained, sliced the air. His smile vanished as he moved toward the commotion, his steps quickening. Rounding the corner, he saw a silhouette—broad shoulders, a strong jaw, a crisp uniform. It was Senior Airman Ramirez.

Ramirez surveyed the mess of scattered books, one polished boot carelessly pushing a hardback. The smirk on his face matched the gleam on his boots. He was the squadron's golden boy, a mechanical genius and an insufferable show-off. He had earned respect for his abilities and disdain for his attitude. Today was proving to be no different.

"You don't need these stupid books, Doc," Ramirez said, voice mocking. "They'll just slow you down."

Roo's stomach tightened. Dr. Franklin Terracotta was the target: reclusive, brilliant, and easily flustered. The civilian radio engineer huddled, clutching his books as if they were a shield. His glasses perched askew, and his unruly hair seemed to defy gravity.

Roo stepped forward, voice calm but firm. "Ramirez, leave him alone. Don't you have prep to do for the war games?"

Ramirez turned with that familiar grin. "Well, if it isn't the king of the snack bar. What's the matter, Roo, out of popcorn? Why do you even care about this guy? All he does is fiddle with telephones."

Roo exhaled, fists clenching, then released. "It's radios, you moron. Radios that keep pilots alive and missions running, or do you think jets just coordinate themselves by magic?"

Ramirez waved him off. "Whatever, man. I've got better things to do than argue with rejects from the island of misfit toys."

He glanced once more at Terracotta. For just a second, the smirk faltered—something unreadable flickering behind his eyes—before he turned and walked away.

Terracotta hummed under his breath. A nervous tick that Roo recognized. "At first I was afraid, I was petrified..." he sang, his voice shaky but sincere.

Roo kneeled beside him, offering a hand and a grin. "Don't worry about him, Doc. If his head were any bigger, we'd need a larger hangar to fit it in."

Terracotta gave a sheepish smile. "I'll swing by later with some Reese's Pieces," Roo added. "You can tell me about the time you tried to rewire the vending machine to play Sinatra."

Roo caught back up with the UK crew and heard laughter, loud and pointed, not the good kind.

He stepped in, voice steady. "What's going on here?"

The group fumbled to stifle their grins. One of them spoke with a chuckle. "We told Lizzie to ask Marvin for a left-handed hammer, and she did it! Can you believe that? I mean, if she had two brain cells left, they'd be fighting for second place. Did you know she holds the base record for simulator crashes? Seventy-two! Bloody hell!"

Roo's eyes flicked to Lizzie. She stared at the ground, cheeks flushed, lips pressed tight. The hurt in her posture said everything words didn't.

Roo stepped closer, tone softer. "Don't worry about it, Lizzie. The guys once sent me walking around the base in January looking for a canooter valve. Spoiler alert... it's not real."

She looked up, surprised. Just a little.

Roo turned back to the group. "Tour's over. Figure it out yourselves. Lizzie, come with me."

He didn't wait for a response—just walked and she followed.

They reached the snack bar and sat in silence, tension still clinging to the air. As soon as he was about to speak, the door banged open.

"Hey, snack hoe! I need a Gatorade and some chips. Make it quick!"

Roosevelt rose without a word, jaw clenched. He got the items, handed them off, then sat again, his focus returning to Lizzie with quiet care.

"As you can see," Roo said, gesturing to the shelves behind him, "I'm not frontline material. Most days, I'm in here manning the snack bar and monitoring radio squawks when jets come in. It's not glamorous, but... it keeps me out of trouble." He paused, meeting her eyes. "You okay?"

Lizzie's gaze dropped. When she looked up, her eyes shimmered. "My father's a decorated pilot. Twenty years in the Royal Air Force—letter from the queen and everything. My grandfather flew in World War II. Flying is in my blood. It's all I've ever wanted." Her voice faltered, but she pressed on. "But these guys... they make me feel like I don't belong. Every mistake feels huge. They're waiting for me to fail, and when I get nervous, I just mess up more. These war games—" she paused, "they might break me." She lowered her head. "I'm sorry, Roo. You didn't sign up to hear all that."

Roo leaned forward, voice steady and warm. "Don't be sorry. Everyone needs someone to talk to." He smiled, just a little. "They used to call me 'Snacks.' I spilled an entire case of chips in the hangar my first week. Took forever to live it down. One day, I figured out that nicknames don't matter. What matters is what you do." He looked around the quiet snack bar. "Welcome to the island of misfit toys. You're in good company."

Lizzie's lips twitched—a near-smile—just as a piercing siren erupted from the radio on the wall.

"We have a real-world event! I repeat, real-world event! Unidentified aircraft in Alaskan airspace. Scramble all jets— prepare for launch!"

Roo and Lizzie bolted upright. Outside, everything was in chaos. The sky was a flurry of activity. Airmen yelled and raced to their posts. Engines sprang to life with a roar. Radios crackled with a cacophony of commands.

Lizzie paused, her eyes sweeping the sky, anxiety fluttering in her eyes.

Roo put a reassuring hand on her shoulder. "You've got this," he said, steadying her. "Stick close and keep your eyes up."

She nodded, still scared but with newfound courage.

A brilliant streak of light flashed across the Alaskan sky. Trails of smoke twisted behind it, a comet of fire and metal plummeting downward. Roo squinted, feeling a mix of wonder and fear.

"We have to investigate," Lizzie said, her voice gaining strength.

They sprinted forward. Above them, alarms blared and voices filled the air.

"Unidentified object approaching! Prepare for impact!"

The escape pod from the ISS hurtled through the clouds, aimed directly at them.

CHAPTER FIVE

The Letter

The escape pod jolted as the parachutes deployed, throwing Tammy forward in the straps. Her breath hitched, shallow and ragged. The cold control panel bit into her palms as she braced herself, knuckles whitening.

A high-pitched hiss filled the capsule, soft yet grating, amplifying every ounce of pressure pressing down on her chest.

Through the small circular window, the Alaskan wilderness stretched out in bleak, windswept waves—scrub grass and stony plains fading into distant snow-capped mountains.

A sudden image flashed in her mind, too sharp to be imagination. A man dressed in flowing purple robes. Standing motionless on the earth below as the pod descended.

She blinked hard. "Am I hallucinating?" she whispered. Her own voice startled her.

Then the pod slammed into the ground with a jarring crunch, snapping her back into the moment. She gasped and exhaled all at once, fingers fumbling at the harness until it came loose.

Crawling out of the pod, she staggered to her feet—then froze.

A sound rose in the wind. Distant at first, then building—a low mechanical roar, growing louder by the second.

Tammy's pulse spiked. Something, or someone, was coming.

She shielded her eyes against the glare of oncoming headlights, a cavalcade of vehicles racing toward her, sirens slicing through the stillness like jagged blades. Her hands trembled as she stepped back, the cold Alaskan air biting at her skin.

Then, as if conjured from thought, the man in the purple robes appeared, standing just feet away.

Tammy froze, the air caught in her throat, her heart skipping. His robes billowed in the breeze, the rich violet fabric whispering like a ghost. He extended a letter—old and weathered—with a mechanical precision that felt almost inhuman.

Fear crawled along her skin, but curiosity pulled harder. She reached out with trembling fingers, brushing the coarse paper. The rough texture sent a shiver through her. Before she could summon the courage to speak, the man turned away. His steps were silent on the soft earth as he disappeared without a word, leaving only questions behind.

She unfolded the letter, her pulse thrumming as her eyes scanned the cryptic message.

"As the veil closes, push the butterflies through."

Her quiet reflection ended with shouts and screeching tires.

"Stay where you are! You are on American soil. Do not run, or we will use force!"

Tammy shoved the letter deep into her pocket, heart hammering. She dropped to her knees, hands raised, the cold earth biting through her jumpsuit.

"I—I'm an astronaut from the International Space Station!"

The armed men didn't pause. One shoved her face-first into the dirt as handcuffs snapped around her wrists.

"What's going on?!" she said, panic flaring.

"You're coming with us," a voice said.

They hauled her up and shoved her into the back of a waiting vehicle. Through the smudged window, she watched the inspection team surround the pod. One brushed dirt from the surface, revealing faint stenciling: Icarus–International Space Station.

The radio crackled. "Transport, this is inspection. The person you're holding is friendly. Repeat: this is the ISS escape pod. Over."

"Copy that. En route to holding."

Outside, a flatbed truck pulled in to recover the pod. The area was already ringed with caution tape.

The convoy rolled onto the base, and guards led Tammy through a series of checkpoints, into a sterile holding room. Her wrists throbbed from the handcuffs, and she was extremely nervous.

A man in a dark suit entered, face unreadable, but his tone was calm. "Sorry about the aggressive approach. We didn't know what we were dealing with. Can I get you some water?"

Tammy's fists slammed on the table, the crack echoing off the walls. Her eyes narrowed, her voice sharp with fury.

"Water? Are you serious?" Her breath hitched. "You pointed guns at me, cuffed me like a criminal, and shoved me into the back of a truck. And now you want to play nice?" She leaned forward, fists clenched. "I want answers. Now."

The man didn't flinch. "My name is Special Agent Richardson, NSA. We received a call after your last transmission from orbit. We have a few questions. This is just a debrief, Tammy."

Tammy's expression shifted—anger fading into fear. "How do you know my name? I didn't tell you my name." She shook her head. "I don't even know what I saw up there. I feel like I'm losing my mind. None of it makes sense."

Agent Richardson pulled up a chair across from Tammy.

"Let's start with your last transmission," he said, flipping open a notepad. "You said the space station is gone. Can you walk me through what happened?"

Tammy's hands trembled on the table. "I saw it happen," she said, her voice shaky but certain. "The mist—it shifted, swallowed the ISS whole. Then there was this flash, an explosion so bright I had to shield my eyes. But the fire—it didn't last. The mist smothered it, like it never happened."

Richardson raised an eyebrow. "That's unusual. Are you certain? Could it have been an equipment malfunction? Maybe you hit your head during ejection?"

Tammy cut in, sharp and defensive. "Of course I hit my head. I slammed the button without even thinking about it. I was trying to survive."

Richardson leaned back, pen hovering mid-note. "So... it's possible you were hallucinating. A concussion could've distorted your perception—"

Her fists slammed the table again. "I know what I saw, damn it!" Her voice cracked as she leaned forward, locking eyes with him. "I didn't hallucinate. I didn't imagine it. The station's gone, and something—something not from here—made it happen."

Agent Richardson, unfazed by Tammy's outburst, leaned forward toward her. "Let's move on. Why did you feel the need to use the escape pod?"

Tammy sank back into her chair, shaking her head as if to clear the memory. After a long breath, she spoke. "This is going to sound insane. Captain Gonzalez and I were troubleshooting comms with Houston when we heard this... rush of air, like something ruptured. Gonzalez went to check it out, and the next thing I knew, he was screaming at me to get to the pod. He said we were under attack. He sounded terrified."

Richardson held up a hand. "Under attack by what?"

Tammy's voice tightened. "How should I know? I've never seen anything like it."

He studied her, then said in a gentler tone. "Just tell me what you saw."

Tammy let out a shaky laugh. "You're going to love this. It looked... human. Sort of. But wrong. Over seven feet tall, built like a tank. Its skin shimmered—like it couldn't decide if it was solid or smoke. And its eyes..." She paused for a moment before she continued. "They were pale. Unblinking. Like it could see through me—everything I've ever been." She gripped the table, knuckles white. "And its voice..." Her tone dropped to a whisper. "It didn't just speak. It pushed the words into my mind and said: 'He is coming, and we can't escape the inevitable.'"

Richardson paused, his pen frozen above his notepad. "He? Who is 'He'?"

Tammy's hands curled into fists, her nails digging crescents into her palms. "How should I know? I didn't stick around to play twenty questions with it!"

Agent Richardson scribbled something in his notepad. "Did you see anything else during all of this, or is that it?"

Tammy closed her eyes, sifting through the chaos of memory. "Well..." she said. "I saw what looked like an old spacecraft flying past the window of the station." She opened her eyes and met his gaze. "It said Voyager 2 on the side. There were strange markings—a giant tree with thick branches full of leaves. Wrapped around it was a snake. A big one. In the center of the tree was the letter 'E,' and below that, a large 'A.'" She paused, irritation creeping into her voice. "No, I don't know what it means. I'm not a hieroglyphics expert."

Richardson's pen moved back and forth in rapid movements. He glanced up. "Are you sure it was a snake?"

Tammy rolled her eyes. "Yes, I'm sure." Then another image flickered in her mind—clear and jarring. "Oh, and there was a man." She leaned forward, her voice rising. "He was wearing purple robes. I saw him on the ground during the descent. He was standing there, just... staring at the pod. And when I got out, he was there again. Then he just walked away."

She hesitated, stopping short of mentioning the letter still hidden in her pocket.

Agent Richardson's pen froze mid-air. His expression darkened, and the air in the room felt heavier.

"Tammy," he said, "are you certain it was a man in purple robes? One hundred percent?" His voice was almost above a whisper, but the weight behind it made Tammy's stomach twist.

"Yeah. I'm sure. He was standing on the ground, staring right at the pod. The robes were bright—royal purple, almost theatrical. But..." she hesitated, "I couldn't see his face."

Richardson's jaw clenched. He pulled out his phone and dialed, speaking in a hushed tone. "He was there. Yes, sir. Purple robe. It's been over forty years. How should we proceed?"

A brief pause. He nodded, then hung up. He stood, ignoring Tammy's startled look. "You're done. The debrief is over."

Tammy shot to her feet. "What? That's it? Who is this guy? What the hell is going on?"

Agent Richardson turned to the guard at the door. "Take her to this address. NSA safe house. Make sure she has food, water—whatever she needs. I want a twenty-four-hour detail. She doesn't leave unless cleared by me or another authorized agent. Understood?"

The guard gave a sharp nod, then asked, "Is this the same location where the first lady and her kids are staying? Should we house her with them?"

Richardson didn't hesitate. "She's not a threat. For now, she stays with them. Once we verify everything, we'll arrange transport back to D.C."

The guard nodded again and stepped toward Tammy, reaching for her arm.

Tammy yanked it away, eyes blazing, shoving the chair back with a screech. "This is insane! I have a family—people who think I'm dead! You can't just lock me up! What the hell is happening?!"

Agent Richardson's gaze was unwavering as he looked at Tammy, his expression firm yet controlled.

"You can't leave until we understand what's happening. We need to verify your story. I promise you'll be safe, and we'll make sure you have everything you need."

Tammy's shoulders sagged as the guard took hold of her arm. Her eyes flicked to the door, chest tightening under the weight of questions no one was answering. Her family's faces flashed in her mind—faces she might never see again.

She clenched her fists, nails digging into her palms as the walls seemed to close in. Tears welled in her eyes, but she refused to let them fall. Without a word, she followed the guard out of the room.

A door burst open behind her, the sharp sound snapping through the tension like a whip. A woman strode in, urgency carved into every step. "Sir, we've just received reports—Voyager 2 has crashed in a cornfield in Iowa. Teams are on-site and recovering debris. Early analysis shows strange markings. They're beginning reconstruction for closer study."

Richardson's face hardened. "Thank you," he said, reaching for his phone. As he dialed, his voice turned clipped, authoritative. "Get me the situation room."

Hours later, Tammy sat in the back of the vehicle, her hands resting in her lap, fingers twitching. The rhythmic hum of tires on cracked Alaskan roads did little to calm the storm inside her. The wilderness stretched in front of her, a vast sea of darkened trees closing in with every mile.

Despite the guards' stoic silence, she couldn't shake the feeling of being watched—not just by them but by something else.

Her thoughts drifted to the man in the purple robes. His unmoving gaze, the way he had appeared and vanished like the earth itself had conjured him sent chills crawling up her spine. How did Richardson know about him? Why had he reacted like that?

Her fingers brushed the folded letter in her pocket, its cryptic words burning through the fabric like embers

"As the veil closes, push the butterflies through."

She hadn't dared read it again, but the line repeated in her head like a whisper.

Up front, the guards exchanged clipped words—too quiet to catch. Tammy shifted her eyes, scanning the smudged window. A shadow moved across the tree line. It was nothing, but it didn't feel like nothing.

Her pulse quickened. "How much further?" she asked.

The nearest guard didn't turn. "Not long," he replied.

Unease bloomed into suspicion. The weight pressed again on her chest: her family, the explosion, the voice...

"He is coming."

It was all building toward something. Something she couldn't escape, no matter how fast the car moved.

She turned back to the window. Darkness crawled across the glass, her breath fogging its surface. Her reflection stared back and behind her, she thought she saw an outline. Faint and indistinct.

When she blinked, it was gone.

Her fingers trembled as she gripped the letter.

Whatever was happening, it wasn't over.

CHAPTER SIX

A *Situation in the Situation Room*

Agent Richardson's report had traveled up the chain of command like wildfire, triggering an emergency briefing in the Situation Room of the White House.

A red phone rang, slicing through the tense silence. An aide to a general snatched it up. "Name and credentials, please?"

"Special Agent Richardson, National Security Agency. Clearance code Alpha-Charlie-Zulu-Whiskey-seven-nine-eight."

A brief pause, then the blunt reply, "We clear you for a briefing."

Before Richardson could speak, a sharp voice barked through the line. "What the hell is going on, Richardson? These reports make no sense!" It was General Henderson, Chief of Staff of the Army—his tone like a hammer striking steel.

"General," Richardson said, keeping his voice steady despite the onslaught, "my team is prioritizing this as we speak. We're merging all relevant—"

"Prioritize faster," Henderson said. "I want answers, and I want them yesterday."

"Understood, General. I'll escalate this now."

In the Situation Room, the muffled scratching of pens and the low hum of monitors underscored the tension. No one spoke. Everyone was holding their breath.

The room buzzed with tension—a symphony of military precision layered over raw urgency. Uniformed officers and intelligence leaders exchanged clipped phrases and sharp glances, while NASA's top brass scribbled notes. Satellite imagery flickered across monitors. The Situation Room was a hive of movement, but at the head of the table, President William Davidson remained still. He didn't need to raise his voice to command the room. His dark hair, streaked with the earliest hints of gray, was trimmed in a no-nonsense military cut. He looked every bit the former general—broad-shouldered, sharp-jawed, and solid. There was a quiet intensity in his eyes that came not from politics but from the battlefield. This was a man who had once led troops through sandstorms and firefights, who'd earned loyalty that didn't fade when the bullets stopped flying.

His presence grounded the room.

He was in his late forties—old enough to carry the weight of his decisions, young enough to still fight if he had to. That balance made him dangerous in the best way.

By his side stood Dr. Michael Solomon, the president's unprecedented choice for a religious advisor. Solomon's piercing blue eyes flickered with a mix of intellect and quiet faith as he studied the room's tension. He was a man of contrasts: his scholarly air tempered by a calm conviction, his trimmed beard offset by hands worn from decades of handling ancient texts and sacred scrolls. His presence—understated, but magnetic—reminded those in the room that wisdom often whispered where power shouted.

President Davidson raised a hand, and the murmur of voices died down. He spoke with the quiet force of someone accustomed to obedience. "Agent Richardson," he said, "what's the status on the spacecraft that crash-landed in Iowa?"

Over the speakerphone, Richardson's voice came steady and composed.

"It's Voyager 2, Mr. President. So far, we've recovered and reassembled about half of it from the debris." He paused. "The craft has markings. Strange ones. They resemble hieroglyphics, but our analysts say they've seen nothing like them. I've sent the images to your secure inbox, sir."

Davidson's brows knit as he opened the email on his tablet and turned the screen toward Dr. Solomon. "Doctor, do these symbols mean anything to you?"

Solomon leaned in, his sharp gaze narrowing as he studied the image. A flicker of something—recognition, perhaps—passed across his face but vanished just as quickly. The room held its breath.

"These markings are... unfamiliar," he said, "and yet they stir something. I've studied sacred texts for decades, but this feels older—ancient beyond written record. As if it came from a time before scripture itself."

The president tilted his head. "What's your recommendation, Doctor?"

"With your permission, sir," Solomon replied, his voice calm but intent, "I'd like to consult my colleagues. Someone may know more."

Davidson nodded once. "Do it."

Solomon rose and strode out of the Situation Room, already turning pages in his mind no library had touched in centuries.

The president turned his attention back to Agent Richardson, his tone edged with concern. "What's the latest on the International Space Station? Why would the astronaut jettison the escape pod if the station is still operational?"

Richardson spoke in a measured tone, but uncertainty edged into his words. "Sir, she claims the station is gone—said it exploded after being swallowed by some kind of mist. But we're still receiving transmissions, so we can't confirm anything yet."

Davidson narrowed his eyes. "Is it possible she's right? Could the station send signals even if it's destroyed?"

"Not with any tech I've ever seen," Richardson said. "There's no known system that could fake transmissions like that if the station were gone. Until we know more, I'd advise caution."

Davidson nodded, then turned to the NASA advisor seated at the far end of the table. "I want your best people on this. Run diagnostics. Try sending a coded message to the ISS. If someone replies, verify the origin and confirm the station's location. I need answers."

The advisor stood without hesitation, exchanging a quick look with his colleagues before rushing out of the room.

The president's tone sharpened as he addressed Agent Richardson. "Agent, this next question requires a direct answer. No gray area. Understood?"

"Understood, sir," Richardson replied, steady.

Davidson's eyes narrowed. "Were there any reports of a man—unusual, mysterious—near the landing site?"

There was a brief pause of hesitation. "Yes, sir. The astronaut reported seeing a man in purple robes as she was landing. Just a glance—when she looked again, he was gone."

Davidson's jaw clenched. He rubbed his temple and began pacing. "I can't believe it... I thought the briefings were exaggerations. Folklore." He paused, scanning the room. "Everyone who isn't an advisor—leave. Now."

Chairs scraped. Within seconds, the Situation Room emptied, leaving only the president and his inner circle.

Davidson rose, his movements slow and deliberate. "What I'm about to share does not leave this room. It is top secret. In the 1970s, we launched Voyager 2. The public knows it as a deep space probe meant to photograph the cosmos. That's only part of the truth." He paused, letting the silence stretch, then continued. "Voyager 2 was also a listening device—a probe sent to make contact. The program was championed by a special advisor... a man in purple robes. He appeared at the White House and met with the sitting president. His insights were extraordinary. Based on what he shared, Congress approved the launch with record funding." Davidson's voice lowered. "He left us with a warning: 'When you see me again, the prophecy will begin, and the Right Hand's arrival will be near.'"

The room fell silent.

"When asked who the Right Hand was," Davidson continued, "he answered: 'The Right Hand is the end of what we know and the beginning of Revelations.' He left specific instructions. If he ever returned—we were to prepare. Everything we know... would change."

The advisors exchanged uneasy glances, but before anyone could speak, the door burst open. Dr. Solomon rushed in, clutching a stack of papers, his face pale.

"Mr. President," he said, "we found something."

Davidson turned to face him, brows tightening.

"One of my colleagues uncovered an ancient text—one of the oldest tied to the Old Testament. It describes the Tree of Life. Adam. Eve. The forbidden fruit..."

He paused, holding up a photo from the Voyager wreckage.

"That same symbol is on the spacecraft. The letter 'E'—we believe it stands for Eden."

Davidson's expression hardened. "Eden," he repeated. "What else?"

Solomon's voice dropped. "And the snake? Likely Lucifer. Evil incarnate. The same serpent that tempted Eve." He hesitated, then pointed to another symbol. "This one—'A.' It's ancient. Predates scripture."

The president leaned forward, voice low and deliberate. "Does it suggest anything... significant?"

Solomon's hands trembled as he answered. "Sir... it aligns with an apocryphal tale. A being known as the Right Hand—said to have stood beside the Creator before time began."

Davidson stiffened. "The Right Hand," he said. "The warnings passed down... is this what they meant?"

Solomon's eyes widened. "You've heard of it?" he asked, voice cracking. "I thought it was a myth. A fragment of lore..." He stepped back, shaking his head. "But if this is real..." His voice trailed off. Then, just above a whisper, he said, "Then the Right Hand is real."

Silence filled the room, heavy and electric.

Davidson gripped the edge of the table, his voice quiet but unwavering. "I'm not saying I want to believe it, but the evidence is too consistent to ignore."

Solomon swallowed. "And the tale... it includes a warning." He leaned in, his voice like the hush before a storm. "When He arrives... and the trumpets sound... the end begins." A tremor ran through him as he added, "Mr. President, this isn't just a revelation. It's a reckoning."

Davidson straightened, the weight of leadership settling on his shoulders. "Then we've run out of time to doubt," he said.

"Prepare for the unthinkable."

Dr. Solomon's words hung in the air, plunging the Situation Room into a suffocating silence. The president gripped the table's edge, knuckles white, a storm of possibilities tearing through his thoughts—national security, prophecy, the terrifying unknown.

Around him, nervous glances flickered. No one spoke.

Adrenaline surged. Davidson clenched his fists, his breath shallow. The tension was a living thing, crawling across the room like static. Even Solomon, who moments ago had delivered the revelation with fire, now stepped back, his face pale.

"This can't be happening," he said, raking a trembling hand through his hair. His voice cracked, eyes scanning the room for reassurance—and finding none. Every person sat frozen, the weight of the unknown anchoring them in place. Goosebumps rippled across arms. A collective chill moved through the room like a premonition.

The president paced, slow and mechanical. Each step matched the rhythm of his pounding heart. His brow furrowed; his jaw tightened. The information swirled in his mind like a gathering storm. This wasn't politics or military strategy. This was something older. Something cosmic.

As the silence stretched, it pressed harder—until something inside Davidson shifted. Beneath the fear, a fire burned. It spread through his limbs, stiffening his spine, focusing his mind.

They stood on the edge of something they couldn't yet name. And the president knew hesitation would cost them everything.

The sharp slam of a door shattered the stillness.

Scientific advisors flooded into the room, their footsteps quick, faces pale. The room's tension—which had only just settled— spiked again.

One advisor stepped forward, eyes flicking between the president and the gathered staff. "Mr. President, we sent a coded message to the International Space Station. The response came back in less than a minute. It said, 'He is coming.'"

A stunned silence followed.

"We believe the astronaut may be right. The station might be... gone. But somehow, it's still transmitting. We can't explain it."

The president froze mid-step. His jaw tightened. "How could she be right?" he said. "I thought none of this was possible." He turned to Dr. Solomon. "Doctor... What do we do?"

Solomon's voice was steady, but the weight behind it was unmistakable. "We act as if every word is true. If this being is coming, we must prepare. I'll reach out to my network."

Another advisor stepped forward, holding a tablet. "Sir, we just received updated images from Voyager. You need to see this."

Davidson crossed the room in three quick strides. The screen flickered to life. At first, only static—then a shimmer. Faint and shifting. And then, something massive moved behind it: the silhouette of a colossal spacecraft, just visible against the void.

"Where was this taken?" Davidson asked, voice low.

"Just outside the moon's orbit, sir."

The president stared at the image, his face unreadable. After a few seconds, he sank into his chair. "They're almost here," he said.

There was a long, silent pause in the situation room.

"We're too late."

Without warning, the Situation Room exploded with sound.

The monitors and TVs erupted in a blaring screech that slammed into the room like a shockwave. People staggered, clutching their ears as the noise vibrated through their chests—a sonic assault that drowned out every voice. General Henderson yelled something, but the roar swallowed his words whole.

Then, just as abrupt, there was silence.

Breaths came in gasps. Rustling uniforms, the scrape of a chair—small, human sounds rushing in to fill the void. A low hum pulsed from the monitors. One by one, the screens flickered back to life, casting harsh light on stunned faces.

A single message appeared on the largest monitor in stark white letters: "THE PROPHECY IS UNDERWAY. HE IS HERE."

The screens blinked again. Grainy footage flickered to life—of the International Space Station. For a single heartbeat, it drifted against the stars. Then, in a flash of white fire, it exploded. The feed dissolved into static.

A voice followed. Deep and resonant. "He has arrived."

The lights flickered. Sirens wailed. The room erupted into chaos. Secret Service agents burst through the doors. Two of them grabbed the president by the arms and began pulling him toward the secure exit. Radios crackled with commands.

"There's a situation in the Situation Room. The Eagle is en route to the bunker. All units, converge now. Secure the cabinet—move!"

President Davidson resisted for half a second, locking eyes with his generals. "Sound the alarm. I want every asset on alert within the hour. Prepare for an invasion." His voice sliced through the panic like a blade.

Somewhere, on the other side of the earth, far from the White House, a pair of girls sat in a living room... like butterflies beginning to stir in their cocoons.

CHAPTER SEVEN

Butterflies

Hours later, after the chaos in the Situation Room and the shattering footage from space, a sleek, black SUV with windows tinted so dark they could hide the world glided to a halt in front of a house on the edge of the Air Force base.

Tammy pushed the door open and stepped out. Her knees wobbled with the first step, and she caught herself on the edge of the door. She didn't lift her feet so much as slide them forward, her shoulders caved in, spine curled under the invisible weight she carried. Sweat streaked her brow, smudging the dirt she wiped away.

Her breathing was shallow and uneven, each inhale a struggle she had to will herself through. For a moment, she tilted her head back, her unfocused gaze landing on the pale sky, its vast emptiness pressing down on her. She dropped her head again, her eyes snagging on the house ahead—a plain, inescapable symbol of her confinement.

The stale tang of sweat clung to her clothes, stifling even against the crisp breeze that carried the scent of pine from the surrounding forest. It sharpened her awareness of her own discomfort—the grit of exhaustion drying in her throat, the faint metallic edge of her breath. She lingered, then moved forward, one slow step at a time.

Her gaze swept the area, pausing on the armed guards stationed nearby. Their presence felt deliberate, their sharp vigilance a reminder of the debrief—and of the cryptic letter folded in her pocket. Her fingers brushed against it, and the chilling words surfaced again.

"As the veil closes, push the butterflies through."

The phrase echoed through her mind, quiet but persistent.

What did it mean? Butterflies—symbols of hope, of transformation... or something darker? Her thoughts spun, catching on fractured images and unspoken dread, but the pieces refused to fit. The words gnawed at her, their meaning elusive yet weighty, like they held answers she wasn't ready to find.

Her pulse fluttered. Her fingers found the crumpled letter again. The paper felt damp against her palm, grounding her without comfort. She gripped it tighter, but the unease slithered back in, coiling beneath her ribs and squeezing until she couldn't take a full breath.

Tammy caught the tail end of a hushed exchange between two nearby guards, their voices clipped but urgent.

"Are we sure this is where she's supposed to be? Isn't this where the president's family is staying?"

"It came straight from the president," the other replied. "He wanted both of them in the same place."

A chill slid down Tammy's spine. The president's family? Her thoughts jumped to the cryptic letter, the phrase that wouldn't stop repeating in her mind: *Push the butterflies through.* But she stuffed the thought away, burying it beneath exhaustion as she forced herself forward.

Inside the safe house, the contrast was jarring. Two young girls sat cross-legged on the floor, crayons in hand, their laughter light and unbothered. Innocence radiated from them, an almost sacred calm that didn't belong in a world like this.

On a nearby couch, a woman spoke into a phone. Her voice was calm, composed, but carried the unmistakable weight of authority. Tammy blinked, a flicker of recognition tugging at her, but her brain was too foggy to catch up.

The scent of brewed coffee met her nose as she entered the dining area, but the sterile bite of fresh ink and paper overran it. A female guard sat at the table, upright and alert, her eyes sharp but not unkind.

"Take a seat," the guard said, motioning to the chair across from her.

Tammy collapsed into it, her body protesting every movement. Her legs ached. Her head pulsed with fatigue.

"Can I call my parents now?" she asked, her voice just above a whisper.

The guard exchanged a quick glance with someone out of view, then handed her a phone.

"It's a secure line. We'll be monitoring. Keep it brief—no classified information."

Tammy took the phone, her grip unsteady. Her fingers hovered over the keypad for a moment before punching in the familiar number. The ring echoed in her ear, distant and hollow.

The moment her mother answered, Tammy swallowed a lump in her throat. "I'm safe," she said, the words coming out softer than she meant. "I promise." She paused, trying to sound strong. "I don't know when I'll be home... Things are complicated here." A silence followed, heavy and filled with everything she couldn't say. "I love you both," she whispered, her voice cracking. "I'll call as soon as I can."

She hung up the phone with a sigh. Her hand trembled as she set the phone down. "Thanks," she said to the guards, her voice flat.

"I'll just... sit for a bit."

She nodded toward the living room. The guards let her pass without a word.

Tammy sank into the chair, her body folding into the cushions like a marionette with cut strings. Across the room, the woman hung up the phone, her voice composed and steady, the demeanor of someone accustomed to control. The conversation hadn't even registered with Tammy, her gaze following the woman's actions, unfocused. When the call ended, Tammy glanced over again. The woman's face struck a chord of familiarity again, but her exhausted brain fumbled with the connection.

"Hi, I'm Tammy," she said, voice hoarse and smile worn thin. "You look familiar, but... it's been a long day. Have we met?"

The woman chuckled, a soft, musical sound that felt out of place in the aftermath of so much trauma.

"I'm Alaina Davidson," she said. "My husband is the president. I serve as first lady. It's a pleasure to meet you, Tammy."

Tammy blinked, staring. The realization hit like a splash of cold water. She straightened reflexively and glanced down at her rumpled clothes.

"Oh, wow... You're the first lady? I feel underdressed."

Alaina's smile widened, warm and genuine. "This isn't a formal reception. My husband insisted we come here—said it was the safest place for us right now."

Tammy nodded, the words safest place clanging against the image of the station exploding and the cryptic letter burning a hole in her pocket, but she pushed the thought aside.

"So," Alaina said, "what's your story? How did you end up here—with me?"

Tammy hesitated, glancing toward a nearby guard. "Can I... talk about that?"

The guards exchanged a look and gave a nod.

Alaina tilted her head. "Tammy, the president tells me everything. You're safe to speak."

Something about her voice—steady but kind—loosened a knot in Tammy's chest. She let out a slow breath. "I'm an astronaut," she said. "I served aboard the International Space Station." Her fingers fidgeted in her lap. "We were troubleshooting something. Then it all went wrong. Captain Gonzalez told me to get to the escape pod. He shouted we were under attack... and I ran." She paused, jaw tightening. "I didn't look back. I couldn't. And when I did... there was an explosion and then it was just gone."

Alaina said nothing, letting the silence absorb the weight.

"I was the only one who made it out," Tammy added, her voice cracking. "Everyone else—my entire team... they're gone."

Alaina's expression softened, the gravity of Tammy's words sinking in. "I'm so sorry," she said. "That must be what had my husband pacing earlier. He wouldn't tell me details, just insisted we move here. Now I understand why."

Tammy looked down. "I don't know what to believe anymore. I keep replaying it. Over and over. And then the debrief..." She exhaled, rubbing her face. "They didn't tell me anything. I'm still in the dark."

For a moment, silence stretched between them, broken only by the soft scuff of crayons on paper. Tammy exhaled, glancing at the two little girls cross-legged on the floor. Their giggles had quieted to curious murmurs as they peeked up at her, wide-eyed and cautious. The simple innocence of it tugged at something deep within her—a fragile echo of normalcy she hadn't realized she missed.

Before Tammy could ask Alaina more, the girls rose without warning, their movement slicing through the stillness like a ripple across the water. "Can we go get a drink?" one of them asked.

Alaina nodded. "Go ahead."

They darted toward the kitchen, the bounce in their steps shadowed by the quiet glide of a nearby guard.

Tammy watched them go, a faint smile warming her face. Their laughter carried from the next room—soft, untarnished, a sound untouched by everything unraveling around her. It felt like a balm on raw nerves.

"They seem like sweet kids," she said, surprised by the warmth in her own voice. "How old?"

Alaina's expression softened with pride. "Madison's thirteen. Savannah's ten." Her smile grew wistful. "We came here for the war games. The girls were so excited—they couldn't stop talking about the jets. But..." Her voice trailed off, the smile dimming. "I don't think we'll see them now."

Before Tammy could respond, the girls returned, drinks in hand, their energy skipping back into the room ahead of them.

Alaina stood and gestured toward Tammy. "Girls, this is Tammy. She's an astronaut and been to space."

The words rippled through the air like magic. Madison and Savannah froze, then blinked in astonishment. Their awe was immediate and pure.

"You've been to space?" Madison asked, inching closer, curiosity gleaming in her eyes.

Tammy chuckled. The weight on her shoulders lifted just enough for her to straighten a little. "Yeah, I've been up there," she said, and for the first time in hours, there was a note of pride in her voice. "I worked on the International Space Station. Floating in space... it's like nothing else. You look down and see Earth—this beautiful blue sphere—and for a second, you forget how dark everything is beyond it." Her gaze drifted, caught in a distant memory, the edges softened by fatigue and awe. Then she looked back at the girls, and her smile found a new shape. "It's something you never forget."

Alaina cleared her throat, her voice slipping into a cooler, practical tone. "Tammy, would you mind watching the girls for a few minutes? I need to speak with the security team."

Tammy nodded. "Of course."

As Alaina steps away, the girls wasted no time, inching closer to Tammy with wide, expectant eyes. "What's it like up there?" Madison said, her voice filled with awe.

Savannah clutched a crayon, as if frozen mid-doodle, waiting for Tammy's reply.

Tammy leaned forward, her voice dropping, as though sharing a secret. "It's quiet," she said. "Peaceful, but strange. You don't walk; you float. Imagine flipping upside down and realizing you don't fall." She smiled as their eyes widened. "And when you look out the window... it's like you're staring into velvet. Deep and endless. Like the universe is holding its breath."

The girls hung on her every word, their whispers of amazement blending into the soft shuffle of crayons against paper. Tammy's voice wove tales of the station's corridors and the thrill of spacewalks, carrying the girls into the vast expanse of the universe. For a moment, the weight Tammy carried felt a little lighter.

When Alaina returned, she paused, watching the scene with a faint smile before stepping closer. As she leaned in to kiss Madison's forehead, her blouse lifted, revealing a vibrant tattoo on her side, two monarch butterflies, bright orange and black against pale skin.

Tammy's eyes lingered on the artwork, curiosity flaring. "That's beautiful," she said, tilting her head. "What's the story behind it?"

Alaina's smile widened, a warm laugh bubbling up as she straightened.

"Oh, that... that's a good story," she replied, her voice tinged with nostalgia.

She took a seat and glanced at her daughters.

"When they were little, they started taking dance lessons. My husband, he always marveled at their grace, the way they moved like two butterflies fluttering through a sunlit meadow." Her gaze softened, the memory painting her mind with warmth. "They are my little queens, and I carry that reminder with me always."

Tammy listened, struck by the tenderness in Alaina's voice, the love etched into every word. The tattoo, once just ink on skin, now felt alive, a symbol of something far greater.

Then Tammy's heart skipped, a chill spreading through her chest. The cryptic words, the image of tangled butterflies, and the letter. Its message raced through Tammy's mind.

Her breath caught. With trembling hands, she reached into her pocket and pulled out the crumpled letter, its edges worn from her grasp. She unfolded it, her pulse hammering as she read the words again, desperate for clarity she didn't find.

The words sent a shiver through Tammy, an icy ripple that prickled her skin and settled deep in her spine: "As the veil closes, push the butterflies through."

What did it mean? Her mind spiraled, reaching for answers that refused to take shape. Each beat of her heart pounded like a drum in her ears, echoing the growing urgency. Her breath hitched, shallow and uneven, as though her lungs couldn't hold air. The adrenaline buzzing through her veins sharpened her senses.

Tammy's throat tightened as she looked down at the letter in her hands. The memory of the man in the purple robes lingered— his silence, the weight of his gaze, the way he'd vanished without a trace. None of it made sense, but the letter remained, its presence heavy and undeniable.

She hesitated for a moment, and the air between her and Alaina had shifted. Tammy's gaze settled on the first lady, and something inside her clicked into place.

"I need to tell you something," she said, her voice low, frayed at the edges. Tammy extended the letter toward her. "Please... sit."

Alaina took the paper and lowered herself onto the couch, her eyes scanning Tammy's face.

Tammy drew a breath to steady herself. "This is going to sound unbelievable," she said. "But I need you to hear me out." She rubbed her hands together once before speaking again. "After I landed, I saw someone—this man in purple robes. He didn't say a word. Just handed me that letter. Looked at me like... like he knew me. And then he was gone." She paused, watching Alaina's reaction. "When I saw that tattoo—the butterflies—I remembered the letter. I think... I think this message is about your daughters."

Alaina blinked, then looked down at the letter in her hands. Her shoulders stiffened, the color draining from her face.

Tammy could feel her heart pounding, her thoughts crashing into one another. The letter felt heavier now, its meaning clawing closer. Something was coming. Something big.

Across from her, Alaina was motionless, the silence stretching between them. Finally, Alaina spoke, her voice just above an audible whisper. "Please," she said. "Promise me this stays between us. If anything happens to me... I need to know you'll protect my girls. Take them to their father and keep them safe."

Tammy's eyes didn't waver. She nodded once. "You have my word," she said. "I'll protect them... like they're my own."

The weight of it settled between them.

For a moment, neither moved. Then, from outside, the piercing scream of a jet ripped through the sky.

Tammy turned toward the window, watching as it vanished beyond the clouds. The world held its breath, and she held her promise.

CHAPTER EIGHT

War Games

F ar from the tense quiet of the safe house, the Air Force base
buzzed with activity. Jets screamed overhead, drills barked
across the concrete, and somewhere inside a break room, Roo
scrubbed at a counter like it had wronged him. His movements
were sharp and restless, jaw clenched, forearms taut with effort.
The rag crumpled in his grip, but the stains refused to vanish—as
if they mocked him for every missed shot, every snide comment,
and every second he felt out of place.

Behind him, the TV droned. Then he heard something that
caught his attention.

"Breaking news..." The anchor tried to appear calm, but
the tightness around his mouth gave him away. "Reports show
anomalies over several military bases worldwide. While details
remain scarce, early footage shows strange formations appearing
through cloud cover. The Pentagon has not issued a formal
response."

Roo froze. On the screen, shaky footage flickered—something enormous pierced through clouds before the camera jolted and cut to static. A dark shape loomed just outside the frame.

"What the hell..." Roo said, stepping closer.

The door slammed open, and Roo jumped, spinning to see Lizzie in the doorway. She looked different—shoulders squared, eyes narrowed. No smart remark. Just caution.

"You see this?" Roo asked, nodding toward the screen.

Lizzie stepped in, glancing at the TV and then back to Roo. Her grip tightened on the soda can she held, its aluminum creaking. "It has to be just a test. Some classified hardware or optics glitch," she said.

Roo responded, the nerves could be heard in his voice. "Doesn't look like any test I've ever seen."

Lizzie hesitated a moment before saying, "We can't worry about what we can't control. Let's focus on what's in front of us." Then, with a small sigh, she nodded toward the hallway. "War games are starting soon. You ready for this mess?"

Before Roo could respond, the familiar crackle of the PA system broke the silence.

"We are ready to begin our annual war games. All crew chiefs report to the flight line and prepare to launch your jets for the first mission."

The announcement echoed off the walls, snapping the room back into motion.

The war games were more than just training. Every year, Air Forces from around the globe converged to pit their best against each other—five jets from one country against five from another in simulated combat. Precision, reflexes, and coordination decided winners. For pilots, it was adrenaline-fueled competition. For ground crews like Roo, it was a matter of pride. A flawless launch meant everything.

Roo glanced up. Lizzie still stood in the doorway, helmet dangling from her fingertips. She had rumpled her flight suit at the sleeve, as if she'd suited up in a hurry. She hesitated—just for a second—then stepped inside.

"What are you still doing here?" Roo asked. "Shouldn't you be heading out?"

Lizzie met his gaze. For a moment, her tough shell cracked. "I just wanted to say... thank you," she said, voice lower now. "For showing me around the hangar when no one else would. For listening." She took a breath, her eyes searching his face. "Sometimes it feels like everyone here's just waiting for me to screw up. But you," she smiled, just a hint of it, "you reminded me I'm not alone."

Roo blinked, surprised. The words landed heavier than he expected.

"You're a good person, Roo," she added. "Don't let these guys beat that out of you."

Before he could respond, a voice barked from the hallway. "Miles! What the hell are you doing in here?" Lizzie's commanding officer stormed into view, fury in every step. "War games started five minutes ago! They're waiting on you at the jet!"

Lizzie snapped to attention, spine stiffening. "Yes, sir!" She threw Roo one last look—half grateful, half apologetic—then turned on her heel and jogged down the corridor, her helmet bumping against her hip with every step.

On the flight line, Senior Airman Ramirez stood beside his jet, arms crossed, a smirk tugging at the corner of his mouth. Next to him leaned his supervisor, Technical Sergeant Charles Tipton—

the self-anointed king of the crew chiefs. For these two, war games weren't training. They were a stage.

Tipton lounged against the nose of the aircraft like he owned it, his boots gleaming, his sunglasses catching the morning light just right. He didn't spare a glance at the junior airman nearby fumbling with a wrench. Instead, Tipton barked out his usual sarcasm.

"You planning to retire before you finish that, kid? Christ, you're making me look bad."

The younger airman mumbled an apology and scrambled to recover, his ears burning.

Ramirez let out a low snicker, enjoying the show in front of him.

Tipton nudged him with an elbow. "You see that, Ramirez? They don't make crew chiefs like they used to. Back in my day, we didn't need someone to hold our damn hand."

Ramirez grinned. "Maybe they'll add training wheels to the toolbox next year."

Tipton chuckled, a deep, smug laugh that drew sidelong glances. "Come on, these war games are ours to win. I want perfect. Anything less, and I'll pretend I don't know you."

Ramirez adjusted his gloves with mock precision. "Perfect's easy. I'm just waiting for you to catch up. You sign off on those forms yet, or did arthritis slow you down?"

Tipton laughed louder, slapping the jet in response. "Son, I was fixing birds before you learned to wipe your nose. You're lucky I'm still here to keep you honest."

Their banter snapped like electricity—sharp, cocky, and calculated. Around them, the flight line buzzed with activity, but for Tipton and Ramirez, the rest were just extras in a show starring them.

As Tipton and Ramirez traded jabs, a shuttle rolled onto the flight line and hissed to a halt. A young pilot stepped out, prompting both crew chiefs to snap to attention.

The pilot gave them a once-over. "Everything ready, boys? We need this bird in the air—now."

"Yes, sir," they echoed in unison. "You're clear to enter the cockpit."

The pilot nodded, began his pre-flight checks with swift precision, and climbed into the seat without another word.

On the other side of the flight line, tension bristled as the UK team prepped their jet. Crew chiefs moved with quiet urgency, every motion crisp. Fumes thickened the air, mixing with the whine of turbines and the rising energy of competition.

Lizzie arrived at the British jet, helmet under one arm, her posture focused and unbothered—until Tipton's voice cracked across the flight line like a beer can opening at a frat party.

"It's called a cockpit, princess. You don't have the required equipment to get in there."

Ramirez barked out a laugh.

Lizzie didn't flinch. She rolled her eyes, muttered something under her breath, and got to work on her inspection—flawless and fluid.

Tipton elbowed Ramirez with a smug grin. "Look at that. You Brits brought your A-team, huh?" He raised his voice, baiting the UK crew. "Heard all about her simulator scores. Seventy-two crashes, right? Should've issued her a parachute and a prayer."

More chuckling ensued. The UK crew chiefs shifted with unease, not meeting Tipton's eyes.

Lizzie didn't bite. She finished her checks, and her expression was unreadable, save for the faintest flush in her cheeks. No words.

No reaction. Just a silent promise as she climbed into the cockpit—
I'll show you.

War games thundered overhead as jets screamed across the sky. Ramirez crouched beneath his aircraft, plugging the communication cord into the belly panel. He adjusted his headset, tried the radio—and got nothing. Just static.

He yanked the headset off with a hiss of irritation, then flashed Tipton a sharp chopping motion: comm failure.

Tipton raised an eyebrow and strolled over, leisurely, like the problem didn't even warrant his time. He peeled one side of Ramirez's headset back, the engine noise making conversation near-impossible.

"What's the issue?" he shouted.

Ramirez leaned closer. "Comm's down! Nothing but static!"

Tipton's smirk faltered. His eyes narrowed. "Dammit. That damn Dr. Terracotta," he said, rolling his eyes. "I knew he'd screw us. That son of a bitch gave us a bum cord just to watch us eat it."

Blame was as easy to Tipton as breathing. Ramirez didn't argue. He just nodded, jaw clenched, feeding Tipton's indignation.

Tipton flagged the expediter truck with dramatic gestures. When it arrived, he snatched the new cord like it offended him.

"Leave it to the brainiacs to screw up the one job that matters," he said.

Ramirez swapped the cords with smooth and quick precision, sliding the new one into place. His headset hissed, then crackled to life.

"Chief, you there? Chief, do you copy?" the pilot's voice came through the static.

"Loud and clear," Ramirez responded, calm returned to his tone. He stepped back and scanned the jet. Everything was ready.

He unplugged, raised his hands, and ran through the launch signals.

Across the flight line, the UK crew had already finished their launch. Lizzie's jet surged forward, the crew cheering as it lifted off. One of the British crew chiefs turned, flashing a smug one-finger salute.

Tipton's scowl deepened.

Ramirez didn't need to look to know his supervisor was fuming.

"Unbelievable," Tipton said. "We got beat by crumpet-eaters."

Then the mocking started.

"I've seen two blind men launch a jet faster than you clowns!" one Brit heckled.

"What happened—too busy stroking each other's egos?" another laughed, flipping the bird.

Ramirez stiffened. His knuckles whitened around his gloves.

Tipton's face flushed dark, but his voice stayed cold. "Ramirez," he said, tight and low, "go find that damn doctor and make sure he knows he cost us."

Ramirez nodded and climbed into the expediter truck without a word, the door slamming shut behind him. As the vehicle rolled toward the hangar, Tipton stayed behind, still simmering and blaming... still Tipton.

Ramirez's fury mounted with every bump of the expediter truck. His fists clenched on his knees, knuckles white, boots tapping a jagged rhythm on the metal floor. By the time the truck lurched to a stop outside the hangar, he was a powder keg ready to blow.

He jumped down and stormed inside, barking at every airman in sight. "Where is he?! Where's that damn doctor?" The walls caught the echo and hurled it back. Ramirez didn't flinch. "Dr. Terracotta! Get your ass out here!"

He marched into the snack room like a wrecking ball, zeroing in on Roo, who stood mid-wipe, a rag still in hand.

"You. Where is he?" Ramirez jabbed a finger at Roo. "You protect that loser. Where is he?"

Roo gave a few confused blinks. "I haven't seen him. What's going on?"

"Nothing that involves you, Snacks," Ramirez said. "Go back to selling chips." He spun and stalked off.

Something was off. Tossing the rag on the counter, Roo followed.

Ramirez blew through the hangar, shouting, shoving—until he found Dr. Terracotta near the tool shed with Marvin. Without warning, he seized the doctor by the shoulder and spun him around, finger stabbing the air.

"You gave us a faulty comm cord, Doc! You cost us points!"

Dr. Terracotta stumbled back, pale and startled. "I... I don't assign cords. I just test them. That's all I do—"

Ramirez knocked the book from his hands. It hit the ground with a slap that echoed. "Don't lie to me!" he roared. "You did this on purpose!"

Roo arrived just as the scene unraveled. He stepped between them. "Hey!" he yelled. "That's enough."

Ramirez glanced at him. "Stay out of this, snack boy. It's his fault."

"No, it's not," Roo said, voice calm but edged with steel. "The expediter hands out cords. Doc just makes sure they work."

Ramirez stepped forward, face twisted in fury. "You will not protect him from this."

"Try me," Roo said.

Ramirez shoved him—hard. Roo stumbled but didn't fall. His feet planted. His voice didn't waver. "If you've got a problem, take it to your supervisor. Otherwise, walk away."

A tense second passed.

"This isn't over," Ramirez growled, stabbing a finger in warning before storming out.

The silence that followed rang louder than the shouting.

Roo turned to Dr. Terracotta, who stood frozen, eyes still wide. "You okay, Doc?"

The doctor bent down, picking up his book with trembling hands. "Yeah... I think so. He always blames me. I don't get it."

Roo placed a hand on his shoulder. "Some people just suck, Doc," he whispered. "Some people just suck."

Roo returned to the snack area to find chaos. The trash can lay on its side; popcorn was spilled across the floor like confetti; and torn-open chip bags were scattered like debris from a storm. He sighed, pinching the bridge of his nose. There was no doubt who was responsible—or why. Shaking his head, he grabbed the broom and got to work cleaning up the latest disaster.

The roar of engines still echoed as he scrubbed at the last stubborn stain on the counter, the earlier confrontation with Ramirez replaying in his mind. Outside, jets screamed across the sky in tight formations. The annual war games were in full swing.

Inside the hangar, things quieted. The hum of a nearby radio buzzed, filling the silence with static-laced voices. Roo worked alone, his thoughts drifting.

High above, the sky was alive with motion. Pilots from around the globe wove through the air in a blur of precision and aggression, their jets gleaming like blades under the sun. Vapor trails stitched across the heavens as teams sparred in elegant, deadly dances.

In the middle of it all, Lizzie flew.

The scent of jet fuel clung to her flight suit. Her hands were steady on the stick, her breath tight with focus. Her jet bucked as she rolled through a tight turn, chasing a flicker of movement across her HUD. G-forces punched into her chest, but she didn't flinch. Radio chatter crackled in her ear. Background noise now. She remained locked in.

Then—something tore through the clouds.

A massive structure surged into view above the battle. Black. Monolithic. It punched through the clouds like a pillar dropped from the heavens, blotting out the sun. Its surface shimmered, like it was made of both metal and shadow.

Lizzie's blood ran cold.

She yanked the stick hard. Alarms blared, the Over-G warning flaring red. Her jet groaned in protest, fighting the maneuver as she pulled out of a dive, her body crushed into the seat. The sky spun as the world tilted.

"Control! Control, this is Jet 1097! I've got a level three Over-G—requesting immediate return!"

Her voice was tight but calm. Behind her, the pillar loomed in the clouds, still and absolute.

She steadied the aircraft and turned toward the base, the dark shape shrinking in her mirrors but never disappearing.

Roo was still sweeping up the wreckage in the snack room when the radio crackled to life.

"Jet 1097 is inbound with a level three Over-G. Crew chiefs report to the flight line for recovery."

He froze. 1097 was Lizzie's jet.

Instinct told him to bolt for the flight line, to make sure she was okay—but he stayed rooted, broom in hand. Leaving now would raise eyebrows and invite trouble. He clenched his jaw and continued listening to the radio.

Outside, Tipton's voice cut through the air like a rusty saw.

"Hey, Brits! You better check on your princess!" he yelled. "Broke another jet, didn't she? Too much tea in the system. Our pilots don't snap wings when they fly."

Ramirez chimed in with a snort. "You might've beat us on the launch, but your golden girl doesn't know her stick from her throttle."

The UK crew chiefs said nothing. Focused and silent, they watched as Lizzie's jet approached with a slight tremor in its landing gear. She taxied to the designated spot, and her team flagged her in with crisp, practiced gestures.

As the canopy lifted, Lizzie climbed out. Her face was pale, hands trembling as she removed her helmet.

One of the British crew chiefs stepped forward. "You all right there, ma'am?"

Lizzie gave a faint nod, her voice shaky. "I know it sounds insane... but I saw something up there. A structure, massive—nothing human. I had to bank hard to avoid it. That's what caused the Over-G."

The crew exchanged glances—part skepticism, part unease.

"Get yourself sorted, ma'am," one of them said. "We'll handle the jet."

Lizzie didn't argue. She just nodded again and climbed into the expediter truck. As it pulled away, the UK crew returned to their work in silence—faces tight, their earlier confidence dimmed by something they didn't yet understand.

When Lizzie reached the hangar, she made a beeline for the snack room. Roo looked up from the shattered remnants of popcorn bags and crumpled wrappers. He saw her pale face, the tension in her jaw.

"What's wrong, Lizzie?" His voice was low.

She stared at the floor, eyes distant. "They don't believe me. They never do. They think I'm just a screw-up... like I made up the whole thing because I gave them extra work."

Roo took a minute to let what she said sink in. "Believe you about what? What happened up there?"

She hesitated, lips parting, then closing again. When she spoke, it came out hoarse. "I can't explain it, Roo. It didn't look like anything I've ever seen before. I don't even have the words for it."

Roo stepped forward. His tone softened. "Try. Just tell me what you saw. Best you can."

Before she could answer, the radio above them exploded with static and an urgent voice.

"We have a real-world emergency! I repeat—real-world emergency! An unidentified object is in the air. All personnel report to the flight line now!"

Lizzie's eyes widened.

"That's it, Roo! That's what I saw!"

She grabbed his sleeve and yanked him toward the door. Roo didn't even have time to grab his hat before she was pulling him into a full sprint across the hangar.

By the time they reached the flight line, chaos had erupted. Crew chiefs from every nation scrambled across the flight line, shouting, prepping jets, and barking orders. The air buzzed with adrenaline and disbelief.

Near them, Roo caught snatches of a frantic exchange.

"Unidentified object? Is this part of the exercise?"

"No way. This isn't a drill. It feels too real."

Tipton and Ramirez blew past them in a blur of boots and bravado.

"Outta the way, losers," Tipton yelled. "This doesn't concern you."

Lizzie and Roo ignored them—because overhead, the sky had cracked.

A jagged obsidian obelisk jutted through the clouds, piercing the heavens like a blade. Suspended above it, a colossal craft hung in the air, too massive to comprehend. Its edges seemed to bend the surrounding sky, as though reality itself resisted giving it shape.

Around them, the frenzy slowed. Jets stood silent. Radios crackled and fell quiet. Everyone stared.

Then another message blared across the radios.

"All personnel, stand down," the base radio commanded. "Repeat: stand down. Await further orders. We are coordinating with Washington to determine if the object is friendly or hostile."

Lizzie turned to Roo, her voice trembling. "What... what is that?"

Roo's eyes never left the sky. "I don't know," he said. "Maybe we're not alone anymore."

The obelisk pulsed—deep and resonant, vibrating in their bones. Then the voice came. It was booming, ancient, and inescapable.

"He has arrived. Prepare to meet the Right Hand."

Time seemed to stand still.

Across the globe, similar obelisks tore through the clouds above other major cities—New York, London, Paris, and Rome. Panic rippled like shockwaves.

Back in Washington D.C., deep within the presidential bunker, President Davidson stood with his cabinet. The Situation Room was a storm of reports, satellite feeds, and alarmed whispers.

The president's voice cut through the chaos, grim and clear. "Tell me everything we know. Now."

CHAPTER NINE

The Speech

President Davidson sat at the head of a long conference table, deep within the fortified presidential bunker. Dim fluorescent lights buzzed overhead, casting flickering shadows across scattered folders, steaming coffee cups, and glowing monitors. The recycled air hung heavy with the metallic tang of stress.

Around him, chaos reigned.

Cabinet members shouted over one another, their voices colliding in a storm of panic. One pounded a fist against the table, rattling cups. Another rubbed their temples, eyes squeezed shut, muttering something inaudible. Papers fluttered to the floor as a chair scraped, jolting the tension even higher.

Davidson had had enough.

He slammed his palms flat against the table with a sharp crack that silenced the room. "Enough," he said, his voice low but cutting. "Panic doesn't solve problems. Focus does. If you want to lead, start acting like it."

The air shifted and heads turned. Chairs creaked as everyone retook their seats.

Davidson's gaze shifted to the Secretary of Defense. His tone softened, though the authority never left his voice. "Before we get into protocols and projections—where is my family?"

The secretary straightened. "They're safe, sir. Secured at the safe house outside Anchorage. We've increased the protection detail, and we're preparing a transport route to bring them back to D.C. once it's cleared."

Davidson exhaled, his shoulders easing just a little bit. He gave a quick nod, his voice quieter now. "Good. Thank you." Straightening, he swept his gaze across the room. "Now, I need answers. What do we know so far? How many confirmed sightings are there?"

The Secretary of Defense spoke up, his voice measured but laced with tension. "Sir, our knowledge remains limited. The mysterious objects are transmitting a message: 'He has arrived. Prepare to meet the Right Hand.' Beyond what Dr. Solomon has shared about the symbols, we know nothing about who this 'he' is or what he wants." He tapped a tablet and turned it to face the president. "We now have six confirmed sightings. Five of them center over major cities—Rome, London, Paris, New York, and Berlin. The sixth appeared over the Air Force base in Anchorage, Alaska during the war games. Reports confirm it disrupted operations and unsettled personnel. Elizabeth Miles, a pilot on-site, described a dangerous encounter with the object just before its full emergence. We have enacted emergency protocols, but we still don't know their purpose or intent." He hesitated, then added, "Sir, there's another detail. Satellite imaging shows a dense mist forming around the obelisks in five of those six cities—Rome, Paris, London, New York, and Berlin. It's... atmospheric but also thick and consistent. This matches reports from around the ISS just before contact was lost." He paused again. "Anchorage remains clear—for now. We believe it may be a delayed reaction... or a deliberate exception."

Dr. Solomon, who had remained silent until now, sprang from his chair. The sharp scrape of the legs against the tile startled the room into stillness.

"The Vatican," he said. "One obelisk is in Rome, just miles from the Vatican." He looked around, wide-eyed. "That's not a coincidence. The Vatican is a symbol of faith... that location carries weight. They're sending a message."

President Davidson narrowed his eyes. "Rome and religion," he said. "You're saying this has theological intent?"

Solomon hesitated, then gave a cautious nod. "I'm saying it might. The Vatican holds influence over more than a billion people. If these entities know anything about our world or human culture... placing something like this near Rome could rattle belief systems. Not just governments."

Davidson absorbed that, exhaling through his nose.

"And Alaska? Why show up over our most remote base during international war games? They could have chosen Washington, Beijing, Moscow..." He paused for a moment to think. "Unless it's not just symbolic—it's strategic. That base holds one of the largest concentrations of global air power right now. Maybe they're watching us respond."

The room remained silent for a while before Davidson continued.

"Dr. Solomon," Davidson said, more decisive now, "I can't send you to Europe, we have frozen international travel, but I can send you to Alaska." He turned to the general in charge. "Get Air Force One ready. Dr. Solomon is en route to Anchorage now. I want him working with the team on-site." Then he turned his attention to Dr. Solomon. "Reach out to the scientists you worked with on the Voyager project—the ones who helped you decipher the symbol patterns. I want them flown in under top security. Whatever's happening, I need eyes on that obelisk. Yesterday."

Solomon gave a short, solemn nod, snapping his briefcase closed. "Yes, Mr. President." He exchanged a look with the general, then both moved out of the room.

President Davidson turned to the remaining generals, his tone resolute. "We need a comprehensive plan in case these sightings escalate. I want contingencies for every outcome—analyze all communication channels, assess logistical challenges, and coordinate clear response strategies. And start trying to establish communication with these objects. We need to know if they come as friend or foe."

The room held steady as Davidson's words sank in. Just as the generals rose, one spoke up.

"Sir, military advisors from our allied nations are reaching out. They're concerned about the safety of their troops taking part in the war games in Alaska."

Davidson's gaze sharpened. "Tell them their troops are under our care. We will treat them with the same diligence and protection as our own. Alaska's significance hasn't escaped me, and we're already reinforcing security. Reassure them, General—no one gets left behind."

The generals exchanged firm nods of understanding before exiting the bunker, their phones already in hand, their steps purposeful as they moved to carry out the president's orders.

President Davidson turned to another advisor, his expression darkening. "What do we know about our citizens? How are they handling the news?"

The advisor hesitated, bracing for the president's reaction. "Sir, there are reports of riots and unrest in multiple cities. Some news outlets are irresponsibly throwing around words like 'aliens' and 'Armageddon,' fueling fear and hysteria. Police departments are overwhelmed. We may need to deploy the National Guard."

Davidson's jaw tightened, his face a mask of controlled fury. He rose from his chair, pacing for a moment before stopping cold, eyes locked on the advisor. "The news outlets are pouring gasoline on a fire that's already burning too hot," he said, voice low but sharp. "I don't blame people for being scared. But panic will tear us apart faster than any outside threat."

He took a breath, his spine straightening with renewed resolve. "Get a message to the General. I want the National Guard deployed to the cities that need it most. We're not just restoring order—we're protecting lives. And make this clear to every officer on the ground: Their mission is the safety of our citizens. No heavy-handed tactics. No unnecessary escalation." He turned back to the advisor, tone unwavering. "And the media—contact the FCC and the heads of every major network. Remind them of their responsibility in a national crisis. This isn't the time for fear-mongering or reckless speculation." Davidson's gaze lifted to the glowing monitors—footage of protests, smoke, flashing lights. His eyes narrowed. "The American people need to know we're in control. We will not abandon them to chaos."

The advisor nodded and rushed from the room.

Davidson sat back down, pressing his fingertips to his temples. Though exhaustion flickered across his face, his voice was steady when he muttered to himself, "We're going to get through this."

The president's Chief of Staff approached, his expression taut with urgency. "Sir, I have the leaders of the United Kingdom, France, Germany, Spain, and Italy on hold. They're demanding to speak with you."

Davidson exhaled, pinching the bridge of his nose as if to hold back the storm rising behind his temples. Frustration flickered, but only for a moment. With a steadying breath, he straightened and rolled his shoulders back. "Patch them through to my phone here in the bunker.," he said, voice composed and firm. "I'll take it there."

Moments later, in an office inside the bunker, Davidson adjusted his tie as the secure video call connected. Faces of the world's leaders filled the monitor—each one marked by tension, worry, and rising agitation. Voices overlapped in a rush of concern, accusation, and fear.

Davidson raised a single hand. His voice was calm but carried unmistakable authority. "Ladies and gentlemen. Please." The chatter died in an instant. "I understand your concerns. I share them. We are all facing something unprecedented and unknown. But panic and speculation will only magnify the danger. My team is working around the clock to assess the situation. And when we have actionable intelligence, I give you my word—you'll have it."

A French voice cut in, sharp with frustration. Another from Berlin followed, demanding transparency. Davidson's gaze remained steady.

"I am prioritizing the safety of my citizens—as each of you must prioritize yours. We'll remain in close communication and share what we know. But at this moment, what the world needs is calm leadership. Not fear or blame. Leadership."

He let the words hang in the air, weighted and deliberate.

"Return to your people. Bring calm to your streets. I will do the same here. We will endure this—but only if we lead together." He paused for a brief second—then ended the call. The screen faded to black, and Davidson sat for a moment in the silence that followed, his reflection faint in the polished surface. Then he rose,

93

shoulders squared, and stepped out of the office—ready to face the storm again.

The president strode back into the conference room, his expression steely as he locked eyes with his Chief of Staff. "How's the speech coming?" he asked. "I need to address the American people. They deserve the truth—and they need to hear it from me."

The Chief of Staff hesitated, then handed him a document. "This is the rough draft, sir. We have another version as well."

Davidson took the speech and began scanning it. His brow furrowed deeper with every line. His jaw set tight. "This reads like a funeral dirge," he said, circling phrases with deliberate strokes of his pen. "We are not standing at the edge of the grave—we're standing at a crossroads. This can't be fear-mongering. It has to be about resilience and unity."

The Chief of Staff shifted, nerves visible in his body language under Davidson's piercing gaze. "I thought you might feel that way," he said, pulling a second document from his folder. "This version leans more hopeful with a stronger tone and clearer message."

Davidson took it and read in silence, the tension easing a little from his shoulders as his eyes moved down the page. After an intense review, he looked up.

"This is better. Much better." He held the pages at his side, his voice firm. "Why you led with the doomsday draft is beyond me. If I didn't know better, I'd say you were testing my patience."

The Chief of Staff opened his mouth to respond, but Davidson waved a hand dismissively. "Doesn't matter now. This is the one we go with." He turned, already walking toward the door, the second speech in hand. "Get the press room ready. It's time."

As President Davidson left the conference room, lines of fatigue etched deeper across his face, an advisor intercepted him with cautious urgency. "Sir," the advisor said, holding out a cell phone, "it's your wife. We got through."

Davidson froze mid-step, the chaos of the day suspended in that moment. He took the phone with careful hands, though the urgency in his movements betrayed how long he'd been waiting for this.

"Alaina?" he said, relief and longing mingling in his voice as he stepped into the quiet of the hallway.

On the other end, the first lady's voice flowed through like warm light—steady, Southern, and familiar. Her words softened the edges of a day that had almost broken him. "William," she said, her voice carrying a smile. "You've always been such a worrier. We're fine. The kids understood, though missing the war games disappointed them. This safe house is a fortress. And Tammy—the astronaut—is here with us. She's been good company. Sweetheart, you've got enough on your plate. We're safe. How are you?"

Davidson leaned against the wall, exhaling hard, emotion catching in his throat despite himself.

"It's chaos down here, Alaina. We're being pulled in every direction. Everyone wants answers, and no one has them. Now I'm expected to stand in front of the country tonight and tell people everything's under control."

"You always carry the weight of the world," she said. "But you're William Davidson. You don't have to promise perfection— you just have to speak from your heart. That's what people believe in. You."

A faint smile tugged at his lips, tired but real. "You're right," he said. "You always are."

"Of course I am," she teased. Then her voice softened once more. "I love you, William. The kids love you. Just go out there and do what you've always done—lead with strength and grace. We're already proud."

Davidson's throat tightened. He swallowed hard, grounding himself in the moment. "I love you too, Alaina. Tell the kids I love them. I'll see you soon."

"You'll be fine," she said. "Now go make history, Mr. President."

The line clicked silent.

Davidson stood for a moment, the phone still pressed to his ear, unwilling to let go of her voice just yet. Finally, with a steady breath and the weight of both love and duty in his chest, he slid the phone into his pocket and turned down the hall.

Thirty minutes later, President Davidson emerged from his private quarters with the composure of a man stepping onto history's stage. Every detail of his appearance was immaculate—a visual testament to his discipline and the seriousness of the hour.

His black suit jacket fit like armor, tailored to project both control and confidence. The matching trousers fell in crisp lines with creases so sharp they could cut glass. Beneath the jacket, a pristine white dress shirt shone under the soft hallway lights, its collar stiff, cuffs aligned at the wrists. At his throat, an American flag tie—tied in a flawless half-Windsor—sat centered with military precision. A polished lapel pin shimmered with quiet pride on his left chest, catching the light with each step. His shoes were black leather, buffed to a mirror sheen. The faint scent of polish and leather trailed behind him like ceremony. He had combed his silver-flecked hair; not a strand was out of place. Clean-shaven— he looked every bit the commander-in-chief he was born to be.

As he exited the room, his Chief of Staff met him mid-stride, giving the president's attire a once-over. Every pleat was perfect, every fold where it should be. He clipped the microphone onto

Davidson's lapel, his fingers trembling despite the routine he'd done a thousand times.

"Sir," he said, the nerves threading through his voice, "are you sure you want to do this from the Rose Garden? It would be far safer to deliver the address from inside the bunker."

Davidson paused. He adjusted his already-perfect tie with one last tug, then met the man's gaze with steely calm. "The American people need to see their president—not their fear," he said. "If I hide underground, I send the wrong message. We don't lead from the shadows. We lead from the front."

The Chief of Staff hesitated, then nodded. "Yes, sir."

"I want the Secret Service doubled. No one gets within a hundred feet of the platform unless I say otherwise. If it moves and isn't supposed to, shoot it."

"Yes, sir."

As the Chief of Staff hurried off to give the orders, Davidson took a steadying breath. The hallway stretched ahead like a runway. At the far end waited the Rose Garden, and beyond it, a nation gripped by fear, uncertainty—and hope.

Davidson squared his shoulders and walked forward, every step measured. A leader answering history's call.

President Davidson stepped into the Rose Garden just as the last light of day spilled golden across the white stone columns. The podium awaited at the center, bathed in the warm glow of the setting sun. A hush blanketed the space—a stillness so complete it felt like the world itself was holding its breath.

Above him, an eagle soared across the twilight sky, wings stretched wide against the fading amber. Its silhouette cut a perfect line across the heavens, regal and unhurried. Davidson's eyes tracked the bird's silent flight, something settling in his chest. A sign, perhaps, or maybe just a reminder of freedom and resilience.

The moment stretched, heavy with meaning, before he returned his gaze to the podium.

The sweet scent of flowers from the manicured beds brushed against the breeze, incongruous with the tension in the air. Yet somehow, it grounded him—life persisted, even now.

Secret Service agents lined the perimeter like statues, eyes sharp, hands at the ready. They watched every shadow. Every movement measured.

The seal of the president gleamed on the front of the podium, catching the last kiss of sunlight. Two American flags framed the stage, their fabric whispering as they rippled in the wind, a quiet, reverent sound. The scent of fresh turned soil mixed with the cool air.

Davidson stepped forward. The click of his shoes echoed against the stone. He reached for the note cards resting atop the podium, fingertips brushing their edges. He didn't need them, but their presence was a ritual, an anchor.

The image of the eagle lingered in his mind.

He nodded once.

"Let's begin."

The camera operator gave a silent countdown—three... two... one—and pointed.

Davidson took a slow breath, his shoulders squaring beneath the tailored weight of leadership. He looked into the lens, his eyes steady, his voice ready. And then he spoke—calm, measured, and unwavering—as the world listened.

"My fellow Americans, and citizens of the world, tonight, I speak to you in a moment of great uncertainty. A moment that demands our unity, our resolve, and our strength as a people.

"Just moments ago, as I stood in the Rose Garden, an eagle soared overhead—its wings outstretched against the setting sun.

In that quiet flight, I was reminded of what the eagle has always represented: freedom, strength, and resilience. It is the symbol of who we are as a nation—and who we will continue to be, even in the face of the unknown.

"What we are witnessing in our skies is without precedent. For centuries, humanity has looked to the heavens with curiosity, wonder, and hope. Tonight, we face a new truth—one that suggests we may not be alone in this vast universe. These mysterious objects have appeared over cities across the globe. Their arrival has stirred fear, confusion, and speculation. Though we do not yet understand their purpose, I assure you, we are not powerless.

Your government is working around the clock to uncover the truth. The greatest minds—scientists, military leaders, and scholars—are collaborating across nations to interpret the signs, the symbols, and the cryptic message that has shaken the world: 'He has arrived. Prepare to meet the Right Hand.'

"I know many of you are afraid. I understand the unease. But I ask you, do not give in to panic. Fear divides us. Courage unites us. As a nation, we have faced impossible challenges— wars, disasters, and crises that tested our very soul. Each time, we emerged stronger. This moment is no different. We will not react with hysteria. We will respond with purpose and resolve.

"For your safety, authorities have implemented curfews in affected areas and enacted emergency protocols to preserve order. These are not decisions that are easy to make but they are necessary. I ask for your patience, your vigilance, and your strength. Help one another. Look out for your neighbors. Remain calm, and know this—we are not alone in facing this. We face it together.

"This is not the end of our story. This is the test of our character. And when history looks back on this moment, let it remember our courage, our unity, and our unshakable resolve. Our fear will not define us. Our strength will.

"May He guide us through these uncertain times."

As the president disappeared through the White House doors, his words echoed across the globe. In New York, crowds filled the sidewalks, gathered outside storefront TVs. A teenage boy held his little sister close as the last lines of the speech reverberated from a tiny speaker.

In London, spotlights swept the sky above Westminster. Mounted police stood watch near the Thames as a hush settled over the crowd, staring up at the pulsing obelisk overhead.

In Paris, Notre-Dame's bells tolled. A priest crossed himself beneath the ancient archways as flocks of pigeons took flight.

In Rome, the Vatican lay encircled in a ghostly mist. The pope stood alone on a balcony, his hands clasped in silent prayer as the shape in the clouds loomed far above the city.

In Anchorage, Dr. Solomon stood at a tall window in the command hangar. He sipped a coffee gone cold, notebook pressed against the glass, his eyes locked on the strange monolith in the sky—its surface humming as though waiting.

In Tokyo, Cairo, Johannesburg, São Paulo—people of every faith, every tongue, and every walk of life—turned their eyes skyward, united by awe.

High above the White House, unseen by most, the eagle still circled.

CHAPTER TEN

Phase Three

T he next morning, uncertainty still gripped Washington D.C., its tension mirrored thousands of miles away on the rain-slicked flight line at Elmendorf Air Force Base in Alaska. The crisp air carried the metallic tang of jet fuel and the lingering scent of rain—fitting for a day wrapped in mystery and unease.

It had been twenty-four hours since President Davidson's address, and the world hadn't taken a breath since. In Washington, the president had left the safety of the underground bunker, defying the cautious pleas of his staff. He'd returned to the White House for optics. In a moment of global anxiety, Davidson believed hiding beneath concrete and steel sent the wrong message. The people needed to see their leader standing firm, not buried behind blast doors.

Seated at the head of a conference table cluttered with briefings and satellite photos, Davidson scanned his advisors with steady eyes. His tone was composed but edged with unmistakable urgency. "Has Dr. Solomon arrived in Alaska?" he asked. "What about my family? Are they en route back to D.C.?"

An aide cleared his throat and answered, "Dr. Solomon touched down a few hours ago, sir. His colleagues will arrive by the end of the day. As for your family... they're still awaiting transport. The FAA's freeze on outbound flights has complicated things. We're doing everything we can."

Davidson's jaw clenched. His knuckles whitened against the polished wood of the table.

"I want them on a plane. Now," he said, his voice low and iron-steady. "Get the FAA on the line."

The advisor scrambled to comply, punching in the number with trembling fingers and handing the phone across the table.

*   *   *

The first light of dawn broke over the flight line at Elmendorf Air Force Base, signaling the start of a critical phase in the escalating crisis. General Robichaux stood waiting for Dr. Solomon, his broad frame silhouetted against the soft Alaskan sunrise. His weathered face and cropped gray hair gave him a look of quiet authority, while sharp hazel eyes scanned the horizon with practiced calm. His quiet confidence showed a man who had seen too much to be shaken.

His deep voice carried the distinct drawl of his Cajun heritage, evoking memories of the bayou where he had grown up. The stillness of those waters had taught him to navigate uncertainty, relying on his instincts as much as his training. Now, faced with a global crisis, he drew on that same precision to guide his team through the storm.

As Dr. Solomon disembarked, their eyes met, a silent acknowledgment of the urgency that gripped both the president and his team.

With a firm handshake, Robichaux greeted him. "Good morning, Doctor. How was your flight?"

Dr. Solomon climbed into the waiting vehicle, his movements purposeful despite the exhaustion etched into his features. A life spent navigating cryptic symbols and ancient texts had brought him to this moment. The esoteric had always attracted him, but never had the stakes felt so high. The president's choice to trust him with such a mission wasn't just a professional honor, but also a personal one. He thought of the young pupils he'd lost in the past, their fates sealed by forces they couldn't understand, and a knot of determination formed in his chest.

Settling into the seat, he said, "It was as good as expected under the circumstances. Have my colleagues arrived yet, General?"

Robichaux gave a reassuring nod, though a trace of exasperation colored his tone. "Not yet, Doctor. There were some logistical hurdles with their travel arrangements, but they're airborne now and should arrive by the end of the day."

Dr. Solomon nodded, his expression thoughtful. "Thank you for the update, General. Let's get to the heart of it. What can you tell me about this mysterious object? Has anything significant changed in the past day?"

Robichaux said, "Well, Doc, the only thing we know for sure is the same message keeps coming out of it: 'He has arrived. Prepare to meet the right hand.' But in the past few hours, it started emitting a pulsing sound. It's strange—almost like a tornado siren, except the pitch and volume fluctuate."

Solomon's brow furrowed, his fingers brushing his lips in thought as he processed the information.

"A pulsing sound?" he said, his tone tinged with curiosity. "Have we identified any markings or symbols on it yet?"

Robichaux shook his head.

"Not yet. We're still waiting on clearance from Washington to send in drones or get closer. The restrictions are tying our hands."

"We need those photos, General. I'll call the president and get you the approval myself." Without hesitation, he retrieved his phone, dialing the president's direct number. His movements were swift, his focus unwavering as he prepared to cut through the red tape.

Across the base, activity continued with an undercurrent of anticipation.

Back in the hangar, tension hung like smoke in the air. Military personnel from across the globe paced or leaned against crates, their conversations hushed, their eyes flicking to the radios and sealed doors as though answers might come bursting through. The sharp clang of tools, the grind of loading equipment, and the occasional crackle of static added to the unrest.

General Robichaux's decision to halt all flight operations had left the flight line stagnant—and restless.

Tipton grinned and nudged Ramirez with a casual punch to the arm. "Look around. We're the best. If they send anyone up to check that thing out, it should be us. Load it with missiles and blow it out of the sky. My dad always said, 'Shoot first, ask questions later.'"

Ramirez crossed his arms, watching a jet crew recheck their equipment for the third time. "That's excessive. We don't even know what it is. For all we know, it's part of this year's war games—maybe some test to see how we react under pressure."

Tipton scoffed, shaking his head. "Doesn't matter. It's weird. I don't like it. Just blow it up and move on." He paused, then smirked and jerked his chin toward Lizzie, who stood a few yards away near a grounded UK jet. "One thing's for sure—they won't be sending her bird. She damn near snapped the wings off. That jet's out of commission for a week."

Lizzie didn't respond. She turned without a word and walked away, her posture straight despite the weight behind her silence.

Ramirez watched her go, his jaw tight. Something about the way she walked—unflinching and focused—nagged at him. And for the first time since this began, Tipton's swagger didn't feel like strength. It felt like noise.

Before the banter could escalate further, a sharp crackle burst from the overhead loudspeaker, cutting clean through the hum of machinery and idle chatter.

"All crew report to the briefing room for an update."

The announcement halted movement in the hangar. Conversations ceased, workers dropped their wrenches mid-turn, and people raised their heads toward the ceiling speakers. The peaceful rhythm of downtime evaporated, replaced by a pulse of urgency. Within seconds, personnel moved in practiced formation, making their way to the briefing room with growing anticipation.

Inside, the air buzzed with unspoken questions. Fluorescent lights flickered overhead, casting pale shadows on the rows of seats, filling with crew members from every unit. The only sounds were the quiet creak of chairs and the low rustle of uniforms as bodies settled to attention.

Then came the unmistakable echo of boot steps—sharp, measured, and authoritative. General Robichaux entered, Dr. Solomon at his side. The General's expression was unreadable, the kind that carried weight long before he said a word.

Toward the back, Tipton leaned toward Ramirez and muttered just loud enough for heads to turn. "I swear, I can't understand a damn thing this guy says with that thick Cajun accent. It's like he's speaking a whole other language."

Ramirez chuckled, nodding. "It's... unique."

Robichaux's gaze snapped toward them like a targeting system locking in. "Is something funny, airmen?" His voice cut like steel against stone. "We're on high alert, and you're acting like a couple of clowns at recess. Straighten up—or I'll have you cleaning latrines with a toothbrush instead of prepping jets."

The laughter died in an instant. Ramirez and Tipton straightened in unison, their expressions wiped clean under the General's glare. The rest of the room seemed to freeze, bracing for what would come next.

Robichaux stepped forward and scanned the room.

"Ladies and gentlemen, we've received orders from Washington," he said. "The time for speculation is over."

A stillness settled over the room, thick and expectant.

"We'll proceed with a three-phase approach to communicate with the object. Phase one: we deploy standard drones with visual signal systems and cameras. If we get any kind of response—or if we capture new imagery—we move to phase two."

He moved along the edge of the briefing table, letting the weight of the next phase sink in.

"Phase two involves unmanned jets flying in a controlled pattern around the object, continuing the light signals while collecting higher-resolution data. And if that goes well... phase three brings in our F-15s for manned reconnaissance and radio contact. If that thing can talk, we'll be listening." He stopped, his voice leveling into steel. "If it shows even a hint of hostile intent, we are authorized to engage. Full force."

A ripple of tension passed through the room.

Then, from the back again, Tipton spoke. "Who's the suit next to you, sir?"

Robichaux turned toward Dr. Solomon, his voice measured but pointed. "This is Dr. Solomon. He's the president's religious advisor and an expert in ancient symbology. He's here under direct orders to study any markings or transmissions from the object and provide us with insight."

Tipton let out an audible groan and leaned toward Ramirez. "Great. Another doctor. As if one wasn't enough..."

General Robichaux didn't even blink. "You have your orders," he said, cutting through the murmurs like a blade. "Report to your stations. Phase one begins in twenty minutes."

Chairs scraped back. Boots hit tile. The mission had begun.

The service members filed out of the briefing room to their respective posts, boots echoing against the tiled floor as urgency rippled through the air.

Roo lingered by Lizzie, eyes flicking around the hangar. He leaned in and whispered to her, "Why send a religious advisor?" His fingers twitched against his thigh. "This doesn't feel right, Lizzie. Something bad's coming. I can feel it."

Lizzie placed a steadying hand on his shoulder, her tone low but firm. "Maybe they know something we don't. Just stay sharp, Roo."

The faint scent of oil and metal hung in the air, mixing with the distant whir of machinery as the base shifted into high gear.

Inside the control tower, drones were being prepped for launch within the hour. Screens flickered with telemetry data. The glow of monitors painted the tense faces of flight crews and engineers. General Robichaux stood at the center, conferring with Dr. Solomon and Dr. Terracotta. His polished boots clicked on the floor with each measured step.

Outside, the hum of drone engines swelled, reverberating through the hangar.

Robichaux leaned into the microphone, his voice calm and deliberate—cutting clean through the rising tension. "Begin phase one."

The operators sat hunched in front of glowing monitors, their faces bathed in an eerie blue light. Fifty drones were in motion, guided with precise coordination toward the enigmatic object hovering beyond the flight line. The video feeds displayed its surface—a living mosaic of swirling hues that shimmered and shifted with every frame, as if the object pulsed with thought. Each flicker of light reflected in the operators' wide eyes. No one spoke. Only breathless concentration and the soft click of keys filled the room.

One drone began scanning. As the data on dimensions, composition, and altitude streamed in, a complete picture emerged. The structure was breathtaking: a vast inverted obelisk suspended in midair. Its flat top glowed, emitting an ethereal light, while the pointed base tapered toward the earth like a spear of divinity.

Adorning its glass-smooth surface were radiant, interwoven markings—lines that resembled both branches and veins, glowing like starlight filtered through a canopy. They pulsed in time with no discernible rhythm, suggesting something alive, or aware.

A second drone hovered closer, lenses adjusting as it focused on the etchings. As it neared, the markings responded, subtle at first and then shifting as though disturbed by the drone's presence.

Dr. Solomon leaned forward, his breath catching as the screen revealed more. "Look at those markings," he said. "The lines radiate outward... they split into branches—like the roots of an ancient tree. The Tree of Life." He hit the record button on his voice memo. "This pattern... it spans the entire surface. At the center of each quadrant is a letter—'E'—illuminated on all four faces. These symbols echo ancient myths of origin, knowledge, and judgment.

It's possible this structure was designed to resemble something divine—or is divine."

General Robichaux nodded beside him, eyes on the monitor. "We need more data. Focus on the upper levels."

The drones ascended higher, engines humming as they strained against the altitude limits. One camera feed jittered, then stabilized, revealing a dizzying truth.

"Sir," an operator said, "it extends beyond our atmospheric ceiling. We can't see the top. We're pushing as high as the drone will allow."

The image flickered again. Above the clouds, the object continued—colossal and unknowable.

Despite the proximity and visual probes, the structure remained unresponsive to the light signals intended to prompt communication. Not a shimmer or a shift.

Robichaux's jaw tensed, but his voice remained composed. "It's silent for now."

One by one, the drones cycled through color patterns, beacons flashing in calculated rhythms. The object remained still and mute, as though it had no interest in their language—or just didn't need to speak.

After a long moment, Robichaux turned to the control tower and keyed the radio. "Begin phase two."

The fifty drones descended, touching down one by one across the flight line, their mission complete but their silence unnerving. Within minutes, a second wave launched—sleek, unmanned drone jets now slicing through the morning air.

As they neared the obelisk, the repeating message ceased. 'He has arrived. Prepare to meet the Right Hand—cut off mid-syllable. In its place, the pulsing tone returned. It began as a low vibration, not even noticeable at first, but with each passing second, it climbed in volume and pitch. The sound wasn't just heard, it was felt, rattling through the walls of the control tower and pressing against the eardrums like the warning cry of something ancient and alive.

Inside the tower, operators adjusted their headsets, flinching. No new images surfaced—only repeating patterns, looping footage, and unreadable energy readings.

General Robichaux leaned forward, his eyes never leaving the monitors. His voice crackled over the comms, calm and unwavering. "Begin phase three."

On the flight line, crew chiefs moved with purpose, their boots scraping against the concrete as they completed last inspections. The low hum of jet engines swelled, growing deeper, more insistent.

Then the engines ignited.

Fifty F-15s roared to life, rumbling like a rising storm. One by one, they surged forward, slicing through the overcast sky in perfect formation. The ground trembled beneath their ascent. The air crackled with tension.

In the control tower, eyes tracked every movement. Radios hissed with static.

As the jets neared the object, the lead pilot's voice broke through the comms. "Should we attempt communication, sir?"

General Robichaux's reply came steady and clear. "Communication is a go, pilot."

The pilot keyed the mic. "This is the United States Air Force. This is an attempt to communicate with you. You are in restricted airspace belonging to the United States of America. Please respond."

Silence.

He repeated the message; urgency creeping into his tone as the jets banked around the object, their formation tightening.

Then, after a few moments, a sound occurred. Low at first, like a whisper carried across a chasm. A voice emerged, echoing through every cockpit and speaker in the tower.

"Everything belongs to Him. You own nothing. The Right Hand is here..."

The broadcast cut off without warning. The pulsing sound intensified—erratic, frantic, and alive. With a hiss like steam escaping the bowels of the earth, the sides of the obelisk unfolded, revealing massive vents that glowed with a burning blue light. A violent pulse burst erupted, warping the air with invisible force. The shockwave ripples outward, and the very atmosphere trembled.

One by one, all fifty F-15s lost power, their engines sputtering and dying mid-flight. The formation disintegrated as the jets spiraled downward, lifeless metal falling like a flock of broken birds. Frantic screams and desperate calls crackled across the radio—a final chorus of panic before total silence.

"Mayday! Mayday! We've lost everything, no power—eject! Eject!"

Parachutes bloomed in the sky like dandelions caught in the wind. Fifty pilots floated toward Earth; their silence matched only by the haunting stillness that followed the pulse.

The obelisk moved again. From its underside, cylindrical barrels deployed, rotating with cold, mechanical grace. A soft hum filled the air, like a hymn from another world. Without warning, blue beams sliced through the sky, one after another—sharp, swift, and merciless. Each beam struck a falling pilot. Each impact was precise and terminal. One by one, the parachutes went limp, bodies dropping like discarded toys to the earth below.

In the tower, General Robichaux's jaw clenched, his expression stone-carved with horror. He slammed his hand onto the control panel, his voice thundering through the base. "All available aircraft, take off now! Load every plane to full capacity. This is not a drill. We are at war. Engage!"

The flight line erupted into chaos. Crew chiefs sprinted across the flight line; their faces carved with urgency and fear. There was no time for protocol. Pilots scrambled into cockpits as engines roared to life, systems flickering awake in record time. Hands flew over controls. Safety checks were skipped. Crew chiefs waved them forward with frantic urgency. Within minutes, a fresh wave of jets tore into the sky, their thunderous ascent rising like a war cry against the looming dread.

General Robichaux stood rigid, fists clenched at his sides. His eyes scanned the horizon, reading it like a soldier read a battlefield. Time was slipping through his fingers. Every second lost bled into catastrophe.

The second wave closed in fast. Pilots locked missiles with deadly precision. As one, they unleashed their payload—dozens of missiles screamed through the air, fire trailing behind them like vengeful arrows aimed at a god.

Then there was a sound on the radio. A cold, mocking, inhuman laugh.

The obelisk responded.

The cylindrical barrels retracted, vanishing into the structure's base. A low hum vibrated through the sky as the vents flared open once more. From the heart of the obelisk, the shimmering mist erupted outward like a living veil—the same iridescent fog that consumed the space station.

The missiles hit the barrier—and vanished in blooms of fire. The structure didn't flinch. Not even a flicker. The mist held, unscathed, then, without warning, it collapsed inward, disappearing like it was never there.

And the barrels deployed again.

Blue energy flared in spiraling bursts. The lasers ignited, cutting through the sky with surgical finality. One by one, the jets were struck mid-flight—erased from existence in flashes of light and debris. Screams never had time to form. Black smoke and burning metal rained from the sky.

From the tower, Robichaux watched, horror hardening into fury. His voice blasts over the radio.

"Abort mission! Abort mission! Everyone return to the hangar and take defensive positions!"

Dr. Solomon stood frozen in the tower, his face drained of color, his mouth open just a little as if caught mid-breath. His eyes were locked on the destruction outside, unblinking. He couldn't move or think. His mind, so brilliant and curious hours ago, was now seized under the crushing weight of incomprehensible loss.

Jets burning. Parachutes never landing. Lives erased mid-air.

His chest rose and fell in shallow, ragged breaths.

General Robichaux grabbed him by the arm hard. "Let's go!" he yelled, the urgency slicing through the fog of shock.

Beside him, Dr. Terracotta and the remaining personnel hesitated, but the General's tone allowed no argument. "We need to get you out of here. Now!"

They bolted from the tower, boots pounding down metal stairs. But when they reached the bottom and stepped out into the open air, they stopped cold.

Time seemed to splinter.

The base was a war zone.

Burning wreckage stretched across the flight line—jet engines still spitting flames, wings sheared in half, and landing gear twisted into grotesque angles. Scattered among the debris were bodies— some still strapped to smoldering ejection seats, others crumpled where they fell, limbs bent at unnatural angles, flight suits torn and bloodied.

The air was thick with black smoke and the sharp stench of scorched fuel. Sirens wailed in the distance, but they sounded small, almost drowned out by the roar of burning metal and the occasional dull thud of collapsing equipment.

Dr. Terracotta's knees buckled, and his hands trembled. He tried to speak, but only a rasp came out. "This is... this is impossible," he whispered, his voice cracking under the weight of it.

No one responded. Even General Robichaux—the stoic and battle-tested general—stood still. His jaw clenched tight, eyes scanning the destruction, his breath shallow.

There were no words. Only silence, fire, and the unbearable truth of what they had witnessed.

From beyond the haze and smoke, a group of figures emerged, shadows at first, then their uniforms emerged. Dr. Solomon's breath caught as he recognized Roo and Lizzie from the briefing earlier sprinting toward the wreckage with desperate urgency. Soot streaked their faces, but their resolve was unmistakable. They weren't running from the destruction. They were running into it.

General Robichaux pushed through the chaos with Dr. Solomon at his side, his voice cutting through the roar of distant flames.

"Any survivors?" he yelled. "Anyone?"

Roo slowed, eyes hollow, disbelief etched into every word. "They're all dead, sir. Every single one."

The silence that followed hit harder than any explosion.

Robichaux turned, his gaze sweeping across the smoking ruin of the flight line. His voice rose, sharp and commanding. "Spread out! Search every inch! If there's anything left to salvage— equipment, intel, or survivors—I want it found!" Without missing a beat, he snatched the radio from his belt. "Status report. I want a full account of the damage... now."

The radio crackled, then a voice broke through, breathless and shaking. "Sir... the pulse blast hit more than the flight line. We've got structural damage across the base. Anchorage wasn't spared either—widespread blackouts, multiple aircraft down. The hangar's taken damage. Sir... this is a mass casualty event."

Solomon spun toward Robichaux, his face pale, his voice tight. "What about my colleagues, General? They were en route. Their plane should've been arriving by now."

Robichaux's jaw flexed as he keyed the mic again, his voice a low growl of urgency. "I need confirmation on two flights. PF314, inbound with Dr. Solomon's team. And PF279—scheduled to depart with the first lady and the president's children."

The static lingered, each second dragging longer than the last.

After a few minutes, a voice answered. It was flat and hollow. "PF314... was lost, sir. Total loss. There were no survivors."

The words hit like a blade to the gut. Dr. Solomon dropped to his knees, his breath catching, a sob escaping before he could stop it. His shoulders heaved, silent tears carving tracks down his soot-streaked face. The pain wasn't just grief—it was guilt, sharp and consuming.

The voice on the radio continued. "PF279 never departed. Mechanical delay on the runway. The president's family is safe. They're still grounded and secured."

Relief washed over Robichaux's face, but it was fleeting—overshadowed by the wreckage all around them.

Dr. Solomon looked up through tears, his voice raw. "What do we do now?"

Robichaux crouched beside him. "We get you to the hangar," he said. "You analyze the images we pulled before everything went to hell. You tell us what we're dealing with." Then he stood, his gaze cutting toward the horizon. "And I need to call Washington. The president must know what just happened here."

The hangar was silent, except for the low rumble of the backup generator and the quiet murmur of a television. A small crowd had gathered—mechanics, officers, medics, and survivors—each face streaked with soot and exhaustion. Their uniforms were torn, their eyes hollow. They stood shoulder to shoulder, watching the news coverage unfold in stunned silence.

The broadcast flickered across the dusty screen, showing footage of burning wreckage, drone feeds, and images of the smoldering flight line behind them. The anchor's voice wavered, as if struggling to keep his composure.

Then he paused mid-sentence, one hand pressing against his earpiece. "We're getting breaking news... Just confirmed—a large unidentified spacecraft has entered the airspace above Los Angeles and is now descending toward LAX. Repeat: a massive craft appears to be landing at Los Angeles International Airport. We're receiving live images now..." The camera cut to shaky aerial footage: The sky above LA glowing as a shadow descended, its size dwarfing the skyline.

The room froze.

Dr. Solomon's voice broke the silence, hushed and shaken. He turned to General Robichaux, his face pale, his expression haunted. "That must be him..." he said. "The Right Hand. He is here."

A chill rippled through the room.

Robichaux didn't respond. He pulled out his phone, his fingers already dialing. Without another word, he turned and walked toward his office, the weight of the world pressing on his shoulders.

CHAPTER ELEVEN

The Woman in Shackles

T he devastation in Alaska still hung over every conversation in Washington. At Elmendorf Air Force Base, smoldering wreckage was all that remained. In the White House, the smell of stale coffee and anxious sweat clung to the walls like a second skin.

President Davidson sat motionless at the head of the Situation Room table. Hours of tense coordination and briefings had worn him down. The room was dim, the mood dimmer.

The door burst open, and his advisor appeared, breath ragged. "Sir... you need to see this. Now."

Davidson rose without a word, his face unreadable. He followed her through the hallway, the sound of his shoes tapping out the rhythm of his exhaustion. They reached the conference room. A crowd had gathered, and officials huddled near the screen. No one was saying a word.

On the television, a news anchor spoke over grainy footage of something vast moving through cloud cover.

"...we can now confirm a spacecraft is descending toward Los Angeles International Airport. It entered into the atmosphere five minutes ago. FAA has grounded all flights, and authorities are attempting to clear the area. The military response—if any—is still unknown..."

The feed cut to aerial footage: the massive form of the object, smooth and dark, easing downward through the atmosphere like it belonged there.

Davidson stared, unmoving. His pulse ticked louder in his ears than the anchor's voice.

Someone spoke behind him. "Sir, do we need to mobilize troops? LAX is near downtown. If we don't act—"

He held up a hand. The room quieted.

"They just swatted our planes out of the sky like they were flies," Davidson said, his voice quiet but firm. "Sending more would be a death sentence."

Silence followed but no one argued.

He drew a breath, then looked around the room—really looked at them. Faces were pale and eyes were darting. They were all waiting for him to lead.

"We take a defensive posture," he said. "Alert every available unit in Los Angeles County—military, National Guard, and emergency response. I want them on standby, positioned but not aggressive. They'll line the perimeter of LAX, but they do not engage." His fingers gripped the edge of the table. "We don't provoke. Not unless we're forced. That thing out there... is beyond us. For now, we will watch, and we will wait."

No one dared break the silence.

The room hadn't breathed since the news of the landing.

Then a trembling voice broke through from the back. "Sir... one of those obelisks—it just appeared over Los Angeles!"

118

Gasps rippled across the room. Heads swiveled. The television flickered back to life, bathing everyone in its pale blue glow.

The reporter's voice crackled through the speakers. "We now have confirmation—four more of the obelisk structures have materialized. One over Los Angeles, one over Madrid, one over Atlanta, and one over Houston. That brings the total to ten confirmed across the globe."

It hit the room like a thunderclap.

Davidson's chest tightened. Each name—each city—landed like a blow. He felt a slow, creeping dread as the screen shifted, revealing not only the suspended obelisks but also the ship that was descending onto LAX.

The light above flickered. The room was silent. Even the air felt like it had stopped moving.

Davidson's jaw locked tight. He turned to his Chief of Staff, his voice cold and surgical. "Get me Dr. Solomon. Now."

Dr. Solomon sat alone; the dim office in Elmendorf's hangar swallowed him. Long shadows stretched from cold fluorescents over a desk swamped by drone photos. The air smelled of paper, toner, and old ink and dust. He felt the weariness etched into his posture.

He rubbed at his temples, his fingers brushing scattered prints as his mind reeled from the day's horrors. The low hum of the still-running printer was the only sound, a mechanical reminder of the task he could not set down. Hundreds of photos lay before him, each one frozen in eerie silence, every frame whispering questions that had no answers.

His phone buzzed, breaking the stillness. He glanced at the screen. William Davidson.

He exhaled and tapped the speaker icon. The president's voice filled the room, steady, but heavy with strain. "Dr. Solomon, I'm sorry about your colleagues. Their loss is a tragedy. Please—tell me you've found something. Anything."

Solomon swallowed, his voice hoarse from hours of silence. "Thank you, sir. I've printed everything the drones captured. I'm sorting through them now, but there's a lot... and without the others, it's slower. Some of them specialized in specific symbology, so it'll take time." He paused, running his fingers through the photos. Then... he saw it and froze. One image caught his eye.

At first glance, it was like the rest, distorted shadows and strange geometry, but in the background, hidden among the abstract forms, a figure stood.

A man cloaked in deep purple.

Solomon's breath caught. "No..." he said. His hands trembled as he snatched the photo. "No... it can't be..."

"Dr. Solomon?" Davidson's voice sharpened. "What is it? Who are you talking about?"

"The man in the purple robes," Solomon said, his voice rising with urgency. "He's in one of the drone images. Sir—it's the same man you told us about in the Situation Room!"

A long pause followed.

Solomon moved fast, scanning the image and then sent it to the president.

The silence stretched for what seemed like an eternity.

Then the president's voice returned, now faint and shaken. "What is he doing there? What does this mean?"

Solomon stared at the screen, heart pounding. "I don't know yet, but I'm going to find out. This is important, sir, I can feel it. He's not just a symbol. He's part of this."

"Keep going," Davidson said. "We need answers, and we need them fast."

The line went dead.

Solomon leaned back, the weight of the moment settling over him like a shroud. His eyes stayed fixed on the photo, on the man cloaked in purple.

The truth wasn't just in the sky. It had already arrived.

At Los Angeles International Airport, the ripple effects of the Alaska catastrophe had brought air travel to a grinding halt. What was once a bustling terminal now simmered with unease. Families paced, faces tight with worry and frustration. Announcements had long since stopped. Instead, silence settled in like a fog—thick, tense, and waiting to break.

Then it happened.

A single gasp cut through the air. Heads turned toward the windows. For a heartbeat, the terminal stood frozen.

Outside, something enormous pierced the clouds. A massive spacecraft descended, its silhouette dark and sleek against the dimming sky. Its sheer size eclipsed the setting sun, casting an expanding shadow across the tarmac. A low, vibrating hum followed, a sound that became a presence—rattling floor tiles, reverberating in ribs, and pressing into skin.

Panic was instant. Screams rose. Some people rushed to windows, others ran in the opposite direction—toward nowhere in particular, just away.

The ship was almost six hundred feet long; its black surface laced with pulsing strands of deep blue. The texture appeared alive, as though it breathed. Along the hull, intricate etchings formed a complex pattern—symmetrical and alien, like a language encoded into geometry, and across its wings glowed a single, searing symbol: a luminous "E."

Eight smaller ships broke through the cloud cover, following the larger craft in a perfect arc. They descended in synchronized silence, fanning out as they aligned themselves with eerie precision. Though smaller, each bore the same markings, ancient patterns, and glowing insignia.

With a roar, all nine vessels landed.

The ground convulsed beneath them, tremors rippling through the runways and into the bones of the onlookers. The alien ships now stood like sentinels across the airport, foreign and immovable. Through the glass, the crowd stared, paralyzed by awe and dread. The age of first contact had arrived—and it didn't feel like a meeting of peace.

In the distance, the wail of sirens swelled—rising into a deafening chorus as military vehicles flooded toward the airport. Trucks, jeeps, and armored carriers raced down the roads, packed with soldiers ready to respond. They formed a growing procession, fanning out along the perimeter of Los Angeles International.

The hot air vibrated with tense energy as the troops poured out. Boots thudded a rhythmic tattoo on the scorching pavement. Soldiers, a blur of motion, formed lines, weapons clutched tight, their gazes sweeping the sky and ground. The silence was thick, broken only by the distant drone of the airport. Fear hung heavy and unspoken, a palpable weight.

As the chaos settled, a heavy silence dropped like a curtain. Only the hum of distant engines and the occasional clatter of equipment disturbed the stillness. Time stretched. Anticipation tightened like a wire pulled taut.

A sharp rush of air broke the tension.

All eyes turned toward the massive spacecraft at the heart of the runway. With a mechanical groan, a rear ramp began to lower. The grinding of metal echoed through the open space, each inch descending with glacial weight. The final thud as it met the tarmac was soft, but absolute.

From the darkness at the top of the ramp, a solitary figure emerged.

A woman.

Though small, her presence commanded attention, filling the room with quiet intensity. Her hair—a wild, vivid red—flowed like fire in the breeze, defiant and untamed. Her features were delicate, but her eyes carried the weight of long suffering. Strength etched in silence.

She stepped forward, descending the ramp with slow, deliberate grace. Her hands were bound in silver shackles and yet she carried a large, worn bag at her side. From it, with each step, she released a handful of soft blue petals. They floated to the ground, fluttering like tiny birds, catching the light as they scattered across the pavement.

The moment was haunting. Beauty and sorrow braided into every footfall. A woman in shackles, descending from the unknown, marking the world with something fragile... and deliberate.

CHAPTER TWELVE

Right Hand Arrives

T he crowd remained motionless, the weight of the shackled woman's arrival hanging in the air like an ancient prophecy fulfilled. As she continued her solemn march, silence deepened around her—thick and electric, the atmosphere charged with a breathless anticipation.

A new presence stirred.

From the shadows of the great spacecraft, another woman emerged—her steps deliberate and unyielding. She wore a black suit of armor, its surface etched with a distinctive checkerboard pattern that gleamed under the late afternoon sun, as if forged from something not of this world. Over the armor flowed a black cape edged in blue, made from the finest fabric, rippling with an otherworldly shimmer. Sewn into the cape's back, golden thread formed a single, haunting image: a scale—balanced, precise, and heavy with meaning.

Behind her, a procession followed. They marched in perfect formation, unnerving beings that resembled humans in form, yet something in their features betrayed another origin. Their faces were angular, sharp, and still, as though carved rather than born. Their eyes glinted with a fierce, inhuman light. They wore black linen tops frayed at the edges, garments worn by time and war. Their pants and boots were functional and serviceable, but crude compared to the immaculate garb of the figure they followed.

Each one carried a banner bearing the same golden scale, embroidered with eerie precision.

They marched in rows of five, twenty-five to a group, their movements synchronized with chilling exactness. The rhythm of their boots struck the ground like a slow, deliberate war drum, each step a heartbeat of looming judgment.

As the last row of black-garbed beings stepped down the ramp, a new figure emerged from the ship's shadow.

He was clad in white armor, its surface etched with the same checkerboard pattern, and it gleamed like polished bone beneath the fading sky. Draped over the figure's shoulders was a cape trimmed in fine blue thread and embroidered in shimmering gold was the unmistakable shape of a bow—its presence both regal and chilling.

Behind the second figure marched another group of twenty-five beings. Like the first, they wore frayed black linen and carried banners bearing the golden bow. Though still unnatural in appearance, their features seemed more focused and resolute, their eyes locked forward as they marched in perfect rhythm, each step deliberate, each banner snapping in the wind like an omen.

Moments later, the ramp groaned once more as a third figure appeared.

She wore deep red armor; its surface layered with the same precise checkerboard design. A rich, blue-trimmed cape flowed behind her, bearing the image of a sword in gold. The symbolism was unmistakable—her presence radiated violence.

125

Trailing behind her was yet another squad of twenty-five—eyes hollow, movements crisp—each holding aloft a banner embroidered with the golden blade.

Then came the fourth.

A pale figure, dressed in ghostly armor so light it almost shimmered against the dark ship. The checkerboard was still present but more subtle—like veins beneath skin. His cape was almost translucent, edged in that same electric blue, but on its back lay the last symbol: a scythe woven in gold thread.

The last twenty-five descended behind him in silence, their banners raised without fanfare, their presence no less terrifying for its quiet simplicity.

Stillness filled the air after the last parade.

As the final group stepped onto the runway, a heavy pause settled over the world. The procession halted. A hush fell over the crowd; you could hear a pin drop. No talking or sound. Just the silent thunder of groups marching, occupying the heart of a world that never saw them coming.

The tension in the air remained thick, the mystery of who they were and what they represented hanging over everyone like a shadow. The sound of boots marching faded into the distance, but the silence they left behind felt heavier.

*　*　*

Back in Alaska, Dr. Solomon sat motionless before the TV, bathed in the pale blue light of the broadcast. His breath caught as the camera zoomed in on the figures descending the ramp—each armored in a different color, each adorned with a distinct symbol.

His lips parted, the words escaping like a ghost exhaled from a deep memory. "Black... white... red... pale..." His voice trembled as he leaned forward, eyes widening, hands gripping the desk with white-knuckled force. "Scale. Bow. Sword. Scythe..."

The room felt smaller and the air colder. His heart thundered in his chest with recognition. Dread born from understanding.

"No," he whispered. "No, no, no... it can't be."

The Horsemen. The whispers of myth and metaphor had faded, replaced by the undeniable presence of what was once considered impossible. It was more than just scripture now; a profound truth he felt deep within his soul. They existed.

The symbols, the precision, the order of their arrival all aligned too well. His academic training, years of study, and lectures on prophecy and ancient texts, they'd led him here, to this broadcast, and this nightmare blooming into reality.

He staggered to his feet, pushing back the chair. Paper scattered from the desk as he stumbled toward the screen, reaching out, as if touching it would make it less real.

"They're not just here to intimidate. They're here to begin." His voice was almost not even audible now, breaking with a mixture of awe and raw terror. "We weren't meant to see this. Not in our lifetime. Not like this."

Behind him, the door creaked open. General Robichaux stepped in, his boots echoing like drumbeats of doom. He froze at the sight on the television. He said nothing at first. Then, in a quiet tone, he spoke, the weight of history in every word. "The Germans did the same thing in Belgium during the first World War... marched the whole war machine through the streets. Let the world watch them come."

The two men stood in silence, watching history repeat itself—only now, it wasn't tanks and infantry. It was something older. Something biblical.

On the screen, a reporter walked beside the procession, desperation in his voice. "Who are you? Why are you here? What do you want?!"

The figure in black didn't even turn. She just kept marching forward.

For hours, they marched through the heart of Los Angeles—a river of black flowing across the city. Cameras tracked their every step, the broadcast feeding a world that could not look away. Streets fell silent as the procession advanced, their banners snapping in the dusk wind, their armored figures illuminated by the last glow of a sinking sun. By the time the Coliseum gates rose into view, night had descended. Floodlights and the cold shimmer of television lenses painted their arrival in stark relief, a spectacle equal parts liturgy and invasion.

The woman who first exited the spacecraft reached the gates of the Los Angeles Coliseum and stopped. The silence that followed her arrival was near-sacred.

To her right, Pestilence and Conquest fell into formation, their followers assembling behind them in perfect lines. To her left, War and Death did the same, their own ranks falling in step with eerie precision.

The air thickened with anticipation. The ground itself seemed to hold its breath.

Dr. Solomon watched from Alaska, motionless in his chair, the images on the screen unfolding like scripture he never imagined would come to life. His mind churned with recognition, dread, and one gnawing question: *What happens now?*

The camera zoomed in.

The woman in shackles stood at the head of the procession, unflinching. Her eyes met the lens. For a moment, time seemed to pause.

Then her voice cut through the stillness. "I am Heliosa, historian of the Right Hand."

Her words landed like a commandment. The faint clinking of her shackles echoed through the coliseum, a haunting reminder that even prisoners could become messengers of destiny.

"Forever bound by these chains—a penance for my people's defiance." The atmosphere tightened. Even the sky felt closer. "Today, the world will bear witness to the magnificence of the Right Hand to the Creator." Her conviction was unshakable. Each syllable felt like it was carved in stone. "He will deliver to you all a new canvas. Blank and full of potential. The chance to begin anew... to rewrite the story of your lives."

A hush fell. It wasn't fear alone that gripped the crowd, it was also reverence, wonder, and dread.

Like a blade drawn in silence, she finished. "The Architect is here."

What followed wasn't noise; it was a symphony of silence.

No screams or cheers. Just the weight of arrival.

Back at the airport, a new procession began—one that sent a ripple of awe and dread through the gathered crowd.

Twelve trumpeters emerged from the spacecraft in slow, deliberate movement. Their presence felt regal and imposing. Six took positions to the left, six to the right, each one holding a trumpet behind their back. The instruments gleamed like artifacts of fate, untouched by time.

Without a word, they raised their trumpets in perfect unison.

A single note rang out, piercing the silence. The sound, pure and ancient, filled the air with such force that the sky itself seemed to pause. The haunting melody rolled across the airport with unnatural weight, as if the music were made of memory, prophecy, and power. It was beauty wrapped in terror. Music that didn't ask for reverence—it commanded it.

The trumpeters remained statuesque, their eyes forward and unblinking. Around them, the spacecraft shimmered in the dusk, its surface casting a glow of alien light. The surrounding air warped, as if the fabric of reality was bending in quiet submission to what was unfolding.

The song continued. It fused with the deep hum of the ship's engine, forming a strange symphony—vibrations that seemed to reach through bone and blood, through time and memory. This wasn't performance; it was proclamation. A message from the beginning of creation—or the end.

Then came the scent.

Subtle at first but unmistakable. It carried with it something ancient, something cosmic. A fragrance like dust from long-dead stars and the perfume of newborn worlds. It smelled like reverence and soothed and unsettled in equal measure, like a memory you never experienced but somehow remembered.

And still the music went on.

People wept. Some collapsed to their knees. Others felt an invisible touch, like a breath of air on their skin, a presence that seemed to know their deepest secrets and watched them with an unseen gaze. It wasn't just a song anymore. It was him.

The Architect had not yet appeared, but the world already felt changed.

From the shadows near the top of the ramp, a colossal silhouette stirred. In a slow, deliberate fashion, it stepped forward, and even the air seemed to recoil. Reality bent around him with eerie reverence. This was no man. This was the Architect, and his arrival felt less like an entrance and more like a prophecy that came alive.

His piercing gaze flicked toward the twelve trumpeters, and though he said nothing, the weight of his stare landed like a silent decree. Each footfall rang out in a chilling metallic clang, echoing down the ramp, reverberating across the tarmac. It was the sound of something ancient awakening. Cameras fixed on him. The crowd didn't move. They wouldn't dare.

He stood almost seven feet tall, his physique carved with unnatural precision—powerful, lean, and graceful, as though shaped by divine mathematics. His shoulder-length hair, black as midnight, flowed behind him like a shroud. He radiated inevitability, a presence that pressed against the will of anyone who faced him.

He wore luminous blue armor forged from a metal no Earth-born forge could shape. It gleamed with an otherworldly sheen, flecked with tiny gemstones that twinkled like frozen stars. His gauntlets, boots, and greaves displayed the same elegant, alien craftsmanship, as if constellations coated him.

Trailing behind him was a royal blue cape, its edges rippling like light on water. Embroidered at its center: a massive golden "E," radiant and unmissable. It was an assertion. This was his empire, and he commanded it. The world was just catching up.

At his right hip rested a sword—sheathed in midnight silk, its hilt gleaming gold. Twin blue gemstones anchored the T-shaped grip, and the pommel, a circle carved like tangled roots, spoke of something ancient... something planted long ago, now ready to rise.

In his left hand, he carried a staff of pure gold. Intricate carvings spiraled its length like coiled vines. At its top sat a serpent's head—its mouth agape, revealing two diamond fangs that flashed in the light. Inside the serpent's mouth was a bright blue gemstone that pulsed a faint light with every step the Architect took. Blue stones set as eyes glimmered, unblinking, hypnotic, a gaze that promised ruin.

Four skulls dangled from the staff, swaying with each step, brushing one another in a hollow, bone-on-bone whisper that chilled the blood. Each skull was marked, burned with forgotten runes. They didn't rattle like trophies; they whispered like warnings. Around them clung a scent—aged and ancient—dust from a collapsed tomb.

And fastened to his left side was a matte-black cylinder. Sleek and silent. With each sway of his body, it tapped against his armor—a mechanical tick, like a clock wound too tight. Inside it were his blueprints. The Architect did not plan for war or conquest. He planned for something worse, something final.

The Architect continued his foreboding march toward the Los Angeles Coliseum, where his followers—arrayed in perfect formation—stood in silent reverence. Each step echoed a divine decree, his presence bending the air with invisible gravity. Every deliberate movement, precise and unhurried, suggested a destiny written in the stars and sacred scriptures.

Then, without warning, he stopped.

At the precise midpoint of his journey, the Architect turned his head, his eyes locking onto a solitary figure across the crowd. Draped in flowing purple robes, the man stood alone, unmoved amidst the chaos. For a single heartbeat, the world forgot how to breathe.

The Architect stared, and time faltered.

His expression didn't change, but the air thickened with hostility. Then, in one smooth, terrifying motion, he lifted his golden staff and pointed it at the robed figure. The serpent's jeweled eyes glinted in the light, and for a moment, even the Earth seemed to brace for impact.

But nothing happened.

The staff lowered. No words were spoken, no commands issued, and yet the meaning hung in the air. A warning or a promise?

A chill passed through the crowd as the Architect resumed his march. Cameras continued to roll, capturing every second, but no lens could convey the moment that just passed.

Something ancient had begun.

*   *   *

Back in Alaska, the glow of the television flickered across Dr. Solomon's face. He and General Robichaux sat in breathless silence, the feed from Los Angeles continuing to stream live. The images were chaotic—media scrambling, soldiers holding lines, and civilians paralyzed in fear—but it was the moment between the Architect and the man in the purple robes that seized Solomon's attention.

His eyes narrowed. "That man..." Solomon said, leaning forward, "...he was here, in Anchorage, during the drone launch. I swear it. How could he be in Los Angeles now?"

Robichaux grunted, shaking his head. "Either we're seeing ghosts, or the universe just changed the rules."

Solomon said nothing. Something tugged at him beneath the chaos, beneath the spectacle. His mind raced with a crawling dread that tightened in his chest. The banners, armor, and symbols burned into the capes. Scale. Bow. Sword. Scythe.

He whispered the words like a litany. He reached for his leather satchel and drew out a small, worn Bible. His hands trembled as he flipped the pages. He wanted to confirm what he already feared.

General Robichaux watched in silence as Solomon landed on the Book of Revelation.

"Chapter six," Solomon said. "The first seal... a rider on a white horse, carrying a bow. Then a red horse, its rider with a sword. Then black scales. Then death." He stared at the page, then back at the screen. "But this... this isn't prophecy being fulfilled," he said, his voice cracking. "It's prophecy being performed."

Robichaux furrowed his brow. "What are you saying?"

"I'm saying this is a script. He knows how to mimic what was written. The Architect isn't bringing Revelation to life... he's using it and weaponizing it."

The weight of his words settled into the room like concrete.

Robichaux looked back at the screen. The Architect moved in perfect unison, like a chess piece marching across holy ground.

"That's why people will believe him," Solomon continued. "Because it looks like Revelation. It feels like a prophecy, but this isn't the Creator's design... it's his." He slammed the Bible shut. "This makes him dangerous, General. He's not a false prophet... he's a false god, and he's building a new home in his own image."

On the television, the camera captured the Architect's ascent toward the Los Angeles Coliseum—golden staff in hand. Heliosa watched from the gate like a chained oracle.

Dr. Solomon exhaled. The moment wasn't surreal anymore; it was painful and terrifyingly real. And the world was watching it unfold as if it was already written.

CHAPTER THIRTEEN

Blueprints

"We're back, live from Los Angeles."

The reporter's voice crackled through the television.

Dr. Solomon sank into his leather chair; eyes locked on the screen. The camera zoomed in on the Architect's procession as it reached the steps of the coliseum—his massive frame flanked by the Four Horsemen.

"They're building something," the reporter continued, the feed cutting to activity at the center of the arena. "It looks... ceremonial, but we can't be certain. Officials have not yet released a statement."

Solomon's voice was hoarse. "This isn't just a message, General. It's a show of power."

Robichaux stood rigid beside him, his expression pale and unreadable, eyes flicking from Solomon to the television. He swallowed hard. "It's playing out in front of the entire world." A long silence. He spoke again; this time it was quieter. "The president needs to know. We've got troops on the ground in Los Angeles..."

He paused for a moment; he knew the answer but had to ask it. "Can we kill the Horsemen?"

Solomon turned toward the general. His stare was sharp and heavy. For a moment, he didn't answer—just looked at him like he was trying to understand if the man grasped the magnitude of what he'd asked.

"Kill the Horsemen?" he said, his voice cracked and bitter. A dry, mirthless laugh followed. "You're asking if we can destroy the epitome of power itself? These aren't just beings, General. They're forces. Ancient and relentless." He gestured toward the desk, where a stack of photographs lay scattered like shards of a prophecy. "What we know of them comes from fractured texts and whispers—history written by hands that were shaking in fear. And even those accounts fall short. Throwing military might at them would be like trying to drown the ocean." He met Robichaux's eyes. "They wouldn't even notice."

The General let out a sharp breath and gripped the back of a chair. "Then what do we do?"

"We prepare the world," Solomon said, his voice lower now, almost trembling. "Prepare them for what can't be stopped." Once more, his fingers traced the photographs' cryptic symbols and runes, each glance a fresh taunt. "I need more time to study these. Call the president. Update him on everything." He still hadn't looked up. "I'll see if I can find... anything else."

Robichaux hesitated, then gave a firm nod. The tension between them pulled like a static charge. As he turned to leave, the television filled the silence once more, the reporter's voice growing thinner as the camera continued to broadcast the impossible.

The White House buzzed with frantic energy. President Davidson stood behind his desk, a map of California spread across its surface—littered with pins, notes, and red circles that offered no comfort. His brow furrowed as he scanned the chaos, searching for a strategy buried in uncertainty.

The sharp ring of the phone cut through the noise.

"General Robichaux," Davidson said as he snapped the receiver to his ear. "What's the news from Alaska?"

A long silence followed. When the General spoke, his voice carried a weight it had never born before. "Mr. president... I'm not sure how to break this to you."

Davidson straightened, his tone sharpening. "This isn't the time for vagueness, General. Speak."

A deep inhale. Then the hammer fell. "Dr. Solomon recognized the symbols. Black, white, red, pale... the scale, the bow, the sword, the scythe. He's certain, sir. These beings are the Four Horsemen."

The silence that followed seemed to stretch into eternity. Davidson stared ahead, lips parted, but no words came. When he spoke, his voice was tight. "The Four Horsemen of the Apocalypse?" He cleared his throat, the sound echoing in the otherwise silent room. "Are you saying this is... the Apocalypse?"

Robichaux's reply hung in the air, thick with dread, the silence that followed more terrifying than the words themselves. "We don't know for sure, sir. But Solomon... he's certain. And I trust his judgment."

Davidson's grip on the phone tightened. His eyes dropped to the map as if it might offer answers. The room pressed in. "Thank you, General," he said. "I... I need a moment."

The line went dead.

Davidson stayed still, the faraway voices outside his office morphing into a meaningless drone. He shut his eyes, and for the first time since becoming president, he felt an isolation deeper than politics or diplomacy—it was existential and absolute.

Los Angeles lay in a surreal stillness, hours having slipped by since the Horsemen began their march from LAX. What started beneath a fading sun had stretched deep into the night, and now, in the early hours of morning, the Coliseum loomed under artificial lights. Within the vast arena, the same eerie beings who had marched with the Horsemen moved with unnerving precision. Silent and unyielding, they worked to assemble a towering platform at the arena's center. The wood shimmered, its grain swirling in intricate, unnatural patterns—like a mesmerizing dance, defying human comprehension and smelling of wood smoke and old magic. A faint scent wafted through the air, earthy yet unfamiliar, tinged with a sharp metallic edge. It was clear that this was no earthly material. Perhaps the Architect's vessel carried it, a resource from some alien domain.

Piece by piece, the structure rose. The workers brushed vibrant blue paint across the surface, each stroke deliberate. As artificial light struck the drying paint, it seemed to glow, amplifying the structure's ethereal aura. Etched into the front of the platform was the now-familiar emblem of a tree—its branches forming a precise, curling "E" at the center. Gold-leaf detailing flickered like fireflies with every shift of the breeze.

The Architect stood nearby, his imposing figure framed by the rising edifice. In one hand, he held a bundle of blueprints. With precise gestures of his golden staff, he guided his followers, pointing out specific details. The serpent's head at the tip gleamed, almost alive, its gemstone eyes catching the last rays of light.

With the final brushstroke applied, the beings stepped back in unison, heads bowed in silent acknowledgement of their completed task. The platform now loomed over the coliseum, gleaming beneath the coliseum lights. A low hum of anticipation, like a thousand buzzing bees, vibrated in the air, while the very earth seemed to hold its breath, heavy with expectation.

The Four Horsemen stepped forward. Their presence amplified by the disciplined ranks at their backs, they moved with solemn grace. Each gave sharp, guttural commands that cracked like thunder through the silence. Their followers responded, forming into rigid formations beside the platform.

Pale Death took his place to the right of the podium, ghostly armor catching the dying light and radiating inevitable finality. Beside him, War—clad in blazing red—stood like a flame personified, her presence fierce and unforgiving.

Opposite them, Conquest moved with lethal elegance, his white armor gleaming as though untouched by the chaos he foretold. Beside him loomed Pestilence, shrouded in black, her jagged silhouette exuding cold, unyielding dominion.

Together, they flanked the podium, sentinels of prophecy, statuesque and silent.

Heliosa stood at the base of the structure. Her chains caught the floodlight beams, glinting as she moved with regal resolve. Even among these towering forces, her presence held weight— commanding and unreadable. Above her, the rhythmic churn of helicopter blades disturbed the air, circling the Coliseum where tens of thousands had been driven inside. The stands, once filled with cheers of sport, now held a captive audience—silent, trembling, and lit by the strobe of countless cameras. Flashes erupted like lightning, every lens capturing each movement. The Architect remained still. He adjusted the gleaming plates of his blue armor. The faint creak of metal brushed the air. He held his golden staff in one hand, its serpent head gleaming with ominous authority. With slow precision, he tightened his grip. The faint scrape of metal on metal rang like the drawing of a blade.

Then, responding to an unseen cue, he moved, ascending the platform's steps. Each rise echoed through the vast arena, his boots striking the boards like a war drum. The Coliseum crowd fell into a trembling hush—tens of thousands holding their breath, torn between terror and awe. Some clutched each other, some stared unblinking, others buried their faces in their hands, but none dared to move. At the summit he paused, his towering silhouette stretching long shadows over the polished blue. His gaze swept right... then left... lingering on each Horseman. Then, a single, confident nod.

The moment had arrived.

With a practiced flourish, he planted his staff into its holder beside the podium. A sharp, final, holy clang echoed, the metallic ring resonating like a bell. From beneath his arm, he retrieved the rolled blueprints from their container. In a slow and deliberate manner, he unfurled them across the podium. The faint rustle of parchment broke the stillness, delicate yet immense. A whisper before the thunder.

The Architect stood tall, his gaze sweeping over the crowd. His baritone voice boomed through the coliseum, each word resonating with an almost tangible weight.

"People of Planet Zero..." he began, the disdain in his tone unmistakable. His voice echoed off the coliseum walls, wrapping the audience in its commanding grip. "Behold the perfection before you—the divine beauty that I embody. Weep, for you stand in the Architect's presence; the Creator's right hand, the master planner, the builder of worlds."

He paused, letting his words settle like ash over the trembling onlookers. He raised his arms in a slow, calculated gesture, drawing every eye to him.

"Once, this place was a pristine, tranquil canvas..." His voice softened but lost none of its force. "It was adorned with skies of unbroken blue, waters that danced with light, and lands bursting with vibrant color. A masterpiece—flawless in every way." Then his tone darkened, venom curling through his words. "And then... the Creator gave it to you—pathetic, crawling insects. You, who desecrate my canvas with your blasphemous presence. Towering monuments of arrogance scar the horizon, casting shadows that choke the light. The air reeks of your corruption. The stench of your futile existence is suffocating this once-beautiful world."

His hand moved to the blueprints on the podium. The pages fluttered in the breeze, amplified by the eerie hush that had fallen.

"Fear not, zeros..." His voice climbed, resonating like thunder. "You will not suffer your failures anymore."

The Architect's eyes gleamed with dangerous light as he unfurled the blueprints further, spreading them before him with a flourish. The scent of ink mixed with the crisp tang of paper.

"I will reset this world..." Each word fell like a hammer. "Return it to its genesis. A new beginning awaits—untouched and unspoiled. And on it, my vision will reign supreme." His voice dipped lower, almost reverent. "A world worthy of my genius and my perfection." He scanned the arena. "When I am finished, this planet will not bear the shame of your existence. It will be my masterpiece once more—reflecting only the brilliance of its rightful creator."

He lowered the blueprints, his piercing gaze slicing through the crowd. A faint, chilling smile curved his lips. "Gaze upon your savior—and despair. For I do not offer redemption. I offer obliteration. And from it... creation."

With ritualistic care, the Architect placed the blueprints back atop the podium, smoothing the parchment like sacred scripture.

141

He cleared his throat, a deliberate sound that silenced even the faintest of whispers.

"To achieve this vision, I must cleanse the world of the plague that is your existence." His voice sharpened like a blade. "You have stained my creation with chaos and conceit. I will scrape you from the canvas like filth from a masterpiece." The coliseum trembled beneath his words. His expression remained calm, but his eyes burned with a cold, unrelenting fire.

He leaned forward, voice dropping to a whisper that chilled the blood. "Your children... will not share your fate." The phrase hit like a dagger. "I will pluck the tender flowers of your future from your homes. I will mold them—not to remember you but to forget you." Straightening, he spread his arms wide, his shadow stretching long across the platform. "They will not return to you but to the blank canvas I will create. A world untainted by your failures. They will be my foundation. The architects of a future molded in my image—their minds stripped of the rot you left behind." A faint, humorless smile tugged at his lips. "They will dance to my tune." His voice dripped with malice. "Marionettes of perfection—strings held in my grasp. Every thought they think, every move they make, will echo my design. And they will build my new masterpiece... not as your children but as mine."

Then his voice rose again, resolute and final. "Your time has ended. I cannot control you—and I will not waste my vision on what is irredeemable. I will cast you aside like debris swept from a workshop floor. But your children... they will flourish in the world I forge."

The weight of his vision settled over the coliseum like smoke.

The Architect's laughter erupted—deep, venomous, and resonant. It echoed through the coliseum like a chorus of damned bells, vibrating through bone and stone alike.

"Your Creator thought He could sever His right hand and cast it into the garden... then send you—pitiful, fumbling creatures— to smear your fingerprints across my canvas." The air thickened, charged with a tension that clung to every breath. His voice dropped, coiled with poisonous revelation. "He underestimated me." His eyes swept across the hushed multitudes, their silence hanging like a held breath. "He did not foresee that I would harness the untapped power of Eden itself. It was I who imprisoned His essence—trapped it within the very tree you insects defiled with your greed, arrogance, and hunger for forbidden fruit."

A collective ripple of dread shivered through the crowd. The weight of the moment pressed down like gravity doubled. And then, with a thunderous voice, he proclaimed, "That is why you have not heard from Him in eons!" His voice cracked the air like a divine judgment. The walls of the coliseum trembled, the sky itself seemed to flinch. "He is gone. Forgotten." A purposeful pause ensued. "And soon... I will obliterate even the memory of His existence—wiped from the annals of time."

The Architect paused. His piercing eyes rose toward the heavens, tracing the outline of the looming object that hovered high above. With a grand, deliberate sweep, he extended his arms wide—his silhouette haloed by the lights from the coliseum.

"Behold, zeros!" he roared; his voice laced with divine wrath. "Gaze upon my inaugural masterpiece. Bathe in the resplendence of the Fingers of Eden!"

A thunderous chorus of cheers erupted from his followers— ecstatic cries of worship, fanaticism, and awe. But with a single, sweeping motion of his arm, the Architect summoned silence. The cheers ceased. The sudden quiet was deafening.

"You have seen only a glimpse of their power." His voice lowered, sharpened to a blade's edge. "One Finger, with a mere

143

flick of its might, swatted your pathetic flies from the sky. A demonstration. Nothing more." A cruel smile spread across his face—then laughter, dark and resonant, echoed through the coliseum. "But soon," he said, savoring every syllable, "you will witness the full extent of their magnificence."

Again, the crowd erupted—an ocean of devotion. This time, the Architect let their worship swell. He stood motionless, absorbing it like a god receiving tribute. And when he raised a single hand, silence returned like a thunderclap.

"Your arrogance will deceive you." He paced. "You will believe you can stop what is coming... that you can halt the inevitable. But do not fret, zeros." His tone twisted into mockery. "The Eden Veil shields us—impenetrable to your futile little fireworks."

A low hum pulsed through the coliseum as the Finger of Eden above shifted. A vent cracked open with a deep, mechanical groan. From within, a strange mist poured forth—an iridescent vapor that bathed the arena in shimmering light. It danced across the Architect's armor, refracting in eerie patterns that dazzled and disturbed.

The crowd watched in reverent awe; breath caught in their throats. Every eye fixed on him.

Then, like a dagger through silk, his voice sliced through the glow. "Not even that fool draped in royal purple will stop me." A sneer touched his lips. "He hides in mystery and clings to prophecy—but this world is mine to reclaim. Mine to shape. And none shall stand in my way."

He turned from the podium, his boots striking the platform with deliberate force. Each step was a drumbeat of judgment as he paced with the precision of a war general, the calm of a master craftsman preparing to unveil a divine blueprint.

The silence stretched long, and the world listened.

He halted mid-stride, his towering figure framed by the eerie glow of the Fingers of Eden above. His voice pierced the silence, reverberating with absolute command. "Allow me to introduce you to my harbingers." His tone oozed arrogance. "My commanders in this journey of reset... and genesis." He raised his staff high, the serpent's head glinting, its gemstone eyes flickering like they had a mind of their own. "Hands!" The word cracked like thunder.

In an instant, the Four Horsemen turned. Their distinct armor glinted beneath the coliseum's harsh lights. Moving with mechanical precision, they flanked their master in perfect formation.

The sight evoked awe and dread in equal measures. The faint clink of their armor echoed like a funeral march. And once more, the Architect's voice sliced through the tension. "Every revered deity requires a trusted right hand." He spread his arms. "I am blessed with four."

He turned, sweeping the silent crowd with his gaze. "Across every world we've reshaped, their names have changed. The Four Harbingers. The Four Destroyers. Sometimes... just the Four." A sinister grin curled across his lips. "Your sacred texts call them the Four Horsemen, but I assure you..." He paused for effect, then laughed—a sound both chilling and gleeful. "They have mounted no beasts in ages."

His gaze landed on the first figure, clad in ebony armor. "The Fourth Hand: Rangel." Rangel stepped forward, her movements graceful but steeped in menace. "She will unleash the Blight. It will seep into the soil, purging impurities and transforming the land. Death, yes... but death that gives birth to a new life."

Next, he turned to the figure in pristine white armor, radiant and unblemished. "The Third Hand: Durbal." Durbal moved like

145

a tactician, calm and calculated. "He oversees the Fingers of Eden. Their precision, reach, and devastation—it is his domain."

Then came the figure in crimson armor, every step like a spark ready to ignite. "The Second Hand: Seria." Seria advanced, violence coiled beneath the surface of her poise. Behind her, the ranks of her loyal soldiers stood unmoving—except for the low chorus of guttural snarls that rose behind her, primal and chilling. "She commands the Hounds of War. My purging flame. Where they march, chaos blooms. Where they hunt, nothing remains. They are loyal, merciless, and tear in my name."

His gaze found his final hand, a pale figure, the one who chilled the air by his mere presence. "The First Hand: Prime Regar." Regar stepped forward with deathly grace, each step like the closing of a tomb. "He bears the title of Prime. The others bend to his will. Where he walks, you'll find silence, then—ashes. He is the embodiment of death itself."

The Architect gestured toward the four, now revealed in all their glory.

"Together, they are the hands that carry my vision. In their grip, death and rebirth entwine. Through them, a new world is chiseled into existence."

The air thickened. The crowd could feel it. A shift in the atmosphere. The coliseum, once a stadium, now a throne room for annihilation.

Then the Architect turned, his gaze stretching to the distant airport, where the remaining ships lay silent.

"Ah... but there is still one more introduction." His voice dripped with malevolence. "The Nephilim. My legion. The giants of old, reborn in the light of perfection. They will paint the canvas red."

High above the arena, the Coliseum's massive screens flickered to life, hijacked by unseen hands. Cameras trained on LAX showed the great ships groaning open, their ramps descending with mechanical precision. From the shadows emerged enormous figures, their colossal frames dwarfing the tarmac. The broadcast carried their unveiling into every corner of the stadium, making the crowd feel the weight of giants even at a distance.

The Architect raised his staff. His voice dropped to a whisper that somehow echoed louder than any shout. "Let the end... begin."

CHAPTER FOURTEEN

Nephilim

The Architect's proclamation echoed far beyond the coliseum, reverberating across a trembling world. In Los Angeles, his blueprints took form. From the hulking spacecrafts, the first Nephilim emerged—each step a thunderous drumbeat that shook the tarmac beneath them.

Crowds gathered in grim awe—military personnel with trembling grips on their weapons, journalists whispering into their microphones, and civilians clutching children or standing frozen in wide-eyed disbelief. The Nephilim descended into formation, hundreds of towering beings casting monstrous shadows against the sky. Their gleaming skin caught the floodlights, reflecting deep reds and bruised purples as if absorbing the false dawn cast across the tarmac. They moved in unison, unnervingly synchronized—an army of divine wrath, mechanical and fluid all at once. The tension in the streets was electric. Every click of a camera shutter sounded like a gunshot. Every breath a question.

Then it happened.

A sound like the earth's fury unleashed—deep, guttural, and primal—erupting from within the largest vessel. It silenced the city. Even the Nephilim seemed to pause. With a hiss of releasing pressure, the ramp of the central craft descended.

From the shadows stepped something worse than death.

A titan. Head and shoulders taller than any other Nephilim, his presence seemed to blot out the sky itself. His movements were methodical, each step pressing cracks into the tarmac under the weight of his presence. His skin shimmered with an unnatural glow, catching ethereal hues.

He stopped at the foot of the ramp and raised his head. Eyes like molten steel scanned the crowd. He was a weapon shaped like a man. His colossal spear gleamed on his back, wicked edges kissed by twilight.

Back at the Coliseum, the Architect's voice shattered the silence—booming across the city as though spoken by the heavens themselves. "I present to you... Haligot. Commander of my legion of Nephilim... and brother to Goliath."

The words struck like thunder.

Gasps rippled through the crowd. Some soldiers whispered prayers. Others stared, hollow-eyed and mute. Cameras strained to focus, desperate to capture every moment of the impossible.

And then the Architect twisted the knife.

"These fierce giants—half angel, half human—possess strength beyond reckoning. I rescued them from a flood your Creator sent to erase them. Now, they serve me."

Haligot stood motionless. His silence was terrifying. It carried weight.

A creeping, unnatural cold rolled outward from the Nephilim, thickening the air, numbing the limbs of those who stood too close. Some fainted while others wept.

149

The Architect's final decree struck like a blade through ice. "Tremble in fear, Zeros. This is the beginning of the end."

The crowd's shallow breaths came faster, their unease rising like a tide as the Coliseum's massive screens came alive with the image of Haligot at LAX. He looked out over the cameras, his lips curling into a grim, predatory smile.

Without a word, he raised a single hand.

The legion of Nephilim responded in an instant.

A unified roar erupted from their ranks—deep, thunderous, and soul-rattling. At the airport, the shockwave scattered birds into the night sky and sent vibrations shuddering through the tarmac. In the Coliseum, the broadcast carried the sound so vividly it rattled in the bones of every captive, making the distance between arenas vanish. It was the sound of something irreversible. A moment carved in time.

At the coliseum, the Architect moved with purpose. Gripping his staff—its surface as cold and unyielding as his resolve—he raised it high. The gemstone embedded in its crown burst to life, unleashing a blinding brilliance that drowns the arena in white fire. Then, with a swift, deliberate motion, he brought the staff down. It struck the platform with a concussive blast. The sound cracked through the air like a divine hammer. A surge of raw energy exploded outward, pressing against skin and bone, shaking the breath from lungs. The crowd reeled, shielding their eyes as light seared across the walls, casting grotesque shadows that danced and twisted like spirits trying to flee.

As the radiance dimmed to a steady, pulsing glow, the Coliseum's massive screens came alive again. From the haze on the broadcast stepped Haligot—his titanic frame filling the feed, his predatory smile unmistakable even from miles away. His massive frame cleaved through the glow like a blade through smoke. Each stride thundered against the ground, sending tremors in every direction. Reaching the front line of his assembled legion, he halted—rising above them like a monument carved from fury.

The glow shimmered against his diamond-hard skin, refracting in spectral shards of red, violet, and gold.

Then he threw back his head and roared. A roar born from the marrow of the world itself. "NEPHILIM! LOOK UPON ME!" His voice exploded across the airport, rippling through every living soul. The Nephilim snapped to attention. Their bodies, already colossal, seemed to grow even larger under their commander's gaze.

Haligot raised his arm, pointing toward the line of soldiers, civilians, and cameras on the outskirts of the airport—humanity's last audience.

"These vermin have defiled our master's canvas!" His voice was thunder. His presence, a storm. He turned, his gaze sweeping beyond the crowd to the world itself. "One of your kind stole the life of my brother in the valley long ago. And for that... I have cursed your race. Today... I shall avenge him."

The silence that followed was thick and suffocating. The ground seemed to hum beneath the crowd's feet, matching the fury that pulsed through Haligot's veins.

With calculated calm, he reached over his shoulder, and the metallic rasp of a weapon unsheathing rang out as he drew a colossal spear from his back. Its shaft gleamed as if alive. Twin blue lines ran down the length, glowing like veins. At its tip, the triangular blade—forged of alien metal—shimmered with deadly promise.

Haligot raised the spear high. His grip tightened and his muscles coiled.

"NEPHILIM!"

A roar erupted from the legion of Nephilim.

"UNLEASH YOUR FURY!"

The legion responded as one, a deafening roar that shook the earth like thunder from the heavens. Their mouths twisted into sadistic grins, eyes gleaming with unrestrained bloodlust. Then, without hesitation, they surged forward, a monstrous tide crashing against a fragile shore.

The tarmac cracked beneath their pounding feet, spiderweb fractures blooming beneath their march.

The soldiers didn't move. Fear paralyzed them.

A young private, twenty years old, maybe, his hands slick with sweat, raised his trembling rifle and fired.

The shot cracked through the air like a whip. In that moment, time seemed to hold its breath. It echoed like the first gunshot at Lexington.

But unlike that shot, this one failed to rally hope. It struck the chest of a charging Nephilim and bounced off. The bullet ricocheted with a faint metallic ping, leaving behind a scratch no deeper than a fingernail.

The private's eyes widened, his expression collapsing from grim resolve to sheer terror.

Around him, the truth spread like wildfire. Their weapons meant nothing.

The Nephilim slowed, a slow, satisfied smile playing on their lips as they took in the scene before them.

They savored the moment, the taste of fear thick in the air. Their grins widened, fangs gleaming. Claws unfurled like midnight scythes. They struck the crowd with great ferocity.

The first impact was chaos.

Screams tore through the sky. The impact ripped flesh as armor shredded and bones broke. Claws danced with surgical

152

precision, cleaving through soldiers like parchment. Blood painted the ground in sweeping arcs, pooling beneath boots, staining the fractured pavement.

One by one, the defenders fell. Some tried to run but none succeeded. Their final breaths joined the cacophony of slaughter. The symphony of the Architect's vision was taking form.

Through it all, Haligot advanced behind his legion. His earlier words drifted through the smoke and screams.

"One of your kind stole the life of my brother in the valley long ago..."

That fury had never faded. It had aged like poison—refined, distilled, and multiplied over eons. A curse carved into the bones of humanity. And now, it was being made manifest.

Haligot's gaze swept the battlefield. A slow smile crept across his face as he stepped over mangled bodies and crushed weapons, his every step a drumbeat of finality.

There was no urgency in him. The outcome had always been the same. Humanity never stood a chance.

The air above Los Angeles was thick with death—an invisible miasma that clung to the city like a funeral shroud. Beneath it, the Nephilim's wrath played out with brutal precision. Screams of the dying echoed through the streets, a grim symphony underscoring humanity's helplessness.

Across the world, the carnage unfolded on screens—an unfiltered broadcast of annihilation. In the Situation Room of the White House, flickering images painted the walls with an oppressive glow. No speakers carried the noise, yet the silence itself seemed to echo with screams and the tearing of flesh.

President Davidson stared at the screen, unmoving. A single image—the bullet bouncing off a Nephilim's chest—played on repeat in his mind. His hand trembled as he reached for his coffee mug. It slipped from his grasp and shattered against the floor.

The crash was deafening in the stillness.

Nobody spoke. Some covered their mouths; others wept. Security personnel, trained to remain unreadable, stood frozen, eyes red-rimmed and jaws tight.

Davidson buried his face in his hands, fingers clawing at his temples as if trying to keep the despair from spilling out. Around him, aides and generals sat in stunned silence, grief pressing against their chests like a vice.

The broken mug lay in pieces—porcelain fragments scattered like the lives lost in Los Angeles.

Davidson inhaled a deep, shaky breath. Then another, and as he sat back, his eyes red but sharp, the silence cracked.

"Today," he said, voice rough but resolute, "will not be the day we perish without a fight."

The weight of his words seemed to anchor the room.

"I want every ship, every aircraft, every soldier we have on standby. Mobilize them. Prepare for immediate deployment to Los Angeles."

Chairs scraped back. Phones came alive. Aides rushed from the room like pressure valves released. Officers barked orders with newfound urgency. The White House, shaken but not broken, moved.

Elsewhere, engines roared to life. Convoys rumbled down darkened highways. Boots pounded the tarmac. Soldiers loaded rifles with grim efficiency, their eyes filled with purpose and duty.

"First wave mobilizing now, sir," an aide reported.

Davidson nodded. His voice was quieter now but heavy. "Good," he said. "This is only the beginning."

C-130 transport planes pierced the skies, flanked by jet fighters and circling Black Hawks. Down below, tanks clattered across fractured freeways, while convoys of soldiers braced for battle. Offshore, a U.S. Navy destroyer sliced through choppy waters—guns loaded and radars spinning—its crew braced for war.

The first wave of Earth's counterstrike had arrived.

And then the veil fell.

Without warning, a brilliant pulse snapped outward. A split-second shimmer—silent and cruel—cut across the horizon like a blade made of light.

In the air, a C-130 vanished mid-flight, its tail section sheared clean off by the barrier. The fuselage spiraled into the city, crashing into a bloom of smoke and steel.

On the ground, a marine sprinted forward—his weapon raised, and eyes locked forward. The veil slammed shut mid-stride. One side of his body landed inside. The other never made it.

Offshore, the destroyer struck the veil at full speed. The front half passed through and kept moving. The impact severed the rest with surgical precision and tossed deck crew into the sea. Some of them vanished upon impact.

Just like that, the veil rejected Earth's might.

In the distance, atop the ruined bones of Los Angeles, the Architect smiled.

In the Situation Room, the feed went black.

The images of the destroyer, the marine, and the C-130—all severed mid-motion—seared themselves into their minds.

Aides turned away, some rushing from the room, hands over their mouths. Others broke into uncontrollable sobs, the weight of helplessness crashing in all at once.

Somewhere in the room, another coffee mug slipped from trembling fingers. It shattered on the floor.

President Davidson didn't flinch at the sound. He knelt beside the broken pieces, reaching down with careful fingers. As he gathered the fragments, something flickered behind his eyes. A single tear formed. Just one.

He wiped it away with the back of his hand before it could fall. No one saw it. No one needed to.

Outside, the city lay beneath a star-choked sky. Long shadows stretched across the ruined streets of Los Angeles cast by floodlights and fires burning in the rubble, like mourning veils draped over the dead. The city, once vibrant, now stood in silence, grieving its own annihilation.

Amid the smoldering ruins of Los Angeles, the Architect and Haligot stood atop the battered remnants of a once-proud platform. The cold glow of spotlights and the pale wash of a hidden moon carved their towering forms into silhouette; monoliths etched against the darkness.

Below them, the remnants of human resistance crackled with fading flames and distant sobs.

The Architect surveyed the devastation with a calm, calculated gaze. A faint smile tugged at the corners of his mouth.

"Your legion of Nephilim continues to impress me," he said, his voice smooth with quiet satisfaction. "Tonight, let them rest in my chambers. A well-earned reward for the symphony they've composed in blood. Tomorrow, we turn to the next phase of my blueprints."

Haligot inclined his head in acknowledgment, but his expression remained grim. His molten eyes swept across the broken city. "Your will is my command, my lord," he said. Then, almost as an afterthought, "But I will find no peace while these insects continue to infest the Earth."

The Architect turned, his gaze sharp and analytical. He studied the rage smoldering beneath Haligot's surface like a furnace stoked too long.

"Your vengeance has burned for millennia," he said, voice cool and deliberate. "But do not let it consume you before our work is complete."

Haligot's lips curled into a grim approximation of a smile.

"One of their kind stole my brother's life in the valley long ago. For that, I cursed them all. Their defiance of divine power ends now—under our dominion."

The Architect's smile faded into something colder, more precise.

"Your rage is a weapon," he said. "But you must wield even weapons with discipline. Spare those with the mark of prophecy— for now. The rest belong to you."

Haligot's eyes narrowed, glowing with restrained fury. He turned, his massive frame moving like a boulder set in motion. "Tomorrow," he said, "this world will tremble beneath their screams."

His footsteps faded into the shadowed corridors of the city, leaving the Architect alone beneath the star-swept sky. For a long moment, the dark figure remained motionless, his golden staff resting at his side, his gaze fixed on the horizon where night bled slowly toward dawn.

Somewhere in the distance, a cry echoed through the ruins.

The Architect's smile returned, faint but triumphant.

Everything was going according to plan.

The rhythmic cadence of approaching footsteps echoed through the coliseum, cutting through the stillness like a herald of reckoning.

Without turning, the Architect spoke, his voice low and commanding. "Speak, Regar."

From the shadows, the First Hand emerged. His form loomed with solemn grace as he stepped into view and bowed. "My lord," Regar said, his tone laden with gravity, "one Finger of Eden has observed something... intriguing."

The Architect's eyes gleamed with anticipation. He leaned forward, motioning for him to continue.

"We have located the man you encountered during your march," Regar said. "We saw him conversing with a high-ranking military official. The location is in the north. In a remote tundra known as Alaska."

The Architect's lips curled into a slow, satisfied smile. "Well done, Regar," he said, his words rich with approval. "He seeks the ones marked by prophecy... hoping to unlock their destinies before I claim them myself."

He turned his gaze to the northern horizon, the smog-choked sky stretching far beyond the coliseum's broken walls.

"Remain here," he ordered. "There are countless souls in this city still awaiting harvest. At dawn, I will dispatch Seria and her loyal Hounds of War. They will descend upon the North and tear the answers I seek from the ice."

Regar bowed once more and vanished into the gloom, his departure as quiet and final as a death knell.

The Architect strode forward, his silhouette framed by the broken bones of the once-great city.

He approached Seria, her sharp gaze locked on the snarling hounds standing beside her. The surrounding air was thick with menace, each guttural growl reverberating through the coliseum like the beat of a war drum.

"Seria," the Architect said, "I have a task of great importance. Rally your hounds and head north—to the frozen wilds of Alaska. A man cloaked in regal purple searches for those marked by destiny. Find them... and bring them to me."

A wicked smile crept across Seria's lips, her eyes flashing with savage delight.

"Consider it done, my lord," she replied, her voice as sharp as the fangs that surrounded her.

Turning to the beasts at her feet, she raised her voice in a commanding snarl. "Listen well, you vile creatures! At first light, we march and we hunt. Spare only those with the mark—for our master desires them." She paused, then smiled—a cold, feral grin. "The rest are yours to slaughter. Let the world tremble beneath your claws."

A chorus of howls erupted, the sound rising in a nightmarish crescendo that shook the very stone beneath their feet. Flames from nearby braziers cast their shadows in wild patterns.

The Architect turned to leave, his footsteps thunderous, but glanced back once more. "If your hounds grow hungry..." he said, his voice low and cruel, "let them feast on the bones left behind by Regar's reaping."

Seria bowed once, her smile curling wider. With a burst of snarls and howls, she and her pack dissolved into the shadows.

The Architect stood in the growing silence, his expression unreadable. Then his gaze shifted to the two figures standing nearby.

"Ah, Durbal and Rangel," he said, his voice thick with authority.

They stepped forward—Durbal tall and gleaming in white, Rangel a living shadow in black.

"Durbal," the Architect said, "ready the Finger of Eden over Rome. Let the heavens bear witness to their devastation."

Then he turned. "Rangel, go to Rome with Durbal. When the Finger completes its destruction, release the blight. Begin the transformation. Our waiting ends tonight."

Raising his staff to the sky, his voice boomed one last time. "Eden's power will shake the world to its core. Rest now, my loyal hands. Tomorrow... destiny unfolds."

As the Architect's voice faded, the coliseum emptied into silence.

*　　*　　*

Far to the north, beneath the same cold sky, Alaska slept.

The wind whispered through skeletal trees, its chill biting and unrelenting. Fog clung to the mountains like a shroud, muffling sound and obscuring shapes. It was as if nature itself knew what approached—and sought to hide its children.

In the military hangar, Roo and his companions huddled close, their breath visible in the frozen air. The base, once filled with order and purpose, now felt like a sanctuary built on the edge of ruin.

Around them, dust, rust, and silence settled like omens.

Unbeknownst to them, the Architect's will had already reached across the continent. Seria's hounds would soon descend. The brief calm would shatter, and the fog-covered silence of Alaska would scream.

CHAPTER FIFTEEN

Fog of War

T he next morning, a few hours before dawn, an unsettling silence blanketed Los Angeles. The coliseum loomed in the gloom, its shadow stretching long and ominous across the lifeless streets, a dark crown atop the Architect's throne.

Throughout the night, a fleet of ships had docked along its edges, unloading their grim cargo; slaves to toil under the Architect's command, snarling hounds of war eager for bloodshed, and members of his war band.

Durbal and Rangel had departed the night before; their fates now bound to the schemes unfolding in Rome. But here, in the Architect's stronghold, time held its breath, the moment pregnant with dread.

The Architect's voice, thunderous and unyielding, shattered the silence like a crack of divine judgment. "Wake them. This will be a glorious day."

The drummers moved in perfect unity. Stretched animal skins adorned their cylindrical drums, bound by polished wooden rings. As the first mallets struck, a deep, resonant boom echoed across the coliseum—a heartbeat of war.

The rhythm built. Each strike was louder, quicker, and more primal. The hounds of war stirred. Muscles rippled beneath their hides as they rose, their eyes aglow with hunger. Saliva dripped from bared fangs as low growls swelled into snarls, the drums igniting their lust for battle.

The Architect emerged, tall and imposing, his black cloak trailing like smoke. His eyes found Seria standing untouched among the beasts. Her tranquility was more terrifying than their rage.

"Seria," he said, his voice like iron drawn across stone. "The time has come." He paused, letting the moment settle, the drums thundering beneath his words. "Take the hounds and the drummers. Go to Alaska and find the vermin hiding there. The ones marked by the prophecy are mine. Bring them to me alive." A cruel grin crept across his lips. "As for the fool in purple... make him suffer."

Seria's grin spread, a glint of dark amusement dancing in her eyes. With a hiss of steel, she drew her sword, holding it to the light. The blade mirrored her unyielding gaze. Satisfied, she sheathed it in one smooth motion and stepped toward her hounds, their eyes burning with anticipation. The war drums pounded behind her, each beating a summons to blood.

Her voice sliced through the chaos. "Hounds!" Dark satisfaction curled her tone. "Do you feel it? The drums are in your veins now—calling for carnage and demanding blood. Our master has given us a mission worthy of our name, and we will execute it as we always have... to perfection." She paced before them, eyes gleaming. "You are not beasts. You are instruments of annihilation. Grasp your swords and don your Bloodfang Talons. Spare only those marked by prophecy. As for the rest..." Her voice dropped, silken with venom. "Show no mercy. Rip their flesh. Break their bones. Let their screams paint the trees."

The hounds stood entranced, a hunger for the hunt coursing through their veins.

"And when the sun rises?" A savage smile stretched across her face. "You'll be feasting. Their meat in your bellies, their fear in your bones, and their blood in your teeth."

She stopped before them, eyes burning. "Fifteen minutes. Ready yourselves. The hunt begins."

A guttural roar erupted as the hounds pounded their chests. They drew their swords. A promise of violence shimmered in the flickering light reflected on their blades.

One by one, the hounds fitted their hands with the Bloodfang Talons; forged in the sacred fires beneath Zion's Eternal Flame, where heat burned hotter than any earthly forge. The crimson-veined, blackened steel formed each gauntlet, mimicking the curved, cruel, razor-sharp talons of a falcon mid-strike. Curved like shadow-forged hooks, their claws, honed for ripping flesh and shattering bone, extended over their knuckles. Along with the wrist guards, scorched symbols of ancient war rites pulsed, reacting to the rhythm of the war drums. These were no mere weapons; they were sacred instruments of slaughter, baptized in fire and awakened only by the scent of blood.

The air crackled with primal fury.

Seria turned without a word. Her warriors fell into formation behind her, their heavy boots pounding in perfect rhythm with the drums.

Together, they marched toward the waiting ship. The drummers followed, their rhythm rising to a thunderous crescendo, shaking the coliseum walls.

Above the skyline, the Finger of Eden hung like a silent sentinel; casting its shadow over a city held hostage by fear. Behind that shadow, Seria and her hounds vanished into the coming storm.

Far to the north, a heavy quietness clung to the Alaskan base, the kind of hush that comes before something breaks. Fog rolled low across the flight line, swallowing the ruined aircraft outside in a pale shroud. Inside the hangar, backup generators hummed, powering lights that flickered, trying to hold the shadows at bay.

Roo stood motionless, staring toward the horizon as if he could sense the storm gathering thousands of miles away. A single tear carved a clean trail through the ash on his cheek.

Near him, Lizzie's hands trembled at her sides. In her wide eyes burned the terrible clarity of someone stripped of everything but resolve. Around them, a small group huddled near a battered television. The screen flickered between static and nightmares, live footage of Los Angeles burning beneath the Architect's shadow.

Roo's voice cracked the silence. "So much bloodshed..." he said. "What do we do?"

The question hovered in the foggy air.

Across the hangar, Dr. Terracotta hunched over a pile of frayed cables and old tech, muttering as his hands danced across a transmitter's dials. Sweat beaded on his forehead. "If this doesn't work... no, it'll work. Just need to recalibrate..."

Lizzie stepped toward him, arms crossed, eyes scanning the chaos of wires and tools. "Doc, are you sure? If we don't get comms soon, we're screwed."

Terracotta flinched, almost dropping a wrench. "I've got it! Radios are my thing. These old models, though... they're temperamental. Like cats. You can't force them... gotta charm 'em."

Lizzie gave him a look. Part concern, part disbelief, but let it go. "Then charm faster. We may not have long."

From across the hangar, Roo interjected. "Don't sweat it, Doc. I've seen you pull miracles with duct tape and safety wire."

Terracotta chuckled, adjusting his glasses. "Yeah, well... here's hoping for another miracle. If the Architect's goons find us, this baby might buy us time."

He tapped the transmitter, and a crackle of static sparked from the speaker.

Roo smirked. "Just make sure it doesn't explode in your hands."

Terracotta let out a nervous laugh. "No promises."

Then the signal steadied. A voice emerged from the static, faint, but there.

"There! Got something!"

Lizzie's head snapped toward the sound. Her expression hardened. "Good. But it changes nothing. We survive. We find whoever's left. And we leave this place behind."

A voice spoke up from the shadows near the hangar doors, accented and uncertain. "Are you planning to leave? Can we come with you?"

Roo turned toward the sound. Just beyond the scattered tools and crates, a small knot of survivors stood watching, six in total, their faces streaked with soot and hollowed by exhaustion. Three appeared to be European; one looked Russian and the other two had matching expressions and quiet eyes, looked to be of Asian descent. Each one clutched a tattered backpack like it was the last thread holding them alive; their final lifeline in a world that had stopped making sense.

Roo hesitated, then gave a faint nod. "If you can keep up... yeah. We'll need all the help we can get."

165

The moment passed without further words, but something shifted. A sense of unity, quiet and fragile, like a campfire struggling against the wind.

The fog pressed against the hangar windows. They had little time.

Before they could plan further, footsteps echoed through the hangar. Dr. Solomon emerged from the shadows; his brow furrowed with concern. "Where are you going?"

Roo straightened, sharpening his voice. "We can't stay. It's only a matter of time before they find us. We're heading into the wilderness; somewhere we can regroup and figure out our next move."

Dr. Solomon hesitated, then nodded. "Then I'm coming too. This isn't just survival anymore. It ties to the Genesis era, the earliest bloodlines and lost symbols. I must understand what it means."

As he turned to gather his things, his eyes caught a movement near the hangar doors. General Robichaux stood alone, speaking to a man draped in purple robes. This was the second time he saw the general talking to the man in purple. He witnessed the same thing the night before. The robed figure leaned in close, whispering something only the general could hear, and whatever it was, it drained the color from his face.

Dr. Solomon approached the General. "What did he say?"

Robichaux's voice came low and distant. "I know what I must do... I need to make some calls."

Before Solomon could press further, the general turned and vanished into the fog, his silhouette swallowed by mist and silence. The robed man was already gone.

Solomon stood still, the chill seeping into his bones. He rejoined the group, the memory of that whispered exchange burning in his mind like a prophecy half-heard.

Outside the hangar, the rumble of an approaching engine cut through the fog-drenched silence. A black SUV emerged, headlights casting faint beams across the flight line. It rolled to a stop just beyond the open hangar doors. A security guard stepped out and opened the back door.

From the vehicle stepped President Davidson's wife, followed by their two daughters. Their wide eyes scanned the cavernous hangar, unsure whether to be frightened or just confused. Tammy followed them, her gaze flicking between the guards.

"What's going on?" she asked, her voice tight. "Are we leaving?"

The lead guard shook his head.

"New orders from President Davidson. You'll stay here until further notice."

The first lady pulled her daughters close to protect them. Around the hangar, members of the group exchanged uneasy glances, unspoken tension rising like the fog outside.

Roo stepped forward, calm and collected. "Good morning, ma'am. I recognized you the moment you stepped out. It's an honor. Though I wish we were meeting under better circumstances."

He crouched to meet the girls at eye level, his voice softening. "I bet you two are starving. We've got a stash in the hangar, chips, soda, even a little candy. I was just heading that way. Want to come with me?"

Madison and Savannah looked at their mother. After a pause, she gave a gentle nod. The first lady turned to Roo. "Thank you. That's very kind. I didn't catch your name."

"Roosevelt," he said with a small smile. "But everyone just calls me Roo."

He slung his green duffel over his shoulder and motioned toward the far end of the hangar. The girls followed, hesitant at first but drawn in by Roo's calm demeanor. Behind them, the fog pressed against the glass, but inside, for the briefest moment, there was warmth.

Roo pushed open the break room door. The crinkle of chip bags reached him first; a violent rustling of someone tearing through supplies.

Tipton stood at the center of the snack bar, flinging unopened bags of chips behind him like trash, digging through the cabinets as if hunting for gold.

Madison and Savannah peeked out from behind Roo, their earlier excitement fading.

Roo's voice rose, sharp with disbelief.

"What the hell are you doing, Tipton? We need that food."

Tipton whirled around, eyes wild. "You call this crap food? You couldn't even stock decent snacks. Typical... screw up the one thing you're trusted with."

Roo stepped forward. "It's a snack bar, not a five-star restaurant. What did you expect?"

Tipton's lip curled. He shoved Roo hard, it didn't knock him down, but the sudden movement sent Madison stumbling. Roo caught her just in time, steadying her with one hand.

His voice turned bitter. "Take what you want and get out. I'm not doing this in front of the kids."

Tipton snatched two bags and stomped past. At the door, he paused just long enough to bark out one more insult. "I don't give a damn about you or those brats. Stay out of my way." He vanished down the hallway, his footsteps heavy, echoing with malice.

Roo exhaled and turned back to the girls. His voice softened. "Don't mind him. He's just angry at the world and trying to take it out on whoever's closest." He offered a smile, nudging the duffel bag toward the shelves.

"Go on. Grab what you like. It's not every day the snack bar's open."

In an instant, their fear melted into a giddy motion. They darted between shelves, stuffing pockets with candy bars, sodas, and chips. Roo worked beside them, loading snacks and drinks into his bag, the soft clink of bottles and rustling wrappers filling the air like music.

For a moment, it felt almost normal.

By the time they returned to the hangar, the girls' pockets bulged with snacks, and chocolate smudged their cheeks like war paint. Roo guided them through the haze of noise and motion, his duffel slung over one shoulder, eyes scanning the space like a sentry.

Near the far end of the room, raised voices cut through the static.

It was Tipton bickering with Ramirez. He stood before Ramirez, hands flying with every harsh word.

Roo slowed his steps. He didn't want to eavesdrop, but the conversation wasn't private.

"You're thinking of joining these idiots?" Tipton yelled. "Their big plan is to hike into the woods and get eaten by a bear. Or worse."

Ramirez crossed his arms, unfazed. "We can't stay here. You saw what that thing did. This place isn't safe. And where were you when we were digging out the wreckage? I didn't see you lifting a finger."

Tipton stepped in closer, jabbing a finger into Ramirez's chest. "Don't question me. I'm your superior officer." His voice sharpened. "While you were playing janitor, I was securing food, so these leeches didn't clean us out."

Roo kept walking, jaw clenched.

It was always the same with men like Tipton; loud when others were trying to rebuild, invisible when things needed doing.

Roo said nothing. No time for babysitting egos. Bigger battles loomed. He adjusted the strap on his shoulder and walked on; the girls chattering beside him.

As Roo reached the others, Tipton's voice still echoed through the hangar. A reminder that tensions inside were better than the chaos outside.

The girls ran ahead of him, chocolate-streaked faces glowing with joy. "Thank you so much for taking us, Mr. Roo!" Madison said.

Savannah clutched her snacks with both hands, nodding like her life depended on it.

The first lady laughed, brushing a stray hair from Savannah's face. "Thank you," she said, turning to Roo. "For them. And for this moment."

Roo gave her a warm nod, then looked at Lizzie. "The duffel's full. Chips, candy, whatever I could grab. Tipton was in there acting like a lunatic."

Lizzie rolled her eyes. "So... business as usual."

Before Roo could reply, Dr. Solomon rejoined them, a worn backpack slung over one shoulder, his face lined with tension.

And then.... a sound.

Faint at first, like thunder muffled by earth. The group froze.

Roo's head tilted in confusion. "Do you hear that?" His voice dropped low. "It's... distant but real."

The group fell silent. Even the girls stopped fidgeting. A chilly breeze swept through the open hangar, rustling jackets and raising goosebumps.

Then the fog shifted, peeled back like a curtain.

Boom.

A single drumbeat. Low, heavy, and ancient.

Then another.

And another.

A rhythm, deliberate and unyielding, pounded through the stillness.

Roo stepped toward the edge of the hangar, the wind biting at his face. Each beat struck like a hammer against bone, vibrating in his chest, reverberating through the metal walls.

"Why are we hearing drums?" His voice carried over the thudding rhythm, but the dread in it was unmistakable.

Dr. Solomon didn't blink. "Because something's coming," he said. "And it wants us to hear it."

Around them, the group exchanged haunted glances. Even Tipton's shouting had gone quiet.

The drums marched on. The thunderous beat echoed through the air, each pulse like a countdown to doom. An eerie chorus of howls cut through the rhythm, chilling and otherworldly. From within the fog, shadows emerged, their forms sharpening into view.

Seria appeared first, her vibrant red armor glinting in the dim light, an almost spectral glow surrounding her. Her hand rested on the hilt of her sheathed sword, the weight of her presence suffocating the air. Each of her deliberate steps seemed to command the ground beneath her. Behind her, the hounds of war moved in flawless formation, their eyes locked forward, snarls growing louder with each beat of the drums. Their claws scraped against the ground, leaving deep grooves in the concrete.

Hovering above, the Finger of Eden loomed, an ominous sentinel poised to strike at any moment.

Inside the hangar, the first glimpses of Seria and her hounds sent a ripple of terror through the group. Roo, Lizzie, and Dr. Solomon froze, their breaths hitching as an overwhelming sense

171

of dread settled over them. The haunting rhythm of the drums felt like it was pounding against their chests.

Lizzie's voice broke the silence, sharp and urgent. "They're here! Everyone, run!"

The hangar exploded with movement. A woman tripped over a fallen crate, her screams drowned by the clang of metal as others shoved past her. A man clutched at his chest; his panicked breaths audible over the crashing of supplies and the deafening roar of the war drums. Shadows darted in every direction as terror gripped the crowd. Shouts and screams filled the air as fear took hold, paralyzing some while others fled with reckless abandonment. Roo and Lizzie stood firm, their eyes darting around the mayhem.

Their group clustered behind them, wide-eyed and trembling. Roo's gaze locked with Lizzie's, the unspoken weight of responsibility passing between them. With a sharp nod, they began moving, ushering everyone toward the far end of the hangar, toward the back exit and away from the fog pressing outside.

The group rushed toward the door, their hearts pounding. As they stepped outside, they froze in terror. A hundred yards away stood Seria, her vibrant red armor gleaming, flanked by her war hounds.

Seria unsheathed her blade with a sharp metallic hiss and aimed it at the group. Her voice boomed across the flight line, dripping with menace. "I seek those marked by the prophecy. Surrender them, and I shall grant you a swift death. Refuse, and you will suffer the wrath of my hounds." She paused, a cruel smile curling her lips as she raised her blade high. Its handle, bound in a blood-red cord, bore scorched runes etched into dark ironwood, symbols of forgotten gods and ancient pacts. The onyx blade, forged in volcanic fire, gleamed with the sheen of volcanic glass. Serrated near the hilt and smooth toward the tip, it hummed with an unnatural resonance. A history of slaughter and a promise of more.

"For the fortunate few, death shall come by my hand."

Lizzie stepped forward, confusion etched on her face. "None of us have any marks." Her voice faltering. "We don't know what you mean." As her words faded, her eyes shifted to the right, catching sight of the man in the purple robes standing in the distance, his hand outstretched toward her. The moment hung heavy as Seria followed her gaze. Her eyes narrowed, and fury ignited in her voice.

"You deceitful swine!" The accusation reverberated through the air. "You dare lie to me!" Seria pointed her sword toward the man in the purple robe, her rage searing. "He is here, which means the marked are among you. I will find them."

She turned to her hounds, her voice sharp and commanded. "Ready your swords and talons!"

The hounds responded with guttural growls, their weapons glinting in the light as they prepared for the hunt. As Seria's wrath roared, the group felt a rising tension with every pulse.

The hounds' snarls tore through the air, fingers flexing in their Bloodfang Talons. Seria's eyes gleamed with a savage thrill as she hoisted her sword high before thrusting it forward, pointing at the group. Fueled by the relentless war drums, the hounds bolted past her with terrifying speed, their movements a blur that sent her hair whipping in the wind.

Lizzie's panic-stricken voice cut through the tension. "We have to leave right now!"

Roo turned to her, his voice steady but firm. "We can't abandon the first lady and her children, Lizzie."

Her eyes darted to Dr. Solomon, desperation plain on her face. "Lead the others outside the base gate," she said. "We'll catch up."

173

Dr. Solomon nodded and gestured for the group to follow him. Without hesitation, he led them into the fog, their hurried steps fading into the distance.

Lizzie and Roo dashed back into the hangar, the hounds' snarls and the pounding war drums echoing in their ears. They scanned the space and spotted the first lady and her children crouched behind a stack of supplies.

Roo rushed forward, urgency in his voice. "Come with us... now!"

The first lady grabbed her daughter's hands as Roo and Lizzie led them toward the hangar doors. Tammy, seeing them moving, joined, her footsteps frantic.

Just as they stepped outside, a group of hounds materialized from the fog, their glowing eyes locked onto the fleeing group. The snarls grew louder, the Bloodfang Talons scraping against the ground as they advanced.

Roo froze, fear flickering in his eyes. "What do we do?"

Lizzie's voice trembled. "I don't know... we have to find Dr. Solomon."

The hounds inched closer, their movements slow and deliberate, savoring the fear in the air.

The deafening roar of engines broke through the chaos, and General Robichaux emerged behind them in a rumbling military vehicle, a convoy of armored trucks trailing in his wake. The growl of the engines overpowered the snarls, sending a wave of hope through the group.

Inside the vehicles, three hundred men and women sat in tense silence, their breaths held as they awaited their orders. General Robichaux stepped out, his commanding presence drawing all eyes to him. He locked eyes with Lizzie, his voice sharp with urgency. "Take them and meet up with Dr. Solomon. This is what he instructed me to do. You all are the key. You must survive. We'll hold them off as long as we can."

Before Lizzie could respond, Dr. Solomon rushed toward them, his face pale with panic. "We can't go that way!" he said. "Those beasts have blocked it, too."

Lizzie paused, grappling with the weight of the general's words. She inhaled a deep breath, forcing herself to stay calm. "We need to find another way out. General Robichaux and his troops are going to buy us time."

Dr. Solomon's eyes widened with alarm. "But he'll die! I can't let him die."

Lizzie grabbed his arm, her voice firm. "Look, we don't have a choice. If we stay, we're all dead. We must go. Now!"

The gravity of their situation weighed on them, propelling them into action.

General Robichaux turned to his troops, who had already lined up in formation. The clang of vehicle doors echoed as the soldiers stepped out, their faces resolute despite the looming danger.

General Robichaux stepped forward, his broad shoulders squared against the tide of fear rippling through his troops.

His voice rang out like a battle horn, steady and commanding. "This is our fight. Protect them at all costs!" He looked toward his soldiers, his own gaze unwavering. "We may not make it, but our stand here will be the difference between survival and annihilation. Ready your weapons and fire at will!"

Without hesitation, the soldiers obeyed, the metallic clicks of weapons being drawn filling the air. Moments later, a deafening roar of gunfire erupted, bullets streaking through the air toward the advancing hounds.

But the hounds remained unfazed. Their twisted smiles widened as an eerie shimmer enveloped them. The Eden Veil materialized, a shield of crackling energy that deflected the bullets with ease. The ricochets rang out, a chilling reminder of their invulnerability.

General Robichaux's jaw tightened as he raised his own weapon.

"Keep firing!"

The soldiers obeyed, their determination undeterred even as the air filled with the sound of futile gunfire.

The hounds charged forward, their thundering footsteps shaking the ground. As they reached the group, the shimmering veil dissipated, and chaos erupted. Screams pierced the air, mingling with the grotesque sounds of flesh being torn apart.

During the carnage, Lizzie spotted a narrow escape route. "This way!" Her voice was almost inaudible over the chaos.

Without hesitation, the remaining survivors sprinted toward the opening, their breath ragged as their feet pounded the unforgiving terrain.

Dr. Solomon's breath hitched as his legs locked beneath him. His hands trembled at his sides, clutching the air as though trying to grab hold of courage. The hound's guttural growls filled his ears, and his pulse thundered, drowning out all rational thought. A beast broke from the pack, its bloodlust driving it straight toward him. Snapping out of his daze, he stumbled after the group, but the hound was relentless, closing the distance with terrifying speed.

In one swift motion, the hound pounced, slamming Dr. Solomon to the ground. Pain shot through him as the impact bruised his body against the hard pavement. The beast loomed over him, its talons shimmering in the dim light. With deliberate cruelty, it dragged its claws across his face, leaving three deep, bloody gashes. His screams echoed through the chaos.

Leaning closer, the hound hissed, its voice dripping with sadistic pleasure. "Scream for me again, you weak insect."

Just as the hound prepared to deliver the killing blow, its gaze landed on a faint mark on Dr. Solomon's neck. The beast froze, snarling as it recalled its master's orders. Its hesitation was short-lived as a sudden, earthshaking crash interrupted its intent. General Robichaux collided with the hound, driving them both to the ground in a blur of blood and fury.

"Doctor..." The general gasped, gripping Solomon's shoulders as he struggled to his feet. His voice was steady despite his labored breaths. "Your survival is critical. That group needs you to fulfill their destiny."

Before he could finish, a sword struck through his abdomen. The general's cry of pain cut through the air, his body shuddering as blood soaked his uniform. Dr. Solomon froze, horror washing over him.

"Run!" General Robichaux roared, his voice ragged but commanding.

Summoning all his strength, Solomon turned and fled, his legs pumping as adrenaline overpowered his terror. Behind him, the hound rose, preparing to give chase, until a firm hand gripped its leg, stopping it in its tracks. The beast turned to see General Robichaux on the ground, his face twisted in pain but determined.

The general unsheathed the silver knife at his belt, his grip unwavering despite his failing strength. With a last surge of effort, he drove the blade into the hound's chest, piercing its heart. The beast froze, its glowing eyes locking onto the general in a mix of fury and defeat, before collapsing beside him.

As blood pooled beneath him, General Robichaux smiled, his eyes fluttering shut. The weight of his sacrifice settled over him, and he exhaled his final breath, knowing that he had fulfilled his duty.

Amid the chaos, Lizzie yanked the first lady's hand, pulling her forward as the fog wrapped around them like a living thing. Tammy wasn't far behind. Roo shielded the children with his body, his eyes darting to every shadow, every distant snarl. Each step felt heavier, the ground uneven beneath their frantic strides, as if the earth itself conspired to slow them down. The relentless pounding of war drums reverberated in their ears, a cruel rhythm driving the surrounding terror.

Unaware of General Robichaux's sacrifice, they stumbled through the fog, their breaths ragged, despair nipping at their heels.

Behind them, the guttural howls of the hounds grew louder, each sound a chilling promise of death.

Through the haze, a gate appeared, flickering like a beacon of hope. It loomed closer, their one chance at escape. If only they could reach it before the hounds closed the distance.

CHAPTER SIXTEEN

Exodus

The group's ragged breaths and pounding footsteps seemed to match the relentless war drums echoing behind them. Roo's heart raced as the looming gate came into view. Their last barrier between life and certain death. The dense fog swirled around them, muffling their frantic movements and adding an oppressive weight to the chaos.

The rush to flee drove them onward, worry and dread twisting in their minds. Tammy stayed near the first lady, her calm a slight comfort. Each step was a frantic prayer as the guttural howls of Seria's hounds grew closer, the sound clawing at their ears.

"Just keep running," Lizzie said. "We're almost there!"

The fog thickened, cloaking their surroundings in a suffocating shroud, but the clang of talons and distant snarls made one thing certain—the hounds were drawing near. Roo loosened his grip on Madison and Savannah's hands. Without a word, the girls turned and ran to their mother, disappearing into the fog with one last glance over their shoulders.

Ahead, a lone figure sprinted through the haze, their movements frantic. Even through the fog, Roo recognized the unmistakable arrogance of Tipton. "That coward," he said.

Tipton reached the gate, his labored breaths catching in his throat as a glint of crimson pierced the fog, just as Seria emerged. Her armor shimmered like liquid fire, the vivid red slicing through the haze like a warning. Tipton froze mid-stride, paralyzed by her presence. Behind her, the hounds slithered into view, their talons dragging slow, deliberate arcs through the fog like phantoms on a hunt.

Ramirez stopped dead in his tracks several feet behind Tipton, his face pale as he stared at the scene before him. Tipton squared his shoulders, his bravado surging to the surface. He stepped forward, his arm a blur as it arced through the air. The impact of his hand against Seria's cheek echoed in the silence.

"I won't let a damn woman stop me from leaving this base!" His voice dripped with arrogance.

For a moment, Seria stood motionless, her head tilted from the blow. Then her lips curved into a sinister smile, a guttural laugh spilling from her throat. Without warning, her left hand shot out, clamping around Tipton's neck. His bravado crumbled as she lifted him into the air, his legs kicking beneath him.

"Squirm for me. It's all you're good at," she said.

Her eyes bore into him, her grip tightening with a deliberate slowness that sent his face turning shades of red.

"Do you not recognize me? I am the goddess of war, a harbinger of doom, and one of the feared horsemen."

Tipton gasped, his hands clawing weakly at her armored gauntlet. His arrogance dissolved into pure terror as her smirk deepened.

"You mean nothing to me." Her tone was calm but laced with cruel amusement. "Nothing more than a pathetic waste of flesh. It would take the strength of a thousand men to hurt me, and you can't even muster the courage of one."

Tipton's trembling turned to outright convulsions, his body betraying him in the most humiliating way as Seria held him aloft. The acrid stench of his fear only deepened the twisted amusement in her eyes. Her lips curled into a mocking smile, and she leaned in closer.

"You've defiled yourself in fear of me, you insignificant worm," she said. "Allow me to introduce you to my sword."

With a slow, deliberate motion, she unsheathed her blade, the onyx-black steel glinting in the dim light. Tipton's tear-streaked face contorted in sheer terror as his sobs turned into broken wails. His pitiful cries only seemed to heighten Seria's satisfaction. She tilted the blade, allowing its edge to catch the light.

"When you get to Hell," she said, "I want you to remember..." She released him without warning and Tipton crumpled to the ground, wheezing like punctured bellows, his limbs flailing against the dirt in a desperate crawl. Seria followed, slow and deliberate, crouching beside him like a predator savoring the last moment. Her armor shimmered in the shifting fog, but it was her whispering voice that froze him in place. "That it was a woman who sent you there."

She straightened, her imposing form casting a shadow over him.

Tipton's wide, tear-filled eyes locked onto Seria as she loomed above him, her sword gripped in both hands. She moved at a slow pace, savoring every second as she brought the sword down with surgical precision, severing his right hand at the wrist. Blood spurted from the stump as Tipton's anguished scream tore through the fog, the sound reverberating like a broken plea for mercy.

She pivoted, elegant and exact, and drove her blade downward again, severing the left with the same ruthless precision. The second scream was weaker and gurgled, almost swallowed by the agony.

Tipton's body jerked, limbs flailing in a chaotic dance. Ramirez crumpled, his knees hitting the gritty ground with a soft thud. Tears streamed down his face, leaving glistening trails as his trembling hands clutched at his chest. Each ragged breath emerged in quick gasps.

Seria stepped back just a little, tilting her head as if appraising her work. She traced the edge of her blade with one hand, its sharpness catching the faint light. The cruel smile that played on her lips deepened as a pack of hounds emerged from the fog, their eyes fixated on her.

With a casual flick of her wrist, she hurled one of Tipton's severed hands toward the beasts. They snarled and snapped at each other, tearing into the grisly offering. She repeated the gesture with the other hand, her movements calm and measured, as though she were feeding scraps to pets.

Tipton's chest heaved with shallow breaths as he glanced down at his handless arms, his mind unable to process the horror unfolding around him. He whimpered, his voice a broken whisper. "Please... stop..."

Seria's eyes narrowed, the plea only fueling her sadistic delight. She strode forward, her boots crunching against the blood-soaked dirt, and knelt beside him. Her voice dropped to a venomous hiss. "Stop? We're far from done, you pathetic worm."

She rose to her full height; her blade poised with predatory precision. One by one, she severed his feet at the ankles, her strikes clean and deliberate. Tipton's screams grew weaker; each one

182

wrung from a body that couldn't endure the pain anymore. His sobs turned to incoherent murmurs as shock overtook him, his head lolling to one side.

The hounds growled as Seria flung the dismembered body parts toward them, their howls of satisfaction rising into the air. Blood stained their jaws as they feasted, the gruesome display only adding to the suffocating dread that hung in the air.

Tipton's shallow breaths rattled in his chest as Seria crouched over him one final time.

"You are a coward. You will die a coward's death. Let this moment be your legacy."

With one fluid motion, she raised her blade high and brought it down, severing his head with almost ceremonial precision. The detached head rolled to the side, its lifeless eyes wide in a frozen mask of terror. Seria's lips curled into a cruel smirk as she kicked the head toward the hounds. Their howls of acceptance echoed through the fog as they descended on the remains, tearing flesh from bone with savage delight.

Seria straightened, flicking the blood from her blade with a practiced motion. She turned her attention to the remaining hounds, her commanding presence holding them in thrall.

"Feast well, my beasts. There will be more to come."

Behind her, Ramirez trembled, his body shaking as he fought to stifle his sobs. Seria didn't even spare him a glance. For her, the hunt had only just begun.

As the group moved toward the gate, the sound of Ramirez's muffled sobs reached Dr. Terracotta's ears. He paused mid-step, glancing back through the fog. There, amidst the carnage, he spotted Ramirez on his knees, his shoulders shaking as despair gripped him.

Dr. Terracotta hesitated.

Roo noticed and tugged at his arm. "Come on, Doc. We can't stop now."

But Terracotta didn't move. Instead, he pointed toward Ramirez. "Roo, we can't leave him like that to die. He doesn't deserve that."

Roo turned, following his gaze, his expression hardening. "Yes, we can. Ramirez is an asshole. He's made his choices. He deserves what's coming to him."

Terracotta folded his arms, his voice steady but filled with conviction. "I won't argue that he's an asshole. But he's still human. And maybe, just maybe, he'll surprise us. If there's even a chance he can help us later, it's worth it."

Roo's jaw tightened, the conflict clear in his eyes. He glanced back toward the group pressing ahead, then to Ramirez, who looked broken. With a reluctant sigh, he nodded. "Fine, but this is on you."

Dr. Terracotta gave a quick nod of thanks, his voice steady. "Go get him. I'll make sure the others keep moving."

Roo sighed again and crouched low, slipping through the fog and debris in silence. The guttural growls of Seria's hounds gnawing at Tipton's remains sent chills down his spine, but he pressed on. Timing his movements to avoid Seria's gaze, he crept up behind Ramirez and tapped him on the shoulder.

Ramirez flinched, his tear-streaked face turning toward Roo, his eyes wide with disbelief.

"I'm only going to say this once. You need to come with me. Now. We're heading out of the city and into the wilderness to find shelter. This is your only chance."

For a moment, Ramirez seemed frozen, his breath hitching. Then, as though something in Roo's tone pierced his haze of despair, he nodded. Wiping his face with trembling hands, he managed to squeeze out one simple word. "Okay."

The two moved at a quick pace but were careful not to alarm Seria, weaving through the chaos as the hounds feasted and Seria remained absorbed in her grim work. Roo kept his steps quiet, his muscles tense, ready to react at any moment. Ramirez followed, his movements sluggish but obedient, the weight of his near-death experience still bearing down on him.

When they rejoined the group, Dr. Terracotta looked up, relief washing over his face at the sight of Ramirez alive.

Ramirez lingered a few steps away, his shoulders slumped. He glanced from Roo to Terracotta, confusion flickering in his eyes. "Why... why did you come back for me?" Ramirez's voice trembled, laced with disbelief.

Roo crossed his arms, his expression sharp. "I didn't want to, but the Doc here? He wouldn't leave you behind."

Ramirez turned to Dr. Terracotta. "Why? After the way I've treated you..."

Terracotta met his gaze, his voice calm but firm. "Because sometimes even assholes deserve a second chance."

Ramirez looked down, his hands clenched at his sides. He opened his mouth to respond, but no words came. Instead, he gave a small, shaky nod before falling in step with the group.

They continued forward, leaving Seria and her hounds behind.

Roo cast a glance at Ramirez, muttering under his breath. "Don't make me regret this."

Ramirez nodded once, keeping pace, his steps heavy with unspoken gratitude.

As the group continued their exodus, the sounds of carnage behind them grew fainter, yet the urgency in their steps didn't waver. Roo glanced over his shoulder, his jaw tightening at the faint glow of Seria's armor through the fog. The relentless pounding of the war drums and the guttural howls of the hounds seemed to haunt the air.

A rustling in the shadows halted the group.

Roo raised a hand, signaling silence, his other tightening around the strap of his duffel.

A figure stumbled into view, his breath ragged and shallow.

"Dr. Solomon!" Lizzie's voice cracked.

As he stepped into the light, gasps followed. Three deep, bloody claw marks slashed across his face. His movements were strained; his steady gait reduced to a limp. One hand clutched his side; the other held his balance.

Tammy rushed forward. "What happened?"

He waved her off, his voice hoarse but urgent. "There's no time," he said. "We have to move. They're coming."

The group exchanged uneasy glances, fear tightening around them like a noose.

Solomon's wounds—and the memory of Tipton's brutal end—hung in the air like smoke, choking any hope of calm.

Roo took a step forward, his voice steady. "Can you keep moving?"

Solomon nodded, though his expression was grim. "I'll manage. Just... don't stop."

Without hesitation, Lizzie motioned for the group to press on. "Let's go. Now."

As they began their desperate dash for the gate, Roo fell into step beside Dr. Solomon, his hand brushing against Solomon's arm to steady him. Solomon's labored breaths came in sharp gasps, but he pushed forward, determination etched into his bloodied face.

The pounding war drums seemed louder than ever, reverberating through the fog like a sinister pulse.

The group quickened their pace as the towering gate rose into view, its steel frame a distant promise of safety. Behind them, the snarls drew closer spurring a ripple of panic through their ranks.

"Run!" Lizzie shouted. "Don't stop!"

With what felt like a miraculous stroke of luck, or perhaps fate, they stumbled through the gate, the metallic clang of its edges echoing behind them as they crossed. A collective sigh of relief escaped their lips before a furious roar cut through the air.

Seria's voice rang out from the fog. "After them!"

The snarls of her hounds grew closer, their predatory growls slicing through the group's fleeting sense of safety. Each heavy footfall of the beasts seemed to echo like a death knell.

Roo turned his head, seeing their eyes tearing through the fog. "Keep going!" he said.

Exhausted, the group stumbled forward, some collapsing as they darted by. Roo stole a glance back, his mind racing with questions.

On the other side, the man in the purple robes stood unmoving, a staff gripped in his hand. With deliberate precision, he raised the staff high before slamming it into the ground with a resounding boom.

A sudden, deafening gust of air erupted from the point of impact, sending the pursuing hounds sprawling backward with surprised yelps. The force of the blast shook the ground beneath the group's feet, and for a moment, an eerie stillness fell over the battlefield.

The man in the purple robes strode forward, his movements deliberate and unhurried, as if unaffected by the chaos. He approached Dr. Solomon. Without a word, he reached into his robe and pulled out a weathered book. Its cover bore a strange symbol that seemed to pulse in rhythm with the surrounding tension.

He placed the book into Dr. Solomon's trembling hands, then turned, lifting his staff once more and pointing toward the distant wilderness. His intent was clear, leaving no room for argument or hesitation.

With a shared glance, the group obeyed, breaking into a sprint again. The man in the purple robes moved with them for a moment, his pace measured but purposeful, before vanishing into the mist just as quick as he had appeared.

As the group raced further from the gate, a flicker of hope mingled with the unrelenting fear driving them forward. The pounding war drums still echoed in the distance, but for now, they had a chance.

Looking back, Roo saw the first lady and her children falling behind. Just yards from the gate, she stumbled hard, collapsing onto the ground. Her daughters skidded to a stop, trying to lift her. The Eden Veil was closing fast—they were running out of time.

"Go!" she said. "Get to Roo!"

The girls hesitated, their small hands clinging to their mother's arms as tears streaked their faces. Before they could move, Seria emerged from the fog. Her piercing eyes locked onto the children, a cruel smile playing at her lips.

"Are these tiny bugs your offspring?" Seria said. "They would make delightful servants to the Architect. Perhaps I'll bring them back as gifts for my lord."

The girls shrank back, trembling as Seria's gaze bore into them, but before she could strike, a blur surged through the fog. Tammy's boots pounded against the dirt like thunder; her eyes locked on the children.

As the veil closes, push the butterflies through.

The words from the letter echoed in her mind.

With a cry of defiance, she reached them in an instant, grabbing both girls and shoving them through the Eden Veil just as it closed.

The light sealed shut behind them, leaving Tammy alone with the first lady... and Seria.

"Go! Now!" Tammy said.

The girls stumbled but obeyed, running as fast as their legs could carry them. Roo caught them just on the other side. They looked back only once, their tearful eyes locking with their mother's.

The first lady managed a weak, exhausted smile, her lips forming the words I love you. Her stare lingered on her two daughters for a fleeting moment before flicking to Tammy. "Thank you," she whispered.

Tammy nodded, her jaw set as she turned back to face Seria.

Seria stood motionless, her sword at her side, her head tilting in amusement. "How noble," she said, her voice dripping with mockery. "But noble deeds often end in blood."

With a swift, fluid motion, Seria drove her blade through Tammy's chest.

Tammy gasped, her body jolting from the force. Her eyes widened, then steadied. As Seria twisted the sword and withdrew it, Tammy collapsed to her knees. Blood bloomed across her shirt, her breaths shallow and ragged.

She slumped to the ground, her vision dimming, but her thoughts were clear. Her lips parted in a last whisper. "The butterflies... I fulfilled my purpose." A tear slipped down her cheek, catching the faintest sparkle of light.

A small, peaceful smile played on her lips as she stilled, her body fragile but triumphant.

The first lady let out a strangled cry but didn't have time to react before Seria's blade struck again. It pierced her heart with brutal precision. She collapsed beside Tammy, their bodies almost touching; they both had fallen for the sake of her children.

Blood pooled beneath her as her breaths grew shallow. Her eyes, wide with pain, searched the foggy air, searching for a glimpse of her daughters beyond the veil. Her lips trembled, her voice a whisper almost lost to the wind. "My babies... I'm so sorry."

Her hand twitched once, reaching for the place they had vanished. A tear traced a final path down her cheek.

And then she was still.

Just beyond the veil, the girls screamed, piercing, primal cries that shattered the silence like broken glass. Their small bodies trembled with grief; eyes locked on the spot where their mother and Tammy had just stood... and now they were gone.

"Momma!" Madison yelled, her voice cracking as she reached out, her fingers clawing at the empty air.

Savannah dropped to her knees, sobbing so hard that her breaths came in gasps. "They didn't make it... they didn't..."

Roo caught them both, pulling them into his arms, his own eyes burning with helpless fury. "Don't look back," he whispered, his voice rough but steady. "Keep moving. They did this for you. We can't let it be for nothing."

The fog swallowed the silence again. Only the girls muffled sobs remained—two fragile hearts shattered at the edge of a dying world. Roo, clutching them as tight as he could, turned and led them into the unknown ahead.

Seria's gaze burned as the group vanished into the wilderness beyond the veil. She raised her hand, fingers curling with command, willing the veil to open.

Nothing.

The veil shimmered... but held.

Her eyes darkened. One of her hounds had fallen, wounded in battle. The veil, loyal to its soldiers, would not yield while one was unaccounted for.

She lowered her hand, rage simmering just beneath the surface.

"So... even the veil mourns its own," she muttered. "How touching." Her grip tightened on the sword, veins pulsing with fury. "Let them run. It won't save them."

From the corner of her eye, she caught sight of the man in the purple robes standing in the distance, his staff held tight by his side. The rage within her ignited like wildfire. She raised her sword, pointing it at him.

"This is your fault!" she roared, her voice shaking with fury. "We shall cross paths again, you fool!"

The man in the purple robes remained silent, his enigmatic presence unbroken as he turned and strode off into the fog. Seria watched him go, her blade trembling in her grip as the seething rage within her simmered. She took a deep breath, letting the weight of her anger settle, then turned back toward her hounds. With deliberate steps, she walked toward the hangar, her mind already calculating her next move.

The group pressed deeper into the dense wilderness. The faint howls of the hounds echoed behind them, fading with distance but never disappearing. Roo adjusted the duffel bag on his shoulder; his other arm wrapped around Madison and Savannah. The girls clung to him in silence, their small hands clutching his jacket. Lizzie led the way, her sharp gaze scanning the dim forest for any sign of danger. Ramirez trailed behind, his steps hesitant and head bowed under the weight of his guilt.

The silence was suffocating, broken only by the crunch of twigs underfoot and the occasional sob from the children.

Dr. Solomon spoke, his voice hushed and weary. "Who was that woman... the one who saved the girls?"

Madison's voice came after a pause, small and trembling. "Tammy. She was an astronaut. She stayed at the house with us."

Dr. Solomon nodded, unseen pressure heavy on his shoulders. His gaze fell to the book, its cracked leather cover a warm, tangible presence, almost alive, pulsing with a silent, deep weight.

"I can't believe..." he said, more to himself than the others. "Tammy. The first lady. They didn't deserve that." He stared at the book, his fingers tightening around it. "Now this... What am I supposed to do with this?"

Roo looked back at him, then at Ramirez. "You still think following Tipton was the right call?"

Ramirez stopped in his tracks. For a moment, he didn't answer. The tension held like a bowstring. "I thought I was doing the right thing," he said. "I've spent my life following orders, but none of that matters now. We left people behind and let them die." He looked down, his voice hollow. "I didn't know what we were walking into."

"Stop." Lizzie's voice cut clean through the air. She turned to face him, her eyes blazing. "No more excuses. Tammy didn't hesitate. She threw herself into danger to save two little girls she didn't even know, and now she's gone. You don't get to collapse while the rest of us carry the weight."

Ramirez looked away, jaw clenched, but he didn't argue. His guilt was apparent on his face.

The group moved forward again, the weight of sacrifice pressing upon them with every step.

A few moments later, Madison tugged on Roo's sleeve. "Mr. Roo," she said. "Are we going to be okay?"

Roo stopped for a moment, trying to think of the right words to say. "You're brave, Madison. Braver than a lot of adults I know. We'll figure this out, one step at a time."

Ramirez spoke again, his voice quieter, almost reluctant. "Look, I know I've been... wrong. I know I've been a jerk, but I want to help. Let me carry the duffel bag or something."

Roo hesitated, studying him for a long moment before handing over the bag. "You can start by contributing your fair share."

Ramirez nodded, slinging the bag over his shoulder. He glanced at the children, then at Lizzie, his voice uncertain but sincere. "For what it's worth, I'll try not to screw this up."

Lizzie didn't reply, but a flicker of something passed across her face—acknowledgment, perhaps, or the faintest trace of hope.

Ahead, Dr. Solomon slowed his pace, his fingers brushing the strange symbol embossed on the book's cover. The intricate design seemed to pulse. He touched the claw marks on his face. "What if this thing has answers?"

Lizzie turned back to him, her voice steady. "Then we'll figure out what it means. Together."

The group moved forward again, their steps more purposeful this time. Though the shadows of their loss lingered, a fragile thread of determination wove through their shared burden.

* * *

Upon returning to base, silence hung heavy on the flight line. The air, thick and metallic with the coppery scent of blood and the acrid bite of burning metal, pressed against Seria. Her hounds, who most of the time were restless, were still, forming a tight, protective circle, their fur bristling.

She moved toward them without a word.

The circle parted at her presence, revealing the lifeless body of the fallen hound, slain by General Robichaux. A thin shimmer of energy hovered above it, the Eden Veil, still intact, shielding its remains.

Seria knelt, the veil's crackling hum vibrating through the air as it vanished at her touch. Reaching out, she laid a trembling hand on the beast's blood-matted brow, feeling the coarse fur. With one slow, deliberate motion, she closed its vacant eyes.

A single tear slid down her cheek; it was a silent gesture, unnoticed by all but the dead.

She leaned close, her voice a whisper of reverence. "Sleep well, my hound. May your spirit find the great hunt in the next realm... and run forever without chains."

Rising, her sorrow hardened into command. She turned to face the rest of her pack; her tone sharpened to steel. "One of your brothers has fallen. We will remember his name. His death will not go unanswered." She gestured to the broken corpse of General Robichaux, discarded nearby like waste. "There lies the coward who dared to raise his hand against our blood. Rip him apart. Let his bones scream for what he's done."

The hounds snarled, their loyalty ignited.

"Then tend to your fallen. Prepare him for Regar's Reaping. Lay him on the ship with honor." Her gaze swept across the pack, the authority in her voice absolute. "Tonight, we mourn. Tomorrow... we hunt."

Without another word, Seria turned and strode toward the waiting ship, her cloak snapping behind her like a banner of war.

The hunt wasn't over. It had only just begun.

CHAPTER SEVENTEEN

The Worst Day in the History of the World

As the veil closed behind Roo and his group, sealing their escape into the wilderness, the chaos they left behind was but a ripple in the storm brewing far to the south. In Los Angeles, beneath the harsh glare of floodlights and the eerie shimmer caused by the Finger of Eden, the Architect's machinations stirred like a storm on the horizon.

Regar moved alone through the battlefield's wreckage, his pale armor gleaming in the dim light. His cape trailed behind him, rippling like a shroud of mist. Souls drifted from lifeless bodies, their faint, iridescent forms spiraling toward his scythe.

His presence was otherworldly, the embodiment of inevitability. With every step, Regar carried the weight of finality—the clang of his boots underscored by the soft, sorrowful wails of the souls he had claimed. He paused, lifting his pale, armored hand to guide a stubborn soul into submission. The shimmering wraith hissed as it dissolved into his scythe.

Regar's fingers traced over the scythe's surface, its obsidian sheen reflecting the pallid faces of those he had reaped. His presence was an aura of inevitability, a weight that seemed to press against the very ground he walked upon. Yet he moved with measured, almost reverent steps as he conducted his macabre symphony.

A voice, sharp and commanding, cut through the quiet. "Regar." High above, the Architect watched as Regar paused and turned his hooded head toward him. "The time has come," the Architect said, his voice cutting like iron. "Inform Durbal that Rome will be first. Let them see the Finger of Eden... and understand what true power is."

Regar inclined his head, his eyes gleaming beneath the shadows of his hood. "As you command, my lord."

He turned, his cloak billowing like a shroud as he strode toward the ship. The souls he had harvested clung to his scythe, their faint cries trailing behind him like ghostly echoes. Each step was an assertion of the unavoidable, a reminder that death served only the Architect.

From the opposite side of the coliseum, the sound of rhythmic, thunderous steps filled the air. Each step resonated like a drumbeat, steady and purposeful, as Haligot emerged.

The ground seemed to tremble under his weight; his colossal frame bathed in the shifting light of the coliseum. Haligot's diamond-hard skin shimmered, refracting the glow into a spectral array. The golden spear slung across his back gleamed with an unnatural brilliance, its twin blue lines pulsing. He carried himself with the gravitas of one who had endured millennia of rage.

Haligot approached the Architect and came to a halt, towering even over his master. His voice, a deep rumble that carried the weight of ancient wrath, broke the night. "My lord, what do you need from us? The Nephilim are ready."

The Architect met Haligot's gaze, his expression unreadable as he leaned on his golden staff. "I want the Nephilim to search the city—every house, building, and vessel. Eliminate anything that poses a threat. Equip them with scanners from the ship. If they find any young ones without imperfections... bring them to the Ark."

Haligot's brow furrowed. His lips pulled into a tight grimace.

"Must we search the boats, my lord?" he asked, voice low. "The memory of the flood still haunts us."

The Architect's gaze sharpened like a blade. His golden staff flared with a cold light as he drove it into the ground. "Do as you're told, commander."

Haligot grunted, jaw clenched as he bowed his head in reluctant submission. "It will be done." He spun, the clink of his spear echoing through the air as his heavy steps receded into the shadows.

The Architect's laughter rose behind him, a low, resonant sound that echoed through the coliseum.

"The long-awaited day is here!" he said, his voice swelling with fervent delight. "Watch as this world quivers under my power as my blueprints come to life!" The Architect's words hung in the air, a proclamation of triumph that reverberated through the coliseum and beyond, a herald of the destruction to come.

* * *

Far from the coliseum, across the ocean and under a gentler sky, another man stood before a crowd— faith was his weapon of choice. In Rome, the sun rose over the Eternal City, its warm light slipping through the only gap that remained above. Around the city, the Eden Veil's shimmering walls already loomed, encircling the horizon like a living fortress. For now, the heavens still looked down upon the domes and spires in a golden glow, though the tranquility of dawn seemed almost sacrilegious in the face of the impending catastrophe. Within the Vatican, the pope stood before a sea of faithful followers, his robes immaculate yet weighed down by the gravity of the moment. His weathered hands gripped the edge of the balcony as he gazed down at the throng gathered below. Their eyes turned to him in desperate hope.

"My children..." the pope began, his voice steady despite the tremor that threatened to break it. "Our faith has endured the trials of centuries. This moment... this trial... is no different. If it is the Creator's will, then so be it. We remain together here in the heart of our faith."

The crowd murmured, their prayers rising like a hymn to the heavens. Tears streamed down the faces of some, while others clasped their hands until their knuckles turned white. The pope's gaze swept over them, his heart heavy with the weight of his decision.

"Even in the face of such overwhelming power, remember this... the Creator's plan is beyond our understanding. Trust in Him."

Above Rome, the Finger of Eden loomed—its imposing silhouette casting its long shadow over the city below. The morning sun still reached through the open sky, but its light was fractured by the veil shimmering like molten glass around the city's borders, sealing its fate in radiant confinement

The air thrummed with a low, metallic hum, a vibration that tickled the skin and resonated deep within the chest, making the ancient stones of Rome seem to tremble. The sound, a palpable presence, echoed through the narrow streets, a metallic whisper that felt like a prophecy taking form. Vents along the Finger's sides opened with mechanical precision, and a swarm of vessels emerged, darting through the sky in synchronized arcs. Their mission was clear—activate the final sequence: drawing the walls inward and sealing the heavens shut.

The hum grew louder, shifting to a deep, resonant thrum that seemed to press against the very bones of those who heard it. The Vatican Square fell silent as the crowd turned their gaze skyward, captivated by the spectacle unfolding above them. Some knelt in awe, their faces illuminated by the veil's ethereal light, while others shouted warnings, their fear driving them to push through the streets to escape the encroaching barrier.

Inside the Vatican, the pope knelt in prayer, the polished marble cool beneath his knees. "Guide us in this moment," he said, his voice trembling now as he sought solace in the divine. "Grant me strength to shepherd Your flock, even as the storm closes in."

The Eden Veil locked into place with a deafening clang that echoed through the city. As the hum built to a crescendo, the Finger of Eden sprang to life, its surface lines erupting in a brilliant blue. The glow intensified, bathing Rome in an otherworldly radiance that was both mesmerizing and terrifying.

The pope rose to his feet and stepped toward the balcony once more. His voice carried across the square, clear and unwavering despite the chaos. "Do not despair! Do not falter! For even in the darkest hour, His light will guide us!"

His words hung in the air, a fragile beacon against the mounting terror. Above, the Finger of Eden loomed, its presence a

199

grim reminder of the fragility of human faith in the face of divine power.

Durbal approached the veil with measured steps, its shimmer dancing in his eyes. He watched it respond to him with reverence. In his hand, he clutched a small box, its light gray surface bearing intricate ancient markings. The etchings seemed to pulse, their precision suggesting a craftsmanship far beyond human capability. Horizontal lines wrapped around the box like a forgotten language, whispering secrets of destruction.

As he neared the veil, it responded, parting with an eerie fluidity. A soft hum accompanied the movement, and the barrier shimmered as Durbal passed through. With a sharp hiss, the veil closed behind him.

Durbal stood beneath the towering majesty of the Finger of Eden. Its monumental structure loomed above him, a silent sentinel of annihilation. Kneeling with calculated care, he placed the small box on the ground. His gloved hand hovered for a moment, as if savoring the weight of the moment, before pressing a concealed button along its surface.

The box trembled. At first, the movements were subtle, a faint vibration against the stone ground. Then it jerked, twisting and lurching with unpredictable ferocity. The markings glowed, casting flickering shadows on Durbal's face. With a resounding thud, the walls of the box collapsed outward, revealing its contents: a radiant blue sphere of energy. The spark shimmered with an intensity that seemed to draw light from its surroundings, pulsating as if alive.

Reaching into the folds of his robes, Durbal produced a small vial. The glass shimmered, its contents a vivid green liquid that seemed to swirl of its own accord, defying gravity. With meticulous precision, he uncorked the vial and tilted it over the sphere. A single droplet of the liquid fell, and as it made contact, the sphere convulsed.

The sphere twisted, its form warping as though struggling against the infusion. With each passing moment, it grew larger, its light intensifying to an almost blinding brilliance. Its size swelled until it dominated the space beneath the Finger of Eden, a writhing mass of energy that seemed to eclipse even the light of the sun. Waves of heat and static rippled outward, stirring the air and sending tendrils of electricity crackling along the ground.

Durbal straightened, his piercing stare sweeping over the gathered crowd that had dared to watch. Fear and confusion etched onto their faces; their eyes remained fixed on the impossible scene before them. The corner of Durbal's mouth curled into a sneer, his voice cutting through the tense silence with disdain. "Behold the Spark of Genesis," Durbal said, his voice like a blade. "This is not power... it is the breath before creation and the scream before the end. It's meant to erase you." He took a step back. "When the Finger of Eden strikes, this city—this cradle of your legacy—will not fall. It will be erased. Your monuments, memories, and bloodlines... consumed by silence."

The spark pulsed behind him like a heartbeat to Armageddon. A sinister grin spread across his face as he savored the crowd's mounting despair. Without another word, Durbal turned and strode toward the veil, his movements precise and unhurried, as though time itself bowed to his command. The veil opened for him once more, its shimmering surface rippling as he passed through.

And then he was gone, leaving only the Spark of Genesis, its searing light and violent energy, a precursor of the annihilation yet to come.

The sun climbed higher over Rome, its golden rays illuminating three sides of the ominous Finger of Eden. Yet one

201

side remained cloaked in impenetrable darkness, a stark reminder of the balance between light and shadow, hope and despair. Panic rippled through the city like a tidal wave. Crowds surged toward the Papal Palace, their desperation palpable in the chaos of shouts and hurried steps. Strangers clasped hands in a fleeting bid for solace, their voices merging into a fragile symphony of prayers that carried through the ancient streets.

The pope emerged onto his grand balcony, the ornate folds of his papal attire gleaming in the morning light. His presence was a steady force against the rising tide of fear. He raised his hands, and the anxious murmurs quieted. Tears streaked the faces of many as they turned their gaze upward, seeking refuge in his words.

"My beloved children," he began, his voice unwavering. "This city has endured countless trials; its stones are filled with the faith and resilience of generations. Even now, when the shadow of despair looms large, let us not falter. Trust in the divine plan, for His light will guide us through the storm."

The pope's words hung in the air, fragile yet defiant against the impending darkness. Below, the crowd fell to their knees, clutching rosaries and whispering fervent prayers. Some wept, their tears falling onto the cobblestones like rain. Others just stared, their faces etched with a quiet resignation as their gaze drifted to the monolithic Finger of Eden dominating the skyline.

The fourth side of the Finger of Eden glowed, its surface igniting with an otherworldly blue hue that intensified with each passing moment. A collective gasp rose from the crowd as the towering structure began its descent, moving with an almost deliberate slowness. The city seemed to hold its breath, the weight of inevitability pressing against the air.

Time itself appeared to pause as a needle-like appendage emerged from the bottom of the Finger of Eden. Its surface shimmered with a divine, unearthly radiance, as though forged from the fabric of the heavens. The onlookers screamed, their cries of despair cutting through the suffocating silence as the appendage drew closer to the pulsating Spark of Genesis.

The moment they touched, the world seemed to shatter. A blinding light erupted from the contact point, its intensity so fierce it obliterated shadows and painted the city in stark, searing white. The sheer brilliance was visible for miles, a beacon of destruction that pierced the morning sky. For a single, agonizing moment, everything was pure, consuming light.

Then came the wave.

A surge of energy exploded outward, consuming Rome in an instant. Historic landmarks, ancient streets, and countless lives were swept away in a heartbeat—reduced to nothing but memory. The ground split and the sky seared until only one thing remained...

Silence.

Not the quiet of the aftermath or the hush of awe but a silence that followed extinction.

The Finger of Eden hovered in the dead air, motionless above the smoldering void. Its vents hissed open. From it, smaller vessels descended—scavengers meant to clean up the aftermath. They swept through the ruin like carrion feeders, devouring what remained of one of the world's greatest cities. Ash, shattered stone, and the final fragments of millions of lives were funneled into their holds—repurposed as fuel for the Architect's next creation. Rome wasn't a memory anymore. It was raw material.

Where there had been a vibrant, bustling city now lay a barren wasteland. No laughter, cries, or history remained... only emptiness. The once-eternal city had been wiped clean, left to the whims of time and those who might one day seek to reclaim it. For now, it was nothing more than a void, awaiting the Architect's next move.

The veil dissipated, its shimmering surface fading into nothingness as the destruction and cleanup reached their grim conclusion.

Rangel stepped into the stillness, her eyes scanning the scorched terrain. At the edge of the smoldering wasteland, she stood motionless—her slender fingers clenched around a set of golden scales. The cool metal bit into her skin, its weight a solemn reminder of the judgment she alone delivered.

She stepped forward, her movements deliberate, each footfall sinking into the ashen ground. Kneeling with quiet reverence, Rangel placed the scales on the scorched earth. Their golden surface caught the faint glow of the smoldering horizon, reflecting faint, fractured light like a relic unearthed from another world.

She drew a handful of gritty dirt, the particles coarse and jagged against her fingertips. With measured precision, she sprinkled the soil onto both sides of the scales. The moment the last grain settled, the scales shuddered, their stillness broken as they swung with unnatural vigor. Metallic clinks echoed in rhythm, the sound reverberating like a heartbeat through the hollow silence.

Rangel's eyes remained fixed on the scales. The air grew taut, charged with an almost electric tension as the scales' movements quickened, their pendulous rhythm building to a fever pitch. With a sudden, decisive motion, the left side dropped and the right side rose.

Blight's Judgment had been rendered.

Her breath caught as the verdict was delivered. The scales' motion stilled, their once-rhythmic whispers silenced as the left side rested against the ground. A faint tremor rippled through the air, carrying the weight of the decision.

With practiced care, Rangel kneeled closer, brushing the dirt from the scales with her fingertips. The gritty particles cascaded to the ground, their descent unremarkable yet final. She retrieved the scales and reached into a pocket, producing a sleek black glove adorned with a flawless emerald set into its center.

Sliding the glove onto her right hand, she flexed her fingers, marveling at the way the fabric clung to her skin. The emerald's cool surface pressed into her palm, radiating an otherworldly energy. She crouched lower, her gloved hand brushing against the scorched earth.

A surge of power coursed through her body the moment the emerald made contact, a force that resonated deep within her. The ground beneath her hand responded in an instant, the darkened soil twisting and churning. A spreading shadow unfurled from the point of contact, tendrils of blackness creeping outward like an encroaching tide.

The blight advanced, consuming the infected areas marked by the scales. The transformation carried with it the cold certainty of finality, the earth itself succumbing to the verdict rendered by Blight's Judgment. Rangel straightened, her gaze steady as she watched the cleansing process begin, her presence as silent and inexorable as the power she wielded.

*   *   *

The Fingers of Eden moved without pause, cutting across the globe in a relentless cascade of destruction. One by one—Rome, London, Paris, Berlin, Madrid, New York City, Atlanta, and

Houston—each was erased under the Architect's grand design. No survivors, monuments, or memory remained. Only silence and the bitter trace of something sacred turned to ash.

In the heart of every ruin, Rangel appeared. Her black glove shimmered in the light of the ruined cities, and in her other hand, the golden scales trembled with purpose. Where others might have wept, she stood in quiet judgment—her gaze cool and her resolve unflinching.

Behind her, the blight crawled forward like a living tide, devouring what little remained. City by city, she moved—never in a hurry. At each site, she knelt, gathered a sample from the shattered earth, and let the scales decide. When the verdict came, it came without question. One plate dropped while another one rose, and the world around her changed forever.

With slow, ritual grace, Rangel placed her gloved hand against the ground. The earth responded. Black veins split outward beneath her touch, twisting through stone and ash. The blight spread like wildfire.

She didn't look back. There were more cities to judge.

When the last city fell silent, the world seemed to hold its breath. And then, the heavens opened.

Rain poured in torrents. It soaked the barren landscapes, washing over ash and ruin as though the very soul of the Earth was weeping for what had been taken.

There was no thunder or wind. Only the steady rhythm of sorrow falling from the sky. It didn't cleanse or renew. Only mourned.

*   *   *

Later that night, in the deserted sprawl of what use to be Los Angeles, the Architect stood with his most trusted hand, Regar. The cries of infants punctuated the night air as the Nephilim returned from their harvest, carrying wailing bundles to the ship. Regar stepped forward to deliver his report.

"My lord..." he began and bowed his head.

"We deployed eight Fingers of Eden."

The Architect nodded, his sharp gaze fixed on the distance. Two Fingers of Eden remained, one hovering above Los Angeles, the other poised over Anchorage, where Seria waited. He turned toward Regar, his expression dark with contemplation.

"Inform Seria to unleash the Finger of Eden on her location," he said, his voice cold and deliberate. "Prepare a ship with the Spark of Genesis onboard and send it to her. As for Los Angeles..." He paused, his tone sharpening. "I will deliver the Spark of Genesis myself to the city's heart."

Regar bowed, acknowledging the plan. "It shall be done, my lord."

As Regar departed to fulfill his orders, the Architect lingered, his gaze fixed on the horizon as though lost in thought. His voice shattered the silence, sharp and commanding. "Heliosa! Where are you, my faithful servant? Heliosa!"

Startled, Heliosa rushed to meet him, her heart pounding in her chest. She bowed low before him, her voice trembling. "Yes, my lord?"

The Architect's eyes narrowed, his words cutting like a blade. "Were you hiding from me, you wretched pest?"

"No, my lord," Heliosa said, her head still bowed. "I was sleeping in my quarters."

"You sleep when I tell you to sleep," the Architect said, his rage palpable. "You have three menial tasks, you filthy bug. First, you must bathe in the resplendence of my glory, basking in its blinding light. Second, you must announce my arrival with a voice trembling with reverence. Third, you must document my victories in the sacred Testament of Eden. Go retrieve the book and fulfill your worthless duties!"

The oppressive weight of his commands settled in the air. Heliosa bowed once more and turned, her shame clear in the stiffness of her movements as she retreated to the ship.

Alone in her dim quarters, Heliosa sat hunched over the Testament of Eden. The air felt thick and suffocating, each breath a reminder of the violence that had stained the land. Heliosa's trembling hands traced the edges of the Testament of Eden, her fingers brushing against the ancient papyrus. A single tear slid down her cheek, falling onto the parchment like a silent plea.

With a deep, steady breath, she took her quill, dipped it into the inkwell, and wrote. At the top of the page, she inscribed the title:

'The Worst Day in the History of the World.'

Her strokes were firm but heavy with emotion, each word etched with the weight of the day's devastation.

As she wrote, her thoughts churned. This day was one of many the Architect had wrought upon countless worlds, each a chapter in the Testament bearing the same grim title. Her quill moved with a determined rhythm, documenting the horrors and losses as her heart ached with the burden of truth.

When she finished, Heliosa set the quill aside and gazed at the entry, her reflection rippling in the ink. This was her duty, her penance, and her torment, a witness to the Architect's unrelenting vision of destruction.

CHAPTER EIGHTEEN

The Wake

I n the wake of the worst day the world had ever known, the Earth did not scream. It was silent.

Where once stood cities filled with life—Rome, London, Paris, Berlin, Madrid, New York, Atlanta, Houston—now stretched empty plains of scorched soil and silence. Not silence as humanity once knew it, the kind that calmed the soul or settled the nerves. This silence was heavier. It was the kind that made you feel like the world had stopped breathing.

Eight cities were gone, erased from the annals of time. No rubble or wreckage. Just flat, lifeless ground where history once walked. The air still carried warmth from where the Finger of Eden had struck, and the rain that followed hadn't cleansed it.

Birds still sang in the distance, but even that felt wrong now. Their melodies, once comforting, now echoed like eulogies given beside a rainy grave. The world wasn't just quieter, it was lonelier.

The sun rose, but it brought no warmth.

Somewhere, in the middle of all that emptiness, the survivors began to realize... the world hadn't just changed, it had ended.

Heliosa didn't need to see the aftermath. She hadn't walked the ruins of Rome or felt the heat where Paris once stood—but she didn't have to. She had already lived through the end of the world.

Long before Earth, there was Zion. Her home. A planet of twin moons and lavender skies, where music drifted from the cities like wind through glass. She could still remember the scent of rain on the dark soil, the laughter of younglings echoing through a field of flowers.

And she remembered how it ended.

The veil came first, just like here. Then the sky turned silent. Next came the Spark. A light so bright it devoured color, sound, and memory. The Architect hadn't conquered Zion. He erased it.

Now, as the Finger of Eden rested above Los Angeles and the final blueprint fell into place, Heliosa didn't need to look. The signs were already there.

The Testament of Eden sat before her, its ink still glistening, the words bleeding like fresh wounds across the page. Another chapter written and another world gone.

Heliosa stared at it, unblinking, as if the parchment might disappear if she looked long enough. Her hand trembled, the quill still gripped between her fingers like a weapon she didn't remember picking up. The weight of it—of all of it—pressed down on her shoulders, sinking her deeper into the floor.

Her eyes, ringed with shadows, drooped beneath the strain. It wasn't just exhaustion. It was depletion. Her body ached in quiet rebellion. Every step, every breath felt earned. Her feet dragged like they were tethered to blocks of stone. Her arms heavy from days spent carrying burdens she hadn't chosen.

Around her wrists, the shackles remained. Always. The Architect had loosened them just enough so she could hold a quill—but never enough to forget they were there. The cold metal bit into her skin, a quiet reminder: You are allowed to write but never to be free.

She didn't need invisible chains. He had given her real ones.

With a slow breath that caught halfway through, she set the Testament on its pedestal, her fingers lingering on its cover as if hoping it might draw some of the burden from her. But it didn't. It never did.

Outside the narrow porthole, the city still breathed. Los Angeles remained intact—for now—its lights blinking beneath a smog-laced sky. The world carried on, unaware that its days were numbered. Heliosa lingered for a moment, watching it through the glass. What tormented her wasn't yearning or compassion. It was simply the calm knowledge of what was coming.

She turned from the Testament of Eden, the ink still drying on its pages, and stepped into the corridor. Her boots made no sound on the cold floor. That was by design—everything in the Architect's domain was built to muffle noise—even grief.

As she walked, memory and reality wove together in fragments she couldn't stop.

A golden canopy of trees beneath twin suns... ash falling like snow. A sky so bright it peeled the color from her skin. Laughter echoing through crystal courtyards... The silence of a street where no one moved or breathed.

An Oracle who whispered, "You have a purpose." The same Oracle that shrieked in anguish, fading into darkness.

She blinked hard and swallowed.

The corridor bent, leading to the darker and colder lower deck. Her hand brushed the wall for balance, craving something real to hold onto. The wall gave nothing back.

She passed a broken mirror affixed to the corner—a punishment from a time she'd flinched when he raised his voice.

Her reflection stared back, warped and tired. Her face was thinner than it had been on Zion and her eyes older. Too old.

The memories came slower now, heavy as stone.

A marketplace humming with song... a girl with violet eyes handing her a ribbon... The first sound the veil made as it descended was like glass shattering underwater.

She reached her quarters and stepped inside.

It wasn't a room, more a suffocating box. The walls, a dull, metallic gray, seemed to press inward. The air hung heavy, stale with the sharp, metallic tang of rust and the oily reek of machinery. Only the weak, flickering light from the corridor dared to penetrate the gloom. The cold, unforgiving slab of metal beneath her feet felt familiar, a harsh greeting. She sank into it, pulling the scratchy blanket around her shoulders, its fabric as rough as her thoughts.

Zion lingered in her mind. A loss that pulsed beneath her ribs like a second heartbeat.

She closed her eyes, and a single tear streaked down her face. She didn't wipe it away.

Outside the ship, the Architect stood motionless, his golden staff resting next to him. Beside him, Regar loomed in silence.

From the shadows, footsteps began to echo. Rangel and Durbal emerged in unison, their silhouettes sharpening as they stepped into the glow of the ship's exterior lights. Rangel's scales swung at her side, the soft *clink, clink, clink* cutting through the quiet like an old clock counting down. Durbal's fingers tapped against the curve of his bow,—the rhythm, a habit he'd never lost.

Neither of them spoke.

The Architect's chin lifted a fraction, and his grip on the staff tightened. A long pause stretched between them, long enough to feel intentional, before the Architect spoke.

"My faithful hands," he said, "your missions were not only executed—they were etched into the memory of this world. The Fingers of Eden did not whisper. They roared and the Spark of Genesis burned away the rot."

Rangel bowed first, one knee touching the ground with ceremonial precision. Durbal followed, slower, but just as controlled—his head low, his hands still resting on the bow as if reluctant to let it go.

The Architect shifted his weight, the soft scrape of his boot against stone the only sound he offered as reward. "But," he continued, the warmth draining from his tone, "our work is far from complete."

He lifted his golden staff and swept it toward the northern horizon, the metal tracing a slow, deliberate arc through the air.

"All three of you will board the next ship and head north. Seria awaits in Alaska. The Finger of Eden will descend upon her location, and Rangel, you will deliver Blight's Judgment again."

He paused, letting the weight of his words settle.

"Seria and her hounds failed to capture those marked by prophecy. You will assist her in finding them. Do not kill them." His voice lowered, each word sharpened with venom. "They cannot fulfill the prophecy once shackled. I want them alive."

He leaned on his staff, his tone shifting from command to fury. "If you see that wretched pest in the purple robes... make him suffer."

Regar took one step forward. The air seemed to chill as he did. "It will be done, my lord," he said, his voice calm and resolute. "But if I may... why do we not know this mysterious man's name?"

The Architect let out a low scoff, one corner of his mouth curling in irritation. He turned away from them, the metal end of his staff tapping the ground with slow, purposeful weight as he

213

walked a few paces. "Rumors and whispers," he said. "That's all I've ever heard of him. In every world we've conquered, people spoke of him—but no one ever saw him." He came to a stop. "This world is different. Here, he stepped out of legend. Seria saw him, as did I on my march to this arena. She and her hounds chased the marked ones, and when they found him..." He drew in a slow breath, his fingers tightening around the staff until the metal hummed. "... his staff struck once—and scattered her hounds like leaves in a storm. That kind of power is not to be dismissed. According to the prophecy..." He hesitated. The air grew still around him. "... the Oracle of Zion spoke of this. A disciple in purple will rise. He will guide the nine bloodlines. Together, they will fulfill their destinies... and defeat me."

Regar's brow creased, his voice dropping into something more careful. "The Oracle of Zion? I was there, my lord. Beside you. I never saw you speak with her."

The Architect turned back toward him, a dry, bitter smile tugging at his lips. "You weren't supposed to." He stepped forward. "Not all battles are fought in fields, Regar. The Oracle came to me in the dark, her cloak drawn and head bowed, riddles clutched like offerings. She believed I would show mercy." He shook his head, the smile fading. "She thought her visions might move me. So naive. Instead, she handed me what I needed," the Architect said, the edge of his voice curling into contempt. "She offered names and warnings. In exchange for her pitiful life, she begged one mercy." He lifted his staff. "Spare the girl," she said. Take her and use her. Make her your historian. Let her live to witness the fall." He chuckled, low and cold. "So, I did. Not out of pity but because even the condemned have their uses."

He came to a stop inches from Regar, the faint golden glow of his staff illuminating the lines of his face. "Do you understand now? Knowledge is power. I took what I needed, and Zion still fell. But her words… they echo. They cling. And until I burn the prophecy from memory, they will continue to cast their shadow."

His hand reached out and came to rest on Regar's shoulder, firm and commanding. "You have served me long and well, Regar. Do not waste thought on this city. We have already chosen its fate. I will deliver the Spark of Genesis myself."

He turned toward the coliseum; its outline etched against the horizon like a crown of stone.

"That structure will remain. I'll remake it into an arena, grand and eternal. A monument to what I've built. A stage for spectacle. The blueprints are already in motion. My servants work even now."

The Architect's words hung in the air, heavy and final. In unison, the three hands bowed. They turned and walked toward the ships, their footsteps steady, the quiet scuff of boots swallowed by the rising hum of engines coming to life.

The Architect stood alone for a moment, his shoulders squared, the wind catching the hem of his cloak as it curled around his boots. The horizon ahead was dark, but he stood as if he could already see the world remade, as if it were just a matter of time catching up to design.

Then he turned. His stride was smooth and measured as he moved toward another waiting ship. The metal ramp groaned beneath his steps, closing behind him with a hiss of hydraulics. Inside, the quarters were dim and cold, the recycled air stale with the scent of steel and something chemical. The silence was broken only by the slow, rhythmic breathing of a sleeping giant.

The Architect's voice boomed through the air. "Haligot. Wake up! I need you."

A deep grunt echoed from within the shadows. Haligot emerged from his chamber, massive shoulders filling the narrow

215

frame of the doorway. He rubbed a scarred hand across his face, dragging it down over his jaw as if trying to peel the sleep away. His skin, as hard as a gemstone, caught the faint golden glow of the staff the Architect held, and in that flickering light, his features looked as though they were carved from ancient stone.

He dropped to one knee, the floor creaking beneath his weight. "Yes, my lord?" he said.

The Architect stepped closer, the staff now casting long shadows against the curved walls. "Gather your Nephilim," he ordered, his words clipped and cold. "Find the leaders of this world and bring them to me—alive. They will entertain me in my new arena. I want them squirming and broken. And when they kneel, we will laugh."

A hunger flickered in Haligot's eyes, the thrill of the hunt excited him. "With pleasure, my lord," he said, already rising to his full height.

His footsteps fell like distant war drums, slow and thunderous, each one echoing with the promise of ruin.

His door slid shut with a hiss.

The Architect moved with calculated purpose back to his ship, the low hum of the ship's engines pulsing through the floor like a heartbeat. The sound was steady. A reminder that everything here was bent to his will.

He entered the storage chamber, where the air was cooler, still carrying the sterile scent of metal and something older. His fingers brushed across one of the boxes housing a Spark of Genesis. The surface throbbed beneath his touch, its etched symbols flickering like veins of light. He cradled it beneath his arm.

He passed into his private chambers, each step muffled by the thick carpeting, thick enough to absorb the weight of empires. Gold and crystal shimmered from the walls, casting light across the floor. The resplendence of Eden wasn't just a design choice—it was a declaration: You are standing in the room of a god.

At the far end of the room, resting atop its pedestal, sat the Testament of Eden.

He stopped.

The book's presence seemed to call to him. He stepped closer and lifted it with both hands, the worn leather spine familiar beneath his fingers. It was heavy in weight and in meaning. The histories of fallen worlds lived within it—his victories, design, and order carved into the bones of chaos.

He turned a few pages, flipping past ancient entries until fresh ink caught his eye.

Heliosa's most recent account.

The lines were precise. Clean and written with the trembling care of someone who knew every letter was a risk—and a responsibility. His lips parted as he read, drinking in the devastation she had described. It wasn't enough to remember the fall of those cities—he wanted to feel it again, through her words.

A slow breath filled his lungs, the scent of parchment and ash lingering in the air. His lips curled in dark, satisfied hunger. This wasn't a record—it was fuel. A sacred text of domination. Every word she'd written made his desire to destroy burn hotter.

He placed the Testament back on its pedestal and set the Spark beside it, as if consecrating an altar.

"The future of this world is already written," he said, "Now to ensure it bleeds into reality."

He didn't glance back, summoning the pilot with a single command, his tone authoritative and final. "Take us to the Los Angeles airport."

The engines thrummed louder, responding like trained beasts eager to be unleashed.

When the ship touched down, the Architect descended the ramp with solemn precision. The Spark of Genesis rested in his hands like a sleeping god. He walked onto the tarmac, the vast concrete expanse stretching before him, with a silent, ominous presence hanging above.

He reached the center of the runway and knelt. It was a ritual he knew all too well. The Spark was placed with care, its glow pulsing brighter in response to the energy rising around it.

He stood, lifted his golden staff, and raised it toward the sky.

A beam of light erupted from the staff's tip, slicing upward, its radiance painting spectral runes across the clouds. The Finger of Eden twitched, a subtle shift that quickly became movement. Its massive form began to descend.

The Architect tilted his head, watching in eager anticipation. Then he turned, his cloak trailing behind him as he ascended the ramp without a word.

Once inside, his voice broke the silence, calm and unshaken. "Return to the coliseum."

As the engines roared to life, the Architect stood near the viewing window, one hand braced against the frame. The hull vibrated beneath his fingertips. Outside, the Finger of Eden moved with slow, deliberate grace, drawn like a blade toward its scabbard. Inching closer by the second.

The Spark of Genesis pulsed below, waiting. The moment of connection was near and, as always, it would be perfect. This was art—a final stroke on a dying canvas.

The ship touched down at the coliseum, its platforms unfolding like petals. The Architect descended first, his cloak trailing behind him, every step placed with ritualistic precision. At the edge of the platform, he lifted his arms wide, his voice cutting through the still air like a commandment.

"Come forth, my faithful servants," he yelled, "and behold the might of Eden as it removes this city from existence."

From the coliseum's cavernous shadows, they emerged—dozens strong. Their tattered clothes clinging to their skin as they formed a semicircle around him. No one dared to speak.

The Architect moved to the center. His staff creaked beneath his fingers. He closed his eyes in deep focus, and he drove the base of the staff into the ground with a dull thud.

Light surged from the gemstone and went up the walls of the coliseum, refracting until every surface shimmered in gold and blue. The glow grew, pulsing like a heartbeat, washing over the gathered crowd.

"O mighty Eden," the Architect said, "wrap this sacred coliseum in your veil. Let us witness glory, unscathed."

The energy burst outward in a radiant wave. A dome of translucent light unfurled over the structure, snapping into place with a low, resonant hum. The faithful stared upward, awestruck, their hands raised as if to touch it.

The Architect opened his eyes just as the connection struck.

A searing light ignited the horizon—pure and divine. The Spark and the Finger met, and the city of Los Angeles vanished. Buildings, streets, voices, and memories—gone.

A roar erupted from the coliseum floor. His followers broke into thunderous applause, some laughing and some weeping. Their cheers reverberated off stone and steel, echoing like hymns in a temple of annihilation.

The Architect stood motionless.

He exhaled a slow breath. A single tear slid down his cheek and vanished against the edge of his smile.

"What a breathtaking sight," he said. "Eden has gifted me a blank slate once more."

He turned back to the crowd, his voice sharpening, regaining its edge.

"Today marks a turning point. My blueprints are being fulfilled. Take your moment and savor this triumph. Then return to your work. This arena must be ready."

The crowd cheered again, and one by one, they dispersed, their chants fading into focused movement—hammers, chisels, and machinery humming back to life.

The Architect remained where he stood, eyes fixed on the distant stretch of horizon, where a city had once been.

In the far north, another city awaited its end, the Eden Veil already clawing toward it, but here, surrounded by gold and echoes, the Architect basked in his moment. Unaware that something had shifted and that somewhere, in the quiet fringes of his perfect plan... the unraveling had begun.

CHAPTER NINETEEN

The Reaping

F ar to the north, the Eden Veil shimmered like a second aurora, coiling across the sky before cascading downward in silent finality. The moment the Finger of Eden pierced the Spark of Genesis, the ship's hull trembled—a deep, resonant hum that thrummed in the bones. The three hands of the Architect rushed to the observation deck, their boots striking metal in sync.

They saw a blinding light. It swallowed the world.

Anchorage disappeared in a breathless instant. Towers, streets, and rivers—all consumed in a bloom of incandescent finality. The veil didn't tear through the city with violence; it erased it with precision, an almost reverent sweep that left only silence in its wake.

Durbal squinted, one hand pressed against the glass. "Even after all this time... it never stops feeling like a funeral."

Rangel crossed her arms. "Not a funeral," she said. "A cleansing. But this one feels... heavier."

"This world bleeds different," Durbal replied. "The bones are older."

Regar's eyes tracked the last remnants of light as the veil sealed the city's fate. Below, the once-proud skyline of Anchorage was nothing but ash and absence.

He exhaled. "They'll call this the day Alaska wept," he said, voice low and edged with grim amusement. A faint smile touched his lips. "Fitting, don't you think?"

No one replied. There was nothing left to say.

The ship descended through the northern clouds like a dagger slipping between ribs, its hull slicing through the sky. As it touched down outside the veil, the landing struts hissed against the damp, uneven ground, sending shallow tremors through the mossy terrain. For a moment, all was still—until the ramp extended with a metallic groan, slicing open the silence.

Outside the veil, Seria's hounds prowled in restless patrols, their shrill howls rising and falling like a requiem for the dead. The earth bore deep footprints—human and monstrous—and a faint shimmer still clung to the edge of the veil.

The three Hands of the Architect emerged in unison, their boots striking the ground with urgency. They moved without words, their presence commanding the broken silence like a funeral procession.

Seria stormed toward them, her movements rigid with fury. Every step she took seemed to charge the air, and when she jabbed a finger at Durbal, the force of it might've cracked stone. "Durbal! Why did you add that ridiculous secondary protocol? I was this close to capturing them!" Her voice lashed through the air like a whip. "The veil sealed itself because one of my hounds fell in battle!"

Her breath steamed in the cool air, the rage behind her eyes hotter than the sun that never quite set.

Durbal didn't flinch. He let the words settle, unbothered, as if listening to the wind complain about the dirt. When he spoke, his tone was flat and surgical. "The veil serves to protect. It does not mourn your strategy. It shields against the rupture caused by the Fingers of Eden and any threats. It detected a loss within your pack and responded."

Seria's lip curled, her finger trembling with restrained fury. "That loss cost me everything! I refuse to take the blame for this failure."

Durbal tilted his head, voice gaining enough weight to sharpen the tension between them. "The veil does not recognize blame, Seria. Only input. Perhaps..." he let the words settle, long enough to cut "if your hounds were more than teeth and noise..."

"Enough." Regar's voice thundered through the clearing, deep and immovable. He stepped between them, the folds of his cape stirring in the low wind. "We have more pressing matters than bickering like children."

Seria's expression twisted into a snarl, but she said nothing.

Regar turned his full attention to her. "In which direction did those with the mark flee?"

With a scoff and a bitter laugh, she pointed toward the dense tree line beyond the veil's edge. "Cowards. They ran into the trees." Her voice dropped low, malice curling around each word like ash on embers. "But when I find that fool in purple again... I'll cut him in half and feed him to my hounds."

The wind stirred again, carrying her threat into the endless hush of the Alaskan wilds.

The silence between them spoke louder than the commands. The hunt wasn't over. It had only just begun.

A few moments passed as Seria composed herself, her fiery demeanor subdued for a moment. She turned to Regar, her voice softer now, edged with a rare note of reverence.

"One of my hounds has perished, Regar. Could you perform the reaping before we depart—so the others may find closure?"

Regar inclined his head, his movements deliberate and unhurried. "Where is the body?"

Seria gestured toward a nearby pyre, where the lifeless form of the hound lay atop an arranged mound of timber. Around it, the other hounds stood in solemn formation, torches gripped in clawed hands, their flames casting jagged shadows across the terrain. Low growls soared through the air like a dirge, but their usual ferocity had softened, replaced by a stillness that felt almost sacred.

Regar stepped forward, framed by the pale shimmer of the Eden Veil on the horizon. He sauntered, every step measured. The wind stirred as he reached for his scythe, the weapon sliding free with a whisper. At seven feet tall, the scythe dwarfed even him—its ivory handle polished smooth from centuries of use. The blade, a sweeping crescent of silver and onyx, caught the flickering firelight and shimmered as though it hungered.

He paused before the pyre. In his mind, a thousand reaping grounds blurred together, some forgotten, others etched into the marrow of his bones. Zion, where the Eternal Flame once lit the souls of its people like starlight. The reaping there had been blinding, each soul resisting with hymns turned to screams. Abyssia, drowned beneath poisoned tides; its priests fought to the last breath, clinging to their drowned gods even as the scythe pulled their spirits from the deep. And Edom where fire didn't burn, it begged, and the reaping came with a heat so intense it melted the soul before it could be claimed.

224

On Noctis, the shadows fought back. Souls there didn't flee—they watched, whispering in a language older than time as Regar carved them from the dark. And Sinarath, whose pride clung to its towers even in death—those souls chained themselves to their machines, resisting extraction like rusted gears refusing to turn.

Each world carried its own kind of defiance. Earth felt different – less sacred and more ancient. Here souls didn't resist; they remembered, and in their remembrance, death became a story.

His hand tightened on the scythe. "Let it be done," he said—his words falling to the unseen remnants beneath the dirt.

He closed his eyes. The world held its breath. When they opened again, his irises burned white-hot, casting a harsh light across the clearing. His pallid skin seemed drained of all color, as though death had borrowed his body for a moment's work.

He raised the scythe. Its blade hummed—an ancient resonance that vibrated in the bones of every creature present. With a deliberate, reverent motion, he lowered it until the tip kissed the hound's chest.

A shock of energy shot outward.

The hound's body jolted. The pyre creaked in protest. From its mouth, a shadow uncoiled—writhing and resisting, shrieking without sound. It twisted into the air like smoke caught in a storm. The hounds watched, unmoving. Their torches didn't waver.

The shadow circled the blade, furious and desperate, trying to break free. But the etchings along the scythe began to glow, absorbing it with patient inevitability. The shade spiraled down the shaft, inch by inch, toward the base. Then it ripped free in a violent burst. The soul hovered and then dove, vanishing into the earth with a soundless ripple. The ground dimpled where it disappeared.

Regar let out a long breath. The light in his eyes dimmed, returning to its usual hollow gray. He lowered the scythe and planted it in the dirt beside the pyre.

"The reaping is complete," he said.

Seria nodded once. She raised a hand, and the hounds understood. One by one, they approached the pyre and laid their torches on the wood.

The fire ignited with a low roar.

Flames danced up the body of their fallen kin. Their eyes didn't stray. They watched until flesh turned to smoke and memory.

Without a word, Regar turned and strode back toward the ship, his scythe resting across his shoulder, its blade dark once more. The clearing behind him flickered with firelight and farewell.

As the Eden Veil shimmered and thinned above them, its last remnants evaporating into the endless Alaskan twilight, a single, hollow howl rose from the pack—a sound of grief, reverence, and endings.

From the ship's ramp, Rangel stepped into view, her silhouette haloed by the dying fire. She said nothing, but the hounds shifted at her presence, bowing their heads.

Without a word, Rangel stepped past the gathered group, her movements unhurried but purposeful, silent and deliberate, as if she were moving across a sacred space known only to her.

She stopped at the edge of the clearing, beyond the reach of the pyre's dying glow, where the earth lay undisturbed. Kneeling, she placed the golden scales upon the barren soil. Their surfaces shimmered in the dim light, humming with dormant power. With practiced care, she gathered a handful of gritty earth and let it sift through her fingers, dusting the scales in a fine layer.

The air shifted.

A quiet tension settled over the clearing as the scales swayed, their motion slow at first, then quicker and steadier. A metallic rhythm echoed in the silence. Then a clang. The left arm of the scales dropped as the right shot skyward.

Rangel's expression didn't flicker.

She gathered the scales, brushing the dirt from their polished surface with reverent hands. Slipping on her glove, she pressed its emerald centerpiece into the soil. The gem pulsed once, deep green flashing against the darkness.

A ripple of shadow bloomed from the point of contact.

Tendrils of living blackness twisted across the ground, spreading in all directions. The grass withered. Moss curled into ash. The very color of the soil bled away. What remained was scorched earth stripped of its memory. A mirror of what the Finger of Eden had left behind.

Rangel stood, her cape stirring in the wind, and turned back toward the ship. She passed Seria, Regar, and the silent hounds without a glance. The fire's remnants flickered across her armor as she disappeared into the hold. Behind her, the blight remained—a dark wound carved into the earth.

*   *   *

In the vast Alaskan wilderness, the group that had escaped the base stopped to catch their breath. The air stung their lungs, and the silence of the forest pressed in from all sides, broken only by the faint rustle of leaves whispering through the trees. Huddled close, they leaned against thick trunks, exhaustion carved into every line of their faces after running for a full day and most of the previous night.

227

A faint tremor rippled beneath their feet.

Lizzie looked down and froze.

The earth was darkening. Veins of blackness snaked through the soil like living shadows, pulsing with a slow, deliberate hunger.

"What's happening to the ground?" she said.

Roo dropped to one knee beside the creeping blight. His hand hovered above it, close enough to feel the unnatural cold radiating from its center.

"It's spreading," he said. "Whatever they did back there... It's still moving."

Panic rippled through the group as they backed away, the forest floor wilting and rotting beneath their eyes. Madison and Savannah clung to each other, eyes wide as they scanned the forest ahead.

Lizzie's voice broke through the rising dread. "The ship we saw earlier—it was heading this way. Whoever was on board... they're coming, aren't they?"

Roo didn't answer right away. He stared up into the treetop. After a few minutes, he nodded. "They'll come, and we don't know how many or what they'll do when they find us."

The weight of his words sank into the group like a stone. No one moved.

Savannah spoke, her voice small but unwavering. "We can't stay here. What if they catch us?"

Lizzie knelt beside her and placed a steady hand on her shoulder. "We'll keep moving. But for now... we need to rest."

No one argued.

With the creeping blight behind them and unknown threats ahead, the group settled into the shadows of the trees.

Roo unzipped the worn duffel bag he'd hauled from the base and pulled out a few snacks. "Eat what you can," he said, passing it around. "You'll need it."

They took turns. Shaky hands and quiet chewing, with blank stares into the trees. The silence fractured again—this time by howls. Low, distant, and mournful.

The sound made the group stiffen.

When the bag reached Madison and Savannah, they stared at it but didn't move. Roo approached and crouched beside them, his voice low and warm.

"I know it's hard right now but eat something. Just a little. You need your strength." He added, "I won't let anything happen to you. That's a promise."

For a moment, they did nothing. Both girls lunged into his arms, clutching him tight. He held them, drawing strength from their trust. They each picked something small from the bag—crackers and a fruit bar—and unwrapped the food with trembling fingers.

The howls sounded again, louder this time. Madison and Savannah froze, their eyes scanning the trees. Roo pulled them close again.

"We're okay," he said. "We're safe for now."

He rose and joined Lizzie, who stood with her arms crossed and her shoulders tense. She looked at him, then toward the sound.

"They're getting closer," she said.

Roo nodded. "Still sounds far. We've got some time."

Lizzie didn't argue. Her fingers brushed the strap of her bag.

"We need shelter soon. It's going to get cold again tonight. We won't last long out here like this."

"I know," Roo said. He sighed and reached back into the duffel for a small bag of chips. "Five minutes. That's all. Let's rest while we can."

Lizzie hesitated, then dropped beside him. She opened a pack of crackers and took a deep breath. "I'm sorry, Roo. I've been on edge. It's... hard to process any of this. I keep trying to focus on survival, but I forget we're still human."

Roo smiled and crunched a chip. "Stopping won't make the end of the world any worse."

That pulled a soft laugh from her. After a few bites, she tilted her head toward him. "So... tell me about you. Where're you from? You got a family?"

Roo chuckled. "Hell of a time to get personal."

She shrugged. "Why not?"

He leaned back against the tree, a flicker of something faraway drifting into his eyes. "Tiny town in Missouri. The kind where people know you're going to get grounded before your parents do. I had a little brother." He paused. His voice lowered. "Jefferson. He died when I was twelve. Playground accident. It was one of those stupid freak accidents."

Lizzie placed a gentle hand on his knee. "I'm sorry."

Roo's lips twitched into something like a smile. "It's okay. It's been a long time, but I still think about him from time to time. I wonder what life would've been like if he were still around." He turned to her and tried to change the subject. "What about you? UK, right?"

"Born in London. Moved to Manchester. One older sister. My parents used to joke that after me, they knew two was enough."

Roo laughed. "I don't believe that for a second."

His eyes drifted to the edge of the clearing, where the newer members of their group lingered beyond the firelight. They sat in silence, keeping to themselves, expressions unreadable, their posture tense but alert.

Roo lowered his voice. "What do you make of them? The ones that joined us in the hangar."

Lizzie followed his line of sight and shrugged. "Hard to say. They've been quiet since we left the base. I haven't asked questions."

"Think they're hiding something?"

"I think everyone is," she said. "But they're not slowing us down, and they haven't tried to run. That counts for something."

Roo nodded, unconvinced. "I want to know who's with us when things go bad again."

She smiled, but the moment passed as she rose and moved to check on the others.

Dr. Terracotta came to Roo next, nodding toward Ramirez, who sat alone at the edge of the clearing, hunched over with his head in his hands. "Look at him," Terracotta said. "He hasn't said a word. Think we should talk to him?"

Roo followed his line of sight. "He watched Tipton get torn apart and fed to monsters. Let him grieve in his way. He'll talk when he's ready."

Terracotta frowned but nodded, his eyes lingering on Ramirez before walking away.

Roo turned toward Dr. Solomon, who was tending his face, blotting at his wounds with gauze. "How bad is it?" Roo asked.

Solomon gave a dry laugh. "Hurts like torture. Might leave a hell of a scar."

"Ladies dig scars," Roo said, nudging him in the arm.

His attention drifted to the strange book beside the doctor. "That book the guy in the purple robes gave you—any idea what's inside?"

Solomon picked it up, running his fingers across the embossed symbol. "Pages are blank. Doesn't make any sense. He handed it to me and disappeared. Didn't say a word."

Roo shrugged, but before he could respond, a sharp crack echoed through the trees. He froze. Another sound. This time it was closer. Leaves rustled and a branch snapped.

Roo raised his hand, signaling everyone to stop. Then there was a roar. Deep and primal.

A massive brown bear exploded from the brush, charging into the clearing with terrifying speed. The group scattered in a panic. Birds took flight, screaming overhead as the bear's roar tore through the forest.

Roo grabbed for the duffel, but he fumbled it. Panic set in, and he abandoned it and bolted. Adrenaline surged through his body as branches whipped past. Roots tore at his boots.

Without warning, a sudden jolt. His foot caught on a hidden stone, and the world spun. He hit the ground hard, smashing his head against a gnarled tree root.

The pain was intense.

The world spun some more.

The bear's roar distorted, growing distant and higher in pitch, until it was something else...laughter.

A child's laughter.

The forest vanished.

The air smelled of sun-warmed mulch and peanut butter sandwiches. He could hear the swing creaking. Sneakers scraping on pavement. Someone was calling his name.

It was Jefferson.

CHAPTER TWENTY

Two Brothers

R oo's eyes blinked open. *Where am I?*

He didn't awaken to the feel of cold dirt or the crackle of fire. Instead, Roo opened his eyes to sunlight that felt like it belonged to another life. A playground stretched around him, with grass that was bright green, too vivid to seem real. Laughter echoed from a distance, mingling with the smells of sweat, woodchips, and hot metal baking under the summer sun.

He blinked again, feeling disoriented.

The roar that had haunted his ears seconds ago was gone, replaced by the sounds of children. Roo's fingers dug into the cool, damp soil beneath him as he struggled to make sense of his surroundings. The rustle of grass brushed against his skin, while the blades slipped through his fingers like silk at a weaver's loom. Confusion swirled in his mind as he took in the unfamiliar landscape.

I remember this place. This is where... No. It can't be. Not again

A voice called from above. "Hey, Roo! You coming or what?"

He looked up. At the top of the slide stood Jefferson—his little brother, alive and beaming, with his hands gripping the sides like a pirate captain surveying his ship.

"Better tuck in that birthmark," Jefferson said, pointing to Roo's shirt where it had ridden up. "Might scare everyone away."

Roo's face flushed in a bright shade of red. He tugged his shirt down and stood, now aware of the other kids nearby. Some of them turned to look, and a few giggled.

"It's just a mark," Roo said. "Shut up."

Jefferson grinned wider. "Aw, come on. Don't be such a baby. What, you gonna cry again?"

Roo's grip tightened on the ladder rail. "I said, knock it off."

"Or what?" Roo climbed the ladder. Each rung was hot to the touch from the midday sun. When he reached the top, he didn't yell. He just stepped forward and, without warning, gave Jefferson a gentle shove—just enough to say, "I'm done."

After the shove, the world seemed to move in slow motion. Jefferson's foot slipped.

"Roo!" he shouted as panic filled his voice.

I tried to grab him. I swear I did.

For a moment, Jefferson balanced between Roo and the ground below. He tipped backward, legs flipping up, arms flailing like a marionette with snapped strings. Roo's breath caught in his throat as he watched Jefferson fall to the ground below.

I will never forget the sound he made.

A sharp thud echoed through the air.

One second, Jefferson was laughing. The next...

No, not this again.

Jefferson lay in the grass below; his limbs limp and his head tilted at an unnatural angle. Blood pooled beneath him, soaking into the earth like spilled paint.

I didn't mean to push him. I didn't mean it.

A single gasp sliced through the silence. Then another. And another.

Laughter vanished, and the playground became a vacuum; every sound was swallowed except for the ringing in Roo's ears.

"Jefferson!"

Roo's voice cracked as he scrambled down the ladder, his hands slipping and knees banging against the metal rungs. He missed the last step and fell hard beside his brother.

"Jefferson, please..."

He reached out but hesitated, his hands hovering just above Jefferson's chest, uncertain and afraid to touch him.

"Get up. Please, get up."

The blood kept spreading. It crept through the grass in slow, steady tendrils, tracing patterns Roo would never forget.

This wasn't supposed to happen. He wasn't supposed to fall.

Children gathered around. A few stood at a distance, their faces pale and mouths trembling. One girl clutched a stuffed rabbit to her chest like a shield, while another boy backed away, shaking his head, with tears already welling in his eyes.

"Is he... is he dead?" A small voice whispered.

Roo couldn't answer.

I just wanted him to stop.

His heart thundered, each beat louder than the previous one. He could feel it in his temples and fingertips.

"Get someone! Help! HELP!"

The words broke through the chaos. A boy dashed toward the parking lot, his legs pumping as fast as they could, voice shrill with panic.

Roo leaned closer to Jefferson, searching for any sign of movement or any indication of life.

"Jefferson," he whispered again, voice trembling. "You're okay. You're okay. Please be okay."

Jefferson didn't move.

I'd give anything to take it back.

A man burst through the park gate, drawn by the cries. His face twisted from confusion to horror the moment he saw the boy on the ground.

He dropped to his knees beside Jefferson. Two fingers pressed to the neck, eyes flicking between his watch and the boy's face. Roo held his breath, every muscle locked in place, waiting.

The man's shoulders eased after a sign of life.

"There's a pulse," he said as he snapped open his phone.

His voice sharpened as he barked into the receiver.

"I need an ambulance at Millstone Park! A child has fallen and is unconscious with head trauma. Please send someone now!"

There's a pulse.

He heard his parents before he saw them. He could hear their footsteps pounding and his mother's voice screaming.

"No, no, no!"

His mother dropped beside Jefferson, her knees slamming into the dirt, hands trembling as they hovered above her son's blood-matted hair. Her sobs tore through the stillness.

"Jefferson!"

Roo's father stopped in his tracks, eyes wide and pale. His eyes first landed on Jefferson, then drifted to Roo's hands, which were sticky with red.

His lips parted, but no words came.

Say something. Say anything.

"I... I didn't mean to..." Roo whispered.

The sirens swallowed his voice. Red and white lights spun across the grass like frantic ghosts. The ambulance skidded to a stop, and paramedics poured out, moving with hurried purpose.

"We've got a child, male, unresponsive," one said, kneeling beside Jefferson.

Roo took a step back, and then another.

Another paramedic said, "Head trauma. Stable pulse. Breathing's shallow."

Everything moved too fast, but at the same time, it wasn't fast enough. Roo watched their hands as they checked the vitals, secured a neck brace, and unpacked their gear.

His mother clutched his father's arm like she was drowning. Roo shrank behind them, trying to make himself invisible so the world wouldn't notice what he did.

"We need to move him now."

Jefferson was lifted from the ground and secured onto the gurney, the cool metal beneath him contrasting with the heat of the moment. Straps were fastened across his body, ensuring he remained stable during transport.

Roo's parents turned toward him.

His mother's face was soaked and her eyes bloodshot. His father said nothing, but Roo felt the weight of it in his bones.

They didn't have to say it. He'd already said it to himself a thousand times.

I didn't mean to push him. I just wanted him to stop.

The ambulance doors slammed shut.

Roo sat on the bench seat in the back, between his parents. His mother gripped his hand with the desperation of someone trying to hold back the end of the world. Roo didn't squeeze back.

The hospital loomed ahead, cold and towering, its facade illuminated by flickering fluorescent lights.

Inside, the wheels of the stretcher clattered against the tile like bones tossed in a jar. Roo followed behind, unsteady on his feet.

His breath came in short, uneven gulps.

Please let him be okay. Please let this all rewind.

The emergency room swallowed them whole as the doors flew open. The fluorescent lights above felt bright, humming like angry wasps in Roo's ears.

Jefferson disappeared beneath a storm of scrubs and gloves. The medical team descended without hesitation, their faces calm but urgent. Hands moved in fast rhythms, voices clipped and precise.

"Head trauma. Suspected internal bleeding," a doctor said, tightening the straps across Jefferson's chest.

Roo hung back, like a shadow standing just inside the door. He watched the scene unfold as if someone were pressing their face to the glass. He couldn't move or speak, and his fists curled so tight that his fingers turned pale white.

A nurse stood near a monitor.

"Heart rate's irregular," she said. "We're holding stable, but we need to move fast."

His parents clung to each other near the doorway, pale and shaking. Roo's mother gasped every time someone raised their voice. His father didn't blink.

Jefferson didn't move.

He's still breathing. That means something.

Machines beeped in uneven rhythm—one monitor let out a high-pitched chirp, then a stutter. Tubes snaked around Jefferson's body, wires trailing to screens that blinked like warning lights. He looked so small, engulfed by the bed and everything around him.

Roo couldn't look away.

Please don't die. Please don't let this be the last thing I do for you.

A voice cut through the air. "Vitals are stabilizing."

A nurse adjusted an IV with steady hands, her movements fluid and almost gentle.

"Prep him for transfer to ICU," the doctor said. "We need scans. Full diagnostics."

The gurney jolted as the team wheeled it forward, their footsteps crisp against the tile.

Roo's parents followed, one step behind. Roo trailed after them like an afterthought.

They don't even see me.

Every step felt like dragging chains. The hallway stretched for what seemed like forever. Roo couldn't stop staring at the slight rise and fall of Jefferson's chest. It was the only thing anchoring him.

For just a moment, the world slowed again.

Roo's breath caught as his eyes locked onto Jefferson's pale face, motionless like porcelain amidst the chaotic blur.

Please... just wake up. Please let this be a nightmare. Let me open my eyes.

The ICU was shrouded in an uneasy silence, a stillness that hung in the air like a ghostly presence in a graveyard at midnight. The sterile environment had a pungent, plastic-like smell. It clung to the walls like vines in a garden.

Jefferson lay still, pale against the sheets, a tangle of tubes coiled around his limbs like vines. Machines beeped in a slow, steady rhythm, each sound a lifeline.

His mother sat beside the bed, her hand trembling as she brushed a stray curl from Jefferson's forehead. Her lips moved, mouthing a prayer as she leaned down and kissed his forehead.

His father stood near the wall, arms crossed, eyes locked on the monitors as if he could force them to change by staring at them long enough.

Roo sat in the corner with his back against the cold wall and his head in his hands. The fall kept replaying over and over, the sound of it splitting his mind open like a dropped dish.

If I hadn't pushed him and just walked away. If I'd been stronger.

Time seemed to warp as the hours passed.

The door creaked, and a doctor entered, clipboard in hand, footsteps soft against the tile.

Roo's parents straightened, but Roo didn't move.

"We've run preliminary tests," the doctor said. His voice was gentle but practiced. He'd delivered this kind of news before. "There's significant swelling. We're going to monitor him overnight."

Roo's mother gasped as her hand flew to her mouth.

"But he's stable?" she asked. "He'll recover, right?"

The doctor paused for a moment, searching for the right words. "It's too early to say," the doctor said. "For now... he's holding on."

The words landed with a dull thud. They didn't offer comfort or clarity, just the purgatory of "wait and see."

Roo's father nodded once, but his jaw was locked, tight with emotion he refused to show.

Roo shrank further into himself.

Say something. Anything. Tell them it wasn't your fault. Tell them he slipped.

His mother turned, eyes glassy and rimmed in red. She looked at Roo as if she were seeing him for the first time in hours.

"What happened?" she whispered. Her voice cracked like thin ice. "Roo... tell us."

He tried to speak, but nothing came. Then, like a dam opening for the first time, the words spilled out, shaking and broken.

"He was teasing me. I—I got mad and pushed him. I didn't mean to. I didn't mean for him to fall. I swear."

Silence filled the room for what seemed like ages.

His mother turned away, her whole body folding in on itself as fresh sobs overtook her. She reached for Jefferson's hand and gripped it like it was the only thing tethering her to the earth.

His father said nothing. Just exhaled—low and raw—and pressed his fists against his thighs, the tendons in his hands straining beneath his skin.

I didn't mean it. I didn't. But saying it doesn't change a thing.

Roo wanted to disappear, to crawl out of his skin. But instead, he stayed—silent and broken.

The next morning bled into the room through slatted blinds.

The door creaked open, but Roo didn't lift his head. He didn't have to. He could feel the shift in the air.

The doctor's footsteps were quiet and deliberate. His white coat whispered as he crossed the room. He paused at the end of Jefferson's bed, flipping through the chart like he already knew what he'd find but had to look.

Roo's parents straightened, hollow-eyed and sleepless. Roo remained on the floor, his back against the wall and arms wrapped around his knees.

The doctor closed the chart. His eyes rose to meet the parents.

"This is the hardest part of my job," he said, his voice steady, but low. He took a deep breath. "Overnight, the swelling increased. We repeated the scans early this morning. There's been a catastrophic brain bleed—most likely a delayed secondary hemorrhage. The damage is extensive and irreversible."

Roo's mother covered her mouth with both hands. Her body shook before sound even reached her lips. "What does that mean?" she said. "He's... still breathing."

"The machines are breathing for him," the doctor replied. "His brain is not functioning. We've run all confirmatory tests—there's no response to pain and no brainstem reflexes. We've done the apnea test. He's gone."

A silence fell so thick that it drowned even the machines.

"No," Roo's father said, stepping forward. "There has to be something. Another scan or maybe a specialist. It could be a coma, right? We can wait. He's strong. Jefferson's always been strong."

The doctor didn't look away. "I'm sorry," he said. "There's nothing more we can do."

Roo watched as his father's shoulders fell like a collapsing wall. His mother let out a sound that wasn't a sob—it was something more profound. Something that shook the room.

Roo closed his eyes.

Why did I push him? Why couldn't I just laugh it off like I always did before? I didn't mean to...

The grief returned in waves.

"Can you give us a minute, please?" Roo's mother said after a while, her voice paper-thin.

The doctor nodded and stepped out, leaving them alone with the hum of machines and the faint beep of borrowed time.

Please let this be a dream. I'll do anything. I'll take it back or trade places. Just don't let this be the end.

Time stretched on, with minutes feeling like hours.

The doctor returned. Roo's parents stood hand in hand.

"We're ready," his mother said, the words like stones in her throat.

"We've made our decision," his father added. "Please... make it peaceful."

The doctor's eyes shimmered. "I'll make sure of it."

He moved to the machines. With steady hands, he began disconnecting the web of wires and tubes. One by one, the rhythmic beeps faded until there was nothing. Nothing but the somber tone of the flat line on the monitor.

Roo's mother let out a low sob and collapsed into her husband's arms. They bent over Jefferson's still form, whispering their goodbyes with tear-filled eyes.

Roo stood frozen, the silence pressing against his chest like an iron weight.

He took two steps forward. His legs felt like they were walking through quicksand.

"I'm so sorry," he whispered. "I'm so sorry, Jefferson."

He reached out with a trembling hand and touched his brother's arm. "I love you," he said, voice cracking. "I always have."

The nurse in the corner bowed her head, tears brimming in her eyes. She had seen families break before—but this... this was different. This was the shattering of a boy.

The doctor turned to exit the room. On his way out, he managed to offer one more condolence. "I'm sorry for your loss."

Time slowed again, and the air thickened. The moment etched in Roo's brain—as the world exhaled without Jefferson in it.

The days following Jefferson's death passed in a blur—filled with faces, flowers, and a silence that offered no comfort, only a sense of accusation. Roo moved through it all like a ghost, acknowledging the phone calls, the casseroles, and the empty condolences that stung like paper cuts.

Now, a week later, he stood in the dim light of the funeral home, his parents on either side, though neither of them felt present. The scent of fresh flowers clung to the air.

Roo shifted his weight, glancing around the room. Conversations hummed around him in tones too soft to understand but heavy enough to bruise.

"It's as if there's a curse on this family," someone said behind him, just loud enough to land in his ears.

"Tragic accidents and brothers lost. Some at the hands of their own blood."

The words cut clean through him.

His stomach churned as he turned away, shoulders stiff and jaw clenched. The whispers weren't new, but here, among black suits and trembling hands, they felt as sharp as knives.

They know, or at least they think they do.

Amidst the mourners, Roo felt trapped between two tides: grief and guilt. One tide pulled, while the other crushed him.

His father stood stiff beside him while his mother dabbed at her eyes, each motion slow and deliberate. Roo stood small and unsure if he was part of the family or the cause of its undoing.

You were supposed to protect him. Not punish him for laughing.

Time slipped forward. This wasn't just a memory; it was a nightmare that repeated itself.

The house became a mausoleum.

Where there once were birthday banners and framed photos, there was now silence and shadows. Roo felt it first in the quiet—how it pressed against the walls like fog.

His father drifted into the bottle. Once full of loud stories and warm hands, he now stumbled home late, reeking of whiskey and rage, his eyes glassy with unspoken regret.

Roo became the closest target.

His mother faded away in a haze of pills. She moved through the house like mist. Her voice grew slurred, and her smile never returned. Roo could hear her cries every night.

Roo withdrew; first to his room, then to himself. The boy who once begged his brother to stay awake now barely whispered a word to anyone.

Every hallway held an echo, and every photo looked like a lie.

Weeks blurred into months. Months into years. But the pain didn't fade—it just changed shape.

I didn't mean it. But that doesn't matter, does it?

Time folded in on itself. Years collapsed into seconds.

Roo wasn't a child anymore; he wasn't surrounded by fresh flowers or whispered blame this time.

He stood alone in a bustling hotel lobby, twenty years old, dressed in clean jeans and a polo, hands twitching at his side. His heart thudded in his chest like it hadn't in years. The air buzzed with the energy of strangers—sounds of chatter, luggage wheels, and the hiss of espresso machines bounced around the lobby—but Roo didn't hear any of it.

He kept glancing at his phone. No missed call to say goodbye or a text with words of encouragement.

His parents' silence had stretched over the years like a fault line.

He took a slow breath. The hotel's scent mingled with brewed coffee and polished wood, yet those comforts still felt distant, as if they couldn't quite reach him.

He told himself he was ready. Basic training would be a clean slate, and he could earn back their love and make them proud.

A voice came from behind him. "Roosevelt Washington?"

Roo turned to see a bike courier approaching. The courier looked winded and was lopsided, with his helmet tilted to one side as he held out an envelope.

"Yeah... I'm Roo."

"This is for you. I went to your room first. The receptionist said I might catch you here."

Roo took the envelope, which was heavier than it seemed. The paper felt old and thick, the kind that conveyed importance and authority. His name was written in dark ink.

In the corner, a symbol caught his eye: An ornate "E," circled by three stars.

One above. One to the left. One to the right.

Something about it stirred a sense of déjà vu.

With cautious fingers, he opened the flap. The paper inside shimmered in the light, its edges worn, as though it had been waiting a long time to be read.

The words danced across the page, each one sharp and strange.

'Your brother's memory will not fade—it is the shadow you must carry. When the Eagle falls, you will become a father to the butterflies. Death will dance with you, and the Nine will awaken.'

The hair on the back of his neck stood up. Someone was watching.

He turned around in circles, looking for anybody who seemed out of place. The lobby bustled with tourists, bellhops, and a woman dragging a pink suitcase, but no one was looking at him.

Still, the weight of the letter clung to him.

Death will dance with you.

He didn't know why, but those words settled in his chest like a premonition.

He folded the letter, careful not to crease the words, and tucked it into his backpack. The moment felt important, like the first step into something much larger than the weight he'd been carrying.

The memory broke like glass, and the hotel vanished. Jefferson's laugh faded into nothing. Roo's subconscious clutched at the last echoes of the dream, but they slipped through him like smoke.

And then came warmth, the scent of pine, and whispers calling his name. The dream was gone.

CHAPTER TWENTY-ONE

Brutus and the Bear

Roo woke with a sharp gasp, his chest heaving as though the fall had knocked the air from his lungs. Jefferson's scream still echoed inside his skull, that awful thud still replaying behind his eyes. He didn't move at first; he just lay there, staring at a wooden ceiling, afraid that if he blinked, he'd still be in the hospital hallway or beside his brother's bed.

The air around him smelled unusual, not like antiseptic, sorrow, or hospital rooms. He smelled pine, and something else, something faint and floral, like lavender and peaches.

The room was too warm, too still. The faint crackle of fire replaced the shrill wail of machines. Something snored nearby, low, wet, and unbothered.

He sat up, wincing at the dull ache in his skull. The blanket slipped from his shoulders as he swung his legs over the edge of the bed. His heels met cold wood. He let his toes press into it, feeling the uneven texture of the log-planked floor beneath his bare feet.

Split logs made up the walls, their grain raised and uneven. Moonlight filtered through thin curtains, casting silver puddles on the floor.

Outside of the room, he could hear snuffling and snorting; something stout and determined was just beyond the door. Roo's shoulders tensed in anticipation.

He rubbed his eyes and let his hands fall into his lap. He should've felt grateful to be alive, but all he felt was the weight of the letter still tucked inside his bag. Be a father to the butterflies...

Jefferson's name hovered just behind his lips.

He didn't know if the ache in his chest came from the dream or the waking.

A voice, soft and familiar, cut through the quiet. "You're awake."

Roo turned his head toward the sound, but it felt like dragging his thoughts through syrup. Lizzie stood a few feet away, wrapped in firelight, her eyes tired but warm.

"How are you feeling?" she asked.

He groaned as he shifted, every joint crackling like old wood. His body felt used—like he'd been folded and left in the rain.

"I've been worse," he said, rubbing his neck. "What happened? What is that awful sound?"

From somewhere beyond the walls came a thick, wet snore—something between a chainsaw and a leaky accordion.

Lizzie chuckled under her breath, stepping closer. "Sit down before you fall. This is going to sound... unbelievable."

Still foggy, Roo blinked at her, then lowered himself into the chair beside the bed. "How long was I out?"

"About ten hours," she said. "You hit your head hard on the root of a tree. It was a nasty fall."

249

Images came back in flashes: the startled bear, the duffel bag slipping from his hands, and the rock that he tripped on.

"Right... I remember the bear. I was trying to grab the duffel bag, and then everything just... went black." He rubbed the back of his skull, fingertips brushing a tender lump. His brow pulled together. "What happened after that? How did we end up here?"

Lizzie's smile twisted into something between disbelief and amusement.

"Well, Ramirez saw you fall and carried you for miles. He continued until he just couldn't anymore."

Roo blinked, squinting like the words didn't quite add up.

"Ramirez? Carried me?"

Lizzie nodded. "Swear on my life."

Roo leaned back, eyes narrowing. "Are you sure I'm not still dreaming?"

That pulled a full laugh from her. "Oh, trust me—it gets even weirder." She lifted her hands, gesturing as she spoke, the firelight catching on her fingers. "So there we are, trying to figure out what to do, when we hear this wheezing, panting sound—like someone running a marathon through a kazoo. Out of nowhere comes this pudgy little bulldog, barreling through the trees like a bowling ball with legs."

Roo stared at her, expressionless. "A bulldog?"

"Not just any bulldog," she said, leaning in. "Brutus." She said the name as if it carried a legend. "This stumpy, soaking wet tank of a dog charged right at the bear, barking and snorting. He looked like he was going to take it down himself. He smelled like he'd rolled in a swamp and then dared nature to do something about it."

Roo let out a disbelieving laugh, shaking his head. "You're kidding."

"I wish I were. We were standing there, frozen, when we heard a voice shout, 'Brutus! Where are you, boy?' Out of the brush came this gigantic man—wearing a flannel shirt and suspenders, with a shotgun already raised. He fired once, then again, and the bear dropped."

Roo blinked, trying to follow the absurdity of it all. "So, you're telling me... a fat bulldog picked a fight with a bear... and then his lumberjack owner came out of the woods and saved the day?"

Lizzie grinned, nodding. "Pretty much."

Roo shook his head again, rubbing his temple like the impact had somehow knocked the realism out of the world.

"That's..."

"Ridiculous?" Lizzie said. "Yeah. It was, but Brutus—oh man, he thought he did it all. Strutted around like he'd just saved humanity. Wagging tail and puffed-up chest, looking like he expected a medal." She chuckled again, softer this time. "I'm not sure he even heard the shotgun blasts. He acted as if he were the one who brought the bear down."

Roo opened his mouth to respond, but before he could, he noticed that the snoring had stopped. A moment of silence followed, and then he heard it.

Thud. Thud. Thud.

It had a rhythmic quality, heavy and purposeful.

Lizzie straightened, eyes wide. Roo blinked toward the door.

"No," he said, sitting up straighter. "No. What is that?"

The thudding grew louder, now accompanied by a frantic snuffling and the distinct sound of nails scrambling for traction on the hardwood.

"Lizzie..." Roo said, backing further into his seat. "What is coming through that—"

WHAM.

251

The door burst open as if it had been head-butted by a bowling ball, and in barreled a blur of damp fur, flapping jowls, and pure, unfiltered confidence.

"No, no, no—!"

It was too late.

Brutus launched himself like a furry missile. Roo shielded his face before the bulldog landed in his lap with the grace of a cannonball.

"GAH—get him off me!"

What followed could only be described as an assault of slobber. Brutus's tongue was everywhere—cheeks, nose, eyes— moving with the chaotic energy of a busted fire hose. His whole body wiggled with glee, tail wagging like it was trying to take flight.

"He's licking my eyeballs!" Roo said in between half-laughs and choked protests. "Why is he so... wet?"

Lizzie had collapsed against the wall, clutching her stomach in laughter. "That's the hero of the hour!"

Brutus paused only to inhale, then doubled down on his affection, snorting like a hog at a buffet. Roo flailed half-heartedly, trying to push him off, but Brutus just oozed deeper into his lap like a melting bag of sand.

"You've got to be kidding me," Roo said, wiping a long streak of drool from his temple.

Still giggling, Lizzie bent down and gave Brutus a proud pat. "He's got the soul of a warrior and the breath of a sewer grate."

Brutus let out a triumphant snort, turned in a slow circle (half on, half off Roo), and collapsed with his full weight across Roo's thighs. Satisfied with his victory, he resumed his nap. The sounds of snoring once again enveloped the room.

Roo stared down at the snoring heap of flesh. "This is my life now."

Lizzie beamed. "Thank you, Brutus. I needed that laugh."

She looked at Roo, her smile lingering. "If we survive all this, I'm telling everyone about the legend of Brutus and the bear."

Roo sighed, wiping one last smear of drool from his chin as Brutus let out a satisfied grunt in his sleep.

"You're impossible," he said.

Lizzie's expression shifted, softening into something quieter—more intimate—as her eyes drifted back to Roo. "While you were out," she said, "you were talking in your sleep. You kept mentioning your brother... and something about a letter."

The smile fell from Roo's face like a dropped stone. His hand rested on Brutus's back, the dog now a warm, snoring lump across his lap. He looked away, staring at the floor and then beyond it—toward a memory still smoldering in the dark.

"I wasn't honest with you," he said. "Earlier, when you asked."

Lizzie didn't move. She just listened.

He drew in a long breath, bracing himself.

"I caused his death. My brother, Jefferson, was ten years old. It was a stupid accident. We were on the playground, and he teased me. I shoved him just once, not even hard, but he fell."

The words came easier than he expected, but they still burned on the way out. He paused, swallowing against the burn in his throat.

"He hit his head, and I watched the life drain out of him. My parents—" His voice faltered. "They couldn't even look at me after that. I kept telling myself it was an accident, but deep down, they didn't believe it... neither did I."

He risked a glance at Lizzie, then looked away again, afraid of what he might see—pity maybe, or worse, fear.

Why did I tell her?

He felt the weight of it now—the shame crawling up his spine, pressing against his ribs. He half expected her to shift away, to find an excuse to leave the room.

To his surprise she didn't. Instead, she reached out, resting a hand on his arm.

Her touch was warm and comforting. "Roo," she said, her voice breaking, "I'm so sorry. That's awful. I don't know how you've carried that all these years."

He shrugged, his fingers brushing through Brutus's fur again, grateful for the distraction. "It hasn't been easy," he said. "The guilt... it doesn't fade. It just settles in like dust on old furniture."

"You were just a kid," Lizzie said. "Blaming yourself won't bring him back, and it sure as hell doesn't mean you deserved to be abandoned."

"That's what I try to tell myself," Roo said. "My parents... they made their decision. After that, I wasn't their son. I was just a reminder."

"It's not fair of them to put that on you," she said. "You needed them."

Roo's voice cracked. "It's been lonely without them."

"You're not alone anymore." She said it like a vow. "I'm here, Roo. Whatever this is—whatever's coming—we'll face it together."

His throat tightened. He nodded, not trusting himself to speak.

For the first time in a long time, something inside him shifted. The first flicker of peace —like a light seen from far off, breaking through the dark.

A moment of silence passed and then a smell wafted through the air like smoke through a window.

Roo's nose wrinkled, and Lizzie blinked.

"Do you smell that?" she said, half-choking.

Roo turned toward Brutus, who hadn't moved an inch—still sprawled across his lap like a sandbag full of pudding, snoring like a locomotive.

"Oh no," Roo said.

Lizzie fanned her face with one hand. "Is that him?"

Roo gagged. "It's gotta be. That wasn't me—I'd be dead."

They both looked at the bulldog, who snorted once, pleased with himself.

Roo groaned, pressing his sleeve to his face. "Unbelievable. I open my soul, and he opens his—ugh."

Lizzie cracked up, her laugh muffled by her shirt. "Emotional support and biological warfare. What a guy!"

Brutus twitched in his sleep, his tail giving a lazy little thump-thump against Roo's leg.

After their laughter died down—fanned away by the last lingering whiff of Brutus's betrayal—Lizzie leaned back, her smile fading into something more thoughtful.

"You mentioned a letter in your sleep," she said. "What was that about?"

Roo's hand drifted toward the bag near the bed, fingertips brushing its strap before he motioned for her to bring it over.

"It's in there," he said. "I'll show you."

She fetched it without a word, handing it over with a look of cautious curiosity. Roo unzipped it and pulled out the letter with both hands.

The paper was worn, creased, weather-stained, and soft around the edges from excessive handling. He turned it once in his fingers before passing it to her.

Lizzie unfolded the letter with care, the pages whispering as they opened. Her eyes moved across the words.

"'Death will dance with you...'" she said, her voice catching on the phrase. She glanced up at Roo. "That's... comforting."

Roo gave a humorless chuckle. "Keep going."

"The butterflies... are they people? Or actual butterflies?"

"I don't know," Roo said. "I've tried to throw it away more times than I can count, but something always stops me. Every time, it just... feels wrong."

Lizzie flipped the envelope over, her thumb brushing a faint mark on the back. She held it up toward the firelight.

"There's a symbol here," she said. "It's hard to see—but it's... ornate. Like something from a seal or a crest."

Roo leaned in but didn't take it back.

"I've seen it before, on the envelope, and once in a dream. I don't know what it means, but it feels important."

Lizzie squinted at it, tracing the edges. "Maybe Dr. Solomon could help. He's good with symbols. He's got that whole 'ancient texts and weird trivia' vibe."

Roo arched an eyebrow, a half-smile curling at the corner of his mouth. "That's... a good idea. I'll show it to him as soon as I can."

She nodded, still studying the page. After a few moments, she folded it and offered it back to Roo. "It might be more important than you realize."

He tucked the letter back into his bag, and Brutus let out a low, contented snort that echoed in the silence like a punctuation mark.

Lizzie smiled. "Of course, he's still asleep. Saves the world, ruins the air, then knocks out like a champion."

Roo glanced down at the dog draped over his legs like a furry sandbag. "This is the stuff of legends."

Despite the weight of the conversation, the moment felt lighter. Roo sensed it: the start of something genuine, delicate, and unusual—hovering between the warmth of the fire, the handwritten letter, and the sound of the snoring dog.

The door creaked open, hinges protesting like old knees in winter. A broad-shouldered man stepped into the frame, nearly filling it—tall, weathered, and carved from a life outdoors. His black hair was streaked with silver; his beard was trimmed but wild enough to suggest he cared little for mirrors.

He smelled of pine, smoke, and something rich and earthy—like soil after rain. The warmth of the fire met him halfway, crackling louder as if acknowledging his return.

Thick boots thudded against the wood floor with each step. His flannel shirt was rolled at the sleeves, suspenders creaking as he adjusted them with a practiced tug. His clothes were worn but clean, the kind that told stories without saying a word.

He paused, taking in Roo and Lizzie with a sweep of sharp, clear eyes, and then he smiled—a wide, genuine smile that turned the room a little warmer.

"Well, look who joined the land of the living," he said. His voice was deep and smooth, like coffee laced with a hint of laughter. "I was thinking you were gonna sleep right through winter."

He gave his suspenders a dramatic snap and strode forward, extending a rough, calloused hand. Roo reached up and shook it, surprised by the sheer solidity of the man.

"Norman Markus," he said. "Folks around here just call me Big Norm."

"Nice to meet you," Roo replied, his voice still a little raw.

He could feel the strength in Norm's grip, it was steady, like a tree that didn't mind the wind.

257

Norm turned to Lizzie next, his eyes softening. "This one here hasn't left your side," he said, nodding toward her with a half-grin. "Even shooed me out once when I got too close. You two must mean a lot to each other."

Lizzie's face went red, and she chuckled in embarrassment. "Just wanted to make sure he woke up with both kidneys."

Roo shifted in his seat, acutely aware of both Brutus's dead weight on his lap and the teasing glint in Norm's eye.

"You two hungry?" Big Norm asked.

A savory aroma drifted into the room—roasted meat, herbs, and fresh bread. His stomach let out a low, unmistakable growl that echoed louder than intended.

Norm raised an eyebrow. "Well, I reckon that's a yes." He chuckled and clapped his hands together. "Come on then. Supper's ready. You'll need your strength—especially if Brutus plans on using you for a mattress again tonight."

He turned and disappeared down the hallway, boots stomping against the floor.

Brutus slid off Roo's lap with a dramatic grunt and waddled after Norm with his usual swagger, nails clicking like an overconfident metronome.

They followed him into a dining room that felt like something out of a storybook—walls lined with shelves, jars, and hand-carved ornaments. A large wooden table sat in the center, worn smooth by use and time. Steam curled from bowls of food in the middle: venison stew, thick-cut bread, roasted root vegetables, and something that smelled like apple pie.

The warmth of it all—the light, the smell, and the company—settled over Roo like a blanket. For the first time in days, he felt something close to safe.

As the rest of the group trickled in, it didn't take long to realize there weren't quite enough chairs to go around. A few members claimed spots along the walls, balancing their plates while leaning against timber beams or crouching by the hearth. No one complained. The food smelled too good, the fire warm, and the company comforting.

Brutus, of course, had claimed his spot early, sprawled beneath the table like a furry landmine, his eyes locked on the meat above like a soldier watching for movement.

"Ah, there he is!" Norm yelled, clapping his hands together with a grin. "The man of the hour. History tells us Brutus killed Caesar—now they'll say he went toe-to-claw with a grizzly."

A ripple of quiet laughter circled the room.

Toward the far end of the table, Madison and Savannah sat side by side, their hands folded in front of them, eyes wide as they took it all in. Norm placed a stack of old paper and a weathered box of crayons between them—edges frayed and colors half-used.

"I figured you might like these," he said, his voice softening. "My granddaughter left them here years ago. Thought they'd be more fun in your hands than collecting dust."

Madison gave a polite "Thank you,"

Savannah dove in headfirst, already arranging her crayons by hue like a tiny curator.

At the table, Norm reached over his plate and plucked a thick strip of meat, tossing it underhand beneath the table. Brutus caught it midair with a lazy chomp, his jaws snapping shut with surgical precision. He gave an appreciative grunt, then resumed his curled position, snoring like he hadn't just been fed like royalty.

Roo smirked, glancing across the table. "So... are we eating grizzly bear tonight?"

Norm let out a belly laugh that filled the room, his shoulders shaking, hair catching the firelight. "Hell no, boy! That beast was too much work for me and Brutus to drag back, and trust me, he wasn't offering to help." He jabbed a thumb toward the dog under the table. "This here's venison. I took it down myself a couple of weeks ago. Little garlic, a bit of rosemary, and a lot of patience."

He gestured toward the spread, steam rising off stew pots and platters like fog on a mountain trail. "Go on, make a plate. You'll need the energy."

The group didn't need a second invitation. Conversation picked up—quiet but easy—as spoons clinked, bowls passed hands, and the aroma of roasted meat and warm bread filled the cabin like a blessing.

Roo scooped stew onto his plate, grabbed a thick slice of bread, and took his seat again. For the first time in what felt like days, he let himself exhale. No battles or dreams and no guilt clawing at the back of his throat.

Just warmth, food, laughter, and Brutus curled up under the table, still convinced he was the reason they were all alive.

Dr. Terracotta eased into the chair beside Roo. "Ramirez is on the front porch," he said, his voice low. "He hasn't said much since he carried you."

Roo paused, his spoon halfway to his mouth. He glanced toward the front door, guilt creeping up the back of his neck. "I'll talk to him in the morning," he said. "I owe him that much."

He let the words hang there for a moment, then turned back to Terracotta with a gentler tone. "Go on, Doc. Grab some food. You're gonna need it."

Terracotta hesitated—just for a breath—then gave a quiet nod and rose without another word, slipping into the line near the hearth.

Across the table, Dr. Solomon was still, tracing the rim of his plate with a fingertip, lost in thought. His meal sat forgotten, the edge of his bread dipping into the cooling stew.

"Your scar's healing up," Roo said, breaking the silence.

A faint smile tugged at the corner of his mouth.

"Any luck with that book yet?"

Solomon offered a half-shrug. "No luck," he said. "Not yet."

Roo reached into his bag and pulled out the letter—the one that had haunted his thoughts for years and somehow felt heavier now than ever before. He slid it across the table.

"You're good with symbols," he said. "Thought you might recognize this."

Solomon's gaze sharpened as he picked up the letter with careful fingers. He turned it, studying the edges, then angled it toward the firelight to catch the faint design stamped on the back.

"I've never seen this before," he said after a long moment. "But it's... deliberate. Whoever made this didn't want it recognized by accident."

He traced a finger along the edge of the symbol.

"Mind if I keep it for a while? I've got some older texts I can compare them against. Maybe something will turn up."

Roo nodded. "Sure," he said, the word carrying more weight than it should.

Solomon tucked the letter away with practiced precision, as if he were shelving a classified file, then returned to his meal without another word.

Roo watched him for a moment, then picked up his spoon.

A quiet minute passed, filled only with the soft scrape of spoons and the occasional clink of ceramic.

Lizzie glanced up from her plate, her eyes scanning the room. "You know," she said, breaking the silence, "I don't think we all know each other yet. What are your names? Where are you from?"

There was a beat of hesitation—then the tall man at the far end of the table sat a little straighter. "Hans," he said. His voice was crisp, his German accent light but unmistakable. "Weapons specialist. German Air Force." He gave a slight nod, more military than friendly.

Next was the man beside him, broader in build, with dark stubble and a grin that came easy. "Viktor," he said, placing a heavy hand over his heart. "Loadmaster, U.S. Air Force—but my blood's Russian. My parents came to America before I was born. I cook better than I fight, but I'm decent at both."

A few chuckles rumbled around the table.

Salvador leaned forward, his posture relaxed, fingers steepled as if he were used to briefings. "Salvador, Spanish Navy," he said, his voice smooth, almost musical. "I was stationed in Alaska to observe a new radar system. Got caught in Armageddon—never expected to end up here."

Haru spoke next, his tone quiet but assured. "Haru," he said. "This is Akira." He gestured to the woman beside him, who offered a quick nod. "Engine specialists. Japanese Air Force. We were on a temporary exchange when..." He trailed off, waving his hand toward the window.

"Everything changed," Akira finished in a gentle voice. "It is good to still be breathing."

The woman at the edge of the table—slight, elegant, with piercing green eyes—offered a small smile. "Charlotte," she said. "Weapons systems, French Air Force. I was in Anchorage for war games, and then I wasn't." Her voice was smooth, but her fingers toyed with her fork.

When the circle came back around, Roo, Lizzie, and the two doctors kept it short. Lizzie just gave her name. Solomon muttered something vague about religious texts. Roo's explanation was brief—until he spoke of Ramirez.

"That's Ramirez outside. He's been through a lot in the last few days."

There was a pause. No one pressed further.

As plates emptied and bellies filled, conversation picked up. Slowly at first, like warm water over frozen ground. Viktor told a story about losing a crate of supplies over the Bering Sea. Salvador added one about a misfired flare that lit up a general's house.

Even Hans cracked a dry joke about German rations being worse than snow. Haru and Akira shared a rare smile between themselves. Charlotte asked Norm for more tea and surprised everyone by adding a cube of sugar and a drop of milk.

Brutus, ever present, let out the occasional grunt or snore beneath the table, only stirring when Norm flicked him a piece of meat.

For a little while, the world outside didn't exist. There was warmth, laughter, full stomachs, and calm voices. A moment people hoped would last forever.

One by one, the group trickled away—dishes clinked in the kitchen, beds creaked behind hallway doors. Roo lingered at the table, watching the firelight dance across the grain of the old wood.

Brutus let out a final, victorious snort and shifted position with the weight of a stone.

The room fell quiet, but it wasn't empty.

Roo and Lizzie lingered as the others drifted toward sleep, their quiet goodnights fading down the hall like the end of a song. The warmth of the fire remained, its light flickering across the log walls. Brutus stretched beneath the table, snoring in sync with the crackle of burning wood.

"Big Norm?" Lizzie asked, turning to their host. "You got a minute?"

Norm glanced up from the sink, hands wet and sleeves rolled. "Always," he said, wiping his hands on a towel. "What's on your mind?"

Lizzie hesitated, her brows pinching. "How are you so calm with everything happening? The world feels like it's falling apart."

Norm chuckled—a low, chest-deep sound that filled the cabin. "Out here?" he said, sweeping a hand toward the walls. "It's just me and Brutus. No phones and no panic. Just the wild and its rhythms. We hunt and hike. Sometimes we tangle with a bear, but even chaos has a rhythm if you know how to listen to it."

Lizzie's expression tightened. "So... you don't know what's happening? The flying ships? Those... howls?"

Norm nodded, his tone turning graver. "I've seen things in the sky and heard sounds that didn't belong in any forest, but I've learned not to chase what I can't catch. If this is the end of the world, then I'll go down fighting—so long as Brutus is by my side." He paused for a moment. "But I didn't bring you here out of pity."

Lizzie tilted her head. "Why did you bring us then?"

Norm looked down at the floor, his thumb brushing over a rough patch on the edge of the counter. "I did twenty-four years in the Marines. Saw the worst men could do to each other—and sometimes what we did to ourselves. When I came back, I wasn't really back; not until I found him." He nodded toward Brutus, whose snoring now sounded like slow thunder under the table. "I found him in the woods—scrawny, limping, and stubborn. I took him in, and somehow, that dog taught me how to breathe again." His voice cracked. "He doesn't care who I used to be. Just that I'm here. When he ran at that bear for you... I saw something in his eyes. He knew you were worth saving."

Lizzie's eyes glistened. "Thank you," she said. "From all of us. We wouldn't have made it without you or him."

Norm waved a hand. "You don't owe me anything. Just rub his belly once in a while. That's all he's ever asked."

He stretched with a groan, joints popping. "I'm headed to bed. Make yourselves at home for as long as you need." With that, he turned and disappeared down the hallway, leaving Roo and Lizzie in firelight and silence.

After a moment, Roo shifted. "Lizzie," he said, "there's something I've been meaning to show you. It's what Jefferson was teasing me about on the playground." He lifted the edge of his shirt, revealing a birthmark just above his hip. Dark red, almost the color of dried blood, shaped like a crescent moon.

Lizzie leaned in to take a closer look.

"Is that...?"

"I don't know," Roo said. "Maybe? It always felt like it meant something, even before all this."

Lizzie hesitated for a moment before lifting her shirt to reveal a mark near her ribs—a star of the same shade of red. "I have one too," she said. "No idea what it means, but we're not alone in this."

Before Roo could respond, Lizzie yawned. "I haven't slept much since you knocked yourself out," she said with a tired smile. "I'm calling it a night. Goodnight, Roo."

"Goodnight, Lizzie."

He watched her retreat down the hall. Only after she was gone did he whisper, "In the morning... I need to talk to Ramirez. I owe him more than thanks."

He sat for a while, listening to the crackling of the fire. After a while, he stood up and wandered into the living room.

Madison and Savannah sat cross-legged on the floor, heads bent over scattered crayons and paper. Roo leaned down beside them.

"What are you two drawing?"

"Butterflies," Savannah said without looking up. Her coloring was careful. "Mother used to call us her little butterflies. She said we danced like them."

Roo froze.

Be a father to the butterflies.

The words from the letter crashed into him like a tidal wave. His breath hitched. He gripped the back of the couch for balance, the weight of it all pressing hard into his chest.

"It can't be," he said. "Is this... is this how I honor him?"

Savannah looked up with curiosity but remained silent. She returned to coloring, the wings on her paper glowing in orange and purple.

Roo lowered himself to the floor beside them, lost in thought, while their laughter and the soft scratch of crayons grounded him to the moment.

Elsewhere in the cabin, Lizzie moved through the hallway, preparing for bed, but something outside the window caught her eye.

A shadow. It didn't move like an animal.

She stepped closer, heart skipping, and pulled the curtain aside just enough to see the trees.

Moonlight filtered through the canopy in pale ribbons, and there stood a figure cloaked in deep purple at the forest's edge. He watched like a sentinel carved from the night, patient and eternal.

She couldn't see his eyes, but she felt them.

He tilted his head, then turned and melted into the trees, swallowed by darkness.

Lizzie stayed frozen at the window, her breath fogging the glass.

I'm overtired, she told herself. *It wasn't real.*

She closed the curtain and stepped back, but the feeling didn't leave her.

Sliding into bed, she pulled the blanket tight and listened to Brutus snoring in the next room. The sound should've comforted her, but it didn't.

Her eyes stayed open long after the fire died.

Beyond the cabin, in the shadows of the trees, the night deepened. Leaves rustled without wind.

Far away, rain fell over Washington, D.C.—a quiet beginning to something far louder.

In the woods behind the cabin, unseen eyes remained fixed on the house.

A storm was coming, and even here—deep in the wilderness—no one would be safe.

CHAPTER TWENTY-TWO

Monsters in the White House

The skies above Washington, D.C., opened with a steady, unrelenting rain. It fell in cold sheets, blurring the monuments and washing the city in a gray that felt permanent. Thunder rolled overhead—low and distant, like something ancient clearing its throat.

Far beneath the soaked streets, in the war room beneath the White House, the air felt just as heavy. Fluorescent lights buzzed overhead, casting a sterile glow on every pale face around the table. The bunker was sealed, secure, and suffocating.

President Davidson stood near the center, silent and unmoving. His eyes weren't on the screens, maps, or blinking alerts; they were fixed on the hands of the men and women around him—some trembling, some clenched, none at ease.

The room smelled of metal and recycled air. Every breath felt filtered and dry, like the taste of old pennies. In one corner, someone whispered a prayer, while another person rubbed the bridge of their nose until it turned red. No one spoke above a whisper.

Davidson sat down, as if the weight on his shoulders didn't move with him. His jacket, still damp from earlier, clung to his back. He ran his fingers across the tabletop out of habit—like tracing the edge of a cliff he'd already fallen from.

"Any word from Anchorage?" he asked without lifting his head.

One aide cleared his throat. "No, sir. The channel is still dark. We've tried every frequency."

Davidson nodded once, but the silence that followed made the answer echo. "Let me know the second that changes," he said, his voice low and raw. Every person in that room could feel the storm outside, but it was the storm inside him they feared most. They knew it wouldn't erupt.

The president leaned forward, his elbows on the table, with his forehead resting in his hand. The monitors in front of him flickered—satellite feeds, encrypted maps, and a white outline of the city vanished beneath a blanket of static.

Somewhere above them, something massive moved through the clouds.

The Finger of Eden emerged first, cutting through the storm like a dagger through cloth. Its vents released streams of shimmering mist that curled downward in graceful spirals. However, the Eden Veil didn't follow. There was no shimmer of light or suffocating dome, only the steady and relentless rain remained, drenching the city below.

Beneath the storm, the streets of Washington stayed still. The downpour drummed against rooftops and pavement, filling gutters and pooling in the fractured concrete. It was as if the world knew what hovered above it and chose silence as its only defense.

One of the Architect's ships followed, descending through the clouds with a predator's grace. Lightning split the sky, casting its jagged silhouette in strobing flashes. Its underbelly pulsed with an eerie green light, illuminating the drenched stone of the Washington Monument. Rain hissed against the ship's surface, boiling into steam where it met the radiant heat of its engines.

With a groan that echoed like thunder, the ship's ramp unfurled. A blast of pressurized air hissed into the storm, the sound sharp and final, like the opening of a sealed tomb.

The first of the Nephilim stepped into the light. Its skin was mottled in shades of ash and crimson, stretched tight over muscles that flexed beneath like coiled ropes. Water cascaded down its elongated limbs, catching flashes of lightning and reflecting them in brief glimmers—like firelight in a grave.

Claws as dark as midnight scraped against the metal ramp, each step leaving deep grooves in the steel. Its chest expanded with a deep, guttural inhale before it roared—primal and unnatural. The sound didn't just fill the air; it pushed against it, vibrating through the city's bones.

The Nephilim crouched low, its grotesque frame coiled tight— more jungle predator than soldier, perched in the canopy, locked on its prey.

For a moment, the city stood still. Even the rain seemed to pause.

Then a primal roar erupted as it sprang into action, plunging downward from the ramp. Its dark claws flared wide, catching flashes of lightning as it twisted in midair. The sky roared in protest as the Nephilim hurtled toward the monument.

For a moment, it was suspended—its grotesque body outlined against the storm-split sky. It collided with the Washington Monument with a thunderclap.

The stone splintered downward like roots from a tree upon impact.

The creature latched on with ease, its claws carving deep into the marble. It scaled the monument with twisted precision, limbs contorting like a spider climbing its web. Rain streamed down its back, tracing the ridges and scars of a body long since abandoned by the divine.

It climbed to the summit. Perched atop the obelisk, it raised one clawed hand high into the storm and screamed—a cry of both triumph and torment that echoed across the city, reshaping the surrounding storm.

One by one, more Nephilim emerged from the ramp, each one more monstrous than the last. They landed like meteors, crashing into the earth with a bone-rattling force. Some sprinted forward on all fours, while others stood upright, towering silhouettes against the lightning.

They swarmed the monument like locusts.

Claws pierced the stone as they climbed, causing the marble to groan under their weight. Their eyes glowed with a sickly red hue, cutting through the downpour like embers behind a veil of smoke. As they ascended, they snarled and snapped, the noise carrying the weight of a hatred steeped for millennia.

To the world below, the Washington Monument, once a proud symbol of unity, was now topped with monsters, a grotesque mockery of conquest. Yet, the rain continued to fall. It drenched the city, clinging to the monsters and bearing witness to the return of the fallen sons of Eden.

Deep within the bunker, President Davidson stared at the live feed flickering across the monitor. Rain blurred the image, but the horror was unmistakable—the monument to American resilience now crowned with beasts. He clenched his fists as thunder crashed above, masking the gasps of those behind him.

Outside, the ship descended. Its engines exhaled a last sigh as it settled beside the Washington Monument. Rain hissed against its cooling hull, steam curling upward like smoke from a battlefield. The reflection pool rippled, fractured by the relentless downpour and the sickly green light bleeding from the ship's underside.

Haligot came storming out like a Greek god walking out of Olympus. He stepped into the rain as if it parted for him. Each heavy footfall echoed across the pavement with a sense of finality. His spear was slung low at his side, its jagged blade catching flashes of lightning. Raindrops danced across its surface, the rhythm steady and hypnotic—like the ticking of a bomb waiting to detonate.

Behind him, the Nephilim assembled.

Their distorted forms stood in perfect formation, shoulders heaving with anticipation. Claws hung at their sides like unsheathed weapons, and their eyes—deep-set and smoldering—flickered with hatred long cultivated.

Haligot raised his spear and pointed it toward the White House in a slow, deliberate motion. "My loyal Nephilim," he said, his voice deep and resonant, cutting through the storm. "Our lord has given us a mission. The leader of these insects is hiding in that palace." He paused, savoring the mockery in his tone. "Locate and capture him. Bring him in alive. Our lord demands him unharmed... for the arena." The last word dripped like poison.

The legion stirred, massive feet shifting in rhythm, each step splashing onto the flooded pavement with a heavy, deliberate beat. Their movements were synchronized and unnatural—like marionettes moved by one unseen hand.

The rain intensified, pouring off their twisted forms, but it did nothing to hinder their advance. The sound of boots and claws against the waterlogged streets grew like the beat of a war drum. As they spread through the city, the echoes of their passage followed: shattering glass, collapsing walls, and the distant cries of those who were too slow to escape.

Haligot remained behind. His sneer deepened as he watched them disappear into the storm—a storm that, unlike the one long ago, posed no threat. The rain stung against his skin, but it didn't wound him. Not like before.

He glanced upward. The clouds churned above him, thick, but it wasn't the flood. This rain would pass. They were on solid ground now, and on land, they were gods.

Haligot turned toward the Washington Monument, the obelisk now defiled, its stone face carved by claws and crowned with beasts. He tightened his grip on the spear. Its blade pulsed, as if sharing in his anticipation.

"Run, insects," he said, louder than the falling rain. "There is no escape."

In the White House bunker, the tension draped over the room like a wet blanket. The steady hum of monitors mixed with the faint crackle of radio static, each sound a metronome counting down to disaster. President Davidson stood at the head of the room; one hand planted on the table and the other clenched at his side as his advisors relayed the latest updates on the Nephilim's relentless advance.

"They've reached the Washington Monument," a military advisor said, his voice tight with urgency. "Their leader has ordered you taken alive, and a Finger of Eden hovers overhead."

Davidson's jaw tightened. His tired frame straightened with purpose, shedding the weariness of office for the steel of command.

"We don't surrender. Not today." He turned to the head of the Secret Service. "Mobilize all agents. Equip them with everything we have and bring me a weapon as well."

The chief nodded and strode out, already barking into his radio.

Davidson shifted to the generals lining the wall. "Arm yourselves. We make our stand right here."

The room erupted in chaos as chairs scraped and boots thundered. The sharp, metallic clatter of weapons being distributed echoed beneath the bunker's low ceiling. Muffled thunder rolled overhead, blending with the storm's relentless drumming.

Davidson's eyes scanned the room. He noticed the fear etched into the lines around mouths and trembling in hands—but deeper still, he recognized resolve.

"They expect us to cower," he said, his voice firm, cutting clean through the chaos. "But this is our home, city, and country. Let them try to take it."

A charge rippled through the room. Hands gripped rifles tighter. Sweat beaded on foreheads as adrenaline surged. Fear didn't leave but changed shape. It sharpened into purpose.

The sound of weapons locking into place rang out like a call to arms. The ground vibrated beneath their boots as the Nephilim marched closer—a rhythmic tremor that made the walls feel thinner with every passing second.

Davidson put on a bulletproof vest given to him by an aide. His movements were smooth. The burden of the presidency hadn't dulled the soldier within him.

Davidson caught the eye of a junior agent near the rear wall— no more than a kid, his hands trembling as he fumbled with his rifle's magazine.

"What's your name, soldier?" Davidson asked, voice steady with quiet authority.

The agent snapped his eyes forward. "Taylor, sir."

Davidson stepped closer, the clatter of boots and weapons fading into the background. He rested a firm hand on the young man's shoulder to ground him.

"You ever held a weapon in a live op before, Taylor?"

The agent shook his head. "No, sir."

Davidson gave a grim nod. "In my first firefight, my hands shook so bad that I dropped the magazine before I even chambered a round. I thought I was going to get us all killed."

Taylor blinked in surprise.

Davidson continued, his voice low and eyes locked on his. "Courage doesn't mean being calm. It means moving through fear and doing your job. If your hands shake? Let them. Just don't let your feet move."

Taylor nodded, his grip tightening on the rifle.

Davidson gave him one last look—a general's approval, earned in the crucible of war. "Good. Now stand your ground, son. This is our line."

Taylor nodded, swallowing hard as his hands steadied. Around the room, others straightened, drawing strength from their commander-in-chief.

President Davidson turned back toward the entrance, listening as thunder rolled again—closer now, like a war drum in the sky.

The bunker fell silent, except for the rain—a relentless rhythm pounding overhead.

"Hold the line," the head of the Secret Service barked into his radio, his voice unwavering against the dread creeping into the room. The president's eyes flickered to the monitors. A flash of lightning illuminated the Nephilim as they closed in—towering silhouettes framed by the storm, their glowing eyes piercing through the darkness like the gaze of ancient gods.

A team of agents sprinted through the storm toward the White House entrance, their boots splashing against the concrete and fingers gripping their triggers. They only hoped to slow down the nightmare.

They reached the barricades, crouched low, and raised their weapons. Thunder cracked, and rain soaked their uniforms. Deep somewhere within their bones, they already knew the line wouldn't hold.

A voice cracked over the radio. "Perimeter breach!"

The head of the Secret Service leaned in. "Steady. Eyes on the target. Report the moment you—"

He never finished.

From the darkness, movement emerged. The Nephilim crested the iron fence like heavy shadows, glistening in the downpour. Agents opened fire. The rifles roared, but the storm swallowed the sound. Bullets ricocheted off their flesh like pebbles against a battleship.

"They're not stopping!"

The Nephilim surged forward, claws cleaving barricades like paper. The frontline collapsed. Screams erupted and were silenced. The surviving agents fell back, firing as they retreated, radios buzzing with frantic calls for help.

In the bunker, a junior agent gripped his radio with trembling hands, his eyes wide. He pressed the button.

"Sir... There are monsters in the White House." The words echoed throughout the White House. "I repeat... monsters in the—"

The line went dead.

Silence fell like a guillotine.

For a moment, no one moved. The only sound was the rain pounding against the earth with a mournful rhythm.

President Davidson stepped forward, eyes locked on the flickering screen. He saw it but didn't want to believe it.

The front doors of the White House—the same doors Dolley Madison once fled through with the portrait of George Washington in her arms—exploded inward in a shower of shattered wood.

For the second time in American history, the People's House was under siege. It wasn't redcoats or revolutionaries this time.. Monsters had invaded the White House and Washington D.C. would never be the same.

The image on the monitor was a scene of pure chaos—columns were crumbling, marble was scorched black, and paintings were torn from the walls and trampled under clawed feet. Statues of presidents lay cast down like broken idols, and through it all, the Nephilim advanced, their glowing eyes reflecting off polished floors now slick with blood.

The foundation of democracy floundered under the burden of something older than tyranny, never signed a constitution, never pledged allegiance, and never believed in freedom.

Davidson's voice was just above a whisper, yet it seemed to reach every soul in the room. "The last time these walls were breached... they burned them to the ground."

The head of the Secret Service stared at the screen. "This is more than just a fire."

In the entryway, the agents made their last stand. Gunfire flared in rapid bursts, muzzle flashes lighting the marble like a strobe of defiance. The Nephilim were a storm incarnate—hulking shadows moving like predators. One surged forward, razor claws slicing through an agent mid-turn. Blood sprayed across the white pillars like red lightning.

The survivors fled deeper into the White House. Shouts of warning turned into cries of panic, echoing off the shattering glass and collapsing beams. The once-regal corridors trembled beneath the march of the invaders. Antique furniture was destroyed, and chipped portraits of long-gone presidents observed the chaos, witnessing the beginning of a new chapter of American tragedy.

Down in the bunker, Davidson stood unflinching, the chaos above vibrating through concrete and steel.

Silence fell like a curtain.

The head of the Secret Service stepped forward, jaw clenched. "Brace yourselves."

A tremor shook the bunker. Then another followed. And another. Dust rained from the ceiling like ash.

A lone agent, cornered and desperate, grabbed a shattered chair leg and charged at a Nephilim with a war cry that was more a plea than a show of bravery. The makeshift weapon broke against the creature's chest, and it didn't even flinch. With a snarl, the Nephilim seized the agent's throat and twisted.

Haligot entered the White House just as the agent's body fell to the ground. He stepped through the ruined threshold as if crossing into his own throne room.

"Somewhere in this tomb, he is hiding," he said. "Brothers— find him and bring him to me."

The Nephilim roared in unison as the White House fell under siege from within. Walls crumbled, and steel warped. The bunker's secret entrance was torn away like parchment.

Inside, Davidson stood surrounded by what remained of his defenders, their faces smeared with sweat and their guns loaded with false hope. The doors buckled and then gave way.

Gunfire burst like fireworks, but it wasn't enough. The Nephilim tore through the resistance with ruthless precision.

Screams filled the bunker, joined by the chorus of claw against flesh, bone against steel. When it ended, Davidson stood alone—blood on his cheek, a sidearm in his hand, and rage in his breath.

He charged. The weapon cracked—once, twice, and again. A Nephilim flinched, more annoyed than hurt. It seized him by the throat, lifting him as if he were a child's toy.

Davidson pressed his pistol to the creature's head and fired, but when the smoke cleared, the monster still stood.

Haligot's voice echoed through the chamber.

"Enough! Our lord desires him alive."

The creature released Davidson, who fell to one knee. Coughing blood, he gasped, but still he rose to his feet.

Haligot approached, eyes gleaming.

"You call this leadership?" he said. "You can't even stand."

Davidson swayed as he met his gaze.

"You think leadership is about strength? It's about making sacrifices and standing tall, even when you have nothing left. I would die for my people. That's something you'll never understand."

Haligot gave a bitter laugh.

"In just minutes, we have reduced your capital to rubble. Your palace lies in ruin. Your army, mere dust."

Davidson didn't blink. "We fought."

"Fought and lost."

"We'll fight again." A moment passed. Davidson whispered, a last plea to heaven, "Protect my family. If this is my time... so be it."

Haligot tilted his head. With intentional curiosity, he reached forward and tugged something from the front pocket of Davidson's torn shirt—a photo, crumpled and stained with sweat.

A woman and two young girls smiled up at the camera. Wind in their hair, a serene lake in the background. Innocence captured in a moment.

Haligot studied it with mild interest. Then his lips curled.

"Well... would you look at that?" He held the photo up to the dim bunker lights. "I overheard Seria talking with our lord. She mentioned two women with two children in Alaska, stating they were a problem that she dealt with." He looked back at Davidson. "Funny coincidence, don't you think?"

The words hit him like a hammer. Davidson staggered, his knees buckled and then locked. His breath caught in his throat, but he didn't fall. Instead, he stood taller. His eyes, rimmed with blood and tears, burned with fury.

"You will pay for that," he said.

Haligot snapped back. "Shackle him."

Chains clanked as the Nephilim dragged President Davidson from the last sanctuary of democracy. The rain beat down—unrelenting and cold.

The storm extended well beyond Washington, casting its shadow over forests, mountains, and rivers. Yet even in the wilderness, the wind carried whispers of what had begun.

The old world was fading away, and in its place, something monstrous had emerged.

CHAPTER TWENTY-THREE

Alchemy of Friendship

A raven called overhead, its voice hollow and distant, like a memory half-remembered. Roo paused, letting the sound settle before the breeze stole it away.

In the vast wilderness of Alaska, the storm had calmed, turning into a gentle patter as the rain whispered across the leaves like an apology. Dawn broke through the clouds, casting a golden light that touched the tops of the trees. The air was sharp and clean, filled with the scent of wet pine and rich, unsettled soil. Nearby, branches creaked under the weight of dew, and the forest seemed to breathe once more.

They had come here wounded—some with physical wounds, but all of them had emotional wounds. Something in the quiet had stitched them back together. It wasn't medicine or strategy; it was something far more elusive.

The alchemy of friendship.

Forged in fire, through grief, grit, and impossible odds. It was the unseen bond that transformed strangers into survivors and survivors into something greater. Trust didn't come as easy, not after everything they had endured. However, in this pocket of peace, the elements blended. A glance exchanged, a joke shared, a hand offered with no need to ask.

Somehow, against all odds, they were changing. It was more than healing; they were transforming. In a world where everything else was crumbling, that was no small task.

Roo spotted Ramirez near the edge of the cabin, his shirt damp with sweat despite the morning chill. A pile of firewood lay at his feet, split and scattered like shrapnel. He stood over a fresh log, his breath heavy, an axe gripped in his white-knuckled fists.

The blade came down again—hard and with a rage that was palpable.

Crack.

Another swing. Then another.

Each strike was a confession; each splinter a scream he couldn't voice.

Roo approached, stopping a few feet away, watching as Ramirez raised the axe again, then froze mid-swing, his shoulders trembling. His hands slipped from the handle, and the axe tumbled to the ground beside him. For a moment, he just stood there, chest heaving, eyes fixed on the ground.

That's when he broke.

He dropped to his knees, head bowed, and pressed his fists into the soil. A choked sound tore from his throat—part sob, part snarl. Years of buried guilt, bitterness, and pride cracked open beneath the weight of gratitude he didn't believe he deserved.

Roo didn't speak at first. He just knelt beside him.

After a moment, he said, "You don't have to carry it alone anymore."

Ramirez wiped his face with the back of his hand, trying to hide the tears that had already soaked the cuffs of his sleeves. "You should hate me," he said. "After everything I said and did, I wouldn't have blamed you if you had left me to die."

"I thought about it," Roo said, offering the slightest hint of a smile. "Dr. Terracotta talked me out of it."

Ramirez sniffed, glancing side to side. "Terracotta? You mean the guy I treated like crap?"

"He's the reason you're still breathing," Roo replied. "He made the call to save you. I just carried it out."

Ramirez let out a bitter laugh and shook his head. "That man's either a saint or an idiot."

"No," Roo said. "He's just someone who chooses hope over history. Maybe we should try that too."

Ramirez sat back on his heels, staring at the ruined stack of wood. His voice dropped to a whisper. "I don't deserve that kind of forgiveness."

"None of us do," Roo said, placing a hand on his shoulder. "That's why it means something."

Ramirez looked at Roo, his sharp edges softened, suspicion and sarcasm stripped away, leaving only reverence.

"I need to find him," Ramirez said, shaking as he stood up. "I need to tell him myself."

He walked toward the cabin, moving with determination. Roo stayed back, watching him leave. A slow exhale slipped from his lips as he picked up the fallen axe and leaned it against the split log.

"Hell of a morning," he said, then made his way back to the cabin, feeling the ground give under his boots with each step. As he approached, he spotted Lizzie standing just beyond the porch, her arms crossed against her chest and her breath visible in the cool morning air.

She looked up, studying him for a moment, before her lips turned into a tired smile.

"How's your head?" she asked, tilting her chin toward him. "Still feeling rattled from that fall?"

Roo chuckled and rubbed the back of his neck. "Maybe a little, but I've had worse." He nodded toward her. "What about you? Did you get any sleep? You looked like you were about to drop last night."

Lizzie let out a dry laugh. "I tried. But it's hard to sleep when it feels like the sky might fall any minute." She glanced past him, her eyes drifting to the tree line as her voice softened. "While I was getting ready for bed, I thought I saw something," she said.

Roo paused, adjusting his posture. "Something?" he asked.

Lizzie nodded, her brow furrowing in restraint, as though she was trying to keep her thoughts from unraveling.

"I think it was him," she said. "The man in the purple robes. The one who saved us back at the base." A chill rippled down her arms, causing her to hug herself a little tighter. "It didn't feel... threatening. It was the opposite. Like he was just—there. Watching. Protecting, maybe. I don't know. It sounds crazy."

Roo's stomach tensed, an old survival instinct humming beneath his skin. He followed her eyes toward the edge of the woods, where shadows stretched long and silent between the trees.

"Maybe it's not crazy," he said. "We should ask the others to see if anyone else saw something." He paused, chewing on the thought like a splinter in his mind. "Better yet, let's ask Solomon. If anyone has a clue about who this guy is, it's him."

Lizzie nodded, feeling some of the tension leave her shoulders. "That's a good idea."

The two of them turned toward the cabin, their footsteps soft against the forest floor. Birds chirped in the canopy above, and somewhere far off, the distant groan of shifting branches echoed like a warning.

Lizzie couldn't shake the feeling pressing against her spine— the sensation that someone was still watching her from the trees.

Dr. Terracotta sat across from Big Norm, the cabin wrapped in a warm hush broken only by the occasional pop from the fireplace. Shelves lined the walls like monuments to a forgotten era, each spine of faded vinyl a testament to joy, heartbreak, and rebellion. Norm reclined in his chair, boots crossed, a soft grin spreading across his face as he recounted trading a rifle for half of his collection.

Terracotta listened like a man hearing scripture. "Fleetwood Mac, Dolly Parton, and Bowie." His eyes danced along the spines. "I didn't expect to meet someone who appreciates music like this."

"You might be surprised at what people hold onto," Norm said, tapping the ash from his pipe. "Sometimes, a song is the only thing that keeps you sane."

Terracotta leaned forward, his attention caught by something hidden among the stacks—a vintage tape recorder, with dust clinging to its edges as if it hadn't been used in years.

"Is that what I think it is?" he said.

Norm followed his eyes and let out a hearty chuckle. "That old thing? Damn near forgot it was even there. You want it, Doc? It's yours."

"For real?"

"Hell yeah. You'll get more use out of it than I ever will."

With a sense of quiet awe, Terracotta picked it up. His fingers traced the worn buttons and chipped corners as if he were holding a piece of the world before it shattered. "Thank you," he said.

He tucked it into his bag, a soft smile still tugging at the corners of his mouth. As he turned to leave, he stopped on a dime—almost colliding with Ramirez, who stood in the doorway.

"Whoa!" Terracotta staggered back, heart pounding. "You scared the hell out of me. How long have you been standing there?"

Ramirez didn't respond right away. His expression was unreadable, but his voice had softened. "Long enough," he said. "I talked to Roo, and he told me what you did."

Terracotta shifted the strap on his shoulder, unsure of his footing. "What did I do?"

"You saved me, Doc," Ramirez said. "You told Roo to go back for me."

Terracotta hesitated. "You needed help. That's all."

Ramirez stepped forward. His hands weren't clenched as usual. His voice lacked its typical sarcasm. He looked... vulnerable.

"Don't do that," he said. "Don't downplay it. After everything I put you through—calling you dead weight, accusing you of sabotage during the war games... hell, I even tried to get you reassigned. You had every right to leave me behind."

Terracotta looked away. His voice was low, but steady. "You weren't the only one who wanted me gone."

Ramirez's throat bobbed as he swallowed. "I was the loudest." He took another step closer, and his voice cracked. "I treated you like garbage, and you still vouched for me. I don't get it."

Terracotta met his eyes as he finished. "Because you're human. Whether you believe it or not, there is still good in you. You're an exceptional mechanic, Ramirez. We need you on our team. I wasn't focusing on your past; I was thinking about what you can still do."

286

Ramirez's jaw tensed, and then, it unraveled. The walls he'd built for so long came down one at a time. "It takes a better man than me to do that," he said. "I'm sorry for everything. I hope one day you can forgive me."

The silence that followed was heavy, carrying only a sense of weight.

Without warning, Ramirez gave Terracotta a playful jab in the arm—easy, but enough to startle him.

Terracotta flinched, then relaxed when he saw the hint of a grin. "Try not to make me regret it," he said, smirking as he nudged him back.

They both laughed, the tension breaking like a fever. Ramirez leaned against the wall and let out a relieved breath. "You know, I've got a hidden talent," he said. "Bet you wouldn't guess."

Terracotta gave him a sidelong glance. "Let me guess... passive aggression?"

Ramirez chuckled. "Close. I play the drums, and I was in a band back in high school. We played shows in my buddy's garage."

Terracotta raised an eyebrow. "You? Behind a drum kit? I figured the only thing you could hit was someone's books."

"That's fair," Ramirez said with a grin. "But I wasn't bad. Who's your favorite drummer?"

Terracotta shrugged. "I enjoy the rhythm—the heartbeat—of the song."

"Well, that's gotta change," Ramirez said, throwing an arm around him. "Come on. Let's dig into Norm's records. I'll show you the legends."

Terracotta chuckled. "This I've gotta see."

They disappeared back into the cabin, voices rising in easy banter as the firelight flickered behind them—two men who had every reason to hate each other, now standing on the ashes of that hatred, building something new.

On the front porch of the cabin, Haru and Akira sat side by side, the old rocking chair creaking beneath their weight. A gentle breeze rustled the trees, and Brutus lay sprawled between them, snoring in rhythm with the wind, his jowls twitching as he dreamed.

The world was quiet for once.

"You know," Haru said, leaning back and watching the pale orange stretch of the horizon, "it's wild that we worked together for two years and never exchanged anything more than nods and data reports."

He glanced at her with the honest interest that came when the world forced you to slow down. "Do you have anyone waiting for you? Assuming there's still a home to go back to."

Akira hesitated before speaking, as if the words were too delicate to rush. "My parents and my twin sister. She has always been the brave one. When things went wrong, she was the one who held us together. She's holding them together now."

Haru sat in disbelief, his mouth agape. "You're a twin?" He sat up straighter. "No kidding. So am I."

Akira turned to him with a look of genuine surprise on her face. "Yeah?"

He nodded, rubbing the back of his neck. "Yeah, my brother is the golden child. He works for a tech giant and made our parents proud before he even turned eighteen. I was the one who enjoyed maps, puzzles, and taking the long way around."

"You were the explorer," Akira said.

"Yeah." He looked down, a quiet laugh slipping out. "And also the screw-up. They'd never say it, but it was always there in the way they looked at me."

Akira reached out and placed a hand on his arm out of kinship. "You're not a screw-up, Haru. You're still here, still standing. That means something."

For a moment, neither of them said anything. The air between them was light but full.

Laughter echoed through the woods, and footsteps crunched on the pine needles. From the trees emerged Viktor, Charlotte, and Hans, their jackets dusted with dew, arms cradling rabbits like trophies of old-world survival. The crisp scent of pine mingled with the faint musk of game.

Charlotte held up her rabbit like it was a prize at a fair. "Picture this in the history books: a Frenchwoman, a German, and a Russian emerge from the woods with breakfast. No punchline. Just post-apocalyptic life."

Hans chuckled, adjusting the strap of his quiver. "I still can't believe Norm let us borrow his bows. Charlotte... you're an excellent shot. Remind me not to get on your bad side."

"Smart man," she said, flashing a grin. "French precision, mon ami."

Viktor let out a loud laugh. "I've never eaten rabbit before. In Russia, we hunt things that hunt back."

Charlotte rolled her eyes, smirking. "Typical. And let me guess—you would follow that up with vodka?"

"Of course," Viktor said. "Ice cold, like my ex-wife."

Hans rubbed his stomach, relishing the thought of a meal "Forget fancy flavors. I'd do anything for a bratwurst right now."

Charlotte shot him a mock glare. "Don't start, big guy. You Germans have already caused enough trouble over the centuries."

That earned a round of laughter, the kind that filled the cold air with something almost forgotten... normalcy.

As they climbed the steps to the cabin, their playful banter faded behind them, reminiscent of a world long gone. Even in the shadow of what they had endured, for one morning at least, they still felt human.

Inside the cabin, Roo and Lizzie found Dr. Solomon hunched over a table buried in half-open books, yellowed notes, and curling maps. His glasses sat askew, forgotten at the edge of a cluttered page. He didn't even look up at first.

"I know it sounds unbelievable," Lizzie said, stepping closer, "but I saw him. The man in the purple robes. The same one who gave you that book. Have you figured out anything?"

Solomon's hand froze mid-note. He looked up, and for the first time, they saw not only weariness in his face but also a sense of defeat. "I've torn through every book I brought," he said, voice flat with exhaustion. "Historical records, religious texts, and even folklore. Nothing. Not a single clue."

He reached for the blank book and tossed it to Roo. It landed with a soft thud. "That? That is a mockery. It's nothing—nothing more than an empty journal."

Roo caught it, running a thumb across its cover. He didn't say much, just handed it back.

"Doc," he said, "maybe it's not about figuring it out right now. Maybe it's time to take a breath, go outside, and clear your head."

Solomon rubbed his temples, fingers pressing into the skin as if he was trying to hold his thoughts in. After a long pause, he nodded. "You're right." He stood with the book clutched in one hand and walked toward the door—but then he stopped. "You know," he said, softer now, "this isn't the first time I've seen him."

Roo and Lizzie shared a look, their attention sharpening.

"What do you mean?" Lizzie asked.

Solomon stared down at the book, thumbing the corner. "Back at the base, I reviewed the images we took. He appeared in them, in the background and in the shadows. I didn't notice at first; I thought it was a smudge or a trick of the lens. But now..." He trailed off.

Roo took a step closer. "Why didn't you say anything?"

"I didn't want it to be real," Solomon said. "I was still trying to make it make sense. This?" He held up the book. "This doesn't belong to logic or reason, and neither does he."

"Then we need to figure out who he is... before someone else does," Lizzie said.

Solomon nodded, his grip tightening on the book as if it might run from him if he let go. "I'm going for that walk, but this isn't over." He stepped outside, the door creaking closed behind him.

Roo turned to Lizzie, voice low. "That man in the purple robes... he's not just connected; he's the one in control. Somehow, he's steering this."

Lizzie said nothing.

Deep in the wilderness, four shadows moved like wolves on the hunt. The horsemen marched beneath the trees, their boots crunching on wet needles, flanked by Seria's hounds—silent yet watchful. Their eyes swept the terrain like razor blades.

Regar paused, lifting his hand. The others froze behind him.

He saw smoke rise between the trees.

"There," he said, his voice low and tight. "That's them. Let's finish this."

Solomon wandered deeper into the forest, the silence folding around him. With each step, he sank into the rain-softened earth, the scent of moss and petrichor clinging to the air. Branches swayed above him, their limbs whispering secrets he couldn't quite hear. His thoughts were a chaotic mix of unanswered questions, frustration gnawing at his edges like a dull blade.

He stopped dead in his tracks. Eyes wide in disbelief.

Ahead, a figure stood motionless among the trees, cloaked in purple, its outline blurred by drifting mist. He remained still, the fog curling around him—yielding, as if the forest itself acknowledged something sacred.

Solomon's breath caught in his throat. The figure raised a hand summoning Dr. Solomon to come closer.

Something ancient stirred in Solomon's chest.

Compelled by a force he couldn't name, he stepped forward, his fingers tightening around the blank book clutched to his chest. His voice cracked the silence.

"Who are you?"

The figure didn't speak. He extended only a hand toward the book.

Solomon hesitated, his heart pounding in his ears. Yet something inside urged him onward. He opened the book with trembling hands, its pristine pages catching the light.

The figure still didn't take it.

Instead, he reached for Solomon's left hand. His touch was deliberate and almost gentle. A glint of silver flashed; it was an old dagger.

Solomon flinched as the blade sliced across his palm, clean and precise. Warm blood welled to the surface, the metallic scent rising in the damp air. The figure guided his bleeding hand over the page, pressing it down with unspoken command.

As the first drops struck the parchment, the world shifted.

Time no longer flowed in moments but in pulses. The air thickened around him, buzzing with energy that prickled across his skin. Every breath carried a faint tang, electric and metallic, like a storm caught in a bottle.

Solomon's knees almost gave out as he watched the blood spread across the page—transforming it. Droplets bled into elegant lines and symbols, forming letters that shimmered like ink made from the night sky. The language was foreign yet somehow familiar—it was vibrant.

The book had awakened, and it recognized him.

He stared, spellbound, unable to tear his eyes from the script that now spilled across once-blank pages.

"What is this?" he said, his voice hollow and trembling.

The man in purple didn't answer. He stepped back into the mist, his form dissolving like smoke into the folds of the forest.

The book still pulsed in Solomon's hands, its pages warm, humming with quiet power. Each word glowed, waiting for him to understand them, waiting for his blood to remember.

A sound interrupted the trance, echoing from far behind him.

Leaves crunched and footsteps echoed.

He looked up. Through the trees, an eerie green light cut through the fog. The sky pulsed with a sickly glow as a Finger of Eden hovered just above the canopy, its presence undeniable.

Solomon's breath hitched. "I need to warn the others."

He turned and bolted; the book clutched to his chest. Branches slapped against his arms and thorns scraped at his sleeves, but he didn't stop. His lungs burned as he ran, his legs pumped with effort, and his thoughts raced between feelings of wonder and terror.

Behind him, the forest felt like it was collapsing inward.

Above him, the sky trembled.

Ahead, somewhere, were the only people who could help him understand what had just happened, and in his hand... a book born of blood.

CHAPTER TWENTY-FOUR

Fear the Reaper

R oo and Lizzie stood beyond the porch, the morning air clinging to their skin with the faint bite of pine. The surrounding forest breathed in rhythm—leaves rustled like soft whispers overhead, and somewhere nearby, a songbird released a fragile, trilling note into the stillness. For a moment, the world felt cradled in peace, a thin bubble stretched across something darker.

A thunderous crash tore through the trees, splitting the silence wide open. Birds erupted into the sky in a cyclone of wings and panic.

Roo flinched, and Lizzie grabbed his arm. Their heads snapped toward the tree line, which shivered as if something immense was moving behind it.

Branches cracked, and a shadow lunged into view as Dr. Solomon burst from the undergrowth, his coat torn and flapping, one shoe half-off. He stumbled, dropped to one knee, then forced himself upright again. His chest rose and fell in violent heaves, every breath rattling like broken machinery.

His voice came out raw and desperate. "They're here! They're coming this way... we have to go, now!"

Everything shifted. The forest, moments ago a lullaby, now seemed to watch them.

Roo and Lizzie didn't move. The weight of those words cinched around their lungs. The chirps of the birds turned shrill, almost mocking. Wind scraped through the trees like something whispering out of reach.

Dr. Solomon's panicked cries ripped through the clearing like lightning cracking a stormless sky.

Norm shoved open the cabin door, shotgun in hand. Brutus barreled out beside him, his nails scraping against the wood, and a growl rumbled from his chest. The hard-packed earth crunched under their boots as they rushed to Roo and Lizzie's side.

Behind them, there was more movement. Charlotte and Hans stepped out first, squinting in the changing light, followed by Haru and Akira. Viktor was the last to duck under the doorway, his shoulders tense and his broad frame rigid with alertness. Salvador lingered at the edge of the porch, his eyes scanning the trees as if he expected something to leap from them.

Solomon stumbled to a stop, legs wobbling as if gravity had doubled. He bent forward, hands on his thighs, sucking in shallow, desperate breaths. Sweat slicked his skin, trailing down his cheeks and neck, his lungs rattling with each inhale.

Lizzie stepped closer. "What did you see? Who's coming?"

He didn't give an answer right away. He just stayed hunched, trying to fight the tremors that made his limbs feel like jelly.

His voice was frayed and breathless as he forced the words out—each one chosen over a gasp for air. "Th–The Finger... of Eden... hovering... above the forest." He coughed, chest hitching. "And... footsteps. So many... coming fast."

His eyes flicked upward, wild with terror. "It's them," he said. "The ones from the base… the ones that hunt."

The silence that followed was loaded. It had a weight that filled lungs with dread.

Norm's voice broke through, steady as ever.

"Do you all know how to shoot a gun?"

Everyone nodded except Dr. Terracotta, who shifted his weight. Madison and Savannah clung tighter to Roo, their fingers like ice as they grabbed his hands.

Ramirez placed a reassuring hand on Terracotta's shoulder. "Don't worry, Doc. I've got your back. Stay close."

Norm gave a sharp nod and turned without another word, vanishing into the cabin. The door creaked shut behind him, silencing the familiar sounds of weapons being prepared.

The air shifted, and a sudden gust of air ripped through the clearing. Brutus stiffened. His ears twitched first—a slight movement—but then his entire body locked into a rigid stance as he lifted his nose toward the trees. A primal growl rumbled from deep within his chest, vibrating against the silence.

Once. Twice. A third time—louder and sharper, cutting through the quiet like a blade. Each bark echoed through the clearing, bouncing off the cabin walls and shattering the calm they had clung to.

A long, agonizing silence followed.

Brutus's last bark cut off mid-growl, like a wire had been yanked from his throat. His lips curled and teeth bared, but no sound came. Only a vibrating snarl that faded into a breathless void.

From deep within the forest, a whisper slithered out like smoke. "We have found you." The words didn't speak so much as creep, weaving between the branches and curling around the trees. Leaves trembled, though no wind stirred.

The group froze.

Another whisper crept from behind the cabin, colder this time, laced with something venomous. "You can't run from us."

A branch cracked somewhere in the distance. Roo flinched. Lizzie gripped his arm like it was the only real thing left.

A third voice emerged from the left, this one was higher, more gleeful and cruel. "The Architect is waiting for you."

The forest went silent. There was no wind or rustling. Even the birds had stopped singing. The world held its breath.

The last whisper came, drawn from the right side of the clearing—closer than the others. It coiled through the group like a serpent, brushing the skin behind their ears and whispering into their bones.

"The Horsemen surround you."

The words fell upon them like a curse. Brutus whimpered and backed up. Savannah buried her face in Roo's side. Somewhere behind them, Charlotte cried. No one spoke. No one moved.

The whispers lingered in the clearing like smoke after a fire—four voices in perfect discord speaking as one.

Death, War, Conquest, and Pestilence had found them.

The cabin door banged open. Norm stormed out, arms loaded with rifles and shotguns.

"Don't stand there! Get a gun!" he yelled, flinging the weapons to the ground in front of them.

The group scrambled forward, hands trembling as they seized the firearms. The metal felt cold and foreign. Roo could feel his pulse in the grip. Each of them readied their weapons, eyes flicking to the shifting tree line, bracing for what would come.

The forest transformed. The air became thinner. Sounds faded away. Even the leaves appeared to stop moving.

A strange shimmer rippled through the clearing like heat rising off asphalt—but it was colder. The light bent, fractured, and then bled into an unnatural glow. A veil of iridescent haze descended, like silk slipping from the sky, draping the Horsemen in an otherworldly cocoon of power.

The Eden Veil had arrived, and through it... they came.

Regar stepped from the tree line, his form a dark outline against the vibrant morning sky. He moved slowly, exuding confidence, the Scythe in his hand dragging through the dirt like an ominous threat. Rangel moved to Regar's left, the only sound the soft rustle of leaves beneath her feet. Durbal emerged on the right, his mass causing the underbrush to crunch and snap with every slow step. Seria brought up the rear, her crimson armor catching the light, as a pack of hounds moved on either side, resembling fierce shadows. The Bloodfang Talons raked against the cabin's walls, leaving a trail of jagged splinters and the scent of fresh-cut timber.

The four horsemen and the hounds of war encircled the group like predators at a sacrificial fire.

Norm didn't wait. He raised his rifle and fired. The crack of the shot shattered the tension—and triggered chaos.

The others followed suit, unleashing everything they had. A volley of bullets screamed through the clearing, tearing toward the Horsemen with desperate speed.

The veil didn't flinch. Every bullet struck the shimmering air and stopped, repelled with a faint chime, falling to the ground like metal rain. Not a single round reached its target.

Laughter echoed through the clearing—cold, resonant, and cruel.

Regar stepped closer, the Scythe glinting in the light. "You are not warriors or even threats. You are souls... and I am what comes to claim them." The words fell like a hammer on an anvil.

A shiver ran through the group. Lizzie tightened her grip on her weapon, her knuckles turning white. Ramirez muttered something under his breath. Savannah whimpered and pressed closer to Roo, who couldn't take his eyes off the figures standing beyond the veil. Even Norm twitched at the appearance of the horsemen.

Regar stepped forward, unfazed by their fear. He gestured toward the other horsemen. "We are the Horsemen, the devoted hands of the Architect. Our existence predates your fragile world. Your weapons?" He rested the scythe on his shoulder like a man leaning on a memory. "They are meaningless. The Eden Veil shields us."

Norm stepped forward, his rifle cocked and leveled at Regar's chest. His voice didn't waver. "You'll have to kill me before you take them."

As Regar moved closer, the smirk on his face widened as Norm pulled the trigger. The bullet struck Regar in the shoulder and bounced off like a pebble on steel. It hit the dirt with a dull thud.

Regar chuckled, brushing off his shoulder with an idle flick of his hand, as if Norm had swatted him with a leaf.

He stepped in, close enough to smell the sweat and defiance on the old man. With effortless strength, he pried the rifle from Norm's hands, studied it, turning it with almost scientific curiosity. Instead of tossing it away, he handed it back—like a judge returning evidence to a defendant.

His expression had shifted. The amusement faded, and his voice dropped to a near-whisper. "Do you not fear the Reaper?"

300

The question hung in the air like a thick fog.

Norm stood there, like a statue in a museum, his heart pounding as he awaited Regar's next move.

With slow and predatory movements, Regar circled him, observing his every move. "You're too old to fulfill a prophecy," he said. "I see no marks on you. That makes you… unnecessary."

He stopped in front of Norm, his shadow falling over him as he lifted his hand. A single finger pointed to the sky. "Tell me, old man… when you die, do you know where your soul will go?" He lowered his finger until it pointed to the ground below.

It felt like a verdict.

The group stood frozen.

Norm straightened. The grip on his returned rifle tightened, but his face was calm. "I've made my share of mistakes," he said. "I've done some good in this world, too. There's a place beyond those gates for me."

Regar's smirk returned, colder this time. "Then let us find out."

Brutus let out a sharp whimper and stepped forward, positioning himself beside Norm's leg. His body trembled, ears flat and teeth bared in a silent growl—but he didn't bark. Not this time. Even he could sense that this wasn't something he could scare away. This wasn't a fight; it was a verdict.

Roo tightened his grip around Madison and Savannah, his throat burning as if he had swallowed fire. His legs ached to move, charge forward, or ake action, but his body remained frozen in place, paralyzed by fear. Norm had always been the one who stood tallest, spoke the loudest, and made everything seem a little more attainable.

Dr. Solomon couldn't move either. He had seen that look before—in books, ancient texts, and depictions of gods and demons who didn't need permission to take lives. His mind raced for something—a symbol, a phrase, or a weakness. This wasn't a puzzle. This was the moment after the riddle, when the answer was death.

Regar's words turned the clearing into a courtroom, and Norm stood as both defendant and witness, his soul the verdict waiting to be cast.

Regar smirked, his expression cold and unfeeling as he turned his gaze back to Norm. He hefted his scythe with an almost reverent grace, the blade shimmering with an otherworldly glow. "Let us begin," he said, his voice dripping with malice. "I should warn you, the reaping process on a living being is beyond painful. My scythe will tear your soul from your body, leaving you with enough life to witness its final judgment." He held the weapon aloft, letting its curved blade catch the pale light filtering through the trees. Regar's eyes bore into Norm as he took a step closer. "Any last words?" He said, his tone mocking.

Norm stood firm, his weathered face calm despite the impending doom. He turned his head, his eyes sweeping over the group. His voice was steady and warm, carrying the weight of a lifetime's wisdom.

"No matter what happens next," he said, his words slow and deliberate, "I want you to promise me something. Promise me you'll care for old Brutus. That dog has been my companion through it all, and he deserves to be loved."

The group stared at him, their expressions a mix of anguish and helplessness. Tears welled in Lizzie's eyes as she clutched Roo's arm for support. Brutus let out a whine, his ears pinned back, sensing the gravity of the moment.

Norm's voice softened, carrying an almost fatherly reassurance. "Each of you has a purpose. I can feel it. It was my destiny to rescue you, just as it's my destiny to—"

"NO!" Lizzie screamed, her voice cracking as she surged forward—only to be held back by Ramirez. "Please don't do this!"

"Stop!" Dr. Solomon shouted, desperation strangling his voice. "There has to be another way—he's not a threat to you!"

Charlotte sobbed, her hands covering her mouth. Hans turned away, unable to bear the sight. Viktor trembled, his fists clenched so tight that his knuckles bled.

Brutus barked once—loud and defiant—but it ended in a whimper as he pressed against Norm's leg, refusing to leave his side.

Roo dropped to one knee, shielding Madison and Savannah with his arms, pulling their faces into his chest. "Don't look," he said. "Don't look and hold on to me."

The forest felt smaller, like it had drawn in to witness the cruelty.

Regar said nothing. He stepped forward, raised the Scythe, and pressed it against Norm's chest.

Norm let out a scream—a sound so raw that it pierced the stillness of the forest. The scream reverberated through the trees, a haunting echo that refused to fade. Then he crumpled to the ground, the impact kicking up a cloud of dust that hung suspended in the air. His body convulsed, every muscle tensing and releasing with a force that defied the limits of human endurance. The sickening sound of bones cracking and ligaments straining filled the clearing.

The ground beneath him trembled, as though the earth itself recoiled at the torment unfolding. His face contorted in a mask of pain.

A flash of ethereal light came next as Norm's soul broke free. It rose from his contorted body like a shimmering phantom, its form translucent and radiant. The group watched in stunned silence as the soul ascended, trailing faint luminescence through the air before it leaped into the Scythe. The weapon pulsed, consuming the essence, before the soul shot skyward, a streak of light disappearing into the vast heavens.

Norm's eyes, heavy and glazed with the pain of his ordeal, followed the light's path. A bittersweet smile tugged at his lips, and a single tear escaped, carving a glistening trail down his weathered cheek. It carried with it the weight of a life lived, its joys and regrets, mingled into one last moment of peace.

The spasms ceased, and his body stilled. His features, tense a moment before, relaxed into an expression of quiet serenity. The forest reacted, its rustling leaves and soft bird calls forming a mournful requiem. Norm lay motionless, embraced by the peaceful rhythms of nature.

The group remained rooted where they stood, their breaths shallow and their faces streaked with tears. Brutus padded forward, his paws silent on the forest floor, before climbing onto Norm's broad chest. He kneaded his chest, the muscles bunching and relaxing as if he were a baker working dough. He slowly lowered his body, mimicking the way a child gets ready to take a nap. As he lay down, the ragged sound of his mournful whimpers ripped through the suffocating silence.

Behind them, a sharp gagging sound cut through the air. Dr. Terracotta stumbled back a step, doubled over, and vomited into the dirt. His hands trembled as he wiped his mouth, and then the sobs came—sudden, unrestrained, and helpless. He collapsed to his knees, tears streaming down his face, his body shaking with each choked breath.

Ramirez moved without hesitation. He crouched beside him, one arm wrapping around Terracotta's shoulders, pulling him in.

"I know," Ramirez said. "Breathe. I've got you."

Terracotta leaned into him like a man crumbling under the weight of grief, his sobs muffled against Ramirez's chest.

For a long, aching moment, no one spoke. There was nothing left to say.

Seria's lips curled into a cruel smile as she glanced at her hounds.

"Tonight, you will enjoy another feast. Go, gather your prey."

The hounds surged forward, their eyes fixed on Norm's lifeless form. Their Bloodfang Talons scraped against the ground, leaving gouges in the earth as they closed the distance. The group watched in horrified silence, frozen as the monstrous creatures approached.

Brutus didn't move. With a guttural growl that rumbled from deep within his chest, he planted himself atop Norm's body. His stout frame trembled with determination, his flattened face pulling back to reveal teeth bared in defiance. The sound was primal, an unyielding declaration of loyalty that cut through the tension like a blade.

The hounds stopped for a moment, then, with snarls that echoed through the clearing, they lunged forward. Their Bloodfang Talons hit the ground with a sharp crack as they attacked Brutus, their aggression clear. However, the bulldog stood firm. His growls intensified, becoming fiercer, demonstrating his determination not to abandon his fallen master.

"Seria, call them off," Regar said, his tone sharp.

Seria turned, brow furrowing. "What?"

Regar's eyes remained locked on Brutus and his defiance. "I said call them off."

305

Seria raised her hand and gave a guttural command. The hounds froze mid-lunge, reluctant, their snarls boiling beneath their breath. They withdrew with visible irritation, pacing along the edges of the clearing.

Brutus remained, chest heaving, paws planted atop Norm's still form.

Regar stepped forward, gaze narrowing. "This beast..." he said. "It doesn't flee. It protects the dead with no hope of survival and refuses the natural order."

Seria scoffed. "It's a dog—a malformed one. It serves no purpose. Let the hounds enjoy it."

Regar didn't look at her. His voice dropped, almost reverent. "No. Not yet. This display... It's wrong. It doesn't fit the pattern." He paused, studying Brutus like a priest examining a sacred relic. "Things that do not fit the pattern must be studied. We will take it to the Architect. He might use it in the arena."

Seria's jaw clenched, but she didn't argue further. She gave a quick signal, and the hounds formed a loose circle around her.

Regar stepped back. "Restrain it."

The hounds lunged again— this time to subdue. Brutus fought them at every turn, snapping and thrashing with relentless fury. His defiance only grew as they closed in, but exhaustion took its toll on him. His growls became labored, his movements slower, until finally the hounds muzzled and leashed him.

As the group watched in helpless anguish, the creatures dragged Brutus off Norm. His eyes never left his master's body, locked with unyielding loyalty even in defeat.

Regar strode around the group, his eyes scanning them with a predator's precision. His scythe rested in one hand, swinging slightly, its presence alone a silent threat. "Amongst you," he said, his voice smooth but edged with cruelty, "there are individuals who bear a mark of great significance. Allow us to inspect you, and the process will be swift and efficient. You will join us on the ship and serve the Architect as slaves." He paused, letting the words settle over them like a suffocating fog. "If you choose to resist," his voice sharpened, "we will inflict unimaginable harm. The choice is yours."

No one spoke.

A quiet ripple passed through the group—trembling hands, shifting feet, and shallow gasps. The scent of fear had grown thick in the air.

Roo's breath caught in his throat. Lizzie's heart raced in her chest. Ramirez whispered a prayer.

Lizzie scanned the surrounding faces, each one strained beneath the weight of disbelief. When her eyes landed on Roo, he gave a slight, almost imperceptible nod.

She stepped forward. "We will comply," she said. Her voice didn't shake but her hands did.

Regar's smirk widened, and with a slight motion, he signaled his companions forward.

The four horsemen moved like wraiths through the crowd, inspecting each person with unblinking, soulless efficiency. When they reached Haru, Akira, Hans, Charlotte, Viktor, and Salvador, they paused.

Each of the six stood frozen.

Seria ran her eyes over them and then shook her head once.

"No mark," she said. Her voice was like ice. "They are of no use to the Architect."

There was a long, terrible silence. Hans looked down, then straightened—jaw tight and fists clenched. "We don't have to go down without a fight," he said.

"Hans, no!" Lizzie cried, panic overtaking her composure. "Please!"

She was too late. He was already moving, lunging at Seria with a roar, his fists raised—but she sidestepped him with ease. Her blade sang through the air in a single, fluid arc.

The sound was sickening.

Blood sprayed across the dirt as Hans fell to the ground, lifeless, beside Charlotte and the others.

Charlotte screamed—a raw, visceral sound. She brought her hands to her face as she backed away. Haru and Akira flinched and clung to one another, while Salvador fell to his knees in disbelief, shaking his head.

Viktor let out a guttural sound, a mix of rage and heartbreak, and stepped forward, his frame trembling with fury. "You monsters!" he roared, then charged at Regar with reckless abandon, grief fueling every step.

Regar didn't move until the last moment. With a flick of his arm, the Scythe rose, and the blade struck.

Viktor's soul ripped free before his body even hit the ground. A shimmering thread of light vanished into the weapon as his massive frame crumpled.

There was no scream. Only silence.

Charlotte collapsed beside Hans's body, sobbing. Haru and Akira stayed locked in a trembling embrace. Salvador sat in the dirt, arms limp at his sides, staring down at his hands like he didn't know how they worked.

"Enough!" Lizzie shouted. Her voice cracked under the weight of everything. "We agreed to comply. Stop this!"

Regar turned to her. His expression was unreadable.

"Compliance will spare only those we need," he said. "The rest are expendable."

Seria stepped toward Haru and Akira, her sword still wet with Hans' blood. "Two more who lack the mark," she said. "Perhaps they will find peace in death."

Roo stepped forward, arms still around Madison and Savannah. "No!" he shouted, his voice breaking. "They've done nothing wrong! Let them go!"

Seria didn't even glance at him. "This is not about right or wrong," she said. "It is about purpose." The strike came quick.

The two of them fell together, still holding hands. Their bodies hit the earth with a finality that crushed whatever breath remained in the clearing.

No one screamed this time. There were only sobs and the sound of the veil pulsing in the background.

Charlotte wiped away her tears. Her eyes were now empty, glassy, and still. She didn't resist or cry out. She stood and stepped forward, as if walking into the arms of inevitability. One foot in front of the other. She had no more strength to run.

Salvador followed behind her, hollow and silent, his shoulders hunched, and his lips parted as if he might speak, but no words came.

They stood side by side. Charlotte looked up at the sky and closed her eyes. Salvador dropped his chin and let out a long, broken sigh.

Seria stepped forward without hesitation, raising her blade. Two flashes and then they were gone. Their bodies crumpled beside the others, forming a quiet, broken line of the fallen.

The group stood paralyzed: six lives extinguished, and no resistance left.

The air hung heavy, a mixture of blood and grief clinging to everything. Only the whisper of the wind rustled through the trees.

The horsemen continued their inspection, their movements methodical as they ignored the growing despair around them. When Seria reached Ramirez, she paused, her sharp gaze raking over him.

She drew her blade, eyes narrowing. "This one doesn't bear the mark. His life holds no meaning to the Architect."

Ramirez squared his shoulders. His breathing was shallow— but his stance never wavered. "Do what you've got to do," he said. "I'm not begging."

Seria raised her sword.

Before it could fall, Dr. Terracotta stepped forward, his knees barely holding him upright. "Wait," he said, his voice trembling with conviction.

Seria turned, irritated. "You dare to interfere?"

Terracotta nodded once. "Yes." He stepped between them, hands raised in a show of submission, but his voice grew firmer as he spoke. "You've already taken six of us. The Architect values order and discipline, right? He needs slaves." His eyes flicked toward Ramirez. "This man is a mechanic, the best I've seen. He can keep your ships flying and your veil functioning. He can take broken scraps and make them work."

Seria tilted her head, unconvinced. "A mechanic? That's your plea?"

Before she could continue, Ramirez's voice cut through. "Then take him too."

Seria blinked. Ramirez's jaw tightened.

"He's a real scientist, not just a lab coat for show, and he understands your technology better than we do. He's already been studying the Eden Veil. If you kill him, you'll lose something you can't recover." He glanced at Terracotta, then at Regar. "If you want slaves, fine. If you're smart, take both of us. Otherwise, you'll waste two good minds for no reason."

A long silence followed.

Terracotta's mouth opened, then closed again. His lip trembled, but he steadied it. "He's right," he said. "We're not warriors, but we're useful. That's all that matters to you, isn't it?"

Regar's gaze shifted between the two men—one trembling and the other defiant. Two survivors who had no marks but held value.

Regar gave a slow nod. "Very well. Take them both."

Seria lowered her blade, though her annoyance was palpable. "You've bought yourselves some time," she said. "We'll see how long you remain useful."

Terracotta took a shaky breath as Ramirez stepped beside him.

Ramirez muttered under his breath. "I should've let you die."

Terracotta half-smiled, his eyes glistening, and his voice low. "You still might."

They didn't laugh; neither of them had the strength for that. But they stood together as the shackles came down.

Regar approached where Roo was standing, his eyes narrowing as he noticed Madison and Savannah huddled behind him. With a calculated movement, he slid Roo aside with the casual force of someone who knew resistance was futile—and knelt before the two girls.

"Were you hiding from me, little ones?" he said, brushing his fingers through their hair. "Do I scare you?"

Behind him, Seria stepped closer, her lips curling into a cruel smile. "I killed their mother while they were trying to escape," she said. "I had planned on offering these two as a gift to the Architect."

Roo's body tensed. Without hesitation, he stepped forward and placed himself between the girls and Regar. His voice was steady, though his hands trembled at his sides. "Leave them alone," he said. "I will protect these two with my life."

Regar rose with a soft chuckle, his tall figure casting a long shadow over Roo. "I admire your bravery, boy," he said, almost amused. "But you bear a mark. You are not yet ready to face my Scythe." He glanced at the hounds and flicked his wrist. "Take the little ones as well. They'll make fine additions for the Architect."

The girls whimpered, clutching tighter to Roo as the hounds moved in to corral them.

Roo crouched beside them, bringing himself level with their frightened eyes. "Hey," he said, his voice soft yet steady. "Don't be afraid. I'm right here with you." He placed a hand on each of their shoulders, shielding them as best he could.

Regar continued his inspection, his steps slow and deliberate. When he reached Dr. Solomon, his eyes locked onto the book clutched in his hands.

He paused. "That is quite an ancient book," Regar said, his voice thick with suspicion. He stepped closer, narrowing his gaze on the intricate symbol embossed across the cover. "It bears the mark of the Nephilim. Where did you find such a remarkable artifact?"

Dr. Solomon hesitated, his knuckles whitening as he gripped the book. "I discovered it inside that cabin," he said, voice tight but composed.

Regar snatched the book from him with a sneer, inspecting it like a predator sniffing out deception. "Do not insult me with lies! Books of this nature do not appear. Someone gave this to you." He held it aloft with both hands, lips curling into a wicked smirk. "I shall present it to the Architect myself. He will enjoy adding such a treasure to his collection."

The horsemen completed their inspections with mechanical precision. When they were done, Regar turned to Seria. "Have your hounds shackle them. We will take them back to the ship. The Architect will want to enjoy his spoils."

Cold chains bound their wrists and ankles. There was no struggle, no fight—only the sound of metal clanking and the heavy footsteps of the defeated. The group marched through the forest, their long shadows broken beneath the moonlight. The cabin, once filled with life, now stood hollow and silent—a monument to grief.

The man in the purple robes emerged from the tree line, his face etched with the horror of the atrocities he had just witnessed. He knew he could do nothing to save the group, not against the horsemen. Their strength was too great for him to control.

His steps were slow, burdened by the weight of what he had seen. He entered the cabin; the floorboards creaking beneath him. On the table sat a soft blanket, and beside it, a battered rubber ball—Brutus's favorite. He grabbed both of them and turned them in his hands to look at them in more detail.

He returned to Norm's body, placing the toy in the old man's stiffened grip. Wrapping the blanket around him, he treated each fold as a gesture of reverence. He lingered for a moment, his fingers resting on Norm's shoulder. No words were spoken.

One by one, he carried the others—Haru, Akira, Hans, Charlotte, Salvador, and Viktor—and laid them beside Norm, arranging them in a row, as if tucking them into sleep. With precision, he built the pyre, stacking dry pine branches and logs until it reached his shoulders. The scent of sap and bark filled the air.

When the pyre was ready, he knelt, his hands coming together in silent prayer. Wildflowers swayed around him in the gentle night breeze, their petals glowing in the firelight.

He struck a match. The flame flared to life—fragile and fleeting—before taking hold. Fire licked across the pyre like a living thing, devouring wood and flesh alike. The heat rose, and the air shimmered in its wake.

The man in the purple robes stood vigil. He didn't weep; his expression was carved from stone. As the flames climbed toward the sky, he whispered something that no one else would hear, and the wind carried it away.

CHAPTER TWENTY-FIVE

New Eden Awaits

T he group limped up the ramp of the ship, their spirits sagging under the weight of cold metal chains that bit into their wrists with each step. The vessel loomed overhead, humming with a mechanical thrum that vibrated through the soles of their boots.

Brutus resisted with every ounce of strength he had left, his claws shrieking against the steel ramp as the hounds barked in frustration behind him.

"Get on the ship, you stubborn beast!" one hound yelled, punctuating his command with a sharp kick.

Lizzie spun around, her face streaked with tears and defiance. "Leave him alone!" she said, her voice slicing through the heavy air like the crack of a whip.

The hounds froze, their snarls curling into growls as the sound of boots echoed up the ramp.

Seria emerged from the shadows, her armor catching the dim light in crimson flickers. She moved with a purpose, fury burning in her eyes. Her gaze locked onto Lizzie.

"You don't get to command my hounds," she said. Without warning, her hand flew out, delivering a sharp slap that echoed through the silent entryway of the ship. Lizzie staggered, raising one hand to her cheek. Her knees buckled, but she stayed upright. The fire in her eyes remained.

"He's just a dog," she said, voice trembling but unbroken. "He's braver than any of you."

Seria leaned in close, her breath hot and venomous. A razor-thin smile spread across her lips. "My hounds don't answer to pathetic rodents," she said. "Speak again, and I'll make sure you regret it."

Brutus, his sides heaving and tongue lolling, let out a soft whimper. His body shook as he took a few hesitant steps forward. His claws scraped against the floor again, now softer, the sound resembling a defeated sigh.

The group watched in helpless silence as the bulldog was dragged up the steps and into the ship—his once-proud frame reduced to a trembling shadow.

Inside the cargo hold, the cold was immediate and unforgiving. The air smelled of rust and fuel, thick with the stink of damp metal and oil. The walls groaned with the ship's slow movements, and the floor beneath their boots vibrated.

The hounds barked and shoved them forward, the clang of chains and armored footsteps echoing in the dim cargo hold. Then came a sharp strike to Roo's back. He stumbled, his footing slipping on the slick steel, and slammed to the floor with a heavy thud. The pain jolted through his ribs, and the sound of impact rang out like a dropped hammer.

He let out a groan, blinking against the harsh overhead lights. Before he could rise, he felt tiny hands tugging at his arm.

"Are you okay?" Madison asked, her voice soft but steady— like a thread of calm in the chaos.

Savannah knelt beside her, her eyes darting between Roo and the hulking silhouettes of the hounds that loomed just beyond the shadows.

Roo forced a breath and pushed himself upright. The cold bit at his palms as he brushed them off. "I'm fine," he said, though his voice was quieter than usual. He reached out, resting a comforting hand on Madison's shoulder. "You two all right?"

Savannah nodded, though her lip quivered. Her voice came in a whisper, fragile and trembling. "Why are they doing this to us?"

Roo lowered to one knee, the chains binding his wrists rattling as they pooled beside him. The girls were shivering, the chill in the air was nothing compared to the deeper frost of fear and grief tightening around them.

"Because they fear us," he said. "Scared of what we might do."

Madison frowned, confusion and sadness knotting her brow. "But... we're just kids."

Roo watched the pacing hounds, their wet noses twitching as they scanned the area. He turned back to the girls, his voice gentler now. "You're more than that," he said. "You're stronger than you think. Both of you."

For a moment, fear loosened its grip on their eyes, replaced by something quieter but stronger. It wasn't bravery yet; it was faith— faith in him. And for now, that was enough. The girls exchanged a glance, then Savannah shifted closer. Her small hand slid into his, squeezing tight, offering comfort, a small sliver of light in a world full of darkness.

Savannah leaned her head against Roo's shoulder as Madison stared into the open space.

Two butterflies fluttered through the cargo hold.

317

They glided through the ship, their delicate wings glowing in the dim light. One butterfly was pale gold, while the other was a gentle lavender. They danced in the air above the girls for a moment before vanishing into the darkness beyond.

Madison's lips parted in awe. She reached up, as if to catch the moment before it disappeared. "Did you see that?" she whispered.

Savannah nodded. "Yeah... I did."

Neither of them spoke another word, but they both knew that something was watching over them.

On the other side of the hold, Dr. Terracotta stumbled as a hound shoved him hard in the back. He pitched forward and slammed into Dr. Solomon, who caught him with both arms, steadying the smaller man.

"Easy," Solomon said, his voice even, though his eyes tracked the hounds' movements. "They're not gentle."

Terracotta straightened, one hand clutching his chest. His glasses sat askew on his nose, and his face was pale with sweat.

"I'm not built for this," he said. "I design radio equipment and troubleshoot signals. I don't get tossed around by monsters."

Solomon adjusted his grip on the wall behind him, helping to keep balance as the ship hummed and rattled. "They're not monsters," he said. "They're hounds."

Terracotta shot him a look. "Was that... sarcasm?"

"A little," Solomon said. "But it's easier to stay grounded if you call things what they are."

Terracotta exhaled, glancing at Roo, along with the girls gathered in the corner. Roo knelt between them, his shoulders tense and his eyes alert.

"They've been through a lot," Solomon said. "You've seen it. Do you think they'll hold together?"

Terracotta hesitated, surprised by the question. He followed Solomon's eyes for a few seconds before answering. "They're just children," he said. "Roo is different. He steps up. When things fall apart, he remains steady. He doesn't even realize he's holding everyone together."

Solomon nodded. "What about you?"

Terracotta fidgeted with the edge of his coat sleeve, his voice quieter. "I'm terrified," he said. "I'm always terrified, but I'm still here. That has to count for something."

"It does," Solomon said.

A sharp bark from the hounds snapped their attention back. One had taken a step too close to Terracotta, drawing a visible flinch.

Ramirez stepped between them, arms folded, his body language daring the hound to try again.

"You boys shove the wrong guy again, and we're going to have words," Ramirez said, his tone laced with anger and just enough humor to make it dangerous. "I mean, is this your first time handling prisoners, or did they just yank you off a leash this morning?"

Seria's head turned. Her boots clanked against the metal floor as she crossed the hold, every step measured and menacing. Her expression was unreadable, but her eyes locked on Ramirez with the slow, seething attention of someone choosing where to slice first.

"Amusing yourself, boy?" she said. Her voice was silk soaked in steel. "Perhaps I should remove those arms of yours and see how well you entertain without them."

Ramirez didn't back down. His jaw tightened, but the bold smirk stayed. "Try it," he said. "I'll still clap when someone takes you down."

The tension snapped tight. Even the hounds paused; they could sense it.

Seria only smiled—cold and joyless—and turned on her heel, her long brown hair flicking behind her like a war banner.

The metallic clang of a door slammed through the tension.

Regar entered with a swagger in his step. "The Architect is waiting for us," he said, his voice rich with satisfaction. "New Eden awaits."

Before anyone could react, Brutus padded forward from the shadows, still breathing hard and still defiant. He stared at Regar.

Without hesitation, the bulldog lifted his leg and urinated on Regar's boot.

For a moment, no one breathed.

A chuckle broke out in the hold. Another one followed. It spread like a spark across dry leaves—small, wild laughs breaking free from the group like pressure being released. Even Roo managed a grin through the ache.

Regar's eyes went wide, face twisting in disgust as he looked down at his soaked boot. "This filthy creature..." he said. "Durbal, prepare for departure. The Architect will decide what to do with it."

Laughter faded as the ship's engines roared to life. The hold vibrated, and the walls groaned. Outside the small viewing slits, the world tilted and vanished beneath them.

They were airborne—flying toward whatever waited in New Eden.

Roo sat beside Lizzie, shifting as the cold metal shackles dug into the skin around his wrists. The chill from the restraints had seeped into his bones. He leaned toward the small, grimy window, his breath fogging the glass as he stared out at the endless expanse of ocean below. The waves churned like shadows chasing each other in the deep.

"What do you think New Eden will be like?" he asked. "We know so little about the Architect... what he's building."

Lizzie didn't answer right away. When she turned to him, her eyes held a quiet storm—equal parts strength and fear. "If we're wearing these shackles," she said, her fingers brushing against the chains around her wrists, "then it won't be anything good."

"What if we're stuck like this forever? The Architect could force us into something from which we can't recover. Something worse than death."

Lizzie reached out, resting her hand on his arm. Her touch was warm against the freezing metal, grounding him in a way nothing else could. "We've survived so much already, Roo. And we did it together," she said, her voice steady. "Whatever's waiting for us... we'll face it the same way."

He didn't answer. Just let the silence stretch between them for a breath or two, long enough for her words to settle in his chest. The knot of dread loosened—not a lot but enough to breathe again.

He turned to her, and for a moment, the flicker of engines and chains faded. All he saw was her. "Together," he said, and the word meant everything.

Lizzie gave a faint nod. Though neither of them said it, they both felt it. In a world unraveling, they'd found something worth holding onto.

Nearby, Dr. Solomon sat, his hands resting on his knees, eyes flicking between the four towering figures pacing the hold. They moved with practiced control, like predators waiting for permission to strike.

He leaned toward Dr. Terracotta, voice hushed but urgent. "Do you realize who they are?"

Terracotta adjusted his glasses with shaking fingers, following Solomon's eyes. "Besides terrifying?" he said. "No."

"They're the Four Horsemen," Solomon whispered. "War. Conquest. Pestilence. Death."

Terracotta froze, staring at him.

"I've studied the myths," Solomon said, his voice steady but strained. "Not just the biblical versions, but the archetypes and symbols. The names may vary here, but the meanings remain consistent. Seria represents War. Regar embodies Death. Rangel symbolizes Pestilence. And Durbal? He represents Conquest."

Terracotta exhaled, his voice somewhere between sarcasm and fear. "You're telling me we're trapped in a metal coffin with the Four Horsemen of the Apocalypse?"

"They are more than mere stories. They exist beyond this place, and they are serving the Architect."

Terracotta leaned back against the wall, his face pale. "Wonderful," he said. "Fantastic. Just when I thought the soul-stealing was peak nightmare fuel."

They sat in silence for a while, the steady hum of the engines a reminder of how far they were from salvation.

On the opposite side of the hold, Savannah clutched Madison's hand. Her voice trembled as she looked up at Roo and Lizzie.

"What's New Eden?" she asked.

Roo turned, surprised by how quiet her voice was. It cut through the tension like a whisper in a thunderstorm. "It's where the Architect rules," he said. "We know little about it... not yet."

Savannah opened her mouth to asked more—but then paused, her eyes widening.

The two butterflies from earlier fluttered above their heads. They drifted down from the rafters, drifting through the cold air like embers on the wind. Roo blinked, watching them pass between him and the girls, unaffected by the rumbling of the engines or the stench of oil and fear that filled the hold.

Madison's grip on Savannah's hand tightened. Her voice came in a whisper. "They're back..."

The butterflies hovered for a moment above the girls—then vanished through the hull.

An eerie silence settled over the cargo hold, thick and unbroken. The ship groaned as it cut through the sky, its engines humming a mechanical drone that vibrated through the floor. Every so often, the clink of shifting chains echoed—a grim metronome marking the weight of their captivity.

Roo sat near the window, his knees pulled inward, eyes fixed on the streaked glass. Raindrops traced crooked lines across the surface, distorting the endless ocean below. His reflection fractured—like a stranger caught in the water's unrest. His thoughts scattered, spiraling into questions he couldn't answer.

Would they be tested? Broken? Changed?

Lizzie leaned back beside him, her arms draped over her knees. Her gaze was vacant and distant. Faces flickered in her mind—Norm, Charlotte, Haru—ghosts stitched into every step they'd taken. The silence forced her to remember and remembering them hurt.

Dr. Solomon sat with a worn notebook resting in his lap. His thumb slid over its corner pages without turning them, his mind drifting through half-remembered prophecies and fragments of scripture that didn't feel symbolic anymore.

Dr. Terracotta was next to him, his fingers adjusting the same notch on his glasses. He whispered to himself—a loop of facts, equations, and prayers. None of them helped.

Ramirez was a statue, elbows planted, knuckles white. His eyes stared down at the floor below. The heat of his anger lingered, a silent, unseen fire, but his lips stayed sealed, not even a trace of the usual sarcasm escaping.

In the corner, Madison and Savannah huddled together, wrapped in the warmth of each other's arms. Their petite frames trembled. Something was coming. Something bigger than even the monsters they'd faced was waiting for them on the other side of the sky.

The rhythmic crashing of the waves far below seemed to rise into the ship like a haunting melody, the ocean itself was warning them to turn back.

New Eden loomed ahead, unseen but unavoidable. None of them—not one—could have prepared for what awaited inside its walls.

Time blurred after liftoff. Hours passed in silence, broken only by the occasional groan of the ship's frame and the shifting of chains. Hunger gnawed, and the cold deepened. Even the girls stopped asking questions. No one knew what lay ahead—only that each passing minute brought them closer to it.

When the ship began its descent, a jolt ran through the floor, followed by a gut-pulling drop. Roo caught his breath, his stomach lurching as gravity reclaimed them. The restraints tightened around his wrists and ankles, pressing him into the cold floor.

The temperature dropped and the air thinned.

With a final, bone-jarring thud, the ship slammed into the earth. Lizzie stumbled, and Roo reached out, steadying her. Their eyes met—no words, just the shared, silent question, *What now?*

A mechanical groan tore through the hold as the cargo doors opened. A blinding, white light flooded in like a blade, slicing through the shadows. They hadn't seen daylight for hours.

Lizzie squinted into the glare, one arm raised to shield her eyes. She stepped forward, her chains dragging behind her. She took a breath, steadying herself, bracing for what came next. "Time to see what's waiting for us," she said.

One by one, the group stepped onto the platform. The sound of clinking metal was drowned out by something else—a roar, swelling and human, the thunder of a crowd.

As their vision adjusted, a wave of gasps and shock rippled through the group.

The Los Angeles Coliseum was gone.

What stood in its place was a colossal structure—a cathedral to war and spectacle. Towering stone walls stretched into the sky, bleached white like bone. Rows of black iron spires jutted from the parapets, piercing upward like the teeth of a magnificent beast.

Massive archways framed the upper tiers, their colossal forms etched with the scent of old stone and lines of ancient scripture. The markings weren't decorative; they pulsed with meaning, carved in a language older than time.

Between the arches, war banners stretched taut in the wind, their fabric snapping like whips in the air. Each bore a sigil of a Horseman—deep crimson for War, black for Pestilence, bone white for Conquest, and pale ivory for Death. Symbols both bold and unmistakable. On top of each banner rested the flag of Eden, a deep ocean blue with a golden tree at its center, its roots sprawling downward like veins, its branches reaching out like grasping hands.

They all rippled in harmony as if the wind obeyed the Architect's design too.

The air felt rehearsed, too pristine and too symmetrical. The stone under their feet had been polished to a mirror sheen, reflecting their broken forms back at them as they approached. It was beautiful in the same way a loaded gun was beautiful—crafted, intentional, and meant to destroy.

Roo squinted upward, trying to grasp the full extent of the scene before him. Massive staircases lined the outer rings like veins, and torchlight flickered even in the daylight. Crowds filled the upper balconies—thousands of silent, faceless figures observing from above like spectators in a coliseum.

"Holy hell," Ramirez said. He turned in a slow circle, awe melting into unease. "This place... It's beautiful, but it gives me the creeps."

Lizzie swallowed hard, the sound echoing in her ears as she stared up at the wrought-iron gates. They were wrapped in ancient chains, each link scorched and blackened. The chains were meant to bind titans, not guard entrances.

Roo didn't know why, but the sight made something in his bones recoil.

"It's meant to," she said. "It's a trap dressed as a masterpiece."

As they stepped closer, Roo felt the shift beneath his feet—stone gave way to polished obsidian. Each click of his boot echoed, then vanished into the vastness. No birds or even a gentle breeze. Only the heavy, shared breath of thousands... slaves, hauled here from the Architect's shattered worlds. They packed the balconies, their silence a mask for fear. Still, they watched, knowing disobedience meant death.

The air changed.

It didn't just grow colder—it thickened, as though gravity itself had warped. Every breath felt heavier. The chains around the gate stirred—enough to be heard. A faint, metallic groan rolled across the outside of the arena, rhythmic and unsettling, something ancient was waking up.

Roo slowed, the hairs on his neck prickling. His instincts howled, a primal warning before his thoughts could catch up. He glanced at Lizzie; her face etched with tension and her lips a rigid, silent line. The air hung heavy. Neither of them spoke, the silence amplifying the invisible threat. Beyond the iron gates, an unseen presence pressed against them, a powerful entity observing their every move.

At the top of the grand staircase, a figure emerged like a shadow peeled from the void. The Architect.

His robes, black as midnight, flowed with an unnatural weightlessness. They didn't move with the wind; they moved with him. His steps were slow but not hesitant, like every inch of space he crossed belonged to him before his foot touched it.

Roo couldn't look away.

"My Lord," Regar said, bowing at the base of the steps. "I present your spoils."

The Architect didn't answer. He scanned the group with cold detachment, as though assessing the value of rusted tools.

He kept his eyes on Roo for a moment before shifting them to Lizzie.

A sneer twisted across his lips—subtle but cruel.

"So," he said at last, his voice smooth as glass but colder than ice, "these are the ones who would challenge me?" He stepped forward. His presence wasn't loud, but it swallowed the space around him. "How... disappointing."

The words hit hard, like a slap. Delivered as a fact.

He raised a hand—just a flick of the wrist—and gestured to the hounds. "Take them to the cells near Heliosa," he said. "They are beneath my interest."

The hounds moved, but Lizzie stepped forward. "You can't keep us locked away!" she yelled, her voice cracking at the edges. "We're not your prisoners!"

The Architect stopped. He turned back with the casual grace of a man unbothered by threats. His gaze locked onto Lizzie, and the world seemed to narrow. "You misunderstand," he said. "Prisoners imply worth. A risk. A need for containment." He took a step toward her, the space around him chilling further. "You are none of those things." Another step. "You are nothing." His voice dropped to something almost... reverent. "And nothing escapes my will."

The chains behind him groaned again—louder this time. It was enough to send a tremor through the stone beneath their feet. The gates seemed to shift, as if bracing against something buried inside.

Lizzie stood her ground, though her jaw clenched with effort. "There's always a way out," she said. "Even from monsters like you."

The Architect tilted his head in amusement. "Then by all means," he said, "try."

He turned again, his robes sweeping across the steps like oil across glass.

Roo felt the moment solidify. They were meeting for the first time. The monster's shape was revealed. It wasn't a tyrant or a brute. It was a surgeon, a designer. A god who thought he owned them.

With a wave of his hand, the hounds shoved the group forward. Lizzie stumbled, but Roo caught her.

As they approached the Coliseum's echoing catacombs, Roo took a final glance back. The chains at the gate twitched again.

In his mind, the Architect's voice echoed. *"Nothing escapes my will."*

As they were herded deeper into the Coliseum, the grandeur outside vanished behind stone walls slick with condensation. The air thickened with dampness and despair. Distant cheers echoed from the arena above—warped by distance yet sharp enough to chill the spine.

Savannah's eyes darted across the dim hallway, scanning the faces of countless prisoners. She froze when she saw him. "Madison," she said, clutching her sister's arm. "It's him. It's Father."

Madison followed her gaze—and there he was.

President Davidson stood among the captives, hunched under the weight of shackles, his once-imposing figure reduced but unbroken. The moment his daughters called out "Father!"— his head snapped up.

He didn't have time to react before they crashed into him. As they leaped into his arms, he crumpled to his knees, arms outstretched. He held them close, burying his face in their hair as tears streamed down his bruised face.

"My beautiful butterflies," he said, his voice cracked and shaking. "I thought you were gone." He held them like a man trying to stop the world from breaking apart again. "How did you get here? Where's your mother?"

Savannah and Madison exchanged a pained glance. Savannah clung tighter.

"That monster," she said, pointing at Seria. "She took Mom away. But... an astronaut saved us. Then—" She glanced back over her shoulder, eyes landing on Roo. "Then he kept us safe."

Davidson followed her gaze. Roo stood there, silent. A boy caught in a man's war.

Davidson's breath caught.

Roo stepped forward. "Name's Roo," he said. "I tried to keep them safe. I still will."

Davidson gave him a nod that felt deeper than words could express. "Thank you, Roo." Then he stood, keeping his arms around the girls. His eyes locked on Seria. "You," he scowled. "You are a monster. I swear on my faith—they will never suffer at your hands again."

Seria turned toward them, her smile razor-sharp. She approached with slow, deliberate confidence, her hair swaying like a blade. She reached out, brushing her fingers through Madison's hair.

The girl recoiled with a small, frightened whimper.

Seria's eyes met Davidson's. "I hope we have the chance to put that to the test."

Davidson's rage exploded as he swung. The punch landed square against her jaw with a sickening crack. Seria staggered back, more from surprise than force. Her smile vanished as her eyes narrowed, and the air vibrated with her fury.

"How dare you strike me?" she yelled, grabbing Davidson by the throat. With one hand, she lifted him off the ground.

"I am the goddess of war. I could snap your neck like dry wood."

"Seria!" The Architect's voice sliced through the corridor, cold and thunderous.

The air stopped moving. Even Seria obeyed.

She dropped Davidson. He collapsed, coughing and gasping but still glaring up at her with defiant fire.

The Architect descended a few steps, his robes gliding behind him like liquid shadow. "Take the two young ones to my quarters. Chain them to the wall." His eyes swept to Davidson. "As for him... place him with the warriors. He'll provide entertainment."

"No!" Savannah cried, clutching her father's arm. "Don't take him!"

Davidson knelt, cradling her face. "Listen to me, Savannah," he said, voice trembling but firm. "Be brave. Look after your sister. Trust Roo."

He turned to Roo. "Thank you," he said, his voice raw with gratitude. "If anything happens to me... please. Keep them safe."

Roo nodded, jaw clenched. "I promise."

The hounds moved in, pulling the girls away. They screamed for their father, but Davidson didn't resist. He stood tall, even as his body trembled.

As the two girls were dragged around the corner, a sudden shaft of light pierced the corridor from a tall window.

Through it fluttered two butterflies. They glided down, circling Roo and then drifting toward Davidson. The girls stilled, as did Roo. Even the hounds paused.

The butterflies lingered in the beam of light, their wings glinting like stained glass in the dust. Davidson's eyes widened. A smile came across his face for the first time in a long time.

Just as quick as they came, the butterflies were gone—disappearing into the light above, leaving only silence in their wake.

The hounds marched the group deeper into the bowels of the Coliseum. Torchlight flickered against the damp, narrow stone corridors, casting grotesque silhouettes that danced like memories of pain. Every footstep echoed like a countdown. Roo's shackles scraped against his raw wrists. He could still hear the girls crying.

One by one, they were tossed into cells—iron bars slamming shut like punctuation marks at the end of hope. The floor was wet, the air thick with the scent of rust, mold, and old screams.

Above, far from the darkness, the Architect stood outside the Coliseum's gates, his black robes flowing in lazy ripples. The wind carried faint wails from below, but he didn't flinch. Regar approached beside him, stiff-backed, holding a squirming mass of muscle and snorts in his arms.

Brutus.

The bulldog growled, refusing to go.

"My Lord," Regar said, his voice tinged with caution and something almost defensive. "This creature... soiled my boot earlier. What would you have done with it?"

The Architect turned his gaze, settling on the bulldog as one might appraise a ruined painting. He reached out and lifted Brutus from Regar's arms, holding him aloft with both hands. Brutus wriggled, snapped, and drooled—refusing dignity but not defiance.

The Architect squinted. "What is this... thing?" he said, his voice dripping with disdain. "It looks as though it was shaped by accident and kept out of pity. Its face resembles a collapsing cake."

Brutus let out a series of congested snorts, then sneezed in the Architect's face.

The Architect didn't flinch. He blinked and handed Brutus back to Regar, wiping his cheek with a silken sleeve.

"Have you brought this to me as a joke?" he asked. "It wheezes like a rusted engine and drools like a broken fountain."

Regar hesitated, then stood tall. "It protected the dead and did not flee. It didn't fit the pattern of a normal animal. I thought you might use it in the arena."

For a moment, the Architect said nothing. His gaze drifted toward the horizon—where the crumbled skyline of the old world clawed at the stormy heavens.

A laugh erupted from the Architect. Soft at first, then sharper. "Pattern?" he said, turning back toward Regar. "Regar, you disappoint me. Do not mistake patterns for significance."

His eyes shot down at Brutus again, who now sat licking his paw with stubborn indifference. "This animal is an offense to the natural order. Fat, malformed, loud... and yet somehow still alive. A parody of purpose."

Brutus stared up at him, head tilted in confusion.

The Architect stared back... then waved a hand, already bored.

"Set it loose. Let the wilderness reclaim its joke."

Regar hesitated. "... Let it live?"

"Let it wander," the Architect replied, turning his back. "If destiny intends this... creature to matter, then fate has grown far more absurd than I feared."

With a last glance toward Brutus, Regar knelt and stared at the bulldog. "Go, you wretched beast," he said.

Brutus didn't hesitate. He bolted and ran toward the now desolate landscape that once was Los Angeles.

Regar straightened, retrieving the book he had taken from Dr. Solomon. "My Lord," he said, holding it out. "One prisoner carried this. It bears the mark of the Nephilim."

The Architect turned, his expression unreadable as he reached for the book. His fingers hovered just above the surface before taking it, as though testing for something unseen. He traced the sigil with a faint smile, then opened the cover with the reverence of a man expecting revelation.

There was nothing. The pages were blank.

His brow furrowed in contemplation. He flipped through more—blank... blank... blank.

"How curious," he said. "A Nephilim seal... yet no voice inside. No memory. Just silence."

Regar squirmed, thinking he had failed again.

"It may be a forgery—"

"No. It's real. I can feel it. It's waiting to be awakened." He snapped the book shut and handed it back to Regar without looking.

"Place it beside my bed. I'll see if it speaks after nightfall."

Regar hesitated. "And if it doesn't?"

The Architect's voice dropped to a near whisper. "Then it's waiting for someone else."

Inside the cells below the arena, the air was thick and unmoving, heavy with the weight of uncertainty. Roo leaned against the cold iron bars, his fingers curling around them, eyes searching the shadows beyond. A faint torch sputtered in the corridor, casting erratic flares of light that danced across the stone walls like restless spirits.

"What do we do now?" Roo whispered.

"We wait," Lizzie said, her voice steady but laced with unease. Her eyes met his. "And we plan."

The silence stretched long and suffocating until a voice emerged from the shadows. It was soft and melodic, eerie in its calm. "You're not alone. I am Heliosa... the Architect's historian and his prisoner."

The group turned. A figure stepped into the light—tall and striking, with her long red hair cascading like molten fire. Her eyes, the color of polished bronze, held centuries of pain and knowledge, and in them, something else... hope.

Ramirez was the first to speak; his suspicion snapped the spell. "What do you want?"

Heliosa didn't flinch. "I've been waiting for you. The Architect has spoken of your arrival... but I wanted to see for myself what could make him nervous."

Dr. Solomon stepped forward. "What does he want with us?"

Heliosa's eyes locked on him—and widened. Her breath caught. "It can't be," she said. "The Oracle was right."

Solomon frowned. "What oracle?"

She stepped closer, voice trembling but urgent. "The Oracle of Zion, on my planet, foresaw this long before the Architect enslaved me. She spoke of a man scarred by fate—three jagged marks on his face. A man who would one day take the sacred books and unlock their knowledge."

Solomon's hand rose to his cheek. The scars burned cold beneath his fingers. "I'm just a man of faith," he said.

"No," Heliosa said, her voice firmer now. "You are the one. The one who can understand the Testament of Eden and unlock its true meaning."

Roo, Lizzie, and the others stood frozen, their grief forgotten in the shadow of a prophecy they didn't yet understand.

"The Testament of Eden?" Solomon asked. "What is it?"

"The Testament is older than the Architect. It holds the truths he's buried—his rise, the fractures in creation, and the key to ending him."

Lizzie stepped forward; fire returned to her eyes. "We need that book. Whatever it takes."

Heliosa nodded. "Listen, while I tell you everything I know— about the Architect, Eden, and the war you were born into."

As her tale unfolded, she told a story of betrayal, creation, and rebellion—the cells seemed to shrink with gathering purpose.

Beyond the Coliseum's towering walls, the horizon bled crimson. The ruins of Los Angeles rose like broken teeth beneath a dying sky. Amid the desolation, Brutus padded forward, his little legs determined, his snorts echoing across the cracked earth.

A figure waited ahead. Clad in purple, the man's robe caught the last light of day.

Brutus paused, his tail twitching. With a snort, he trotted forward.

The man knelt. A gentle hand patted Brutus's head, and then he whispered just above the breeze, "Good boy. Follow me."

With a soft bark, Brutus turned and fell into step beside him. The two walked into the wasteland, vanishing beneath the bleeding sky. The last thing to disappear was the purple robes, fluttering like a banner of rebellion as they crossed into destiny.

CHAPTER TWENTY-SIX

History Lesson

Heliosa sat cross-legged on the cold floor of her cell in the New Eden Coliseum. Dim lights flickered above, casting restless shadows that danced across the concrete walls like ghosts refusing to be forgotten. Across the hall, the group watched and listened—eyes sunken with exhaustion yet gleaming with a spark of curiosity that refused to die.

Heliosa shifted, the chill biting through her thin clothing, and cleared her throat.

"Sit down," she said. "I'll tell you how we ended up here... a history lesson about the rise of the Architect." She paused, letting the weight of her words settle. "Your sacred texts speak of a Creator who shaped both the Earth and the heavens with meticulous care. What they fail to mention is what was lost long before Babel scattered the tongues of man, before the first of the Seven Days, the Creator needed someone to help him design."

Her voice dropped, almost reverent. "Long before Genesis, before time itself had a spark, the Creator spoke a single word into the void. Not in the tongues you know but in the First Language—

the language that shaped light, bound gravity, and sang stars into existence. A language not spoken but breathed." She let that linger. "From that breath, amid the celestial harmonies, a being emerged."

Around her, the cell became silent, and she felt the stones close in.

"He was called, summoned by the Creator's will alone. The Creator gifted his creation with profound wisdom, timeless understanding, and immortality. He looked upon him and, in the First Language, gave him his name." Her eyes narrowed as she searched for something that she dared not speak. After a few moments, Heliosa whispered, "Al'Varaneth."

The syllables vibrated in her throat as if they didn't belong in a mortal mouth. A chill spread through the cell, prickling the skin of those inside.

"It means the one who draws from light and line. With that name, the Creator gave him purpose—but power was withheld. Divine knowledge was his to hold, but the act of creation was withheld. The balance had to remain."

She leaned forward, her voice steady but quiet now. "The Creator gazed at him and spoke—translated best it might be, 'Rise, my faithful companion. You shall serve as my Architect, aiding me in the design of extraordinary realms.'"

"With those words, Al'Varaneth awakened—his mind burst with visions of geometry and wonder, blueprints unfurling behind his eyes like constellations. He rose as the right hand of the Creator, his purpose etched into him like a divine equation.

"Together, they began. The void stretched before them, a canvas untouched by time or law. From the Creator's will, two designs emerged: one for Earth, a sanctuary for humanity; the other for Eden, a realm of order and beauty, meant as a gift for Al'Varaneth.

The Creator's eyes narrowed in awe—as he traced the curvature of rivers not yet formed and the scaffolding of mountains still unborn.

Next came the moment that split nothingness apart.

The Creator raised his hand and spoke words from the First Language into the void.

Or'a veth'elai. Let there be light.

Vibrations pulsed through the void, bending space and time to His will. The sound didn't echo; it became.

The snap came after that.

A snap of celestial fingers—a gesture so simple and so final that the void itself convulsed.

Light exploded outward in ribbons of gold and violet, fracturing the dark. Stars blinked into place like watchful eyes. Gravity took shape, and atmospheres curled around new worlds.

For six sacred days, the Creator and his Architect worked as one—divine hands moving like dancers, each gesture a brushstroke of energy. Together, they started executing the blueprints Al'Varaneth had designed.

Mountains surged upward, their snow-capped peaks clawing at the heavens. Rivers wove through valleys like silver veins, whispering melodies that harmonized with the rustle of new life. The scent of damp, fertile soil rose as creatures emerged, each one a note in creation's symphony.

Birds darted between branches, stirring the air with the music of their wings. Soft paws padded across the forest floor, pressing into soil still warm from the breath of the Creator. Flowers bloomed in a chorus of color, their petals stretching wide to drink the newborn light. Their fragrance, intoxicating and alive, rose to meet the heavens.

Creation had begun.

As with all things divine, they did not remain in harmony for long.

When the time came to shape humanity, the Creator and Al'Varaneth clashed.

The Creator stood in quiet reverence, watching the swirling dust of potential take form. His voice, soft and full of wonder, broke the silence. "They will be grateful stewards," he said. "Caretakers of beauty and carriers of light."

Al'Varaneth stood beside Him, arms folded, his eyes fixed on the fragile outlines of the first humans. His tone, once reverent, had grown cautious. "I see flaws... pride, hunger, and greed will consume them. They will devour everything we have created, leaving nothing, and shape it to their desires."

"They are not complete," the Creator replied, his gaze never leaving the forming figures. "That is where their beauty lies... in choice."

"They will choose destruction."

A pause stretched between them like a canyon. The light dimmed.

Al'Varaneth stepped forward, his voice booming. "You give them Eden? My Eden? A world built by our hands—and hand it over to these... beasts?"

The Creator turned to him at last, his expression solemn. "It is not yours, nor mine, but ours. You call them beasts, but they are my children."

"I would prefer to create a guardian race—one designed for wisdom rather than emotion. Discipline should take precedence over desire."

The Creator raised His hand. "Enough." His voice was still calm, but now it carried weight. Galaxies bent under that word. "This is my decision," he said. "I will give them your test."

At the heart of Eden, a colossal tree emerged, its roots drinking deep from the fountain of creation. Its towering trunk stretched skyward, so high it almost pierced the firmament above. The bark—gnarled and spiraled—was etched with time itself, ancient glyphs from the First Language woven into its grain.

The surrounding air thickened with a heady sweetness— intoxicating and alive. Its vast canopy swayed like a sea of emerald fire, whispering truths no mortal ear could bear.

Birds sang from its highest limbs, and within that beauty, temptation bloomed.

A fruit, vibrant as blood and gleaming like polished glass, hung at the Tree's center. It pulsed, as if alive with knowledge. The scent —a mysterious blend of sweetness —was irresistible.

The price was steep. One bite, and immortality would vanish. Hard labor, guilt, and death would take its place.

The Creator set the terms. "If they eat, they fall. If they resist, they rise. Eden and Earth shall both be theirs—if they prove they are worthy."

The Creator shaped the first humans. One man. One woman. Fashioned from warmth and breath, imbued with intention, far from the cold stillness of marble.

He placed them in the lush embrace of Eden, where leaves rustled in the breeze and water murmured in the distance like a gentle chorus. Beneath the canopy of the Tree of Life, He whispered to them the sacred truths in the First Language. They knew the consequences if they chose wrong.

Al'Varaneth had already made his own choice. In secret, he turned to one of Eden's earliest creations: a serpent named Lucifer. He whispered to it forbidden knowledge—words never meant to leave the tongue of the divine. The serpent shimmered in the dappled light like molten gold, its scales catching every flicker of sunlight like flame on oil. Its eyes, pale and cloudless, gleamed with eerie guile as it slithered through the grass.

The garden itself reacted—flowers shivered in its wake, petals curling inward. The grass hissed beneath it. Even the air tightened as the serpent approached the Tree.

Before the eyes of the man and woman, it did something no creature had ever dared to do. With a slow, fluid motion, the serpent unhinged its jaw and tore a single fruit from the Tree of Life. It swallowed the fruit whole, unfazed by its effects.

The woman, entranced by the snake's actions, stepped closer. The scent of the fruit filled her lungs, crowding out the distant warnings echoing inside her. Her fingers reached upward.

A heartbeat later, the man joined her. Together, they climbed the Tree of Life. Reaching the top, they stretched toward a branch, their fingers brushing rough bark as they grasped the forbidden fruit. They turned it over, the smooth skin cool against their palms. The fruit called to them, thoughts echoed through their minds. They knew they weren't supposed to eat it, but temptation coursed through their bodies. Unable to resist, they bit into it.

Agony split the garden.

The fruit's sweetness turned to ash on their tongues, while pain wracked their bodies. A bitter scent of regret filled the air like smoke after a fire. The Garden came alive, trees recoiled, and the water stilled.

Above it all, a voice rose. The Creator's voice thundered through Eden, shaking the roots of the Tree of Life and sending tremors through every leaf and stone. The man and woman fell to their knees beneath His fury, trembling in shame.

They pleaded with the Creator and told Him of the serpent— how it climbed the sacred Tree and devoured the forbidden fruit; how its golden scales shimmered like sunlight.

Their explanation could not extinguish the fire kindling in the Creator's chest. Betrayal coursed through him like wildfire.

He cast them out of the Garden—exiling them to Earth, where they would labor, weep, and hope. Their immortality was lost, and their innocence burned away like morning mist. He did not resort to violence; He spoke, and the gates of Eden closed behind them forever.

He turned to Al'Varaneth. The skies darkened, and the ground trembled. Flowers wilted beneath His footsteps as He approached.

The Creator's eyes—once warm with purpose—now blazed like suns collapsing. "Did you deceive them?"

Al'Varaneth opened his mouth, but the truth clung to the walls of his throat. His denials were hollow. A flicker of defiance crept into his voice, but it was too late.

The Creator's voice rose in sorrow so profound it fractured the air. "You gave the serpent words not meant for this world." Thunder cracked in the distance. "I trusted you," the Creator said. "You were the first and my right hand."

The Architect flinched at the words. A fissure split inside him – no trace of guilt, only the corrosive bite of resentment.

The Creator raised His hand. Raindrops fell—soft at first, like tears. The first rain the universe had ever known. Eden wept with Him.

"I spoke your name into the void," the Creator said. "I carved it in the language of stars. You are not worthy of a name." He paused. The wind fell silent. "I strip it from you."

Using the First Language—a language that once built galaxies—He whispered a single word. "Sil'kara."

In that instant, the name Al'Varaneth was erased.

The trees bowed and the flowers closed. Stars overhead blinked, as if in mourning.

The Creator's voice was quiet now, but it fell like a judgment across the sky. "You are the Architect now. Not my companion or my right hand. Only... a builder." He turned to leave but stopped. "You can have this canvas," He said, voice like thunder, "but no one will ever see it. This is your curse." His last words stung deeper than any blade. "I will go to Earth and shape humanity in My image. You will never have power over them."

The Creator turned and walked away. With each step, the colors of Eden dimmed—gold turned to gray, warmth to cold, light became shadow.

The Architect's knees gave way, and he collapsed. Silence surrounded him in the Garden, its beauty now lifeless around him.

He pressed his hands to the ground, gasping and shaking.

Sorrow was a delicate thing. It could be broken. What took its place was something far colder.

His trembling fingers found the old blueprints. He traced their lines like scars, once a companion to the Creator, now a rival.

A builder of his own future and a future forged in vengeance.

Days became weeks, weeks became months, and months became years.

The Architect's resentment didn't fade over time—it calcified. Hardened into an unrelenting desire for vengeance. Eden, once a gift, had become his cage. To escape the crushing silence of his exile, he wandered the world he had helped design.

He descended into ancient caverns, where shadows clung to damp stone like regrets left unspoken. The walls bore the scars of time—etched in silence, weathered by years of solitude. The air was thick with the scent of soil and minerals, grounding him in the reality of his banishment.

He scaled jagged peaks, where winds cut like broken promises and howled like mourning spirits. From the summit of Eden's tallest mountain, he saw it: a distant volcano, brooding and smoldering, its black silhouette curling like a sleeping beast on the horizon.

Something inside him stirred.

He descended again. Rivers cut through the valleys, and he plunged into their cold depths. The sea embraced him with salt and weight. Waves crashed against his form like fists, but he endured, driven forward by rage. Even as Eden's beauty tried to embrace him, he walked through it untouched—his thoughts poisoned by betrayal.

Yet his world did not grieve forever.

Over time, the color returned.

Flowers bloomed in quiet defiance of grief. Meadows stretched green beneath a warming sky. Trees reached upward again, their branches whispering memories into the wind, carrying loss without mourning.

Eden healed, but the Architect did not. He wandered through Eden, a kaleidoscope of colors exploding before his eyes. The gentle breeze carried the sweet perfume of blossoms, each blooming petal a visual delight. The sounds of rustling leaves and buzzing insects filled the air. Everywhere he looked was a constant reminder that the Creator's world still thrived... without him.

He walked with purpose, each step fueling his resolve and every breath tasting of bitterness.

One day, he returned to a cavern that had almost collapsed on him months earlier. This time, he went deeper—beneath the bones of Eden, descending into velvet-dark silence. The air wrapped around him like a burial shroud, and the damp stone walls pulsed with secrets etched into Eden's very foundations.

He listened and heard the slow drip of water, a faint breath of wind, and the stillness of something ancient waiting.

A sudden flash of vibrant blue danced across the cavern walls. The jagged rock shimmered as though awakened, transforming into a crystalline, metallic substance that pulsed like a living nerve.

Rivers of energy flowed across the chamber, threading through the stone like veins. The pulses thudded in his chest—echoing like a celestial heartbeat.

He froze, and his breath caught in his throat.

His fingertips grazed the cool, shifting surface of the wall as he edged forward along a narrow ledge. The low hum of the light ahead was the only thing that broke the silence.

The Architect's eyes widened when he saw it.

Suspended in midair—a perfect sphere of pulsing, radiant blue light. Each wave of its glow distorted the surrounding space, bending the air like heat off stone. The crystalline walls around it reflected its brilliance in fractal mosaics that never repeated.

Awe overtook him, but that soon gave way to hunger.

He had discovered something extraordinary, something the Creator had either hidden... or never found.

A force beyond comprehension, one that could rival the First Light.

He spent months carving a hidden network of tunnels around the sphere.

Experiments were ran, each one leading to the same result... failure. The light eluded his control—slipping through his grasp like a phantom.

He wouldn't give up. The burning rage for revenge clawed at his insides, and the light pulsed, the key to it all. Its vibrant glow promised the power to reshape realities, forcing the Creator to his knees. It could shatter the very ground beneath their feet, only to rebuild it in his own twisted likeness.

The Architect's vengeance had found its heart.

One day, as the Architect sat alone beneath the towering Tree of Life, an idea took root in his mind. He didn't know if it would work, but he'd tried everything else. Spoke to the light. Fought it. Begged it. Nothing answered.

The Tree breathed with something more.

It pulsed with the essence of creation itself—a rhythm he could feel under the soil, like a heartbeat.

He rose, his eyes tracing the bark that curled like ancient script around the trunk. The wood shimmered, warm to the touch, as if it were almost alive.

What if he could take a fragment of it? Just enough to fuse with the light?

A crazy idea. It was risky, but every invention began with a sense of desperation.

He looked up into the canopy of Eden's greatest secret and felt it again—a sense that he had once been worthy of it. Once. Not anymore.

Maybe this would change that.

It would take more than force to penetrate the Tree of Life. He'd need fire—the kind that could birth gods or break them.

His mind returned to the volcano he had seen from the mountain's summit—its jagged silhouette, black and sleeping, had haunted him ever since. An embodiment of both death and creation.

His thoughts raced, and his hands sketched as new blueprints for a forge took shape.

Near the base of the volcano, he carved the forge from stone and ash. Jagged rocks ringed the basin like teeth. The air shimmered with unbearable heat, and smoke coiled skyward in thick, twisting columns.

The structure was sacred. It was designed for greatness, not function. Every stone was placed with purpose.

Symbols of Eden were etched onto its face. The circular hearth roared with volcanic breath, fed by molten lava drawn through a lattice of glowing conduits.

The forge lived.

Despite the oppressive heat, natural light streamed through arched openings carved with divine symmetry, casting shifting patterns of gold and crimson across the floor.

The Architect returned to the cavern of light.

With trembling hands, he chiseled at the crystalline metal surrounding the light source. Sparks flew like the dying cries of stars. The cold material stung his skin.

He gathered the shards, combining them with gold he had unearthed from Eden's veins. The mixture irradiated as it melted— otherwordly and molten, like the blood of heaven and hell combined.

He poured it into a sword mold, shaped in a deliberate design. A single blade, meant to pierce the bark of the Tree and fuse with the light.

At last, he unleashed the volcano's fury.

A tempest of flame and pressure engulfed the mold. The hiss of molten alloy echoed like a beast exhaling its last breath. Smoke poured from vents carved into the walls. Charred stone blackened under the pressure.

For a full day, he worked—feeding the flame and shaping the weapon. Upon its creation, the sword groaned.

The Architect stepped forward and struck the cracked mold with a single blow, shattering it.

In the dimming light of the forge, his masterpiece lay before him.

The Sword of Eden.

Forged from creation and destruction, born of light and betrayal; beauty and wrath made of steel.

He lifted it and examined it like a soldier preparing for battle, running his fingers down the center. It was flawless in every sense of the word. A perfect creation.

Its edge shimmered.

His path to vengeance had taken form.

With the Sword of Eden in hand, the Architect approached the Tree of Life.

The air around it pulsed with sanctity, each leaf humming with the memory of the Creator.

He hesitated... just for a moment.

With trembling hands, he drove the blade into the Tree's trunk.

The sword didn't resist. With a clean cut, it pierced the heart of the tree, the wood splintering around the edges.

A deep, green sap bled from the wound. It shimmered with the essence of creation, glowing with a pulse that matched the sphere's heartbeat deep within the cavern. The scent was sweet and primal—older than light and older than time.

He gathered the sap into a reinforced pouch and returned to the source of his obsession.

Standing before the radiant sphere, he hesitated and then poured the sap onto the orb.

Just one drop—that was all it took.

It struck the orb, and blinding light erupted, painting the cavern walls in stark white. A deafening boom echoed, and a shockwave slammed the Architect back, the rough stone floor jarring his spine. Air rushed from his lungs, and a gritty taste filled his mouth. Dazed, he gasped, fingers scraping across his chest, dislodging dirt and debris.

Fury and rage consumed him. He screamed; his voice clawed at the cavern walls. Blue light snaked along the blade's edge, pulsing with the orb's rhythmic throb. He felt a tremor in the air as he stepped forward and touched the tip of his sword to the sphere. The light yielded with a soft hiss. Withdrawing, he saw a fragment cling to the tip.

His breath caught.

The metallic substance surrounding the sphere was the conductor and the container. The key to unlocking Eden's true might.

Over the following years, he mined the cavern, extracting the crystalline metal and shaping it with precision. From this sacred ore, he forged reinforced containment vessels—each box etched with markings and pulsing with the stored light.

He wasn't just a builder anymore; instead, he had become a harvester of power.

The Architect's knowledge expanded. He constructed entire systems to channel the light's energy, embedding it into his designs with masterful precision.

His greatest triumph came next—a colossal ship of the air, built from the light-bearing metal. It hovered over the volcanic plains, its hull illuminated with radiant energy. A leviathan of the skies, powered by stolen divinity.

As the Architect was getting ready to leave Eden and journey into the cosmos in search of the Creator, he looked down at the sword of Eden, and a thought took shape.

He knew one weapon would not be enough.

A blade could cut, but he needed something to bend wills and command.

So, he returned to the forge and crafted a second mold. This time a staff—tall, elegant, and crowned with a serpent's head.

A tribute to his first defiance.

The molten blend of crystalline metal and Eden's gold flowed into the mold. When cooled, he shattered it with a blow from the sword.

The Staff of Eden beamed like living fire, its serpent head frozen in mid strike.

As divine as it looked in his eyes, it was incomplete.

He returned to the caverns in search of the staff's crown jewel. A brilliant blue gemstone caught his eye, its refracting light shimmered in the darkness.

He placed it into the serpent's mouth and, using the sword, pierced the sphere one last time, gathering its glowing residue and letting it drip onto the gem.

The reaction was immediate. The gemstone swallowed the light, then radiated a searing pulse before becoming a hypnotic beacon. As the Architect's fingers closed around the staff, raw power coursed through him, a jolt that made his skin prickle.

The sword would bring death, but the staff would bring dominion.

Armed with both the Sword and Staff of Eden, the Architect looked to the cosmos.

He would seek the Creator carrying vengeance, a weapon wrought from the marrow of Eden itself.

Heliosa's voice broke through the silence. Her eyes were heavy with memory.

"That's enough for now," she said, her breath shallow. "I need rest." She looked toward the cell wall, where shadows still danced in flickers of dying light. "We'll continue later," she added. "There's more to tell..." She paused, her voice dropping to a whisper. "... including the great flood... and the Battle of Eden."

CHAPTER TWENTY-SEVEN

The Flood

After hours of waiting, Heliosa's voice echoed through the cells, low and deliberate, like the first crack of thunder before a storm. The group leaned in closer, drawn by the weight of her tone. Lizzie's knuckles were white as she gripped her knees. Roo sat cross-legged, while Madison and Savannah clung to each other, wide-eyed and silent. A faint chill had settled in the corridor, or perhaps it only felt that way because of the story they were about to hear.

Dr. Solomon cleared his throat. "Before you begin... You mentioned the First Language. What is it?"

Heliosa turned toward him, her expression softening. "The First Language is not just a means of communication; it is power, intention, and the raw material of creation expressed aloud. Each name it provides shapes a destiny, and every syllable is a thread woven into the tapestry of existence." She paused, as if weighing how much more to reveal. "The Creator Himself spoke before time itself. The Architect knows it too, though only in fragments.

That is how he carves and corrupts— corruption masquerading as creation, but never truly his.."

A look of confusion and curiosity swept over Dr. Solomon. "So, if he speaks a name... he alters its very essence?"

Heliosa nodded once. "That is why the Nephilim look different than what they once were. Words can build, but they can also twist."

A heavy silence followed, laden with the unseen weight of that truth.

"Let us continue."

Fueled by rage and Eden's raw power, the Architect soared through the cold, endless dark of the cosmos. Each star he passed seemed to recoil from him, their warmth dimming, as if repelled by his presence. His mind was burning with vengeance, the Creator's name a cursed ember behind his eyes.

He passed by worlds—new creations, vibrant and full of promise, each a wound to his pride. One planet shimmered with rivers of molten gold and forests of crystal spires. Another spun in a void of violet gas, its mountains shaped like spiraling helices that reached for the stars. A third teemed with life that glowed bioluminescent blue, its oceans singing in frequencies too pure for human ears. The fourth was half-covered in shadow, its cities hanging like lanterns beneath floating landmasses that danced across the sky. The fifth appeared as a vast desert, its sands shifting to form living patterns, as if the world itself dreamed.

He charted them all with cold precision, marking their trajectories and weaknesses in his mind.

"So... you've been busy crafting new realms," he said, eyes narrowing as he passed the fifth. "Each one a monument to your arrogance."

A sixth world came into his view.

A pale blue dot off in the distance, unassuming yet somehow pulsing with significance. He slowed, hovering in the void as the sight of it stirred something primal within him. He recognized it immediately because of its history.

Earth.

The world that the Creator spoke of so often. A stage upon which humanity stumbled, the birthplace of disobedience, and the wound that led to his exile.

His lips curled.

"This is the one," he said, his voice a low snarl. "The world that is responsible for my downfall."

Without hesitation, he descended. His body felt light, a burst of energy breaking through Earth's atmosphere like a divine spear. He landed with a reverberation that resonated in the bones of the Earth and in the pulse of the stars.

His movements were fluid and regal, still showcasing the elegance of his former glory. He walked among the earliest humans like a living flame, causing the grass to wither beneath his feet.

The first humans the Architect encountered were mere shadows of life, struggling through mud and misery. Their bodies were hunched and calloused, and the sun weathered them. Skin cracked from hard labor, with ribs visible beneath tattered garments made of woven grass and animal hide. Choking on the dust, they struggled to breathe, their eyes glazed over, and their spirits seemed to fade away.

He watched them toil, dragging stones up hillsides and crafting pitiful huts with trembling hands. No spark of divinity lingered within, no hint of those he had once deceived in Eden, the ones who had tasted the forbidden fruit. These were afterthoughts, the descendants of rebellion, and they repulsed him.

A sneer spread across his face.

"Is this what the Creator calls perfection?" His voice coiled through the air, low and venomous. "Pathetic."

He stepped forward, and the ground beneath his feet recoiled. The humans turned toward him — then fell to their knees, trembling before a force they could not comprehend.

"This world shall be called Zero," he said. "The origin of all that is corrupt. This is where the plague of humanity began."

He turned, eyes raking across the trembling masses.

"You pitiful creatures... I will call you zeroes—a stain upon creation. Had you not defiled yourselves with the fruit of the Tree, perhaps you would've kept your innocence. Now?" He spat the word like poison. "Now you crawl." His voice echoed like a curse etched into the bones of the land itself.

The wind shifted, and the air grew charged, no longer steeped in malice but alive with a force older and purer, so powerful the very skies rippled as though bowing in reverence. The humans fell to the ground in terror, clutching the soil.

A figure descended through the clouds with reverent force. The light surrounding him was neither harsh nor blinding—it was soft and sacred, a glow that could only come from something untainted. His body was tall and statuesque, skin gleaming like sunlit bronze. Wings extended behind him—vast and pristine, every feather etched with divine precision.

His eyes shimmered with purpose.

When he landed, the Earth listened.

"I see you are the Architect," the figure said, his voice deep, resonant with authority.

The Architect was stunned with recognition. He had witnessed power before, but this... this was something different.

356

"I am Goliath—a Nephilim. The Creator has spoken of you. We are the protectors of humanity in His absence."

The Architect's eyes narrowed. The humans were like crawling insects, yes, but this was something more. Something close to what he once was: divine blood coursed through this being's veins, though tethered to mortal flesh.

The Architect's tone softened, slick as oil on still water.

"Protectors?" he said. "Are you protectors, or has someone deceived you into servitude?" He circled Goliath like a predator around a magnificent stallion. "Look at yourself. You are radiant and strong and carry the breath of Heaven in your lungs—and yet you spend your days shielding creatures who grovel in the dirt. Creatures who fear you."

Goliath remained still, but his eyes narrowed.

"Do they honor your sacrifice?" the Architect whispered. "Do they sing songs in your name? No, they kneel to the One who left you behind." Then, as if reaching into some dark well of ancient memory, the Architect whispered something not meant for mortal ears.

"Dor'emin-tel'sar... kharanai."

The fragments of the First Language, twisted and broken, formed words in his mouth that were close but not perfect.

It was an instant reaction.

In the Architect's hand, the Staff of Eden pulsed with a violent blue light, the air around it crackling. A shockwave rippled through the air after the gemstone pulsed twice. The ground cracked, and the scent of dust filled the air as the nearest human collapsed, blood trickling from his nose.

Goliath staggered backward, his wings half-flaring. His breathing caught, and his eyes widened, as though something profound had stirred within.

The Architect froze.

His eyes darted to the staff, then to Goliath. His smile faltered for only a second before returning, sharper this time.

"You felt that, didn't you?" he said. "Even twisted, the words still carry power."

He glanced down at the glowing gem, then back to Goliath, who now stood taller—his light flickering, dimmer than before.

"Interesting," the Architect said. "So, even the imperfect syllables... resonate. What would happen if I spoke them the right way?"

He stepped forward again, slower now.

"You are not their protector, Goliath. You are their future. Their evolution, but only if you break the chains that bind you." He extended the Staff, its light now calm again, like a serpent waiting to strike. "Join me. Walk as a god, freed from the Creator's shadow, radiant in a light that is yours alone."

Goliath said nothing at first, but the flicker of doubt had entered him. The first language—warped though it was—had stirred something inside his blood. A temptation, and the Architect saw it.

The seduction had begun.

Goliath's pride and resentment fed the seed of doubt that sprouted. The Architect's words carved deep wounds in his faith, wrapping ambition around every fracture. A new order; one where the Nephilim would rule as gods.

"Look at them," the Architect said, gesturing toward the shivering humans below. "They live in filth and worship in silence. For what? A Creator who left them to rot? You were born of divine blood, destined for greatness. Power and dominion should be yours."

The words echoed in Goliath's mind like war drums. He had long-harbored questions about the Creator's absence. Now, those questions formed answers—dangerous ones. The thought of forging a world in his image, free of divine constraint, bloomed like fire in his chest.

The Architect saw the flicker in his eyes and pressed forward, eager to seal the moment with a demonstration. He turned, his grip tightening around the Staff of Eden. The gemstone shimmered, like a restrained breath waiting to exhale.

One human stood only a few paces away. The Architect raised the Staff, its head crackling with unstable energy. He muttered another broken phrase in the First Language, one he only half-understood.

"Ves'tar... dom'khalem."

He drove the staff into the ground.

A wave of force burst outward, throwing the human backward like a rag doll. The man screamed and landed hard against a stone wall, alive but broken, blood trailing from his ears. Goliath flinched as the humans wailed in distress.

Confusion swept over the Architect. He walked forward and examined the staff, turning it in his hands like a puzzle. The gemstone had lit up, but it was only a dim glow. It hadn't obeyed, or perhaps... he hadn't given it the right command.

A snarl curled his lip. He stepped closer to the gasping human, eyes narrowing. "That was not enough." He whispered again, slower this time, feeling the shape of the words as if they were alive in his throat. "Dor'emin... tal'grath..."

The gemstone flared.

He raised the staff high, then drove it into the Earth once more.

The result was immediate.

A cone of searing blue light erupted from the Staff's tip, engulfing the human in a flash so bright it scorched the shadows from the rocks. When the light vanished, all that remained was ash... and a single, clean skull resting atop a pile of white bones.

The Architect bent down and lifted the skull from the heap of bones. With a slow, ceremonial movement, he affixed it to the shaft of the staff, just below the gemstone—a grotesque trophy. A symbol of his triumph—and his growing understanding.

He turned back to Goliath.

"Witness my power," he said. "This is Eden's might, and it can be yours. Imagine what you and your brothers could become—unshackled from a fading god's will, shaping the world in your own image."

Goliath stood frozen with awe. He had seen nothing like this. Power not derived from the Creator.

A part of him recoiled—but another part hungered.

He said nothing, but his silence spoke volumes.

The Architect smiled; he knew his words were making an impact.

Goliath returned to his brothers, his steps urgent, eyes burning with conviction. They congregated on a high, holy plateau the Nephilim had once used for prayer and communion with the heavens. Now, the wind carried tension instead of reverence.

Haligot, second-born and closest to Goliath in strength and wisdom, eyed his brother. "You've seen something," he said. "Something dangerous."

Goliath nodded. "I've seen the future." He spoke of the Architect, the Staff, and the First Language—twisted as it was—and the raw, unrestrained power it unleashed. He described the staff's searing light, the instant death it brought to a human, reducing them to ash. He conveyed the intoxicating feeling of standing above humanity as a god.

Haligot's brow furrowed. "You trust this... fallen one? The Creator exiled him for a reason."

Goliath said, "He exiled him for fear of what he could become." "Just as we are shackled. We bleed and suffer for a world that resents us. Why?"

A murmur rippled through the others. These were beings of grace and power, born to bridge Heaven and Earth—and yet for generations, they had been silent stewards, asking nothing and receiving nothing. Resentment had already planted itself in many of them. Goliath's fire only stoked it.

"The Architect showed me that we could become kings."

Despite Haligot's protests, the others listened. When the Architect appeared before them with the Staff of Eden in hand, they beheld his strength for themselves. He showed his might again—cracking a mountain's edge with a word.

Their resistance crumbled.

One by one, they stepped forward. Hungry for power that was promised to them.

"I renounce my role," said Seraphon, the Watcher of the North.

"I will not kneel for the Creator," said Maldek, whose wings were once white as snow.

"I claim my dominion," said Ithariel, whose voice once calmed storms.

When Haligot remained still, Goliath turned to him. "Brother. This is our time."

Haligot looked up at the sky—still vast and open—but felt nothing. No warmth, no answer, only silence. The Creator had not spoken in years.

He stepped forward, and with that, the last protector fell.

361

With the pact sealed, the Architect led them in a ritual.

A mispronounced but powerful phrase in the First Language drew forth a fire—unnatural, burning blue and silver. Around it, the Nephilim stood in a circle, their wings wide and radiant.

The Architect raised his staff.

"You are not bound to Heaven anymore or beholden to men," he declared. "Cast off the burden. Let your wings be your offering."

The first to step forward was Goliath.

With slow, solemn precision, he unsheathed the blade, its sharp edge catching the dim light. As he spread his wings, their feathers reflected the firelight, appearing like smooth marble.

He sliced them off without hesitation.

A gasp escaped him— a sound of release rather than pain. Blood as luminous as starlight poured from the wound as his wings fell to the Earth, burning to ash the moment they touched the fire. He dropped the blade and turned to face his brothers.

"Do it," he said. "Let this be the last day we are slaves."

One by one, they came forward, clipping their wings in defiance of what they had been. Each one shed light and blood, and with every sacrifice, the fire grew darker, hotter, and more violent.

Though their beauty had once been unparalleled, its decline was a slow, creeping process.

Feathers fell from shoulders. Skin cracked and grayed. Eyes lost their divine glow and filled with something new... rage.

Following the Architect's orders, they descended on Earth as conquerors, their arrival marked by fire, fear, and ruin. They swept through villages like human-shaped tempests, leaving chaos in their wake. Some took women, treating them as prizes, while others seized land, establishing their own kingdoms. Some demanded to be worshipped, while others just destroyed.

Their blood mingled with mortals, birthing horrors that walked with unnatural strength and hollow eyes.

The world rotted under their touch.

Once, the people looked to the sky in hope. Now, they hid beneath the Earth in terror.

Above it all, the Creator watched. He took no action, yet His sorrow was profound and unwavering.

The Nephilim—His bold, bright bridges between Heaven and Earth—had become monsters. Their lights extinguished, and all that remained was shadow.

On Earth, Goliath had become the Architect's most devoted emissary, his hammer, his herald, and his shadow cast long across the nations. Where Goliath walked, hope withered. Villages fell silent as monuments to the old ways crumbled beneath his heel. He delivered the Architect's doctrine with blood.

To him, it was justice.

The Creator had abandoned the world. Goliath would remake it through fear, not faith. He was not a protector anymore.

Destiny had other plans.

His last battle came not against an army nor a warrior king but a boy. A shepherd. One that was too young to carry armor and too small to wield a sword. His name was David.

The clash was brief. A single stone, released by steady hands and belief, struck Goliath between the eyes. Heaven held its breath as the Nephilim's body crashed to the Earth like a fallen star.

It was more than just death; it was a break in the myth.

Goliath wasn't just a soldier—he was the first and the greatest. A living symbol of the Nephilim's divine heritage. For a mortal to kill him was unthinkable. Yet there he lay.

The Architect felt the blow in his bones, but even in loss, he saw an opportunity.

David later described the stone as "divine," and people whispered it carried the Creator's blessing. Some said it glowed for a moment in flight. Others claimed it was the hand of the man in the purple robes that guided it.

In the quiet after the battle, David would recall a presence— unseen, yet heavy in the air. A figure, robed in violet, stood at the edge of the battlefield as if he'd always been there.

Now, as Heliosa recounted the tale, a ripple of unease moved through the group.

Roo leaned forward, voice low. "Could it be... him?"

Lizzie turned toward Roo. "The man in the purple robes?"

Heliosa nodded. "He was there when David struck the blow, and he has been watching ever since."

A heavy silence fell.

They all understood what it meant. The man who had appeared to them, guided them, and warned them—wasn't just part of their story; he had always been part of the story.

Heliosa continued the tale.

Far away, when news of Goliath's death reached Haligot, something inside him broke. He had been the last to pledge fealty to the Architect, but losing his brother shattered the last wall between hesitation and hate.

He stood alone on a cliff's edge when the word came. When he screamed, the sky answered with thunder.

"I will see their blood drown the soil," he swore, eyes burning. "I will burn the name David from the memory of this world."

He turned from the heavens to the Architect.

"I pledge myself in full," he said, voice like a blade. "Protector cast aside. Brother cast aside. I am vengeance."

The Architect welcomed him with open arms.

Haligot, now consumed by his thirst for vengeance, led brutal campaigns across the lands of Earth. Cities burned before his spear. Rivers ran thick with blood. His fury was unmatched and personal. Every slaughtered village and every weeping child became twisted monuments to Goliath's fall. Reason had left him; every strike now was a wound to the memory of David.

Following his example, the Nephilim unleashed their cruelty. Their forms, once bright, now pulsed with a sinister energy. They didn't govern; they destroyed.

Months passed, each more terrible than the last. The Earth itself changed—forests blackened, animals scattered, and stars dimmed, as if turning their faces from the world.

A sound boomed through the darkness. No man, beast, or even Nephilim made a sound.

It was a roar—cosmic, primal, and ancient. A sound that came before language, a cry of the divine heart breaking before its creation. It echoed across mountaintops and ocean floors, resonating within the marrow of every living thing. The sun dimmed, and the moon hid behind the clouds.

The sky cracked open, and the Creator descended.

He came wrapped in a radiant storm—lightning that sang, winds that screamed, and thunder that beat like war drums against the vault of the heavens. His form was glory not flesh. His presence burned away the clouds, making the mountains tremble.

White turned into gold, then the world became still.

The Creator stood in the storm's heart, the Earth beneath His feet scorched to glass. His gaze swept across the ruined lands, and His breath trembled with a burden heavier than rage.

He'd shaped this world with love, crafting its rhythms and entrusting His finest creations—the Nephilim—to protect it.

365

The Creator saw ashes, destruction, and failure.

Once, He had sung over the waters. Now, He whispered over the graves.

"No more," He said.

The skies churned.

Storm clouds gathered with a sense of purpose, roaring to life. Rain fell like a thousand needles of judgment. The oceans swelled as if recalling their commands. Thunder cracked, sounding like bones snapping under divine pressure.

This was a divine reckoning.

Yet, amid that fury... the Creator hesitated. For the first time, He wasn't sure if it would be enough.

The rot ran deeper than water could cleanse.

The Creator turned His gaze toward the storm's edge, where lightning kissed the mountains and the sea clawed at the earth. His voice, once thunder, softened to something almost mournful.

"There is one who still walks beneath My light," He said. "He shall not perish in these waters. He will descend into the Cavern of the Comets and wait for My return. In him, the memory of Eden will endure."

His words were a covenant—spoken into the bones of the storm itself.

The winds paused as if stunned by His words.

And as the storm obeyed His decree, a shadow stirred at the world's edge. A man in purple robes walked toward the mountains, his path lit by lightning and destiny alike. He was obeying the Creator's final command.

The skies split as the waters rose, and the world screamed.

For the first time since his fall, the Architect panicked.

He stood atop a jagged cliff, cloak billowing in the storm winds, the Staff of Eden glowing in his grip—lightning splintered across the sky, each bolt like the crack of a divine whip. Rain battered the land with relentless fury.

The flood had begun.

But this was not the flood of Noah — that judgment had come long before. This was the second reckoning, summoned not to cleanse mankind, but to drown the Nephilim and their corruption once and for all.

Beneath him, the Nephilim gathered, their eyes filled with something unfamiliar... fear.

They looked to the Architect as a last hope.

"The Creator comes," one said. "What do we do?"

The Architect didn't answer right away. His thoughts raced. He had never seen power like this. The Creator hadn't just returned— He had unleashed. The very laws of creation bent in His wake.

Yet the Architect still held the staff.

A sliver of the Spark of Genesis pulsed inside it. He had seen that it could destroy, but perhaps it could also shield.

He raised the staff toward the heavens, lips curling into a snarl. Thunder roared overhead.

"No!" he yelled. "You will not take what I've built."

He spoke a phrase—cobbled from the First Language, warped through his flawed memory. The syllables didn't sing—they twisted.

"Kel'votha din'rech..."

The gemstone atop the staff erupted with blinding blue fire, and a dome of shimmering light poured outward, enveloping the Nephilim like a cocoon. For a moment, it worked. The floodwater slammed into the barrier and split around it.

Without warning, the light changed.

It pulsed wrong, like a heartbeat out of rhythm.

The Nephilim cried out in pain.

Their bodies began to shift and contort. Skin mottled, turned gray and black, and scaled. Their voices deepened; some lost the ability to speak altogether. Veins of violet fire crawled beneath their skin, pulsing with the corrupted energy of Eden.

"What's happening?!" one screamed as he clawed at his face.

"You said you would protect us!" Haligot roared.

The Architect watched, unmoving, lips parted in fascination and horror. He hadn't meant for this, but he didn't stop it.

The Staff of Eden was no mere shield. It was a forge, and the First Language, spoken in error, had commanded it to reshape.

So, it obeyed, and the barrier held... but at a cost.

When the waters receded, the Nephilim's divinity had vanished. They were monstrous, hulking, twisted beasts that bore only a faint resemblance to the celestial warriors they once were. Their eyes, once mirrors of the stars, now burned with hatred and hunger.

The Architect descended into their midst.

"You live," he said.

Haligot stepped forward, almost unrecognizable. "We are cursed."

"No," the Architect said, resting the staff against the ground. "You are reborn." He looked out over the ruined world, the drowned cities and the broken mountains. "You are what they fear now."

The Nephilim said nothing, but they didn't turn away, and that was enough.

The Architect stood before them, the storm swirling around his silhouette like a cloak stitched from lightning and ash. "You have a choice," he said, his voice flat and devoid of sympathy. "Serve me—and unleash your vengeance upon the one who betrayed you... or you will be cast aside, forgotten, and exiled by this new world of ruin."

The Nephilim, broken in form but not in will, looked to the sky as thunder cracked across the heavens. The memory of the flood lived within them now—a trauma etched into bone and blood.

Their wings were gone and their beauty lost. Their light had dimmed into something hateful.

Still... they bowed.

One by one, they dropped to their knees before the Architect. Their oaths rose above the storm like a war chant—low, ragged, and bitter. They bound themselves to wrath alone, spitting on the very idea of loyalty.

From that moment on, they feared the waters as much as they feared the Creator who wielded them. Rain would never again be simple, and thunder would always sound like judgment.

Far above, the Creator moved through the chaos—his form incandescent with divine energy, a silhouette of wrath crowned in fire. The clouds split around Him, the storm parting like a curtain as He descended.

His fury had not abated. If anything, it sharpened to a singular point.

He descended to confront, carrying judgment rather than mercy. The Architect saw Him before the others did. Their gazes met across the fractured battlefield.

The Architect gripped the Staff of Eden while the Creator clenched a fist of light.

Before the inevitable could explode, the Architect slammed the staff into the floodwaters and shouted a broken syllable—one last fragmented phrase of the First Language.

A blinding pulse of light erupted from the staff.

The Creator staggered in pause. He absorbed the radiance, analyzing its source and its shape. There was familiarity in it... and

369

something foul. He had not taught this word. Yet it echoed with fragments of truth.

His rage burned hotter.

The Architect turned, seizing the moment. "Go!" he yelled.

The Nephilim raced toward the ship the Architect had landed in. The Architect followed, his boots crunching through ash and rain that came up to their ankles. As they boarded, the ship's protective barrier flickered and groaned.

As the vessel climbed, breaking through the last veil of cloud, the Architect looked back. In the ascent, something slipped from his grasp.

The cosmic map, a celestial tapestry, ripped free from his cloak in the wind's howl, spiraling down. It splashed into the flood, swallowed by the churning water's icy embrace.

He cursed, but there was no time.

The barrier collapsed behind them, and the ship vanished into the cataclysm.

The Creator stood alone in the eye of the storm.

His fury, though not spent, quieted into something colder... resolve.

He had witnessed his children fall, seen his gifts twisted into weapons, and watched the Architect survive once again. He knew now... the war was only beginning.

Lightning flashed one final time, illuminating the drowned valleys and sunken peaks of the world He once loved.

Even in devastation, there was still time to rebuild and resist.

He would need allies with a purpose—those who could endure and believe.

The storm diminished, and the floodwaters withdrew like breath pulled back into lungs.

What remained was a scarred, sodden world—cleansed, but not healed. Yet within its silence echoed the memory of betrayal, of transformation, and of wrath, and beneath it all... something darker still.

Heliosa's voice softened as she brought the tale to its close.

"This," she said, "was the moment that reshaped creation itself; the Creator's fury, the Architect's betrayal, and the Nephilim's fall. All of it set the stage for the world you now inhabit."

The group sat frozen. Lizzie crossed her arms, eyes narrowed in thought. "Wait," she said, breaking the stillness. "You said this was just the beginning. There's more, isn't there? The Architect didn't stop there."

Heliosa nodded. Her expression darkened like a cloud before the rain. "Indeed," she said. "What came next was the greatest battle ever fought on the sacred grounds of Eden. A battle that shook the heavens and changed the fate of existence itself."

Roo straightened. Madison and Savannah exchanged tense glances.

Heliosa's voice dropped to a reverent hush. "The Battle of Eden," she said. "Perhaps it is time you learned the full truth... of that war and of the Four Horsemen who rode in its shadow."

CHAPTER TWENTY-EIGHT

Battle of Eden

T he Architect stood in the cockpit of his ship at the threshold of Eden, his staff humming in his grasp like a compass of divine betrayal. Even though he had lost the celestial map while escaping Earth, the Spark of Genesis, woven into the staff's core, drew him back to this sacred soil like a magnet.

Eden waited for him. The place where the world had begun and where it would now bend to his will.

Behind him, the Nephilim gathered like storm clouds. Twisted and magnificent, they were not echoes of the divine anymore but weapons forged from abandonment. Haligot stood at the front, his scarred face still marked by the grief of Goliath's death. The others waited, a monstrous chorus poised for their conductor's signal.

"You know your orders," the Architect said, his voice low but heavy with purpose. "Prepare the ground and clear the lowlands but leave the Tree of Life for me. When the Creator comes, and he will come... he must find only ruin waiting for him."

He turned away before they could respond. His thoughts had already drifted elsewhere—to a memory unearthed on one of his earliest walks across Eden, before the rebellion. A mountain range carved like the knuckles of a buried giant; its spires shaped like ten titanic fingers clawing toward the sky. He found it peculiar at the time. Now, the staff pulsed with the memory, beckoning him.

The Architect followed the pull.

He found the mountain where the eastern sky bent in permanent twilight. The ten obelisks stood in solemn formation, each one jagged and towering, obsidian-black but veined with a faint inner glow—like cooled lava hiding ancient fire.

As he approached, the Staff of Eden burned in his grip, glowing brighter with each step. A low hum swelled from within the stones.

He smiled. "You were never just stones, were you?"

One by one, he touched the fingers, letting the staff trace their surfaces like a priest with relics. They vibrated at his touch, whispering forgotten syllables.

"Velin'dar..." he tried, invoking the binding word of old.

Nothing happened.

"Zar'Qualem..."

The spark shivered but didn't respond.

As the staff hovered before the tallest obelisk, he whispered an unfamiliar word—one that surfaced from a dark corner of his memory like a buried curse.

"Tor'Zekai."

The mountain screamed.

The first obelisk cracked and transformed. Shards of stone peeled away to reveal luminous inner segments, glowing with the same energy the Architect had once found in the Cavern of Genesis, only now... magnified. The obelisk bent forward, as if bowing to its master.

The Architect let out a sinister laugh.

"Yes, that's the one."

With trembling reverence, he approached the next finger. "Tor'Zekai," he said again.

Another transformation.

He repeated it eight more times, each invocation drawing more power from the staff, until all ten Fingers of Eden stood awakened—they weren't mountains anymore but monuments of subjugation.

A name formed on his tongue, ancient yet perfect.

"Vel'Karith," he whispered. "The Grasping Hand."

The wind stilled, as though Eden itself had heard, and so the mountains were named.

He extended the staff and tried another word, one that surfaced from the same buried stream of memory.

"Kael'Vurin."

The ten fingers pulsed. A radiant shimmer erupted between them—a veil of pure energy. It flowed like liquid glass, forming a barrier that shimmered in hues of gold and violet. The Architect ran his palm across it, marveling at how it neither resisted nor yielded.

From the veil, his reflection gazed back, shaped only as a god. "A shield," he said. "My shield."

He paced to the center of the formation. The staff buzzed again, whispering a new phrase like a lover exhaling in the dark.

"Vel'Tranak."

The fingers bent inward, aligning in a perfect circle, their tips angled toward the heart of the battlefield.

He raised the staff once more.

"Drav'Ulkar."

Ten beams of concentrated power fired in unison, converging at the center. The ground ruptured, scorched black with divine force. The blast shook the valley and then faded.

The Architect stood within the charred ring, eyes wide with awe. He whispered in reverence, "Even gods can be confined."

He looked toward the distant Tree of Life, its silhouette barely visible beyond the veil of power and treachery he had summoned.

"Soon I will have my vengeance."

From the heart of Vel'Karith, the Architect stood encircled by the Fingers of Eden, with the Eden Veil shimmering around him. The trap was set, and his dominion over Eden had begun.

Even in the shadow of betrayal, the Creator stirred.

Across the strands of time, on a plane untouched by corruption, His awareness surged. The Spark of Genesis had flared once more—stolen light dancing in the hands of the defiant. Eden, the birthplace of harmony, now pulsed with war.

The Creator's thoughts were a whirlwind of fury and purpose as He prepared to descend upon Eden. Untouched since creation's dawn, the sacred land now witnessed the Architect's treachery. The Nephilim, grotesque and twisted by his influence, gathered in dark formation, prepared to reclaim the dominion they believed was theirs.

The Creator would not face them alone. From the pure essence of His will, He summoned four beings of unimaginable power. They materialized out of the light, their divine presence shaking the very foundations of Earth. These four would become His champions, the Four Horsemen, destined to determine the fate of creation in the impending battle.

From the light of the Creator's will, the cosmos parted. A brilliance unlike any star or sun stretched across existence. Out of it, they came.

The first figure emerged barefoot, wrapped in flowing crimson cloth that moved as if caught in an invisible wind. She had a tall, sculpted frame, reminiscent of a warrior yet to be tested, and her skin glowed with a warm, fiery hue. Tiny embers dotted her like freckles. Her eyes sparkled with restrained fury, and her hands curled in readiness to defend herself.

The Creator stepped toward her, hand extended with gentle command. "I breathe into you the essence of conflict and valor. You are the embodiment of strength and courage."

She bowed her head in silence.

The Creator lifted His hand to the stars. Light gathered—fractured, spiraling remnants of ancient suns, shards of collapsed novas, and the bones of dead galaxies. They converged, swirling around the woman, wrapping her in a light that crackled and danced like fire born from war.

The cloth burned away, replaced by armor that shimmered like the fire from a thousand suns. Across the robe on her back blazed a sigil older than language. In her hand, a colossal sword descended from the heavens, forged from the wreckage of dying stars. Sparks raced along the blade.

"I will call you War," the Creator said, "for you will lead my armies against the enemies who threaten creation. Your presence shall ignite the spirit of combat, rallying those who fight for righteousness. In every clash of swords and roar of battle, your power shall endure."

War raised her blade high, and the cosmos trembled in approval.

A second figure emerged from the light, draped in silver and white, radiating an aura of calm. His clothing flowed as if caught by an invisible breeze; his steps were both elegant and resolute. As he moved, the world itself seemed to solidify, order blossoming in his path. His keen, silver-blue eyes held the promise of empires yet to be born.

The Creator spoke, his tone rich with purpose. "I grant you the power to inspire, to guide mortals and Nephilim alike toward greatness."

Above, threads of pure energy unwound from the stars—like harp strings woven from willpower itself. They descended in arcs and wrapped around him, lifting him from the ground. Celestial threads bound to an ethereal bow formed, carved from polished starlight and adorned with markings no tongue could pronounce.

Armor grew around his body like frost forming on glass—white, trimmed with gold. His aura shimmered with the gravity of ambition fulfilled.

"I name you Conquest," the Creator declared. "You shall seize dominion over the hearts and minds of those who falter in their faith. Your essence will forge alliances, build empires, and challenge the strong to rise above their limits."

Conquest drew an arrow, its tip a gleaming shard of promise, and let it hover a moment before lowering his bow with reverent confidence. The very air around him pulsed with leadership incarnate.

The light twisted, darkened, and thickened.

A third figure stepped forth, cloaked in robes of shifting shadow and pale green. Her hair floated as if underwater. The air chilled around her with the whisper of change. In her hands, she held nothing—until the light gathered again, coalescing into a set of scales so delicate they hummed with tension.

The Creator approached, slower this time, voice lowered to a sacred hush. "You shall embody the balance between suffering and renewal. You will test the afflicted, and new life will bloom from those trials."

The stars seemed to fade overhead as armor emerged from the darkness. It wasn't crafted but grew, like fungus from decay or bark from a wound. Her breastplate shifted with an oily iridescence, and steel vines crept along her shoulders. The design was a strange blend of beauty and decay.

"I name you Pestilence," He said. "You will reveal the truth hidden in suffering and oversee the cycles of disease and healing. Your hand will decide if what was once broken crumbles... or rises stronger."

She lifted her scales, tilting them slightly. One side lowered, while the other rose. Somewhere across the cosmos, the blight took root.

Shadows clung to the last figure as he moved. No vibrant clothing, no defining features, just pale skin and an echoing silence. He was thin, almost emaciated, yet his stance spoke of enduring patience, not frailty. His eyes were like two moons in eclipse, holding an age-old depth. Time itself seemed to bend around him with each step.

The Creator didn't speak at first. He looked into the being's eyes, as if remembering something already forgotten.

With a whisper that made stars flicker, He said, "You are the guardian of endings and beginnings. The silent witness to life's journey."

The cosmos held its breath. From the blackest edge of creation, something emerged—a blade, curved and gleaming, older than any known metal. It descended like a falling tear. The figure caught it with ease. Around him, threads of dark silk and ivory light wrapped his limbs, congealing into armor so quiet it seemed to mute the air. Where others shone, he faded.

"I will call you Death," the Creator said. "You embody the finality of all things and the promise of renewal beyond the grave. In your presence, souls will find both fear and peace. You shall guide them through the passage from this world to the next."

Death bowed. His scythe rested against the ground while the universe... exhaled.

Together they stood—War, Conquest, Pestilence, and Death. Champions of the Creator.

Their armor shone with determination, and their weapons radiated divine energy. They were the Creator's response to the corruption that had taken hold in Eden. When they raised their weapons in unison, the heavens trembled, and the battle to reclaim existence began.

Together, the four stood before the Creator—no longer mortals wrapped in light but living instruments of divine will.

Each one radiated purpose and bore power woven from the bones of stars and the breath of eternity.

Even now, the Creator hesitated. They were perfect. Almost too perfect.

Purpose is not enough, He thought. *They must prove it. Shaped by light and refined by fire.*

He gestured, and the sky cleaved open again. Four creatures unlike any others materialized. Their hooves didn't stomp; they hummed. Galaxies swirled within their eyes, and their breath left shimmering trails. They were the essence of horses—perfect forms, crafted from divine thought, existing before the world even had words.

"You will ride," the Creator said, "prove yourselves, and achieve balance. You are Horsemen not only by name but also by nature."

The steeds kneeled, and the Horsemen mounted without a word.

"Go," the Creator said. "Go to Earth and make them aware of your presence."

They descended like falling stars.

Across the Earth, the Four journeyed for an age that neither gods nor mortals could recall.

War cleaved through armies of corruption in forgotten lands. Conquest gathered tribes, united feuding kings, and whispered ambition into weak hearts. Pestilence sowed trials—disease, famine, and storms—and then scattered healing in their wake. Death watched, judged, mourned, and reaped.

The Creator watched in silence, moved at times, troubled at others. They were powerful, unified, and brilliant, yet something felt off.

On the last day of their descent, the Creator stood on a quiet hill in the Heart of the Earth and summoned an ancient power buried beneath. The ground shifted and groaned in response. Stones the size of ships tore themselves from the deep and arranged themselves in a perfect circle. A cosmic alignment of mass and meaning.

They pulsed with radiant energy; like a heartbeat in stone.

"Let this be a beacon," the Creator said, "invisible to the eyes of men yet known across the stars. Let it shield this world from what may one day come."

He called it the Sentinel of Balance. In time, mortals would rename it Stonehenge.

The Horsemen arrived, standing at the edge in silence.

War gripped her sword, hungry for more purpose. Conquest's eyes burned with visions of empire. Pestilence's scales trembled— one side dipping lower than the other. Death said nothing, his gaze fixed on the stars above.

The Creator watched them, and though pride burned in his chest, a sliver of unease lodged itself in his soul.

He turned, and in the shadows of time stood the man in the purple robes.

"I do not know if I have chosen well," the Creator said. "If you see two butterflies that feel... out of place, then you know that I have failed. When you see the comet, turn off the beacon, find the bloodlines and the remnants. They are the key to everything."

The man in the purple robes bowed his head, the weight of future centuries settling on his shoulders.

The Creator turned back to his Horsemen. "It is time."

They ascended in a blinding beam of light, the Sentinel of Balance glowing in their wake. The Earth was protected for now, but not Eden.

In the heart of that broken paradise, the Architect waited with his trap set as his Fingers awakened and the stars themselves held their breath.

On Eden's corrupted ground, the Architect summoned his legion. From the shadows they emerged—Nephilim—once radiant beings, now monstrous reflections of their former selves. Their twisted forms writhed with malice, their bodies grotesque and their souls hollow. They moved as one, a monstrous wave of fury and vengeance. Eden trembled beneath their march, their synchronized steps echoing like war drums struck by hate.

Across the battlefield, a light cleaved through the sky.

The Creator descended with his Four. The Horsemen stood at his side, divine in form and resolute in presence. Where the Nephilim were shadow and rot, the Horsemen were fire and judgment.

War stood at the front, her sword gleaming like a fracture in the sky.

Conquest raised his bow, its arrows crackling with judgment yet to be loosed.

Pestilence's scale tilted as unseen forces weighed the battlefield's soul.

Death didn't move; he waited.

At the center stood the Tree of Life, its branches reaching for the heavens as though trying to escape what it sensed coming. The Architect stood beneath it like a mockery of a prophet, the Staff of Eden clutched in his hand, pulsing with dark resonance. Haligot and the Nephilim gathered behind him, vibrating with bloodlust.

Silence fell.

"Let it be written," the Creator said.

War screamed. She surged forward, her blade cutting through the front lines like a bolt of vengeance. Nephilim shrieked as they fell before her, their bodies exploding into ash and cinders. Conquest's arrows rained beside her, each one a silent decree of punishment. Pestilence sowed sickness like seeds, her plagues unraveling the unnatural strength of the enemy. Death drifted through the carnage, claiming souls without cruelty—only certainty.

The battlefield erupted as the sky fractured, and the ground tore open. Light and darkness collided, and the heavens looked away.

At first, the Creator watched with pride, but as the battle deepened, he noticed it.

War's blade flared brighter beside Conquest's arrows. Pestilence's plagues struck harder near Death. They moved in sync, and their powers intertwined, as if an unseen force guided them toward unity.

This is not how I made them... the Creator thought.

A thread of dread coiled in his chest, and then the Architect moved. He raised the Staff of Eden and roared a single word in the First Language.

"KROL'ZENETH!"

The Ten Shall Hold.

Across the field, Vel'Karith awakened.

The Fingers of Eden—ten towering spires—tilted toward the sky like colossal teeth. One by one, they glowed, their cores igniting with blinding light. They turned inward—ten beams converging above the battlefield.

The light formed a perfect sphere of energy.

"DRAV'ULKAR."

Judgment Beam.

The light surged downward, a holy weapon now warped with dark intent. It struck the Creator dead center, the force splitting the sky and sending tremors through Eden's roots. The Horsemen staggered back.

For the first time... they gasped.

War's mouth parted in awe. Pestilence's scale tilted in erratic swings. Even Death flinched.

They had never seen power like this—not even from Him, and the Architect saw it.

He stepped forward, his voice calm and terrible. "You see it now, don't you? This is the power that built the bones of the world... and the power that will remake it. Stand with me. You served balance... but I offer you dominion. You could command the Fingers and help shape creation itself."

His words slid into their minds like honey and ash.

The battle paused, suspended in time.

The Creator rose from the blast crater, his body cracked with light, divine essence leaking from fractured skin. He lifted his hand and replied with a Word.

"ZAR'QUALEM!"

Spark of Genesis.

The surrounding air ignited, and the ground between them shattered. The Architect snarled, countering with another.

"VELIN'DAR!"

It is sealed.

The First Language clashed, not in sound but in reality itself. Trees uprooted, skies twisted, and stars dimmed.

"THAR'ELUNE."

First Light.

"ORUN'VALEK!"

Broken Sky.

Back and forth, their words collided like titans, each syllable rewriting the laws of nature. It wasn't a battle of muscle—it was a war of meaning.

The damage was done.

The Horsemen—watching—craved what they saw.

War stepped forward first, trembling with desire.

"With this power... I could end every war or begin the ones that should've been fought."

Conquest's breath hitched. "I could unite all under one banner.... mine."

Pestilence turned her gaze from the Creator to the Architect. "Life... born of ruin. A new cycle."

Death said nothing, but his scythe shifted. His posture changed. The Creator saw it. His voice cracked with sorrow. "No..."

It was already too late. In perfect unison, the four turned. War raised her blade. Conquest drew his bow. Pestilence's scale tipped toward ruin, and Death... swung.

They descended upon their maker.

The Creator raised his shield, but their blows landed like stars imploding. Every strike tore through his essence as light flared and divine blood struck the soil. Time itself wept.

At the center, the Architect lifted the staff and gave the last command.

"VEL'TRANAK."

Circle of binding.

The Fingers leaned inward.

A cage of divine energy closed around the Creator, its light folding in on itself. The Tree of Life twisted upward, its roots rising and its branches curling like a crown of thorns.

The Creator's essence became trapped inside the tree as it fell back to the ground and landed with a shockwave that rippled across Eden.

Silence settled upon the land as everyone awaited the next move.

From the silence, the Architect spoke. "Join me," he said, his voice both promise and poison. "Together, we will reshape existence. You will reign as true gods, as architects of a new future."

For a fleeting moment, the Horsemen stood still—four statues of divine power caught between their past and future. The Creator's light flickered in their eyes, but the Architect's promise burned brighter.

War stepped forward.

Her blade, once raised in service of justice, now hummed with hunger. Conquest followed, his gaze cast beyond the stars, seeing only thrones waiting to be claimed. Pestilence tilted her scale— once a tool of mercy, now a weapon of chaos. Death lowered his scythe with reverence, honoring the end above all else.

One by one, they struck the Tree of Life.

The Creator, weakened by the convergence of the Fingers, could only raise his shield once more before their final blows shattered his divine connection to the world. His essence unraveled, and his form collapsed in beams of light. He didn't scream; he only watched them, his final breath etched in silence.

The Architect stepped forward, Staff of Eden in hand, and raised it high. Shadow and light spiraled around him, forming a vortex of creation undone. The Tree of Life twisted, its roots rising, its branches bending inward like a divine ribcage. With a guttural command in the First Language—"KOR'VARETH," unseen chains—the Tree became a prison.

Its roots bound the Creator's essence. Its branches formed an ever-shifting cage, siphoning the last of his strength into itself. The divine spark dimmed, and the Architect smiled.

Silence swallowed Eden.

The Nephilim—once guardians, now monsters—fell to their knees. Their loyalty had a new master.

Haligot approached, his form quivering with grief and resolve. He knelt before the Architect.

"I swear my loyalty to you," he said, his voice steady. "Not just for my survival but for Goliath."

The Architect nodded. "Your loyalty will not go unrewarded."

He raised the staff once more and whispered a forging word that cracked the sky. From the molten heart of Eden, he crafted a new colossal spear for Haligot, its shaft gleaming as if alive, twin blue veins glowing down its length. At its tip, a triangular blade, forged from celestial metal, shimmered with promise, wreathed in shadow.

"Take it," the Architect said. "Let his memory burn through those who betrayed him."

Haligot took the weapon and named it himself: Brother's Fang.

The Horsemen gathered before the Architect, their weapons sheathed.

He looked at each one, his expression grave. "He stripped me of my name," he said. "The Creator, in his eyes, I became only a title. The Architect. I see you, and I give you what he never gave me... names."

He placed a hand on War's shoulder. "You... are Seria."

Conquest, "Durbal."

Pestilence, "Rangel."

Death, "Regar. My Prime and my Right Hand. You are my reckoning."

The Four bowed their heads in recognition. They weren't servants of balance anymore but hands of power.

"The world will fear these names," the Architect said. "And the stars will remember them."

As days turned into weeks, weeks into months, and months into years, the realms started to yield to his will.

One day, Regar reported a strange beacon hidden on a distant world—shielded from his sight. Earth, the place that the Creator once cherished above all others.

The Architect clenched his jaw. "So, He hid something from me." A pulse of rage shimmered through the staff. "Then I will search every realm, burn every veil, and tear apart every sky until I find the world He loved."

His war had just begun.

The flames of memory faded.

Heliosa's voice filled the silence, her tone hushed but heavy, like the last page of a book long forbidden.

"So, my friends... this great betrayal shaped the world as we know it. The balance of light and darkness was forever altered. From the ashes of that conflict... new legends rose."

She looked to the floor, eyes distant. A long pause followed.

"According to the Oracle on my world, two butterflies appeared from the darkness one day... on Earth. They fluttered past the man in the purple robes—out of place and out of season—and with that, he knew... the prophecy would need to be fulfilled."

A breath caught in her throat. Her voice dropped to a whisper. "Perhaps one day I will tell you how I became the Architect's prisoner... and how he ravaged my world."

No one spoke.

The silence pressed down like the weight of history itself. The group sat motionless, the echoes of the story still clinging to the walls.

Outside the cell, the world continued, but inside... something had shifted. A prophecy was awakening.

CHAPTER TWENTY-NINE

Book of Solomon

S tunned into silence, the group huddled together in the arena's damp depths, absorbing Heliosa's story. It wasn't a fable or legend but a harsh, ancient history that felt all too real. The air grew thick and stale, clinging to them like invisible chains, heavy with moisture. A musty odor pricked their noses, and the slow drip of water echoed a mournful rhythm in the corridor. No one moved. They just sat in the eerie silence, thinking about everything they had just heard.

Heliosa's voice had gone quiet minutes ago, yet the story she told still pressed against their chests like a stone too heavy to carry. The rise of the Architect, the Nephilim, the betrayal of the Horsemen, and the Battle of Eden. None of them had been prepared for such a truth.

Out of the silence, Ramirez's voice broke through. "I knew aliens built Stonehenge!"

Roo groaned as if someone had punched him in the soul. "After all that, that's your takeaway? She just said the Creator built it."

Ramirez shrugged, unfazed. "Have you ever seen the Creator? I'm just saying, he could be an alien, maybe a tall glowing one with a strange accent."

Roo let his head fall back against the wall with a thud. "We're all gonna die."

Lizzie huddled near the bars, knees pulled up. She watched Heliosa, who sat across from her, unmoving. Her posture was stiff, and her eyes held memories that were impossible to describe. The torchlight danced across her face, creating shadows that made her seem like a statue, frozen in thought.

Her voice cracked the quiet, low and uncertain. "If the Creator and the Four Horsemen couldn't stop the Architect and his Nephilim... then what chance do we have?"

Heliosa didn't reply right away. She rose in a slow, methodical manner, as if just re-emerging from a deep thought. "The prophecy of the Nine is still unfolding," she said. "According to the Oracle, the man dressed in purple holds the key. The Creator entrusted him with knowledge—truths forged at the dawn of creation. It is he who will guide the Nine. Each one will play his or her part in this... cosmic design."

Lizzie hugged herself tighter. "There aren't nine of us, though. Not yet."

Heliosa's expression softened. "Not all have been found, then," she said. "Some among you already bear the mark, while some serve a purpose beyond the prophecy."

She turned her gaze toward Roo, her tone shifting—less like a messenger, more like a teacher. "It's not always about fighting. Sometimes, survival is the only act of rebellion left, and remembrance... remembrance can reshape worlds."

The words struck a chord.

Dr. Terracotta shifted in the corner, his jaw tightening. He stared down at his hands, flexing them as if trying to wring out guilt. Seria's threat echoed in his mind like a song on loop.

He'd promised Ramirez would be helpful. He'd bargained, but had he saved him... or just bought time?

Ramirez nudged him, noticing the tension. "Hey, Doc. Are you good? You look like you saw a ghost."

Terracotta forced a breath through his nose and offered a weak smile. "Just... processing."

Ramirez winked at him to break his nerves. "Don't worry; I've got your back. No aliens, prophecies, or giants will take you down while I'm here."

A chuckle rippled through the group—brief and fragile but real.

The moment passed, replaced once more by silence, though it felt less suffocating now. Still, the words "man in purple" hung in the air like a cipher no one could crack.

Dr. Solomon, who had remained quiet until now, leaned forward. He turned his attention to Heliosa, his eyes searching hers—a plea for trust rather than answers. "You mentioned a book when we first arrived," he said, his voice low and thoughtful. "The Testament of Eden. I need to see it."

Heliosa didn't hesitate. She turned to face him, the flicker of torchlight dancing in her eyes.

"The Oracle foretold I would assist you," she said. "It is my destiny to help. The Architect allows me to transcribe entries into the Testament of Eden, but I'll need a reason to access it—one that won't raise suspicion."

A subtle energy passed between them—unspoken yet felt. The weight that only two people bound by something greater than themselves could share.

Solomon gave a slow nod, then paused. "There's another book," he said. "Given to me by the man in purple. The cover bears the mark of the Nephilim. If there's any chance of retrieving it..."

Heliosa's expression shifted. The name alone caused a flicker of tension behind her eyes. "That will be more difficult," she said. "The Architect won't let me near that one without a good reason. I'll try, but no promises."

Solomon's gaze lingered on her. He nodded once. "Trying is enough."

Time became elastic in the cells, stretching thin between drips of condensation and the shallow breaths of the group. The silence wasn't peaceful, it was oppressive, like a ceiling lowering toward their heads. The weight of what they had heard still lingered, and now, uncertainty pressed in like a second skin.

After a few minutes, they heard faint footsteps, which grew louder with each passing second.

A hound was on patrol.

The familiar scrape of claws against stone grew louder, echoing like a warning bell. The hound emerged from the corridor's shadow, its massive form blotting out the dim torchlight behind it. Its limbs moved with mechanical precision as it passed the cells, nostrils flaring to sniff the air. A deep growl emanated from its throat—a declaration of ownership.

Heliosa stepped forward, the metallic clink of her chains echoing in the stillness. "I have a message for the Architect," she said, lifting a folded piece of parchment through the bars.

The hound paused. Its eyes, glowing like smoldering coals, narrowed at her. It didn't speak. Instead, it bared its jagged teeth in a guttural snarl, a sound that stirred some primitive fear in the gut.

With a snap of its clawed hand, it snatched the message from her grip and continued down the hallway without a word. The click of its claws faded into the dark, replaced only by the soft thrum of silence.

Across the corridor, Lizzie exhaled as if she'd been holding her breath. Her voice, when it came, was quiet. "What did you write in that message?"

Heliosa didn't look at her right away. She remained near the bars, staring into the black corridor as if weighing how much to say.

"I requested permission to add a new entry to the Testament of Eden," she said. "I told him that your arrival needed to be recorded. If he approves, I'll gain access to the book... and a reason to bring it back."

Lizzie hugged her arms around her knees, eyes flicking toward Roo and Ramirez. The implication settled between them—if the Architect agreed, a door might open. Just a crack, but it might be enough.

The group exchanged a few glances, but no one spoke. Hope, as fragile and thin as a strand of hair, stirred—but no one wanted to name it aloud for fear of jinxing it.

About thirty minutes later, the sound returned.

The heavy rhythm of footsteps pounded like drums of judgment. As the hound came into view, the flickering light and floating dust framed its silhouette.

Clutched in its oversized hand was a ring of keys, glinting like fangs in firelight. It stopped at Heliosa's cell and inserted the largest key into the lock. The metallic clack echoed through the corridor like a gunshot.

"The Architect wants to see you," the hound said.

Heliosa didn't flinch. She nodded, her expression unreadable, but her eyes betrayed a flicker of unease.

Chains rattled as she stepped forward. The hound gripped her arm—firm, unyielding, and without care—and led her away.

Each step rang out in the corridor.

The chill in the air intensified with every footfall, crawling across her skin like fingers of frost. The walls felt narrower than before and the path darker. As they turned the corner, the group watched her disappear into shadow, knowing that whatever happened next... they might never hear about it.

As the corridor swallowed the light behind her, Heliosa remembered. A vision long buried resurfaced—one she hadn't dared think about in years.

She was younger, standing beneath the mirrored canopy of the Oracle's chamber on Zion. The old seer's voice echoed in her bones, not just her ears. "You will walk the edge between loyalty and betrayal, child. Your fate is bound to the one who bears three scars on his face."

She had dismissed it. So many carried scars in this broken galaxy. Now she wasn't so sure.

The closer they drew to the Architect's chamber, the colder the air became, like even the stone itself feared what lived beyond those doors. Torchlight flickered ahead, casting long, angular shadows across the corridor. From within, voices carried.

Heliosa slowed her steps, ears attuned.

"My Lord," came Durbal's voice—measured and reverent but tense. "The Fingers of Eden require two weeks to recharge. We must allow them ample time to achieve optimal functionality."

The Architect replied, calm as a glacier, but beneath it... the slightest hint of irritation.

"Two more weeks..." His hand moved to his chin while he processed the information. "Very well. Continue the process and inform me the moment they are ready."

Footsteps faded away—Durbal's deference echoing in the hollow rhythm of his departure. The hound pushed Heliosa forward.

The chamber was cavernous, almost ecclesiastical in design. Pillars of black marble rose to a ceiling veiled in shadow. At the far end, the Architect stood draped in his usual regalia—gold-threaded robes and onyx rings that clinked together as he turned to face her.

His eyes locked on hers. They didn't blink.

"Ah... my loyal servant," he said. "I'm told you wish to contribute to the Testament of Eden." His voice was almost warm. "Enlighten me. What divine truth would you have me immortalize?"

Heliosa dropped to her knees in one fluid motion. Head bowed, she spoke with practiced reverence.

"You are an exceptional ruler, my Lord," she said, letting just enough admiration color her tone. "The stars themselves dim in your presence. I am forever grateful you spared my life and entrusted me as your historian. The universe must bear witness to your magnificence. I wish to document your capture of the prisoners... and your triumph in averting the prophecy."

A hush followed.

The Architect tilted his head, almost as if tasting the words. He closed his eyes to take it all in. "Yes," he said, "bathe in my resplendence... let your ink etch my glory into the bones of history."

He extended his hand toward her. "Pay homage."

Heliosa's stomach turned—but her expression didn't waver. She lifted her head just enough to press her lips to the back of his hand. The cold metal bands bit against her skin.

The Architect withdrew his hand. "Very well," he said. "The universe should indeed know what I have done. I look forward to reading your entry tonight."

Heliosa stood with grace, keeping her eyes lowered. "Your blessing honors me, my Lord."

She turned, preparing to leave—but paused. "There is another matter," she said. "One prisoner mentioned a book marked with the symbol of the Nephilim. Should I include it in the record?"

There was a shift in the atmosphere.

The Architect's hand snapped forward, fingers like talons around her chin. The pressure was intense and immediate— enough to assert its presence. "A book marked by the Nephilim?" His voice was low now. "Regar spoke of this artifact. Why do you seek it?"

"My Lord," she said, "I believe it may contain knowledge... knowledge that could illuminate our path forward. The Creator entrusted it to one who bears a mark. Perhaps he wishes us to study it or use it."

The Architect didn't blink. His eyes, dark as the void between stars, searched her for signs of treachery, but what he found instead was... curiosity.

He slowly released her.

"You speak of mysteries," he said. "Riddles wrapped in reverence, and yet... the thought intrigues me."

Heliosa remained silent, her body motionless and her pulse steady.

He turned away, pacing in a small, thoughtful arc. "A book given by the Creator... it could be poison or a trap." He looked back at her. "Or it could be a key."

She said nothing, waiting to see what his next move would be.

He gave a soft laugh. "You are clever, Heliosa. More clever than I gave you credit for." He gestured toward the side chamber with a casual, sweeping wave of his hand. "You may take it, but know this... it is blank. The pages are empty. It is nothing but a relic of forgotten hope."

Heliosa blinked, confusion etched on her face. "Blank, my Lord?"

"Indeed. A mockery perhaps, or a riddle only fools chase. Take it if you wish, but do not mistake its emptiness for meaning."

She bowed, concealing the spark of tension that ran through her spine. "Even a blank page can hold meaning, my Lord," she said. "With your blessing, I will transcribe it with the reverence it deserves."

The Architect's mouth curled into a slow, knowing smirk. "We shall see," he said, voice like silk over a blade. "Consider it a gift, but know this, Heliosa—I will not tolerate failure."

"I will not fail you," she said, stepping back and offering one last bow.

He waved a dismissive hand. Heliosa turned and walked from the chamber with a slow, purposeful stride, but her mind was already racing—puzzle pieces shifting and snapping into place. The threads of prophecy were fraying and reforming.

With renewed determination, Heliosa walked forward, her steps purposeful despite the storm tightening in her chest. The Testament of Eden and the Book of Solomon were now within reach. She had done what she needed to do and played her part.

As she entered the Architect's private, smaller chamber, her breath caught in her throat.

Chained to the far wall beneath a hanging sigil of Eden were two small children. It was Madison and Savannah.

The girls looked up as the door creaked open, their faces pale and smudged with dirt. The chains rattled as Madison stepped in front of her sister.

"Please," Madison said, her voice cracking but full of fire. "We beg you! You can take us to our father!"

Savannah didn't speak. She just clung to her sister's hand, wide eyes glistening with hope she didn't understand.

Heliosa froze, her fingers twitching at her sides. Every instinct screamed to move and break the chains, but she knew that helping them now would be suicide—or worse, it would doom them all.

Still, she forced herself to kneel, bringing herself to their level. Her voice, when it came, was a whisper—gentle but laced with grief.

"I'm sorry, little ones," she said, her throat tight. "The risk... It's too great, but I swear to you—if I find your father, I'll tell him you're alive. I'll make sure he knows."

Madison's face remained composed, yet Savannah's lip quivered, and tears streamed down her face. She gave a single nod, a silent agreement offered... and it almost shattered Heliosa.

She reached out, her hand hovering, wanting only to be close.

Her eyes burned as she turned away, spine stiffening. Behind her, the chains rattled, and a quiet sob echoed against the cold stone walls.

She didn't dare look back.

Back in the cell block, Heliosa returned, two books clutched in her hands. Although she was focused, the urgency in her steps revealed the risk she had taken. Without a word, she kneeled and slid them across the floor.

Dr. Solomon crouched, lifting the book the man in the purple robes had given him. As he opened the cover and saw the blank pages, his breath caught.

"You need to be quick," Heliosa said, glancing down the corridor like a hunted animal. "I still have to make my entry into the Testament of Eden. If the Architect catches on... it won't just be me who pays."

Solomon nodded, his mind already spinning. The book was here. The one that refused to speak—until now. He stood, the weight of revelation tightening in his chest. An idea formed—strange but undeniable. He turned to Ramirez.

"Alright, Ramirez."

Ramirez perked up from the corner where he'd been sitting cross-legged, humming some half-forgotten tune.

"Oh, is this about aliens?" he said, grinning. "You gonna unlock some kind of ancient alien code?"

Solomon smirked, shaking his head. "Not quite. I need you to punch me in the face."

The grin vanished. "Uh... what?"

Solomon held the book up. "This is an artifact. I'm almost certain it's activated by my blood, but it needs more than a paper cut."

"You want me to deck you just to make the book bleed?" Ramirez raised an eyebrow. "Can't you just, I don't know, poke your finger or smash a hangnail or something? We don't need a full UFC moment."

Solomon sighed. "We don't have time to be delicate. Just trust me. It'll work."

Ramirez rubbed his chin. "Doc... this isn't some ancient alien summoning ritual, right? Like, we're not about to open a wormhole and have Cthulhu walk out wearing a Nephilim name tag?"

Solomon deadpanned his response, "Yes, Ramirez. That's exactly what I'm doing. I'm summoning aliens to possess the Nephilim and take over the universe."

Ramirez held up his hands. "Hey, don't joke. That's how horror movies start. I just don't want my soul probed by a space squid."

"Just focus," Solomon said, pinching the bridge of his nose. "Are you going to help or not?"

After a moment, Ramirez stood and rolled his shoulders. "Alright, Doc, but don't say I didn't warn you. If anything with over four eyes shows up, I'm jumping out the first nonexistent window."

Solomon exhaled. "Just do it. Quick."

With surprising speed and zero hesitation, Ramirez stepped forward and cracked a clean right hook across Solomon's jaw.

Solomon staggered back, catching himself against the wall. Blood dripped from his nose, splattering onto the open book in a crimson bloom.

"Damn," Solomon said, cupping his face. "That really—"

Ramirez laughed. "Hey, you asked for it! I've been saving that one since the base."

The laughter faded as the blood soaked into the pages, and the book glowed—faint at first, then brighter, each letter appearing like smoke rising from ink. Symbols formed as language took shape. The room dimmed around them as the pages pulsed with a soft, ethereal light.

Solomon's eyes widened. "It's working," he said. "It's actually working."

Ramirez leaned in, squinting at the text. "Well, I'll be damned. That's... not aliens, is it? Please don't say it's aliens."

"No," Solomon said, awe thick in his voice. "It's older than that." He lowered himself onto the floor, cradling the glowing book in his lap like something sacred. The words flowed now, vibrant and alive, as if they had waited generations for this moment.

Minutes passed as he read in silence. Solomon looked up, his face pale with wonder. "It's the journal of Goliath," he said.

The air in the cell shifted.

Lizzie sat up straighter. Roo blinked. Ramirez's mouth opened, then shut again.

Heliosa stepped closer to the bars, her expression unreadable.

"This changes everything," Solomon said, staring at the journal's cover. "Pieces are missing and things hidden. Someone's been watching us—nudging the world in place, keeping certain truths buried."

A chill passed through him like a shadow brushing skin. His eyes darted to the corners of the cell. A feeling came over him, as if something was watching.

He shook his head, trying to break the spell, just as Heliosa's voice sliced through the stillness.

"We need to move. I can feel it... Something is stirring. Time is slipping through our fingers."

Shadows flickered on the walls like spirits unsure of their shape. A metallic clang rang out in the distance, sharp and sudden.

Lizzie's breath caught. "What was that?"

Heliosa turned toward the sound, her voice barely above a whisper.

"Something's watching..." she said. "Or waiting."

Solomon closed the journal, pressing the cover shut with care.

"Whatever it is," he said, "it's closer than we think."

Silence fell over them.

Somewhere beyond the cold stone and iron bars, something moved.

CHAPTER THIRTY

Whispers of the Purple Robes

D r. Solomon's eyes, sharp and unblinking like a falcon closing in on its prey, followed each faded line of Goliath's journal. The room was so still that the crisp whisper of turning pages seemed deafening, like the steady tick of a clock measuring out their last safe moments. Dust and the faint tang of aged ink rose from the parchment, carrying with them the ghosts of millennia.

His breath hitched, the words on the page a dark, jagged line that held him. His fingertips, poised to turn the page, now quivered. He raised his head, and the light in his eyes flickered. Curiosity gave way to awe, and a chill, like the premonition of something terrible, prickled his skin.

"This..." His voice was thick, uneven, as though the weight of the words pressed against his chest. "This is astonishing. Beyond anything I could have imagined. It changes everything—our texts, our history... everything."

He drew in a slow breath, gesturing toward the journal as though it were a holy relic. "These pages carry whispers that tie the man in the purple robes to the very dawn of creation. Let me explain..."

"Please." Heliosa's voice cut through the air like the crack of a whip, urgent and sharp. "Hurry. I can feel it; the Architect is close to uncovering my deception. We have little time."

Solomon swallowed, his Adam's apple bobbing, and gave a brief nod.

"Pay close attention," he said, the charged weight of the moment coiling in his voice.

Solomon's voice settled into a steady, deliberate rhythm, the kind used by someone who knows every word will matter.

The journal confirmed what had long been whispered: the Creator shaped Goliath, the first of the Nephilim, to stand as a sentinel over humanity. Meant to guide and protect, not rule. Into this very journal, the Creator had placed more than ink—a fragment of His own essence, a safeguard meant to chronicle the Nephilim's purpose across the ages.

Solomon's gaze drifted down the brittle page, his finger tracing a faded line before he lifted his eyes to the group.

"Here... this is where the man in the purple robes enters the story."

The words carried a weight that made Roo's shoulders stiffen. Solomon's voice held a reverence, as if he were saying a name that was better left unsaid. The Creator spoke of this man, a companion of Goliath, a student and a guardian of knowledge so dangerous that few could handle it. His name was Enoch.

The air in the room seemed to tighten, every member of the group leaning in a fraction without realizing it.

Having learned from the betrayal of the Architect, the Creator withheld the gift of immortality. Instead, Enoch received something far more rare—an understanding of the design of creation, of humanity's nature, and of the vast forces that moved the heavens themselves. With that knowledge came a duty: to stand at Goliath's side when faith in mankind wavered.

In the beginning, Goliath had embraced his mission. Under Enoch's quiet guidance, he taught humanity the will of the Creator, showing them how to live in harmony with the divine. Solomon's voice warmed as he spoke of these days—the journal's pages were heavy with fulfillment, filled with moments where Goliath found joy in seeing humanity rise above its flaws.

Enoch was more than just a teacher; he was a watchful guardian, always observing and evaluating. His notes, brief, straightforward comments designed to steer Goliath clear of pride, doubt, and the slow creep of temptation, were scattered throughout Goliath's writings. Each annotation served as a reminder of their purpose, anchoring them both to the Creator's will.

Solomon's finger rested on a line written in Enoch's hand, the ink faded but the weight of the words still sharp.

Knowledge is not a weapon but a tool, a bridge to understanding. You must wield it with compassion, not wrath. For if you abandon humanity, you leave your own reason for being.

The syllables left his lips like something sacred, hanging in the air before settling into the group's silence. When Solomon spoke again, his voice lost its warmth and sank into a darker register.

But the journal also told of Goliath's growing frustration. Humanity's endless stumbles into sin had worn him down; what once inspired patience now festered into anger. The more he observed, the more his faith dwindled—and in those moments,

404

Enoch's pen returned to the margins, striving to anchor him to his purpose.

Solomon turned the brittle page. Here, someone wrote with distinct handwriting, almost as if they carved it into the parchment. Enoch's counsel was direct:

Do not let anger cloud your purpose, for wrath is the seed of rebellion. Humanity stumbles, but through guidance, it can rise again.

His voice thinned to a near whisper.

It was on the following pages that Goliath recounted his first meeting with the Architect. He described him as having a golden tongue—words like honey laced with poison. The Architect had fed Goliath's discontent, telling him the Nephilim were superior, that their rightful place was not as guardians but rulers.

Heliosa's voice cut across the cell.

"Does it mention Enoch during this meeting?"

Solomon scanned the lines, then nodded. "Yes... he was there. Watching from the shadows. Goliath wrote: I saw him, my guide, silent and watchful—a reminder of the Creator's light. Yet he did not intervene as the Architect's words took root in my heart."

From there, the journal turned grim. As darkness claimed him, Goliath became the Architect's herald, convincing his Nephilim brothers to abandon their charge. What started as guardianship turned into tyranny.

Solomon's voice grew quieter, as though the next part was almost too heavy to give breath. The Nephilim took human women, resulting in children who were hybrids, possessing immense strength, unnatural lifespans, and a propensity for chaos. Goliath wrote of them with pride, yet in some places, his tone wavered, as if the truth unsettled even him.

405

There was one name repeated more than any other. Azra'el. Even as a boy, his ambition rivaled Goliath's own. Cunning, ruthless... and in his father's private words, dangerous.

Solomon's thumb rested on the edge of the page, but he didn't turn it right away. The light seemed to catch the tremor in his hand.

The journal told of how the hybrid offspring became the Nephilim's most ruthless extension—enforcers of their fathers' will. They swept across the land like a plague, razing villages, desecrating temples, and bending entire generations into submission.

Yet even here, in the bloodiest accounts, Goliath's quill sometimes wavered. Amidst the boasts, moments revealed the cracks—laments for the innocents, the ruins of cities, and the rifts splintering his own brothers.

One passage, Solomon said, stood apart from the rest. His voice dropped as he read it.

"I see the weight of our deeds in the eyes of humanity. They do not look upon us with reverence but with terror. We were to be their guardians, the ones who inspired hope. Instead, we have become the architects of their despair. My son, Azra'el, looks upon this destruction and calls it beauty. I see only ruin."

Roo exhaled, his gaze fixed on the floor. Even Ramirez stayed quiet.

Enoch's presence during these years was faint but sharp, a quiet shadow in the margins. The once-gentle teachings in his notes became harsh rebukes, a persistent and unwavering voice opposing Goliath's decline.

You have forsaken your purpose. Turn back before the weight of your actions consumes you.

Another one, stripped of all poetry, was inked beside an account of a slaughter.

This is not the Creator's will.

Still, the darkness deepened. Goliath's fury intertwined with regret, and his words revealed a spark of the protector he once was—but the Architect's influence tightened around him like a noose. The entries grew darker, until one last page broke the flow.

"I fear the path we tread leads only to annihilation. The Architect whispers of a grand design, but his voice rings hollow — a symphony of lies. I look to my brothers, to the children of our blood, and I see echoes of a future I do not wish to face. There are whispers... of a relic that could command even the will of the Nephilim. I would see it destroyed before it falls into the wrong hands. If there is redemption, it lies beyond my reach."

Solomon's voice faltered as he read, the weight of the words seeming to press down on his chest. His fingers hovered over the parchment as though afraid to touch it.

"This wasn't just a fall from grace," he said. "This was a betrayal of everything the Creator intended... and Goliath knew it."

The group stayed silent, the air thick as Solomon turned another page. His tone softened, but the reverence in it was unmistakable.

"The purpose of David's battle with Goliath wasn't just to test strength; it was a testament to his faith. The Creator instructed Enoch to ensure David found the stones in the brook near Saul's camp. It was Enoch who guided him to the flawless stones and stood watch as the young shepherd fulfilled his divine purpose."

Heliosa's gaze kept flicking toward the door, her unease sharpening with every second, but curiosity won out.

"And the prophecy of the Nine bloodlines? How does that fit in?"

Solomon hesitated, the question pulling a shadow across his features. "Goliath's defeat," he began, "was not the end, only the spark of something far greater." His eyes dropped to the page.

407

"When David defeated the giant with the stone, the Creator's power surged through it, shattering the Architect's hold and ending Goliath's mortal form. However, there is always a cost for such force."

He turned the journal toward them, pointing to a faded line.

"A fragment of Goliath's essence—his strength, defiance, and will—bled into the stone and his sword. When David claimed them, that power coursed through him like a river breaking its banks. Enoch understood what had happened, even if David did not."

Lizzie leaned forward, drawn into the weight of the words.

"That essence didn't vanish," Solomon went on. "It passed from one generation to the next, carried forward, hidden in blood. The journal speaks of a prophecy—of nine great bloodlines chosen for a reckoning that would decide the balance between the Creator's light and the Architect's shadow. Among them, one would bear the blood of Goliath himself."

A glance passed between Roo and Lizzie. Ramirez shifted, scratching the back of his neck.

"These Nine," Solomon said, "are bound by more than just their heritage. They will inherit both the strengths and the weaknesses of their bloodlines. Some will embrace the light, while darkness will consume others. The outcome of the prophecy—whether it leads to victory or ruin—will depend on the choices they make."

Heliosa's voice was unsteady. "And Enoch? Where does he stand in all of this?"

Solomon's gaze softened. He turned another page with deliberate care. "Enoch's role was never to fight in their place. He was the keeper of the path—for David, the Nine, and even humanity itself. He understood the stones' power... and the cost of wielding it. After Goliath fell, Enoch vanished, carrying the stone and the sword away to keep them hidden until the final reckoning."

The words seemed to drain from Solomon's throat. He closed the journal halfway, his fingers trembling on the cover.

"This was never just the story of a boy and a giant," he said. "It was the opening chapter of a war that spans generations—creation against destruction—with Enoch, the man in the purple robes, standing guard over it all."

Ramirez broke the heavy silence like a kid blurting out in class, "I knew they were right!"

Solomon blinked, surprised. "Who was right?"

"Alright, alright, I have to say it." Ramirez leaned back, a grin spreading across his face that often signaled impending mischief. "This whole thing about the man in the purple robes? I've heard about him before."

Lizzie groaned, rolling her eyes so hard Roo swore he heard it. "Here we go again. Aliens?"

"No, historical events." Ramirez shifted into full conspiracy-theorist stance, arms crossed, voice low and dramatic. "Have you ever heard of Echoes of the Unknown? Best podcast ever. They say this guy's been showing up all over history, like some immortal weirdo. Creepy, right?"

Lizzie smirked. "So he's a time-traveling historian now? What's next? He built the pyramids?"

"Well..." Ramirez's grin widened. "That's one theory. According to the legend, he was advising the workers, telling them how to stack those bad boys. Efficient and stylish."

Lizzie's jaw dropped. "Oh, come on. Let me guess, he also whispered the recipe for the Trojan Horse?"

"Hey, I don't make the theories, I just report them." He threw his hands up in mock surrender.

Solomon cleared his throat, the sound sharp enough to cut through their banter. "As entertaining as this is, we're dealing with something far more pressing." His gaze fell to the journal in his hands, fingers tightening on its worn edges. "The question isn't where he's been. It's why he's here now."

The grin faded from Ramirez's face. He looked down, the weight of the words settling in. "Fair point, Doc. But doesn't it bother anyone else that this guy's always around when things go bad? What's his deal?"

"Maybe he's a guardian," Lizzie said, her voice softer now. "Or maybe he's just as lost as the rest of us."

"Lost? No way." Ramirez shook his head, a faint trace of unease slipping through his bravado. "If he has been around since Troy or whatever, he knows what he's doing. Is he just watching, helping, or betraying us?"

Heliosa spoke for the first time in several minutes, her voice thin but edged. "If he's as important as you say, why is he here now? What's his purpose in all this?"

Ramirez didn't have an answer. No one did.

"That's the big mystery," Solomon said. "But if history tells us anything…" He closed the journal halfway. "When the man in the purple robes appears, things are about to change."

Roo glanced toward the door without meaning to.

Solomon lowered his voice. "Or perhaps," he said, almost to himself, "they already have."

Lizzie broke the silence. "Enough about podcasts," she said, eyes fixed on Solomon. "Can we get back to the journal? What happened after David defeated Goliath?"

Before Solomon could speak, Heliosa's voice slipped into the space, quiet but edged with something close to fear. "The Creator prepared the flood… to purge the darkness."

Solomon gave a grave nod and turned the page as though it might crumble in his hands. His eyes lingered over the faded lines, his expression shifting into something between awe and caution. "The Creator also forged the Staff of Enoch," he said at last, each word carrying weight. "A beacon of light and weapon of truth.."

He angled the journal so the others could see the sketch within. The drawing was rough, but there was no mistaking its form—a slender rod crowned with a swirling orb of light. Even on the page, the orb seemed to catch some unseen glow, and the etched shaft appeared almost alive with movement.

"The carvings tell a story," Solomon continued, tracing the lines without touching them. "Scenes of creation and harmony, etched with a divine hand. But its true power lies in the orb, a fragment of the Creator's own essence, radiating light no darkness can withstand."

Lizzie tilted her head, curiosity overtaking her skepticism. "Okay, but why give it to Enoch? I thought he was just a guide."

Solomon's gaze met hers. "Enoch wasn't just a guide; he served as the Creator's bridge to humanity. The robes he wears, deep purple like twilight, isn't a sign of royalty. It symbolizes the balance he holds between divine will and mortal weakness. Purple sits between extremes: the heat of red and the chill of blue. Creation and destruction. Divine and human."

"Balance?" Ramirez asked, his brow furrowed.

"It means," Solomon said, "that Enoch's purpose was never to rule or to destroy but to restore equilibrium. To remind both the Nephilim and humanity of their shared place under the Creator's design. The robe isn't just clothing. It's a message."

Heliosa's voice, quiet but confident, cut in. "It's why he is dangerous to the Architect. Enoch never used the staff to command others. He used it to break the Architect's hold, to clear the fog

411

from minds already ensnared. The robe… it is both a warning and a promise."

Solomon's voice filled the dim chamber, each word heavy with the weight of millennia-old truths. The journal lay open in his hands, its pages breathing out the scent of dust and age. He read like a preacher delivering scripture—until the next turn of the page brought with it a sound.

A faint metallic clang.

It came from somewhere beyond the heavy door, too sharp and deliberate to be the shifting of stone or the groan of old hinges.

Ramirez froze mid-gesture; his hand suspended in the air. "Did anyone else hear that?" His voice was a notch above a whisper.

Lizzie's eyes snapped toward him, her hand tightening around Roo's without thought. "It's just the wind," she said, but the uneven edge in her tone betrayed the lie.

Heliosa's head lifted. She was sitting on the edge of her cell's cot, her back rigid. "It's not the wind," she said, her eyes fixed on the door. She got to her feet with a slow movement, as if the air itself could break. "Keep reading," she told Solomon, though her eyes never left the dark seam of the doorway.

He hesitated, eyes scanning the group. The air, heavy and close, seemed to vibrate with the metallic scent of fear. After a brief nod, his eyes went to the journal. His voice, though calm, held an urgent thread that resonated with each syllable.

"The journal speaks more about the prophecy," Solomon began, "one that names the Nine… but that's not all. A final passage…" A sound interrupted him, louder this time—the measured fall of footsteps, each one echoing like a hammer strike down the corridor.

Lizzie cursed under her breath.

412

Ramirez edged toward the corner, his bravado slipping. "We're about to get company, aren't we?"

Heliosa closed her eyes for a heartbeat, lips moving in silent prayer. When she opened them again, there was steel behind them. "Finish it," she said. "We need to know."

Solomon's hands trembled as he turned the page. "It speaks of something... something that even Enoch feared to write. A warning about..."

The door to the cells slammed open as the Architect stepped through.

His dark robes moved like living shadows, trailing an unnatural chill in their wake. His gaze swept across the group, and it felt as though the walls themselves leaned away from him.

"So," he said, his voice smooth but laced with venom, "this is how you spend your last hours? Chasing fairy tales and whispering lies."

The group recoiled. Heliosa took a step back, but the spark of defiance in her eyes flared like a fragile flame in a storm.

"I wasn't whispering lies," she said, her voice steady despite the tremor in her hands. "I was preserving the truth."

The Architect's expression darkened. "Truth? The only truth is the one I allow to exist."

With a motion so fast it seemed to skip time, he tore both the Testament of Eden and the Journal of Goliath from Solomon's grasp.

"This trinket," he said, turning the journal over in his hands, "means nothing. Only I will decide which truths survive this age."

His gaze shifted to Heliosa. Without warning, he unlocked her cell and yanked her out, sending her to her knees. The group flinched as his grip tightened on her arm, his voice dropping to a low whisper.

"You will pay for your treachery, little historian. The arena will teach you the price of betrayal."

He dragged her toward the door but paused in the threshold, turning back with a smile that was more a wound than an expression.

"I had planned to keep you alive," he said. "See if you were worth more than the Creator's mistakes. Now? No, now you'll serve a higher purpose. Entertainment."

The weight of his words settled on them like chains.

"My grand arena is ready. You will fight within its walls, spill your blood, and prove your worth to the Creator, or die for the pleasure of my followers. Either way..." His smile deepened. "...it will be a spectacular show."

He turned, dragging Heliosa out with him. Her panicked eyes met theirs for one heartbeat before the heavy door slammed shut, sealing them in stunned silence.

Ramirez said in a thin, shaky voice. "So... we're screwed, right?"

"Shut up, Ramirez," Lizzie said.

The echoes of the slamming door faded, leaving the group with the chilling truth — their fight for survival would not be in the shadows but beneath the gaze of a merciless crowd.

Through the silence, a voice broke through that didn't belong to any of them.

"You are not alone, for I am here. The time approaches. Nine must gather, or all shall fall."

CHAPTER THIRTY-ONE

Warden of Chains

The air in the cell seemed to thicken as Dr. Solomon's eyes flew open, lit with a sudden, unshakable clarity. "Enoch is with us!"

The words came out firm, almost reverent, ringing in the cramped space. He stepped closer to the others, his voice brimming with conviction. "I know this sounds insane, but I feel it in my bones—this is what the voice meant. We have to endure the trials of the arena. It's part of our destiny."

Silence hung heavy in the air. The group just stared at him, the gravity of his words making the space feel smaller, as if the stone walls were closing in.

Outside, beyond those walls, the sounds of cheers and stomping feet echoed like distant thunder. The Architect's followers were arriving at the arena, their voices merging into a wild, escalating roar.

Lizzie fidgeted, then met Solomon's gaze. "I don't like it, but he's right." Her voice wavered at first but firmed as determination flashed in her eyes. "This is our path. If the prophecy's real, we face it... together. Whatever we see, whatever happens, we survive as one."

Roo shook his head, jaw clenched. "Survive how? We have no weapons, no clue what's going on, and we're walking into a crazy person's game."

Ramirez leaned against the cold stone, arms crossed. "Yeah, Roo's right. Prophecies are great, but without a weapon and a rulebook, we're toast."

Solomon stepped forward, looking at each of them. "We survive by trusting each other and following the voice. It said, 'The Nine must gather.' We're not just here to survive. We have a purpose. This arena might be a test."

Lizzie straightened; her earlier doubts vanished. "Then we treat it like one. We stick together, think, and adapt."

The stomping and cheers outside intensified, rattling the walls and showering dust.

Ramirez whistled softly, sounding more worried than entertained. "Sounds like the crowd's ready," he said. "Guess it's showtime."

The hounds materialized from the darkness, their growls breaking the oppressive silence. Eyes burned like dying coals, fixed and ravenous. Their claws scraped a slow, unnerving rhythm against the floor, a sound that raised goosebumps. The lead hound stepped forward without a sound, its thick fingers curling around the iron bars. It let out a guttural snarl as it tore the door open. The shriek of tortured metal echoed down the hall, a death knell in the stale air.

"The Architect has sent us for you," a hound said, its voice a low growl that resonated in their chests. "It's time to meet the Warden of Chains."

The name hung in the air, heavy and ominous. Lizzie's knuckles tightened on Roo's sleeve. "Warden of Chains?" she said, her voice trembling. "That can't be good."

The hounds, with their hooked claws, pushed them down the narrow hallway. Cruel laughter punctuated every stumble, echoing through the twisting corridors. With each turn, the air grew heavy, and the weight of their impending doom tightened like a vise. Silence reigned. Even their footsteps seemed uncertain as they approached the looming iron door, studded with rivets.

It groaned open, a sound like a beast exhaling from the depths. An oppressive presence swept through the doorway before he appeared, making the air thick, as if the room itself recognized its master.

From the shadows, a figure emerged: Veltharion.

He filled the chamber like a monument of war, forged from nightmares. Chains bound his massive frame, their black iron links as thick as wrists, each etched with glowing runes that pulsed like embers. They moved and tightened on their own, alive with a predatory will. Flesh and blackened metal fused seamlessly across his form—sinew twined with pistons, muscle plated in jagged armor, and seams that hissed faint steam into the dim light. Where skin met steel, heat shimmered, carrying the acrid scent of scorched oil and hot iron. His eyes burned with cold calculation, fixed on them as if assessing their value before deciding their fate.

"So," Veltharion said, his voice a low growl that seemed to shake them to their core, "these are the mortals who dare to defy the Architect. How amusing."

Ramirez defused the moment with a wry grin. "I have to ask... do you get free cable with all those chains, or is this just your thing?"

The smile vanished. The surrounding chains lifted, clattering like swords. "You amuse me, insect." His voice dropped to a dangerous whisper. "Allow me to show what happens to those who mock the Warden."

Before he could move, Roo stepped forward. His voice wavering, but defiance shone in his eyes.

"Who are you? What are you? Why are you doing this to us?"

Veltharion tilted his head, studying Roo as if weighing whether to crush him or indulge him with words. His amusement manifested in a quiet, metallic laugh that filled the area. "Who am I? I am Veltharion, the Warden of Chains. I was once the pride of Sinarath, a world that sought to conquer the stars through might and ambition." He paced, the dragging of his chains like a rhythmic war drum. "I was their champion, their enforcer. My strength was unmatched and my loyalty absolute. When the Architect showed up, he promised power that was incomprehensible. I accepted, arrogant enough to believe I was above it all, destined for godhood." His voice turned grim. "Instead, I became this." He gestured to himself, the runes on his chains flaring.

"The Architect perverted my strength, turning it into a leash. He destroyed my home, the Skyspire, its very chains becoming my weapon... and my prison. I bound my people to his will."

Lizzie's voice trembled. "Why? Why would you serve him after that?"

His eyes blazed with rage. "Because I have no choice!" The chains lashed out, slamming into the wall with a deafening crack. "I am bound by the Architect's power, as you soon will be. You will entertain him in this arena, and when you fall, your souls will fuel his reign."

Silence descended, broken only by Ramirez's quiet muttering. "So... no free cable."

418

Veltharion's chains shot toward him, stopping just before his face. "Mock me while you can, mortal. The arena will break you. You'll be begging for death long before it arrives."

He motioned to the hounds, and they pulled a cart laden with damaged breastplates, cracked shields, and tattered leather straps. The discarded armor clattered, the sound a stark reminder of battles fought and lost.

"You won't die too quickly," Veltharion said, his voice laced with contempt. "The Architect wants a spectacle, and I aim to please. Suit yourselves... if you can."

Ramirez grabbed a misshapen helmet and squinted through a jagged opening. "Right. Nothing screams 'gladiator' like a bucket with a breeze."

The chains rattled toward him again, stopping only when Veltharion raised a hand. "Another comment, and you fight unarmed."

One by one, they donned the mismatched armor. The metal was freezing, digging into their skin and leaving rusty red streaks on their hands. Roo grimaced as sharp edges bit into his palms. Lizzie wrapped a torn cloth around her forearm, her eyes darting toward the towering figure who never looked away.

Veltharion's voice echoed through the chamber.

"Prepare yourselves. The arena awaits... and so does your end."

The hounds drove them forward, their laughter echoing off the stone as the iron doors of Veltharion's chamber creaked open. Beyond lay the coliseum's holding area—and the deafening roar of a crowd craving violence.

A colossal metal door slid open, its gleaming surface reflecting the harsh fluorescent lights. Beyond it, an incessant roar, a living wall of sound, assaulted their ears. The ground vibrated with the thud of countless boots, the chants of thousands echoing through their soles – the same slaves dragged from conquered worlds now fill the Architect's arena. Lizzie scanned the chamber, searching— then froze.

Against the far wall, shrouded in shadow, a familiar figure slumped.

President Davidson.

The man, once a symbol of strength, was now leaning against the cold stone. His tattered clothes scraped against the rough surface. Bruises, a mix of purple and green, marred his stubbled face. Despite it all, his eyes burned with an unwavering fire, a smoldering ember in the dim light.

A hound followed her gaze and let out a guttural chuckle.

"This one," it snarled, gesturing toward Davidson, "has defied us since he arrived. We've beaten him, yet his spirit remains unbroken. He spat in Veltharion's face." The hound's grin widened, its breath reeking of rot and iron. "So, he gets nothing for the arena. No weapons, no armor. Just his pride."

Lizzie stepped forward, her stomach twisting. "President Davidson," she said. "Are you...?"

"I'm still here," Davidson said, but the steel in his voice was unmistakable. He lifted his head, a faint smirk gracing his split lip. "Though I can't say the same for their patience."

Ramirez gave a nervous laugh, glancing between Davidson and the hound. "Guess guts count for something. Even if they're all you have left."

Davidson's smirk widened, his eyes locking with theirs. "Survival isn't about guts, son. It's about not giving them what they want."

The hound advanced, casting a shadow over Davidson, and growled. "Enough. Your time is up."

The door before them groaned open, spilling a harsh glare into the chamber. Heat bled through the widening gap, seeping into their skin. Beyond it, the crowd's roar surged to a fever pitch—a pounding, living wall of sound that seemed to push the air out of their lungs.

"Move," the hound commanded, its claws clicking against the stone. "The Warden awaits."

Davidson stood up straighter, each movement slow despite his fatigue. He faced the group, his expression grim. "Stay together. Trust each other. No matter what, don't let them see you crack."

Lizzie nodded, her jaw tight. "We won't."

The hounds herded them into the sunlight. The arena overwhelmed them—the sun's glare, the heat rising from the sand, and the deafening roar of the crowd. Across the space, massive gates groaned open. The group steeled themselves for an attack. Instead, a wave of people flooded the arena. Men and women from everywhere stumbled forward, their faces etched with fear. Some wore tattered royal clothes; others wore barely anything at all. Dust covered their skin, and chains rattled with each step.

Lizzie frowned. "Who are they? What's happening?"

Dr. Solomon surveyed the growing crowd, suspicion in his eyes. "This isn't random. It's... planned."

Davidson froze. His gaze swept the crowd and then landed on familiar faces. His smirk vanished, replaced by disbelief. "No... it can't be."

Lizzie turned to him, concern in her voice. "What is it?"

"I know them," he said, his voice barely audible over the noise. "That's Prime Minister Hartwell of England... President Durand of France. They must have been taken before London and Paris burned beneath the Fingers of Eden." His eyes found a woman in

421

a scarlet sari, her chin raised defiantly despite her fear. "And that's Prime Minister Ramesh of India."

Lizzie gasped. "You mean…"

"They've captured them all," Davidson said. "Every world leader. Presidents, prime ministers, monarchs... every single one."

Ramirez tried to grin. "Well, at least the Architect didn't forget the VIPs."

Lizzie glared at him. "This isn't a joke. If they're here, his plans are bigger than we thought."

The closest hound snarled. "The Architect wanted everyone with power brought to their knees. Here, titles are meaningless. You're all just pawns in his game."

Davidson's fists clenched, trembling. "You've taken the hope of every nation... and turned it into entertainment?"

The hound's laughter was a low, rumbling sound that echoed through the stands. "Hope has no place here. The Architect has already won. Now you'll perform for his pleasure."

The captive numbers swelled until the sand disappeared beneath their feet. Fear swept through the group, mixing with the bloodthirsty spectators' chant.

Above, Veltharion's voice cracked the air. "BEHOLD!"

Chains clattered like ancient bells, and for a moment, Dr. Solomon thought he heard something else, the whisper of a prophecy on the wind:

All who rule will kneel before the Architect's throne, and the Trinity will stand alone.

Veltharion pointed down at Davidson and the group as if putting them on trial before the world. "These are the rulers of your broken world. Here, they'll shed their titles and crowns. They'll fight to survive. Witness the fall of your pathetic civilizations!"

The crowd's wild cheers—slaves forced to roar under threat and zealots who worshipped the Architect as divine— vibrated the stone walls. Frozen, the group stood, the spectacle stealing their breath. Tension, thick as a shroud, pulsed with each heartbeat. Massive gates yawned, the roars echoing into the arena. Hounds forced more prisoners onto the sand, a sea of humanity—men and women, stripped of all but the terror in their eyes.

High above, the Architect's imposing throne cast a shadow against the brilliant sun. Flanking it were towering spires, each topped with symbols that glowed an unnatural blue. The throne sat empty... for now. From opposite sides, the four hands of the Architect walked out in perfect synchronization, greeted by a roar from the crowd.

Two took positions to the left of the throne, while the other two mirrored them on the right, weapons held still and ceremonial. Their mere presence was threatening, each radiating a distinct aura that could silence the most rebellious.

From the far corner, another figure appeared. Larger than life, Haligot, the Nephilim leader, moved with the slow, inevitable pace of a coming storm. The crowd's cheers turned into a low, hungry chant. His path to the platform stopped as a shadow separated from the throne's backdrop.

The Architect's robes flowed like liquid ink. He moved with measured steps, commanding the surrounding space. The arena fell silent, as if the world itself listened.

"Haligot," the Architect said, his voice smooth and cold, reaching every corner of the stands. "You will not take part in today's games."

Haligot stiffened, then bowed his head. "As you command, my lord."

The Architect's gaze swept across the arena floor, then landed on his general. "The man in the purple robes jeopardizes my vision and control. Take your legion and hunt him. Leave no trace. Find him and bring him to me."

Haligot's eyes hardened to steel. "It will be done."

He turned to the stands where the Nephilim waited in perfect, silent rows. Raising his arm, he boomed across the arena. "Nephilim, rise!"

The towering warriors stood as one, shadows swallowing the light. Without a word, they filed out of the arena with disciplined precision, their departure colder than any battle cry. The crowd murmured at their absence, but the anticipation remained, all eyes turning back to the throne.

The drums started, their deep echoes thrumming a beat against the chest. As the rhythm intensified, trumpets blared, their sound bouncing off the stone walls. The ceremony stirred the crowd into a frenzy. As the Architect descended the steps, his robes billowed like smoke. The Four Hands adjusted their positions, securing the perimeter. The spectators leaned forward, breathless.

A chill swept through the arena in a heartbeat, raising goosebumps on everyone's arms. Time seemed to warp, the crowd's roar fading as if underwater.

You are not alone.

The voice was quiet, assured, and resonated in their minds, not their ears. Even the Architect's head tilted momentarily, his gaze scanning the stands as if he, too, had felt it. The Architect's control faltered.

You hold the key to his downfall. Survive the games, and I will find you.

Lizzie gasped. Davidson remained composed, but a spark of understanding flickered in his eyes.

As if drawn by the cold, Veltharion stepped into their shadows. His chains shifted, their runes glowing brighter in the silence. "Tricks and whispers won't save you," he said. "The Architect's games have begun, and he always wins."

The Architect reached the throne and sat down, as if he owned the world. His voice cut through the crowd.

"Let the games begin."

CHAPTER THIRTY-TWO

Champion of the Butterflies

The arena seethed with cruel anticipation, every roar from the crowd slamming against the towering stone walls like waves against a cliff. Heat shimmered above the sand, carrying with it the sour stench of sweat, blood, and smoke from unseen braziers.

At the center, high above it all, the Architect sat on a dark metal throne threaded with glowing runes, his posture serene and his eyes filled with malice. Beside him loomed the Warden of Chains, iron tendrils slithering around his frame, their clinking a ceaseless whisper of menace.

The Warden raised a clawed hand, and silence enveloped the arena like a shroud. His voice, deep and guttural, echoed across the stands. "Bow! Kneel before the Architect, Supreme Master of Worlds, Scourge of the Unworthy, Lord of the Five Realms, Sovereign of Stars and Shadows, Harbinger of the Eternal Design! Bask in the resplendence of his unmatched dominion and boundless power!"

Around President Davidson, men and women faltered. Some collapsed to their knees, too terrified to resist. Others hesitated, trembling as the hounds prowled close, their glowing eyes promising swift punishment. Shackled and bruised, the captives reeked of despair.

Davidson stood tall. His wrists bled where the manacles had rubbed him raw, yet his chin remained high. The group mirrored his resolve, though fear flickered in their eyes like candlelight struggling against a storm.

Beside Roo, Ramirez leaned, tapping his restrained fingers against the iron cuffs in a nervous rhythm. The sound was faint, defiant, and almost mocking. "Bask in his resplendence?" He muttered under his breath. "Sounds like we're the ones about to get cooked."

One hound snapped its head toward him, lips peeling back to reveal fangs slick with saliva. "Silence, worm!" it said, stepping closer.

The Architect's head tilted. His gaze slid toward Ramirez, sharp and unblinking, and the temperature of the air seemed to drop. A smile curled his lips, cold as frost, though the flicker of irritation darkened his features.

"That one," he said, the words cutting like glass. "Bring me that one."

The hounds froze, silent and still. The Architect rose a little from his throne, his voice taking on a sharper tone. "He thinks he's clever? A performer or a jester? Perhaps…" His eyes bore into Ramirez, venom dripping from each syllable. "…he believes he can rival my drummers?"

The arena held its breath. Even the ever-present growl of the crowd faltered.

The Architect's smile withered into fury. "Very well," he said. "Let us see if his hands command more than just wit. Take him to the Hall of Silence. He may prove his worth after the games begin—or they may swallow him."

Ramirez's throat bobbed with a loud gulp. Still, he forced a crooked grin, whispering out of the corner of his mouth. "So much for flying under the radar."

The hounds advanced, but before they could seize Ramirez, Dr. Terracotta lurched forward, his voice trembling but steady. "Take me too. He's my responsibility."

The Architect's expression softened into something grotesque, a parody of amusement. "How noble." His hand waved, dismissing them both as though they were insects. "Very well. Take them both to the Hall of Silence. Let them reflect on their insignificance. The fool may have his audience... and his witness."

The hounds closed in, their claws clinking against stone as they herded Ramirez and Terracotta toward a shadowed archway. Faint runes glowed along the walls as they passed, casting a ghostly light across their faces.

The place they entered swallowed every sound. There were no footsteps, no breathing, and even the rattle of chains faded into silence. The Hall of Silence pressed down on them, enveloping them in a suffocating stillness that was cold enough to make their skin prickle. The dim light illuminated the intricate etchings on the stone walls, patterns that seemed to shift as if alive, whispering their presence without a voice.

As Ramirez and Dr. Terracotta vanished into the shadows of the Hall of Silence, Davidson's fists tightened until the iron cuffs bit into his skin. He lifted his head toward the Architect, his voice steady and defiant.

"You won't break us."

The Architect leaned forward, his smile widening like a blade unsheathed.

"Oh, I've broken worlds, President. You are nothing more than a footnote."

At a gesture from the Warden, the hounds prowled through the captives, claws raking across the backs of knees. One by one, the defiant crumpled in pain, the crowd roaring its approval. Davidson collapsed onto the sand, teeth gritted, but his eyes remained fierce. Fire still burned within them.

"Good," the Architect said, his voice rich with satisfaction. "See how we bring down the proud. Kneel before me and know your place."

The iron chains slithered and clattered as Veltharion yanked Heliosa into the light. Shackled and pale, she stumbled to her knees before the throne. Her once-proud figure sagged under the weight of exhaustion, but her eyes lifted, smoldering with defiance. Even diminished, she carried herself like a warrior forced to bow but not to yield. A ripple passed through the crowd—they recognized the rebel who had dared to deceive the Architect.

Another sound broke the silence: the deliberate scrape of armored boots. It was Seria, striding into view with her crimson armor gleaming like fresh blood, her sword resting across her shoulder. In her grip, she dragged two small children, their chains clinking as they moved. Madison and Savannah stumbled forward, their faces streaked with tears and their wrists bound in iron. Their terrified sobs pierced the oppressive air of the arena.

Davidson's heart stopped. For one fleeting second, the rest of the arena faded into the background—he could only see his daughters in Seria's grasp. Seria pushed the girls down at the foot of the Architect's throne, a cruel smile twisting at her lips.

429

"Your trophies, my lord," she said, her voice cutting like silk drawn across steel. "Daughters of defiance. Just like their mother."

Davidson's chains rattled as he lunged forward, his voice raw with fury. "You touch them again, and I swear I'll tear you apart with my bare hands!"

The crowd roared at the outburst, some with laughter, others with unease. Seria only smirked, tightening her grip on the girls' chains, dragging them a step closer to the throne. Their small cries cut through the arena, twisting the knife deeper into Davidson's chest.

The Architect rose from his throne, his gaze flicking between Davidson's rage and Seria's cruel delight. His smile widened, feeding on the fire before him.

"Behold, the arena," he declared, spreading his arms as though he unveiled the cosmos itself. "A stage where creation's failures once again serve their purpose: to amuse... and to enlighten." His voice rolled like thunder, silencing the crowd. "Before we begin, let's remember the worlds that have already submitted to me—their lights extinguished, their hopes crushed. Each one a monument to my triumph... and the folly of defiance."

He paced back and forth, savoring every word.

"First, Zion, the so-called beacon of wisdom and light. Its crystalline towers once sang with radiance, their Eternal Flame burning against the void. A beautiful thing..." His smirk deepened. "...but even the brightest flame casts a shadow."

Heliosa's breath caught in her throat. For a fleeting moment, she wasn't in chains; instead, she found herself back among Zion's crystal spires, listening to their crystalline hymn and bathed in the warm glow of the Flame that had once warmed her heart. The memory shattered her composure, and a single tear slid down her cheek.

The Architect's tone sharpened. "It was there I found my fierce beasts—the Hounds of War. Zion's brilliance lies buried beneath its own ashes, its Eternal Flame snuffed out by my hand."

The hounds around the arena howled in unison, a chilling chorus that rattled the stone. The crowd erupted in unison, their voices rising like a wave.

Heliosa lifted her head, voice trembling but sharp as a blade. "Yet you cower behind those hounds, a thief of honor and light. Zion's Flame burns brighter than you'll ever know... even in its ashes."

Gasps rippled through the crowd. The Architect chuckled, though his eyes gleamed with irritation. "A pity, my dear Heliosa. Your home, now nothing more than a cautionary tale.

"There was Abyssia, a kingdom beneath the waves. Its priests claimed dominion over the oceans, their Tidekeepers lording over waters they believed untouchable. When the flood came—not from their Creator, but from me—they drowned all the same."

He lifted his hand, and a guttural hiss echoed from behind the arena gates. A section of the stands erupted into rhythmic chants, like the tidal hymns once sung to the deep.

"I poisoned their waters and bent their leviathans to my will. Abyssia is now a grave of salt and bones. Tell me..." His grin spread wide. "...who among you will drink from these waters next?

"Edom, oh, Edom. A world that burned with ambition. Its Redbringers sought to rival the heavens, dreaming of empires crowned in Flame. How eager they were to wield the fire of their world's heart... and how I turned that fire against them."

The crowd shuddered as a distant rumble, like magma shifting beneath stone, rolled through the arena. Emberforge heat licked the air, and several in the crowd cried out in fervent recognition.

"Now Edom lies in ashes. Its mountains are gutted, its people consumed by their own hunger for power. A crown of embers awaits those foolish enough to seize it.

"Noctis, a world of light, was next." His tone turned mocking. "The Nocturni sang endless hymns to their Creator, their forests alive with bioluminescence, glowing with devotion—a symphony of foolish hope."

The light around the arena flickered, growing dim. A soft, eerie hum rose from one section of the stands, echoing the sacred songs of Noctis. The sound was haunting and beautiful, but then it twisted into screams as the crowd jeered.

"I smothered that light with a single thought. Darkness swallowed their forests, and they turned on one another like rats. Their hymns are gone. Only wails remain."

"Sinarath was the last, a jewel of ambition. They built machines to pierce the heavens, reaching for the stars with their Skyspire. However, arrogance creates fragile towers."

He tapped the Staff of Eden against the ground, and the chains of Veltharion clinked in reply, hissing across the stone like serpents.

"With a whisper, I enslaved their creations. Their Skyspire now hangs wrapped in iron, its ambition shackled to the dirt. Their strength serves me now, as it should."

Veltharion bowed his head, iron tendrils writhing with pride.

The Architect spread his arms wide, his voice swelling, triumphant. "These worlds—Zion, Abyssia, Edom, Noctis, Sinarath—were once proud and defiant. Now, they belong to me. Their flames extinguished, oceans soured, forests drowned in shadow, mountains gutted, and skies chained. They stand as monuments to my dominion and serve as reminders that defiance ends in ruin."

He struck the Staff of Eden against the stone again. The sound rang like a funeral bell, final and damning.

Through it all, Davidson's glare never left Seria. Her smirk lingered as she tugged his daughters' chains closer, savoring his fury. His vow burned behind clenched teeth. *You'll pay for this.*

The Architect spread his arms wide, his voice swelling until it thundered through the arena. "As you kneel, remember this: Your struggles, sacrifices, and even your victories are entertainment to me. Fight hard for your survival. Amuse me with the brief spark of your fleeting lives. And when the dust settles…" His voice dropped to a razor whisper, cold enough to frost bone. "I always win."

From the dust of the arena floor, Davidson lifted his chin. His knees were forced down, yet he spoke like iron. "Win? You subjugate the broken and call it a triumph. You hide behind beasts and blades, claiming it is strength. I see you for what you are—a coward who feeds off fear. Parasites don't last forever."

The Architect's eyes narrowed, but before he could speak, Seria tugged Madison and Savannah forward by their chains. Their shoes scraped against the stone as she leaned towards Davidson, her lips twisting into a serpent's smile.

"Your wife begged before I ended her. Will your daughters do the same? Perhaps I'll have them kneel at my feet before you do, President."

Davidson's whole body went taut, fury flashing through his eyes like wildfire. His voice broke raw against the air.

"Touch them, and I swear I'll…"

"You'll what?" the Architect cut in, his smile curling wider at Davidson's fury. He tapped the Staff of Eden once against the stone, the sound echoing around the arena. "Seria knows how to cut deeper than any blade. Already your temper reveals your inner turmoil, and thoughts of vengeance cloud your mind." He leaned

433

forward, savoring the tension. "That fury, President, is why I will leave you for last. You will witness your allies fall, hope diminish, and your daughters quiver. When nothing remains but ash in your throat… then you will enter my crucible."

Fueled by his venomous words, the crowd roared.

As the Architect leaned back, his eyes gleamed with delight, and the air grew still. The arena seemed to hold its breath. With a groan like shifting mountains, the gates opened.

The crowd's roar reverberated against the towering walls, their bloodthirsty chants swelling into a storm of sound. The floor beneath the sand trembled as five massive gates creaked open, iron grinding like the gnashing of teeth. From each dark maw, something stirred.

From the first gate, a glowing figure stepped into view—crystalline horns catching the arena's faint light. The Ravager of Zion. Its three horns shimmered in alternating hues of white, gold, and silver, pulsing as though alive with their own rhythm. With each deliberate step across the sand, the air itself seemed to bow away from its presence.

A section of the crowd erupted into wild, unified chants, voices blending in reverent harmony. Davidson's head snapped toward them, not random spectators but survivors. Their chants were the war hymns of Zion. He clenched his jaw, rage building within him. These people, who once sang of light were now forced to praise its destroyer.

The ground quaked as the second gate split open. Water hissed across the sand as the Tidebreaker Leviathan slithered forward, its serpentine body glistening with sickly green bioluminescence. Its coils rippled with monstrous grace, and the glow in its eyes cut like knives through the dust.

This time, the cries from the stands rolled like crashing waves. Roo's stomach sank. These were not cheers of joy but the chants of Abyssia's tidekeepers, twisted into a dirge. His eyes caught an old priest in their ranks, his lips moving in time with the chant, tears glistening down his cheeks. Even enslaved, the tide still pulled them.

From the third gate, heat blasted the arena as the Emberforge Behemoth lumbered forward, veins of molten fire burning beneath basalt skin. Each step left smoldering craters in the sand, the ground glowing red where it passed. A guttural roar shook the walls, and the stench of ash and brimstone filled the air.

In the crowd's far corner, the chants rose harsh and warlike, the cries of Edom's Redbringers—now warped into a hollow echo of the armies that once defended their world. Heliosa flinched and turned her head, her lip trembling before she forced her face to harden.

The fourth gate slid open. Out of the darkness stalked the Nocturnis Wraithwolf, a creature of pure shadow. Its fur seemed to writhe like liquid night, absorbing all light, and its eyes burned with a faint, predatory glow. Each breath released a frosty mist, laced with the sickly-sweet scent of rot.

From above, a soft harmony drifted down from the stands— lilting hums, layered together in chilling unison. They were the sacred bioluminescent songs of Noctis, once sung beneath its glowing skies. Now, they twisted the songs into hymns of mourning, offering them to a monster born from their ruin.

With a sudden thunderclap of chains, the ultimate terror descended from above. The Skyshackle Titan crashed into the arena floor, its impact rattling the very foundations. Metal wings unfurled, jagged edges catching the light like shattered glass. Its half-metal, half-organic body towered over the others, the clang of its binding chains sounding like a war drum.

From one section of the stands came a chorus of metallic stomps, the rhythm of enslaved Sinarathi, their bodies moving in unison as though the Titan's chains now bound them, too. Veltharion's smirk widened, his iron tendrils twitching in approval, drinking in the spectacle.

The Architect rose, spreading his arms. His voice rolled above the arena. "Behold my champions. Born of light, twisted by fire, shadow, and steel. Each one is a testament to my dominion—and to your failure."

A deafening cacophony formed from the crowd's cheers, a hymn of despair and cruelty. The beasts prowled across the sand, their massive forms circling.

Armed with rusted blades and broken armor, the world's leaders stared in disbelief. Fear rippled through their ranks, but desperation forced their hands to steady. They tightened their grips, forming a faltering line of defense.

Davidson, fists clenched, forced himself to breathe against the rising tide of dread. His heart pounded as he whispered the vow that kept him standing. *Keep it together... for my butterflies.*

With a low growl, the Ravager of Zion struck first. Its crystalline horns blazed with a blinding light, sending beams slicing across the sand. Shields shattered, armor sizzled, and one leader—a grizzled man clutching a bronze spear—was impaled mid-stride as jagged crystal spires erupted beneath his feet. His scream ended with a sickening crunch.

The Emberforge Behemoth then lumbered into action, its fiery skin sending out waves of intense heat. A leader swung his war-hammer, but the strike vanished into the creature's molten veins. A hiss of fire erupted across the arena, and the man was turned to ash, disappearing in the Behemoth's trail.

The Tidebreaker Leviathan slithered through the chaos, its coils dragging bodies beneath its glistening scales. It lunged, rows of spinning teeth tearing through a cluster of defenders who had tried to flank it. A spray of acidic froth that melted armor, flesh, and sand swallowed their cries into bubbling ruin.

From the shadows, the Nocturnis Wraithwolf hunted with a dreadful elegance. One moment, there was nothing but deep silence; the next, it was a blur of claws and blue fire. Survivors froze in horror as it dashed by, paralyzed by its glowing eyes, their lifeless bodies collapsing like puppets with severed strings.

The sky itself shook as the Skyshackle Titan plummeted to the ground, landing in a storm of dust and metal. Its chained wings snapped open, creating a whirlwind of steel. The chains lashed through the defensive line, reducing shield walls to splinters and flesh to pulp. Spears and bolts bounced off its half-mechanical body with faint clinks, like raindrops hitting iron.

When the dust settled, the arena floor resembled a graveyard. Blood steamed on the sand, and ash stung the nose. In the distance, the crowd howled in ecstasy, their cheers echoing like a thousand drums.

Roo's throat closed as he stared at the ruin. His voice, when it broke free, was a whisper. "This isn't a fight... It's a massacre."

Heliosa turned away, her shoulders trembling, grief and fury warring in silence. Even Ramirez's absence gnawed at the edges of the moment—his sarcastic muttering might have been enough to break the suffocating despair.

Davidson didn't look away. His eyes tracked every movement and every strike. He observed the Wraithwolf's surgical precision, the Behemoth's molten trail, and the Leviathan's defensive patterns as it coiled. Instead of feeling horror, his jaw clenched in focused calculation. While others saw only death, he searched for openings. Where others froze in fear, he committed everything to memory.

His vow burned in silence.

For my butterflies.

The Architect rose from his throne, his dark robes billowing like a storm cloud. His eyes swept over the carnage, and his voice rang out with commanding authority, cutting through the roar of the crowd.

"Stand witness!" he thundered. "This is the fate of defiance! Let it be remembered that strength without wisdom is worthless, and courage without purpose is a spark extinguished by the wind."

The arena howled in bloodthirsty approval, but the Architect's gaze sharpened, fixing on Davidson's group. With deliberate slowness, he lifted his hand and pointed toward Madison and Savannah. The girls huddled beneath Seria's grip at the base of his throne, the hounds growling low beside them.

"Now," he said, his tone soft, savoring each word, "a reward for my beasts. Their performance was… exquisite. These young ones will do."

The words fell like a death sentence. Madison whimpered. Savannah clung to her sister. Roo took a step forward, but Davidson was quicker. Chains rattled as he moved to shield the others, planting himself at the front. He could not stand between Seria and his daughters on the platform, but his eyes blazed upward as if daring the Architect himself to strike. The weight of the chains dragged at his wrists. "No, you'll have to go through me first."

A ripple of laughter moved through the crowd. The Architect's smile widened, but Seria leaned forward, her eyes burning with cruel delight.

"You are nothing," she said. "A broken man clanking in chains, pretending to be a shield. Tell me, President, how many daughters will you leave fatherless today?"

Davidson didn't flinch. His jaw tightened.

"I'll fight them. All of them, if I must, but not like this. I'll need a weapon and my daughters go to him…" his eyes cut toward Roo, "while I fight."

The Architect tilted his head, feigning consideration. "You dare to dictate terms in my arena?"

Davidson's voice was steady. "If I am to be their champion, I fight armed."

The silence was tense. With a bitter chuckle, the Architect leaned back in his throne. "Very well. Your bravery amuses me." He waved a passive hand toward Seria. "Give the little ones to their so-called protector. Let him guard them. It doesn't matter—they will be mine again when your bones are dust."

Seria's lips curled in a smile of pure malice. She seized Madison and Savannah by the arms and shoved them toward the waiting hounds. The beasts seized them with iron obedience and led them down the ramp to the arena floor. As the girls stumbled into Roo's protection, Seria yelled at Davidson,, "You've only made their suffering slower."

The president's fists clenched, but he stayed silent, his eyes burning with fury.

The Architect gestured to Veltharion. "Now, arm our champion."

Veltharion smirked, chains rattling as he rummaged through the pile of discarded weapons. With theatrical disdain, he tossed a spear onto the sand.

"There. Don't stab yourself… champion."

439

Davidson bent down, picked up the spear, and checked its weight. It felt useful—just enough for his needs.

His gaze flicked once more to his daughters, now clinging to Roo. His voice carried. "I'll be your champion. The Champion of the Butterflies."

The crowd hushed for a heartbeat before the Architect's laughter shattered it, rolling through the arena like thunder. "How poetic. Very well, champion of butterflies. Step into my arena… and let us see how long those fragile wings can carry you."

Davidson didn't flinch as the gates to the arena groaned open, the sand shifting beneath his boots. The beasts howled from beyond, their fury rattling the stone like a storm waiting to be unleashed. He gripped the spear, casting one last look at Roo and his daughters.

"Bring them close, Roo," Davidson said, his voice steady. "I'll need a moment before this begins."

Roo obeyed, guiding Madison and Savannah near, the girls clinging to him, their eyes wide with terror. Davidson knelt, his hand resting on their shoulders, and in that fleeting touch, all his defiance found its anchor.

The roar of the arena faded, dissolving into silence that carried weight.

The Hall of Silence lived up to its name. Its walls swallowed every breath, every sound, until only the pounding of Ramirez's restless fingers against the stone dared to break it.

Dr. Terracotta sat slumped opposite him, eyes closed, lips moving in what might have been a prayer, or perhaps a resignation too quiet for words.

"Echoes of the Unknown was right," Ramirez said while pacing. "Aliens, prisons, creepy runes... next thing you know, the chupacabra shows up to sell life insurance."

Terracotta cracked one eye. "Ramirez..."

"What? I'm just saying... conspiracy theories aren't so crazy anymore. My high school civics teacher owes me an apology." His grin faded as the air shifted, becoming colder and heavier. The runes dimmed to embers. Shadows in the corner stirred, folding into shape until a figure in a purple robe emerged, as silent as a memory.

Ramirez stopped drumming. His throat went dry. "...no way."

The figure's eyes fixed on him, deep and endless. Terracotta remained still, his gaze fixed on the glowing script, oblivious to everything else.

Ramirez raised a nervous hand. "So... let me guess. You're here with some prophecy nonsense, right? End of the world, blah, blah, blah. Please tell me there's a pamphlet."

The man tilted his head, voice low but resonant, carrying as if it belonged to the stones themselves. "Your rhythm will silence them. Your sacrifice will save them all."

Ramirez swallowed, sarcasm flickering under the weight of the words. "Sacrifice. Right. You're great at pep talks, you know that?"

The figure stepped closer. His voice deepened, like time itself pressing through the air. "The Eagle will fall, and then the light may rise."

For the first time, the man's hood shifted back just enough to reveal eyes worn by centuries yet burning with conviction. His words lingered like scripture. "I am Enoch the Last, keeper of the prophecy. Bear witness, Ramirez—your part has already begun."

And then he was gone, dissolving into silence as if he had never been. The air warmed, and the runes regained their glow.

Terracotta opened his eyes, frowning at Ramirez's pale face. "What's wrong with you? You look like you've seen a ghost."

Ramirez forced a laugh, his fingers resuming their nervous tapping against the stone. "Ghosts, prophets, immortal weirdos—take your pick. Either way, I'm way over my head." His grin returned, but it was thin. Beneath it, with his thoughts racing, the man's last words replayed on a loop.

Eagles. Sacrifice. Rhythm.

He muttered under his breath, "What the hell did I just get drafted into?"

CHAPTER THIRTY-THREE

Eagle's Crucible: The Protector's Awakening

The air in the arena was heavy with tension, a suffocating stillness settling over one corner of the Architect's grand design where President Davidson knelt before his daughters. The arena floor loomed in the distance, a vast stage of blood and spectacle. His voice was steady when he spoke, but every syllable trembled with the weight of a father's love.

"My butterflies," Davidson said, placing his hands on their small shoulders. "You're stronger than you realize. No matter what, remember this: your strength and courage will get you through anything. Look out for each other. Trust Roo and the others."

Madison's chin quivered, her eyes brimming. "But, Daddy…" Her voice faltered. "What if you don't come back?"

Davidson brushed a tear from her cheek with his thumb, his own eyes glistening. "Then you'll fly higher than I ever could."

Savannah clung tighter to his arm, her little fingers digging into the frayed fabric of his sleeve as if she could hold him in place. Above them, two butterflies drifted through the arena, their wings catching what little light broke through the haze. Davidson followed them for a moment, a small smile playing on his lips, before reaching into the folds of his tattered uniform.

He pulled out an ancient scroll. The parchment, brittle and brown with age, bore faint symbols untouched for generations. It was bound with a purple ribbon, faded but still vibrant against the aged paper. As he offered it, a soft hum emanated from within, like a heartbeat you couldn't ignore. The air held a faint scent of cedar and smoke, as if it had journeyed through time.

Davidson turned to Roo, his expression solemn, carved with resolve. "Every U.S. President has had this scroll, beginning with George Washington. They all received the same instruction: Don't read it. You'll know when the time is right, and when that moment arrives... give the scroll to the Protector."

Roo blinked, his throat tightening.

"Why me? I'm not... I'm not ready for this. I couldn't even protect my brother. How am I supposed to protect them—or anyone?"

Davidson stood before him at eye level, his hand gripping Roo's shoulder with quiet strength. "Every leader questions themselves before embracing their fate. But I've seen you. I've heard about how you looked after Madison and Savannah and how you faced danger. That's what a protector does."

Roo's gaze fell to the scroll, its weight far heavier than its size. His voice cracked. "What if I fail? What if I'm not enough?"

Davidson's tone softened but carried the steel of conviction.

"The protector isn't a perfect one, Roo. He's the one who stands up—even when he's afraid, even when he's certain he'll fail. That's what you've done, and that's what you'll keep doing."

Roo swallowed hard and nodded, his grip tightening on the scroll. "I'll do my best and keep it safe… I'll protect them, too."

Davidson squeezed his shoulder. "That's all anyone can ask. Keep it safe. When the time is right, the scroll will reveal what it must. Trust yourself."

For a fleeting moment, Davidson's eyes grew distant, shadowed by memory. His voice dropped to an inaudible murmur. "He said it would start with a Washington… and end with a Washington."

The words froze Roo in place. His own name echoed like a bell tolling in his mind. His pulse quickened, though his voice came out hollow.

"What does that mean?"

Davidson shook his head, a grim smile at the corner of his lips. "I don't know, but if there's truth in those words… then maybe you'll be the one to find it."

Madison and Savannah clung to him, their sobs muffled against his chest. He kissed the tops of their heads, holding them close for as long as he could. After a few minutes, he stood, composed and resolute, then glanced back one last time at the two circling butterflies, as if a part of him remained with them.

A metallic clang of chains echoed across the arena floor, announcing the beginning of the end.

High above the arena floor, the Architect sat on his throne, his piercing eyes gleaming with amusement. With a single, lazy gesture of his hand, he silenced the crowd. "Well, well," he said, his voice carrying like venom through the arena. "The great President Davidson and his merry band of misfits. How noble of you to march to your doom."

At his command, the hounds stalked forward, claws scraping sparks from the stone walls as they circled the group. Their growls reverberated like thunder, saliva hissing where it struck the ground. One lunged, tearing through the tatters of Davidson's sleeve. The fabric fell away, revealing the tattoo on his arm—an eagle frozen mid-flight, its talons outstretched, etched in dark, bold lines.

The Architect leaned forward, his lips curling into a mockery of intrigue. "An eagle," he said, with a blend of fascination and malice in his voice. "A sky-hunter. I've seen these symbols before— on other worlds, emblazoned on flags, carved into armor. Creatures that soared above, ignoring the tempests brewing below. But no matter how high they climbed… they always fell."

He tilted his head, eyes narrowing. "Tell me, President… what does this fragile bird mean to you?"

Davidson squared his shoulders, the faint echo of his daughters' breaths behind him steadying his resolve. His voice rang clear and unflinching. "This eagle is a symbol of freedom and resilience. It stands for the strength to rise above oppression and the courage to protect the innocent."

The Architect's smile sharpened into a predator's grin. "How quaint. An eagle to save butterflies. Let us see how far your wings carry you before they burn."

He rose from his throne, spreading his arms wide as the crowd erupted into a frenzy of cheers and jeers. The sound rolled like a storm against the walls of the arena.

"Let us christen this moment!" he roared. "A fitting spectacle for your defiance. Welcome to The Eagle's Crucible. Six trials await you, President—each one a dance with the beasts from the worlds I have conquered. Survive them, and you will face the ultimate test."

His voice dropped to a hiss, laced with malice.

"Perhaps a dance with Death itself, a battle with Regar or, more fitting for a man of war, a waltz with Seria, the Horseman of War. Either way…" His grin widened as he stepped closer, his gaze locking with Davidson's. "The outcome will be the same." He paused, letting the silence coil around the words before twisting the knife one last time. "After all, President… no one has ever made it past the first trial."

He flicked his wrist, and the arena gates groaned open.

"Let the crucible begin."

The arena shook, and a blinding shaft of light spilled across the sand. A hulking shadow moved within its outline—jagged and monstrous. The crowd erupted in anticipation, their roars crashing like thunder against the walls of the coliseum.

Davidson stood frozen, spear clutched tight. He spared a last look at his daughters, his jaw clenched. "I'm ready," he said and stepped forward.

High above, the Architect lifted his hand with casual grace, as though he was conducting a symphony only he could hear—a smirk formed on his lips. "The first trial," he said, his voice rolling through the arena like distant thunder, impossible to ignore.

The red dirt at Davidson's feet trembled. Tiny cracks crept outward, glowing with otherworldly light. A deep rumble soared through the air as the ground split and erupted. From the wounds in the earth, jagged crystalline spires burst forth, jutting at impossible angles.

The air shimmered with an ethereal glow, the entire arena transforming into a dazzling, alien labyrinth. The spires bent and twisted as they grew, their mirrored surfaces catching the crowd's reflection and fracturing it into thousands of warped images. Light bent, creating kaleidoscopic illusions that disoriented the eye.

447

Savannah clutched Roo's arm, her voice just above a whisper. "It's like a maze… he can't even see us anymore."

The humming grew louder, rising to a high-pitched, almost musical tone. Each crystal pulsed in rhythm, like the heartbeat of something vast and unseen. Davidson planted his feet, steadying his breath. Deep in the maze, the roars of a ruthless beast took shape, vast and unrelenting.

The Architect's voice then echoed through the crystalline maze. Each word dripped with cruel delight, as though the crystals themselves were speaking his lines. "Behold, President. My first champion, the Ravager of Zion." His smile widened, eyes shimmering with false reverence. "Born of both brilliance and destruction, it has outlasted countless warriors, their names now forgotten, and kings who believed they would live forever. Its dazzling power has brought empires to their knees." His hand extended, palm up, as though presenting a sacred relic to the crowd. "Now… it's going to destroy you. Let's see how long you can soar before you're brought down."

The growl deepened, shaking the crystal walls. Beams of golden, silver, and white light lanced outward from within the maze, crisscrossing like a web spun by some celestial predator. One beam sliced through a crystal spire near Davidson, shattering it into glittering shards.

It emerged from the shifting maze like a nightmare given form. The Ravager of Zion towered above Davidson, its body a jagged mass of living crystal. Each shard along its frame caught the arena's light and bent it, splitting the glow into fractured rainbows that danced across the walls. Plates of translucent crystal overlapped like armor, clicking with every movement, while beneath the surface something pulsed—liquid fire flowing through veins of gold, silver, and white.

Its face was a deathly, angular mask, more animal than human. A wide maw split open, showcasing rows of razor-sharp, crystalline fangs. Three horns spiraled from its skull, one gold, one silver, and one white, all pulsing with light that danced across Davidson's clothes. Burning white embers filled its eyes, emotionless yet hungry. Despite its size, the Ravager moved with a terrifying grace, its massive claws tearing furrows into the crystal floor as it stalked.

Davidson stepped back, sweat already beading along his brow. The creature tilted its head as if studying him, before unleashing a roar that shattered the air. The sound resonated through him, shaking his teeth and causing fragments to fall from the maze.

The horns flared. Golden, silver, and white beams erupted in a sudden lattice of light. Davidson dropped flat, the heat of one ray slicing inches above him and cleaving a spire in half. The shards exploded outward in a spray of glittering knives.

From the sidelines, Roo's voice tore through the chaos. "Watch the horns! That's where it's coming from!"

Davidson grimaced. *Easier said than done.*

The Ravager lunged, claws tearing the ground to rubble. Davidson rolled aside, his shoulder slamming against a jagged wall. He gritted his teeth, forcing himself upright as the beast raked where he had stood, its talons leaving gouges as deep as trenches.

Think. Look for patterns, the rhythm. It's not random.

He watched. The horns pulsed before each strike. It was enough for a small plan to form.

The Ravager crouched, muscles coiled and sprang forward once more. Davidson stood firm, gauging the rhythm, anticipating the telltale flare. At the last possible second, he drove the spear upward. The tip slammed into the central horn, fracturing its surface with a sound like shattering glass. Light flickered. The Ravager shrieked, a mournful cry like splintering crystal.

449

It reared back in a fury, one massive claw lashing across Davidson's side. The blow sent him sprawling, pain blazing through his ribs. He rolled to a knee, blood trickling down his flank, his breath ragged.

The crowd's roar became a frenzy of bloodlust and awe. High above, the Architect leaned forward, lips curling in cruel delight. "Impressive, President, but even eagles bleed. How long before your wings are broken?"

Davidson pushed himself up, his spear trembling in his grip. Sweat stung his eyes, but he didn't break his stare at the beast. The horns were throbbing, but they were gradually slowing down and becoming unstable. The middle one dimmed. A furious whirlwind of motion, the Ravager swirled around him, its crystalline shards clicking. Davidson steeled himself, his heart pounding in time with the light. One chance. One strike.

It lunged. Davidson feinted left, drawing the talons down, then pivoted hard, driving the spear upward with every ounce of strength left in him. The weapon pierced the fractured horn. The crystal detonated in a blinding explosion of golden light, shards slicing across the arena like a hailstorm.

The Ravager convulsed, its movements erratic and jolting, sparks flying as veins of light flickered within. A deafening roar ripped through the air, making the ground tremble, and then it imploded. Its crystalline form exploded into a cloud of shimmering dust, rising like fading starlight.

Davidson staggered back, panting, his side burning with every breath. His arms trembled from the force of the strike; his knuckles split and were raw, but he was standing. He looked through the fading haze toward the sidelines, where Roo and the girls pressed against the crystal walls. Relief softened their faces, and that sight alone steadied him.

For now, the eagle still stood.

The Architect spoke, his words measured, and they filled the arena. "Well done, President. Your eagle's wings remain… unclipped. Do not make the mistake of thinking that survival is a victory. The next trial will not be so forgiving."

The crystalline spires groaned and retracted into the earth, vanishing into silence. A low rumble followed as the arena floor softened. Water seeped up through cracks, pooling around Davidson's boots. The air grew thick, humid, and suffocating. Within moments, the red dirt gave way to a festering mire, the arena sinking beneath a swampy expanse. The stench of decay clung to the air, rank and choking, and a veil of mist crept low across the surface of the water.

Davidson tightened his grip on the spear, shifting his footing. With each step, he sank into the mud, which sucked at his boots. The cheers of the crowd muffled into something distant, drowned beneath the weight of the swamp itself.

From the haze, a serpentine shadow unfurled. The water trembled as the beast slid forward, scales shimmering with bioluminescent light.

The Architect's voice cut through the silence, silken and proud.

"Behold, the Tidebreaker Leviathan. It consumed the rivers of Abyssia and dragged the great ships of man into the depths. Its coils crushed the palaces of kings, its breath scalded armies into bone. Where it swims, even oceans surrender. Tell me, President— will your eagle's wings carry you through the storm… or will they be broken and drowned?"

The water churned as the creature surged into view. The Leviathan's body stretched longer than any serpent Davidson had ever seen, coiling and uncoiling with hypnotic grace. Its scales

451

glowed green and blue, casting the swamp in an otherworldly light. Along its sides, rows of jagged fins jutted outward like the blades of a sunken crown. Its head loomed high above him, wedge-shaped and armored, with gills that glowed each time it inhaled. Its maw split open, revealing spirals of rotating teeth—razors that ground together with a sound like grinding stone. Acidic saliva dripped into the water, sizzling on contact, filling the air with a sharp, metallic tang.

Davidson braced himself as the Leviathan attacked, its jaws closing just where he'd been a second ago. He dove away, hitting the muddy ground with a thud. The beast's massive body slammed into the swamp, sending waves over him, the murky water stinging his skin. He pushed himself up, spear in hand, gasping for air.

The creature attacked again, its tail cracking across the water with incredible force. Davidson tried to hold his ground, but the blow sent him sprawling. A cry escaped him as pain shot through his ribs. His spear vanished into the mud, and he scrambled to regain his footing just as the Leviathan's head rose for another attack.

Find the weakness.

The glow. The gills. They open with every breath.

The Leviathan lunged, its teeth spinning like drills. Davidson rolled, seized a shard of crystal still lodged in the mud from the first trial, and slashed hard across the glowing gills. The beast shrieked, a sound that vibrated through the swamp like a bell tolling underwater. It thrashed, coils lashing, waves crashing across the arena. Davidson's hand shot back to the mud where his spear had sunk. Fingers closing around the shaft, he ripped it free, slick with muck but unbroken.

Davidson lunged forward, driving the spear into the wound, and acidic blood sprayed across his arms, burning his skin. The stench was harsh and choking. He gritted his teeth through the pain, shoving the spear deeper.

The Leviathan's tail whipped across his side, sending him sprawling again. His ribs screamed, and for a moment, the world blurred, but he forced himself up, gasping, mud and blood slick on his hands.

The beast's glow dimmed, its movements faltering. Davidson charged once more, plunging the spear deep into the same gill. The Leviathan roared, coils crashing, before collapsing into the swamp. Its body dissolved into shadow and steam, the glow extinguishing as though the swamp itself swallowed it whole.

Davidson shuddered, gasping for air. His forearms burned with the searing acid, blood mixing with the grime coating his skin. He stared at his hands, slick with swamp water and the burning, viscous fluid.

Above him, the Architect leaned back on his throne, a smile playing at the corner of his lips, still amused but less careless now.

"Still standing, President," he said, voice curling with quiet disdain. "How long can the eagle's heart beat before it bursts?"

The swamp drained away in a hiss of steam, leaving Davidson gasping in the sudden silence. He tightened his grip on the spear, chest rising and falling in ragged breaths. Two trials survived. Four more loomed. His body screamed at him to stop, but he clenched his jaw. He would not fall without a fight.

The ground split with a thunderous crack. Heat blasted upward, suffocating and pungent with sulfur and ash. Fissures spread like veins of fire, spitting molten rock into the air. Rivers of lava coursed across the arena floor, their light shimmering in the haze, warping Davidson's vision. Jagged spires jutted upward, glowing red at the edges. The heat wrapped around him like a heavy shroud, every breath burning his throat.

From the deepest chasm, a growl echoed, sounding like it came from the earth itself. Lava churned, then exploded as a colossal shape emerged from the fiery heart.

The Architect's voice slithered across the inferno, quieter now but edged with cruel reverence. "Behold, the Emberforge Behemoth. Born from the ruins of Edom, it drank their rivers of fire and split their mountains into ash. Its breath scorched their cities into silence. When it walked, kingdoms burned. Now..." His lips curled into a bitter smile. "...it will consume you, President."

The Behemoth dragged itself free of the lava, a towering hulk of molten muscle and stone. Its body pulsed with fiery veins, rivers of magma flowing beneath cracked plates of basalt. Chunks of molten rock dripped from its shoulders and arms, sizzling as they struck the blackened stone. Its chest glowed like a furnace, the molten heart visible between fractured plates. Its head, horned and jagged, was crowned in fire. Eyes like twin furnaces fixed on Davidson, unblinking and merciless. Each step shook the ground, and the very air around it shimmered, too hot to breathe.

Davidson raised his spear, sweat streaming into his eyes. His ribs throbbed, his forearms burning from the Leviathan's acid, and his legs trembled under the oppressive heat. The Behemoth roared, a sound like bellows igniting a forge, shaking the very walls of the arena.

It charged.

Davidson dove aside, the Behemoth's molten fist slamming into the ground where he had stood, spraying a wave of molten shards. He rolled behind a spire of rock, only for it to explode as the Behemoth's next strike reduced it to fragments. A shard sliced across his arm, searing his flesh. He bit back a cry, forcing himself forward.

454

The Behemoth inhaled, its chest glowing brighter, before exhaling a torrent of heat and flame. Davidson dropped flat, rolling across the blackened ground as the blast scorched the rocks above him.

Find the weakness.

He watched. Just before it attacked, the fiery veins dimmed— its core drawing in energy. A half-second window. Small, but enough.

The Behemoth lunged again, its massive fists hammering down. Davidson darted aside, swinging his spear into the glowing fissure at its chest. Sparks erupted, and the Behemoth staggered with a roar, its molten veins flaring and dimming.

A wave of heat radiated outward, searing Davidson's leg. He stumbled, teeth clenched against the burning pain, his pants scorched and smoking. His body screamed for rest, but he pressed forward, gripping the spear in both hands.

The Behemoth slammed both fists into the ground, opening new fissures. Davidson leaped across the jagged terrain, seizing a chunk of rock dislodged in the blast. As the beast charged again, Davidson thrust the rock forward, using it as a shield. The molten fist shattered it, sending shards flying into its furnace core.

The Behemoth's howl wavered, and its motions became clumsy as its chest pulsed. Davidson seized the chance, plunging the spear deep into its heart. The beast shuddered, fracturing and crumbling as lava, like blood, gushed forth. With a deafening roar, it dissolved into a pile of molten debris, its fiery arteries fading until extinguished.

The rivers of lava cooled, and the ground blackened, hardening beneath his feet. The air reeked of sulfur and smoke, heavy and choking. Davidson yanked his spear free from the beast's smoldering corpse and leaned on it, sweat pouring down his face, his body trembling. Burns seared his arms and legs, and his ribs stabbed with every breath, but he was alive.

The Architect rose from his throne, his expression a mask of cruel fascination. He clapped his hands once, the sound echoing through the arena like a judge's gavel.

"Well, well, President Davidson," he said, his voice a mix of disdain and cold amusement. "Fortune seems to stumble at your feet. Three trials endured, but luck is a fickle thing... Tell me—how would your precious protector hold up?"

Davidson stiffened, his battered frame tightening with fury. "Leave them alone."

The Architect chuckled, a sound that slithered down into the bones of all who heard it. "Why deny us this moment of discovery? If the eagle has carried you this far... let us see if the fledgling can spread his wings."

With a wave of his hand, casual and cruel, he summoned movement from the shadows. A guttural growl rolled across the arena as a hound stalked forward, its glowing eyes fixed on Roo and the girls. Its claws scraped against the stone, leaving trails like scars in the earth.

"Let us see," the Architect whispered, his tone silk and venom, "how long wings of borrowed courage can carry him."

Madison and Savannah clung to Roo, their fingers digging into his shirt as though they could anchor themselves to him. Madison's voice trembled.

"He's hurt, Roo... he can't keep going."

Roo's jaw tightened, though his voice betrayed him with its thinness. "He'll make it," he said. He must.

His mind dragged him back to the words scrawled in that long-ago letter: *You will honor your brother and be a father to*

456

the butterflies. The memory of Jefferson's fall clawed at him—his brother's scream and the silence after. His stomach churned.

A second growl rumbled closer, and the ground shivered beneath their feet. Roo spun, shoving the girls behind him as another hound lurked from the gloom, saliva spattering across the dirt in thick, streaming ropes.

"Roo!" Savannah screamed, clutching his arm.

The beast lunged, and its impact drove him to the ground, claws tearing across his shoulder in a burst of fire and blood. Its jaws snapped inches from his face, teeth flashing like daggers. Roo grunted, locking both hands around its neck, straining to keep those jaws from closing. The weight crushed down on him, hot breath filling his nostrils with the stench of rot.

Blood slicked his fingers. He was losing.

"Get away from him!"

Madison's voice was shrill with desperation. She snatched a shard of crystal from the dirt and hurled it with all her strength. The shard struck true, glancing off the hound's flank. It howled, staggering for a heartbeat.

Roo seized the opening. Summoning everything he had, he twisted, throwing the beast off. His arm screamed with pain as he lurched to his feet, crystal shard clutched in his hand.

"Stay back!" he shouted, his voice ragged, as the hound lunged again.

This time, he sidestepped, driving the shard deep into its throat. The creature convulsed, eyes flickering, before collapsing in a heap at his feet.

Roo staggered, blood running down his arm, his body trembling from the effort. Madison and Savannah rushed to his side, faces pale, tears streaking their cheeks.

"You're hurt," Savannah whispered, voice breaking.

"I'm fine," Roo said through gritted teeth, though agony burned his shoulder. "Are you two okay?"

They nodded, clutching him tight. Roo pulled them close with his good arm, holding them in a desperate embrace.

Across the arena, Davidson watched, battered but determined. A faint smile touched his lips, pride cutting through his exhaustion. Roo met his gaze, and for a moment, something unspoken passed between them: a mantle shifting.

The Architect's laughter shattered the stillness, cold and cruel.

"Ah, the fledgling protector spreads his wings. How touching." His voice curled like smoke. "Wings are fragile things, boy. Tell me... how long before yours burns to ash?"

Roo's fingers grazed the ancient scroll. The prophecy echoed in his thoughts: *You will be a father to the butterflies.* His heart hammered against his ribs. He wasn't ready for this. He knew he'd never be.

Madison's tear-streaked face looked up at him. Savannah's small hand squeezed his. They were terrified but alive.

They need me.

"You're wrong," Roo said, his voice low but steady, strength coiling inside him like a drawn bow. He rose, standing between the girls and the arena, his bloodied arm screaming in pain, but his back straight.

"I won't let them fall. Not again."

CHAPTER THIRTY-FOUR

Eagle's Crucible: A Waltz with War

D avidson's legs trembled as he emerged from the arena floor, his hands gripping the spear like a lifeline. Every step sent a bolt of pain through his battered ribs. The roar of the crowd slammed into him like a wave—a grotesque symphony of jeers and cheers that rattled his skull. Blood trickled from cuts along his arms, warm against the chill that clung to the vast arena, staining the tattered remains of his clothes. His breaths came shallow, each one scraping like glass down his throat, but his eyes refused to waver.

From the sidelines, Roo's voice cut through the chaos, raw and desperate. "You're still standing, Mr. President! Keep going!"

Davidson's eyes found him. Roo was a wall in front of Madison and Savannah, their little hands gripping his arms so hard their knuckles were white. The girls were ashen, tear tracks marring their faces, but their wide, glistening eyes were fixed on their father with a mix of fear and wonder. Just for a second, Davidson drew strength from them. He stood up straighter, battling the fire in his side, pushing his body to keep going when it wanted to give out.

Above them, the Architect rose from his throne. His dark robe unfurled like smoke as he stepped to the edge of his platform. The crowd hushed as though his voice carried the weight of command itself. "Three trials completed, yet here you stand." His voice dripped with mocking sarcasm. "Remarkable, President, but do not fool yourself. Your defiance is nothing more than a flicker—a candle fluttering in the wind, delaying the inevitable."

Davidson's jaw tightened, but he kept silent. He knew the Architect's game: words sharpened into knives, meant to slip beneath the skin and fester.

The Architect's smile deepened as he spread his arms wide, reveling in the spectacle. "Now, let us see if your wings can carry you through what comes next. The final two beasts will test your resolve, your strength... and your will to protect those you love."

His gaze slid toward Roo and the girls, lingering just long enough to twist the knife.

"One at a time, though. We wouldn't want the Eagle to go down too fast."

Davidson's grip tightened around the spear until his knuckles whitened. His voice rasped, low and defiant. "Bring them out. Let's get this over with."

The crowd erupted in laughter at his boldness, a cruel, rolling sound that shook the air. Some jeered at his arrogance, others cheered his bravery, but all were hungry for blood.

The Architect's smile didn't falter. He leaned forward, eyes gleaming with sadistic delight. "Very well. First, the darkness that devoured the light of Noctis..."

His hand swept toward the gate, his voice resonating like a judge delivering a sentence. "Witness my Wraithwolf."

The gates groaned open, their hinges shrieking like tortured metal, and the arena dimmed as if the lights themselves recoiled from what approached. Shadows spilled from the entrance in thick, writhing tendrils, spreading across the sand like an encroaching tide.

A low growl rumbled from the shadows, a vibration that snaked down Davidson's spine and settled in his chest. The Nocturnis Wraithwolf solidified, a creature born of nothingness. The form writhed, a shifting mass of liquid night. Icy tendrils of shadow seemed to ooze and reform before his eyes, a silent ballet in absolute black. Smoke writhed where fur should have been, and hunger pulsed where muscle should have been.

Electric blue eyes flared in the blackness. Its jaws opened, revealing bioluminescent fangs that crackled like frozen lightning. Drool hissed as it hit the sand, dissolving the grains as if its saliva was venom. The creature's snarl was a grotesque grin, broad and human in its mockery.

From above, the Architect's voice cut across the hush, rich with amusement.

"A predator of shadows, President. Do try to entertain us."

The Wraithwolf threw back its head and howled. The sound wasn't just noise; it was an intrusion. It slithered into Davidson's thoughts, pressing against the fragile edges of his will, freezing the blood in his veins until his hands almost slipped from the spear. The crowd gasped as he faltered, their jeers and cheers mixing into a savage chant.

Davidson forced his body to obey, tightening his grip and raising the spear in defiance. His chest heaved, sweat and blood mingling on his skin.

The wolf moved. One instant it stood before him; the next it dissolved into the shadows, leaving only a ripple of cold in its wake.

It reappeared at his flank, claws lashing with silent fury. Davidson barely avoided the talons, which tore his clothing and cut his skin, causing a trickle of blood to appear on his chest.

He spun, slamming the butt of his spear into the sand to kick up a circle of dust. For a split second, the mist allowed him to be seen against the gloom, showing a fleeting image of the beast.

It lunged again. Davidson sidestepped, spear driving toward the glowing core at its chest, but the Wraithwolf twisted in mid-air with inhuman grace. The weapon met only air. It vanished once more, leaving him spinning, ears straining for the whisper of claws, nose filled with the acrid scent of its saliva burning through sand.

For what felt like an eternity, Davidson waged a desperate dance with the Wraithwolf. His spear slashed shadows while his muscles screamed with every evasive move. Sweat stung his eyes, his breath came ragged, and fatigue dragged at his arms. Every miss bled more of his strength away.

A flicker of hope emerged. He saw it just before the beast attacked. Its claws and fangs shone with a brighter light.

He stood firm, anticipating, with his spear ready. The Wraithwolf prowled the perimeter, its growl vibrating in his bones. It charged, a blur of claws and luminous fury.

Davidson lunged to meet it. He drove his spear upward, catching the beast at the exact instant its glow flared brightest. The tip pierced the shadow-flesh of its core.

A burst of ghostly blue light engulfed the arena as the Wraithwolf shrieked — a cry that clawed at the ears and seemed to echo inside every skull. Its body unraveled into wisps of darkness that twisted and thrashed, then dissipated like smoke on the wind.

Davidson staggered, chest heaving, the spear almost slipping from his slick palms. He dropped to one knee, gasping for breath as the crowd erupted—some in furious boos, others in wild, disbelieving cheers. The sound washed over him in waves, distant and hollow.

He had survived, but at what cost?

The Architect's laughter rolled across the arena, sharp and brittle; it didn't hold the same easy amusement as before.

"Impressive, President," he said, his tone tightening at the edges. "The night has passed, and now... the day breaks with chains. Bring forth the Skyshackle Titan!"

The ground shuddered. From the far gate came the shriek of grinding metal, like the wail of some ancient machine torn back to life against its will. The gates split open, and the Skyshackle Titan emerged, dragging the darkness with it.

It was colossal—a living fortress of iron and shadow. Chained wings unfurled with the scrape of steel on stone, casting jagged reflections of light across the arena's walls. Sparks cascaded from its joints with every movement, its clawed feet gouging trenches in the earth. Each step sent tremors through the ground, rattling bones and hearts alike. In its chest burned a mechanical core, pulsing with cold, merciless light—the rhythm of a heart that had never been alive.

Davidson pushed himself to his feet, legs shaking as the Titan lurched forward. Agony shot through his ribs and lungs, but he held his stare. The spear felt tiny, useless, but he lifted it. Roo and the girls were watching; he wouldn't give up now.

The Architect rose from his throne, robes billowing as he gestured to the beast like a showman introducing his finale. His voice cracked through the charged silence.

"Behold, President, Sinarath's jewel, now reduced to a chained relic of ambition. Witness what becomes of those who defy the Eternal Design."

The Titan roared, a metallic screech of grinding gears and tortured iron echoing across the arena. It then slammed its massive claws into the ground. A crushing, invisible wave of gravitational force surged outward, slamming Davidson to the ground and stealing his breath. Dust erupted into the air.

"Rise, Eagle," the Architect said, his voice ringing with irritation masked as command. "Or the weight of your defiance will crush you."

The Titan's assault began in a blur of metal and fury. It spun its chained wings in a whirlwind, the massive links lashing out with shrieking discord. Chunks of stone flew as the arena floor split under their force. Davidson dove, rolling across the sand just as a chain smashed where he'd stood, leaving a trench deep enough to bury him.

He landed hard, agony ripping through his side. His hands shook as he staggered upright, sweat blurring his vision. The Titan loomed, lifting a massive fist before crashing it into the earth. The blow unleashed a shockwave that sent him sprawling once more, his spear sliding across the dust.

The air was a storm of grit and sparks. Coughing, Davidson searched for his weapon. Each breath was a struggle, and every action was a negotiation with the pain. He couldn't match the Titan's strength, only outthink it.

The chains... they moved in rhythm. Each swing left a fleeting gap, just enough for a desperate man to gamble on.

Davidson feinted left, baiting the monster's strike. The Titan swung wide, the wing's chain tearing through the air with a sound like the scream of a thousand anvils. At the last instant, Davidson rolled beneath it, snatching the length of chain as it passed. He heaved with every shred of strength, wrapping it around a rock spire.

The Titan jerked, caught off balance. Its core flared and became exposed. Davidson lunged, driving his spear into the seam of its armor. Sparks exploded and metal shrieked—but the core held.

The beast roared in fury and lashed out with a backhand the size of a battering ram. The blow caught Davidson full in the chest. He flew through the dust and hit the ground with bone-cracking force. White-hot pain lanced his ribs, air tearing from his lungs. Something inside him gave way.

He saw the Titan coming, fists raised to deliver a deadly blow. With a roar, Davidson rolled away as the Titan's fists slammed down, pulverizing the ground. The shockwave sent him flying, but he regained his footing.

Desperation drove him. He seized the chain again, this time looping it around the Titan's leg. With a final, desperate pull, he wrenched the beast off balance. It staggered, wings flailing, core flaring bright in its moment of weakness.

Davidson roared and thrust his spear with all the fury left in him. The tip punched into the glowing core.

The Titan convulsed, molten light bursting from its chest as sparks and shrapnel rained down. Its scream was metallic agony, a thousand gears tearing free at once. With a crash, the colossus fell, its chains thrashing before going still on the sand. The impact shook the arena like an earthquake, dust boiling upward as the beast collapsed into ruin.

Davidson fell to his knees, clutching his ribs. For a heartbeat, the arena went still, the silence deafening. Next came the eruption—a cacophony of boos, cheers, and disbelief.

High above, the Architect stood unmoving, his jaw tight though his smirk remained. His applause was slow and deliberate— every clap was like a thunderclap of disdain.

The Architect's voice sliced through the chaos, cold and mocking, though his tone now carried a hard edge that hadn't been there before. "A victory, President... but at what cost? You can barely stand, and your trials are far from over."

Davidson gritted his teeth, forcing himself upright despite the fire tearing through his ribs. He leaned on his spear, his breath shallow but steady. From the sidelines, Roo and the girls watched in silence, their faces pale and their eyes wide with a mixture of fear and awe.

As the Titan's corpse smoldered, Davidson lifted his gaze toward the Architect with unyielding defiance. His body faltered but his eyes did not.

The Architect descended from his throne with exaggerated grace, though the tightness in his jaw betrayed his frustration. His applause echoed across the arena, slow and venomous, each clap like a blade of mockery.

"Incredible. Even with its wings in tatters, the Eagle still flies." His voice hardened, frustration clear despite his attempts to sound otherwise. "But your tenacity, Mr. President, only delays the inevitable... and I'm losing my patience."

Davidson wiped blood from his mouth with the back of his hand, his grip tightening around the spear. "Get to the point."

The Architect's chuckle was brittle, his robe flaring as he gestured toward the gates. "Very well. You've reached the last act before the curtain falls. The question, President..." He leaned forward, eyes narrowing. "...is with whom you wish to dance. Shall it be Regar, the stiff embrace of death? Or Seria... the unrelenting fury of war?"

Davidson didn't hesitate. His knuckles whitened on the shaft of the spear as his voice growled through clenched teeth. "Seria."

466

The crowd erupted in a storm of gasps and cheers, their voices shaking the rafters. The Architect's lips curled into a dangerous smirk, though his eyes gleamed with a sharp, seething intensity.

"Ah… predictable. A man chasing vengeance for his departed. How poetic."

The gates at the far end of the arena groaned open, their iron hinges wailing like a funeral bell. The roar of the crowd fell into reverent silence, a tension so thick it pressed against the lungs. Then came the drums—slow, thunderous, and relentless. Each beat rattled the bones, summoning something primal.

From the shadows, she emerged.

Seria stepped into the light with the poise of a conqueror. Crimson armor gleamed like fresh blood under the light, her sword catching the glow in cruel flashes as though already drinking from unseen veins. Her cold eyes swept the arena as if it were already hers.

The crowd broke into a frenzy. Edenflower petals rained down in a crimson-and-gold storm, their sickly-sweet perfume coating the battlefield like incense at an execution. The blooms scattered across the blood-stained sand; a grotesque carpet laid at the feet of War.

Above, the Architect's voice thundered, sharp with irritation. "Seria… end this embarrassment. My patience is wearing thin."

She tilted her head, acknowledging him with the faintest curl of her lips. Her gaze fixed on Davidson next. "Still standing, President?" Her tone dripped with mockery. "You look like a drunk clinging to the last drops in his cup." Her eyes flicked toward Roo and the girls, who clung to each other in terror. "Tell me… do your daughters weep the way your wife did? Will they beg when I come for them?"

Gasps rippled through the stands, a savage wave of delight and horror. Davidson froze, his grip tightening until his knuckles flinched. Rage burned through his pain.

"You killed my wife," he said, voice raw and cracking. "And you'll pay for it."

Seria laughed, a sound as hollow as an empty grave. "Your wife? That pitiful creature who whimpered at my feet? I don't even remember her... except for the beautiful moment the light left her eyes."

Davidson trembled, his whole body seething with fury. He leveled his spear at her. "You'll remember her name when I'm done with you."

The crowd erupted, drums quickening, the arena vibrating with anticipation.

Seria's cruel smile widened. "Yes. That's the fire I want." Her voice cut like a blade. "Let's see how long it burns before I snuff it out."

She attacked. A crimson blur met a flash of steel as her sword clashed against Davidson's spear, the clang echoing through the arena. Sparks erupted. The drums quickened their pace, mirroring her furious assault as she pushed him back, each strike a brutal testament to her skill.

"You're weak," she said, her strikes a symphony of precision. "A broken man clinging to a broken dream."

Davidson roared through gritted teeth, parrying the strike. His arms shook with the impact, pain shredding through his ribs, but he found one chance... one thrust. His spear grazed her cheek, drawing a line of red.

The crowd gasped in unison, the sound swelling into thunder. For a heartbeat, Roo and the girls' eyes lit with fragile hope.

Seria touched the wound, staring at the smear of her blood against her gauntlet. The crowd hushed, the drums pausing for a single second. Her smile vanished, and her eyes, now icy with fury, met Davidson. "Impressive," she said, voice low enough to chill the sand. "But it won't save you."

With another thunderous beat of the drums, she unleashed a vicious swing. Her sword met Davidson's spear, ripping it from his grasp. The weapon clanged away, and she followed up with a hard kick to his chest. The crowd erupted as Davidson slammed into the sand, groaning and clutching his broken ribs.

Seria loomed over him, her blade catching the light, poised for the killing stroke.

"Stay down," she said, her voice cruel and calm. "At least die with dignity."

Davidson didn't stay down. With a guttural cry, he forced himself to his knees, then to his feet, swaying but upright. The crowd went silent, holding its collective breath. Even the drums stilled.

From the sidelines, Roo whispered, "He's still standing."

Madison clutched his arm, her voice trembling. "He can do it."

Seria's fury flared, her lips curling in disdain. "You should have stayed down. Now I'll make sure you regret it."

Davidson met her glare, his voice breaking but defiant. "You've taken everything from me, but I'm still here, and as long as I'm breathing, I'll fight you."

The crowd surged again, torn between awe and bloodlust. The drums rolled like thunder. Something stirred in those watching—the sight of a man who refused to fall, who rose against the impossible.

Seria screamed in fury and swung her sword down. Davidson tried to block her, but her blade bit deep. He staggered, blood spilling, his body failing at last.

From the sidelines came a piercing cry—Madison and Savannah's voices breaking together, shrill with terror.

"Daddy!"

The sound cut through the arena, silencing even the crowd for a moment. Davidson's legs buckled, and as he fell to his knees, his dimming vision caught two butterflies rising from the sand—fragile wings glowing as they drifted upward into the light.

A faint smile touched his lips. For an instant, the pain faded, replaced by the quiet certainty that his daughters would endure.

The drums cut off with a final, brutal beat.

The Architect rose from his throne, voice triumphant.

"So, the Eagle falls—not without a fight but falls all the same. A fitting end for a defiant soul."

Seria lowered her sword, cold and unreadable. "You were never a match for me," she said, her voice flat with certainty.

She turned, cape flaring, and strode away as Edenflower petals rained upon her victory.

Davidson kneeled in the blood-soaked sand, vision dimming, the cheers of the crowd crashing over him like a storm. His breath came in short, ragged gasps as he sprawled across the blood-soaked sand. The world around him blurred, sound muffled to a distant roar. For a second, there was only silence—then he heard the cries.

"Daddy!"

Two small voices pierced the arena, raw and desperate. His vision cleared just enough to see Madison and Savannah break free from Roo's grasp, their clothes streaked with sand as they stumbled toward him. Roo was close behind; his face twisted with anguish.

The girls dropped to their knees beside their father, tears splashing onto his battered face. Madison clutched his arm, her hands shaking.

"Daddy, don't leave us. Please... don't go."

Davidson's lips curled into the faintest smile, though the effort cost him almost everything. His voice came as little more than a breath.

"My girls... you're so strong. Keep going. Protect each other."

Savannah got close and cried in his embrace. "We need you. We can't do this without you."

"You can," Davidson whispered, his tone weak but certain. His eyes turned toward Roo, who knelt beside them, guilt and grief carved deep into his features. "You have Roo. He'll look after you."

Roo's voice cracked as he pressed a trembling hand to Davidson's shoulder.

"I'll do it, I swear. I'll protect them with everything I have."

Davidson's hand shook as he gripped Roo's arm with the last of his strength. His voice broke, hoarse and fragile. "You're their protector now. Keep them safe... my butterflies..."

Roo's tears spilled as he nodded, his words a vow. "I promise."

Davidson's eyes drifted back to his daughters. Pride, sorrow, and love mingled in that last glance. His lips moved once more.

"I love you... Both of you. Always remember that."

Madison and Savannah clung to him, their sobs echoing in the hushed arena. And as his body went still, the two butterflies flew into the sky. They spiraled upward, drifting through the falling petals as though carried on a breeze no one else could feel.

Davidson's faint smile lingered even as his eyes dimmed.

Roo pulled the girls into his arms, his shoulders trembling with the weight of his promise. Their cries mingled with the

471

muffled roar of the crowd until a sharp sound split the air—the metallic click of boots against sand.

Seria approached, her crimson armor gleaming as if polished with blood, her sword dragging through the sand in idle menace. The crowd hushed, the petals still falling like funeral confetti. She stopped a few feet away, tilting her head with cold amusement.

"So, you're the protector now?" Her voice was like a knife. "How quaint. Do you think you're up to the task… protecting his butterflies?"

Roo's jaw clenched as he shielded Madison and Savannah. He said nothing, but the fire in his eyes was enough.

Seria chuckled, pointing her blade at him, the steel glistening like a predator's fang.

"I hope for their sake you're stronger than you look, but don't get too attached. The Architect has a way of turning hope into ash."

With a flourish, she returned her sword to its sheath, her cape billowing as she turned. The crowd roared again, blanketing the arena in Edenflower petals as Seria walked away, each step measured, as if she owned the world.

Roo clutched the girls tighter, his chest heaving with rage and helplessness. Madison buried her face against him, Savannah's sobs shaking her petite frame. For their sake, he forced himself to steady, though the weight of Davidson's last words threatened to crush him.

Above them, the Architect rose, his voice slicing through the air like a blade.

"So, the Eagle falls, leaving the butterflies to flutter alone, but the show must go on."

He gestured to the shadows. The arena gates groaned open, and a pack of hounds stalked forward, claws raking the ground, eyes burning with hunger. Their growls echoed as the crowd fell into an expectant hush.

The Architect's smile widened, cruel and cold. "Fetch the next contestants. Bring forth those in the Hall of Silence. Let us see if they can amuse me... or die screaming."

The hounds howled as they vanished into the dark. Roo's arms tightened around the girls, his heart pounding as dread seeped into his bones.

The Eagle had fallen—and now the weight of his promise pressed down like iron.

CHAPTER THIRTY-FIVE

Terracotta Drummer

Ramirez and Dr. Terracotta felt the Hall of Silence press in on them, the shadows seeming to twist and listen. The scrape of unseen claws echoed down the corridor, eating away at the silence.

Ramirez leaned against the wall, crossing his arms across his chest.

"Doc, keep fiddling with that recorder and those glasses, and they'll fall apart before we do." He let his grin flicker, then forced it to steady.

Terracotta shot him a dry glance. "Would you rather I fidget with my hands or my sanity?"

Ramirez let out a short laugh, the sound bouncing in the oppressive stillness. "Fair point. Just... don't lose it on me. I kind of need you."

Terracotta arched an eyebrow. "Didn't expect to hear that."

For once, Ramirez didn't volley back with a joke. He leaned forward, elbows on his knees, and the grin slipped away. Shadows

474

hid his eyes, fixed on the dark corridor, his breath tight, as if bracing himself for old regrets.

"You know," he said, his voice dropping, "back at the base, I wasn't your biggest supporter. Hell, I gave you more grief than you deserved. You were an easy target. Quiet. Too smart for your own good. And I..." He exhaled, shaking his head. "I was wrong, Doc. About a lot of things."

Terracotta's lips parted, surprise softening his features.

Ramirez's hand moved under his shirt, the fabric rustling against his skin. He withdrew a chain, the metal cool against his fingers. Two tiny, golden drumsticks swung, catching the faint light and gleaming. He extended his hand, steady and unwavering, while his voice rasped, a rough sound in the quiet.

"These... They have been with me since the day I thought I was going to end it." His jaw clenched, voice breaking for a fractured second. "My buddy gave 'em to me after I came back from a tough mission, said they'd keep me drumming no matter what life threw. Dumb, right? But every scrape I survived, every close call—these were there." He blinked, silence tightening around him. "They've carried my sins longer than they should. Maybe it's time they helped somebody better."

Terracotta stared, his hand hovering. "Ramirez, I can't..."

"Yes, you can." Ramirez pushed the chain into his palm. "You always see the good in people and try to figure out the 'why' when the rest of us are just trying to survive. You have a chance of getting through this. I don't know if I do." Ramirez's eyes welled up, tears threatened to spill, a sight Terracotta had never witnessed before.

With a crooked smirk, he blinked them back, lips trembling. "Don't make me regret it, Doc. When you make it out... buy a round for me."

475

Terracotta slipped the chain over his head. The tiny drumsticks rested against his chest, their weight far heavier than gold should be. His throat tightened. "I won't forget this."

Ramirez swiped at his watering eye with the heel of his hand and straightened as a growl rolled out of the corridor. Claws scraped stones, closer this time.

The first hound emerged from the shadows, its eyes glowing, followed by others.

"Great," Ramirez said, rising from the floor. "Looks like we've got company."

Terracotta pushed himself up, brushing the necklace for courage.

"Do you ever not antagonize things that want to kill us?"

Ramirez flashed his grin. "Where's the fun in that?"

The lead hound barked, sharp and commanding.

Ramirez tilted his head. "Sorry, Cujo. I don't speak bark. I'm guessing you want us to follow."

Terracotta said, "Why do I feel this ends with us getting mauled?"

"Nah," Ramirez said, tapping him on the shoulder. His voice softened just for a second.

"You've got that necklace now. Maybe some of my luck rubbed off."

Terracotta drew in a breath, the weight of the drumsticks heavy against his heart. Together, they stepped forward, swallowed by the silence.

Ramirez and Dr. Terracotta stepped out of the Hall of Silence and into the arena. The air carried a heavy, stinging stench of sulfur and burning flesh that clawed at their throats, prickling their skin. Bones littered the sand, crunching underfoot like dry fall leaves. Blackened crystal shards jutted from the ground, glinting in eerie flickers of light. Acid hissed from craters, sending faint plumes into the air that shimmered with an otherworldly iridescence.

In the center, Roo knelt beside President Davidson's lifeless body. Madison and Savannah clung to him, trembling, their sobs drowned by the thunder of the crowd. The sound wasn't just noise—it reverberated in their chests, a living storm demanding more blood.

Terracotta froze, fists clenched at his sides and shoulders tense.

Ramirez, stepping closer, placed a steady hand on his shoulder, his voice quiet but firm. "Keep it together, Doc. They want us to break."

Terracotta nodded, though the strain on his face betrayed him.

Ramirez moved forward, each step deliberate and measured. Roo looked up as Ramirez approached, his eyes swollen and hollow, his shoulders hunched beneath the weight of his grief. The two men locked eyes for what felt like an eternity, a weighty silence between them: foes on base, rivals on the flight line, and now, against all odds, they were both alive in this nightmare.

Ramirez broke the silence first, his tone stripped of sarcasm.

"You kept them alive, Roo. I was wrong about you back then... all of it. You've got more fight than half the men I served with."

Roo swallowed hard, bowing his head again. His voice cracked.

"I couldn't save him."

Ramirez's jaw flexed. He glanced at Davidson's still form, then laid a hand on Roo's shoulder. "Doesn't matter, brother. You stood your ground. That's what he'd remember."

Madison clutched at his sleeve then, her eyes red and wet.

"We can't leave him here," she said, her voice breaking.

Ramirez crouched, balancing on the balls of his feet, and his sharp expression softened as he looked at Madison and Savannah. He reached out and brushed a strand of hair back from Savannah's face with surprising gentleness.

"Listen. Your dad would be proud you're still standing. Keep walking, no matter what. That's how you honor him."

For the first time, the girls nodded through their tears, clinging to each other tighter. Roo's hand closed around theirs, steadying them.

Only then did Ramirez push himself to his feet, the mask of swagger sliding back into place.

At the far end of the arena, the Architect rose on his throne. His robes rippled, as if stirred by a wind no one else felt. His Four Hands stood like statues at his side, eyes cold and unreadable.

"Ah, the drummer arrives," the Architect bellowed, his voice carrying with unnatural clarity.

Ramirez squared his shoulders and smirked, brushing the dust from his clothes. "Nice to know I've got a fan."

The Architect's lips curved into something that wasn't quite a smile.

"Are you ready to perform, little drummer? Show us if your defiance carries any meaning... or if it's as hollow as the sound you'll make."

Ramirez glanced around the arena. "What, no regular kit? Guess I'll have to improvise."

The Architect's hand twitched. Hounds slunk from the shadows, dragging grotesque drums behind them, crafted from stretched skins, cracked bone frames, and glinting shards of metal. They dropped them at Ramirez's feet like offerings to a twisted god, the air thick with a strange, pulsing energy.

Ramirez crouched, kicking one of the drums. The hollow, discordant sound rattled up through his boot. His smirk faltered for a split second, but he covered it with a quip. "Who tunes these things? I want a refund."

The Architect's voice cracked like a whip. "Play, or the next sound you hear will be your friend's final breath."

Terracotta stiffened, fingers brushing the necklace Ramirez had given him.

Ramirez lifted his hands in mock surrender, the grin curling back. "Alright, alright. Don't get touchy."

He knelt among the warped instruments, running his fingers over their surfaces and testing their resonance by tapping one and then another. His eyes narrowed with concentration, and a grin returned— brimming with intent.

Terracotta's voice was tight. "You're not serious. These?"

Ramirez flicked him a glance. "Got a better idea, Doc?" He twirled the mallets handed to him by the hounds. "Didn't think so. Just... keep your eyes on the big guy."

The Architect's patience was thinning, his eyes narrowing as Ramirez picked up the mallets. He twirled them again, then struck the first note.

The air vibrated with an ugly sound—jagged and discordant notes clawed at the ears. The crowd, a sea of faces, hissed and jeered, their voices a harsh, collective rasp. Ramirez's grip, slick with sweat, faltered; the mallets felt loose, slipping in his palms. His heart hammered a frantic rhythm against his ribs, a panicked drumbeat.

"Steady," Terracotta said, clutching the golden drumsticks at his chest. A pressure built within him, a feeling more than a thought. His hand acted on its own, delving into his bag. The tape

479

recorder emerged. His thumb hesitated, then hit record. The click was loud, as if the arena itself wanted him to preserve the instant.

"You've got this," he said, voice trembling despite the words. His hands shook as they gripped the recorder.

Ramirez squeezed his eyes shut, inhaled, and struck. The next notes were harsh, stumbling—but vibrant. A rhythm emerged, odd and flawed, yet purposeful. The crowd's roar lessened, the very air seeming to lean in, hushed, to listen.

The hounds twitched first. Snarls ebbed into whines. Their massive heads swayed as if the sound tugged invisible strings inside their skulls.

Terracotta's chest tightened as the tape rolled. He didn't decide to say it; the words spilled out like a revelation. "It's not noise. It's order... It's the key."

The phrase hit Ramirez like lightning. His hands faltered for half a beat, and then memory crashed over him—the Hall of Silence, the suffocating stillness, the man in the purple robes.

Your rhythm will silence them. Your sacrifice will save them all.

His chest clenched. He had dismissed those words as riddles, but now they rang true. His rhythm wasn't just defiance; it was salvation.

Terracotta edged toward Roo and the girls, clutching the necklace as if it were a lifeline. "Keep going!" he yelled, his voice breaking.

Ramirez's jaw set. He leaned into the drums, striking them harder and faster. "Silence them," he said to himself, voice raw with determination.

The arena bent to the sound as the hounds rocked like puppets on strings. The crowd's cries dulled into murmurs, their movements sluggish, like sleepers caught between dreams. Even the Architect's Four Hands shifted, their eyes flickering with something close to doubt.

Ramirez's heartbeat matched the rhythm. He wasn't afraid anymore. A defiant grin spread across his face.

He cast a glance toward Terracotta, caught his eye, and winked.

"Guess you were right, purple dude," he said, voice dripping with swagger. "Let's see how far this rhythm can take us."

The Architect's roar cracked across the arena like thunder in a tomb.

"Enough!"

The sound buckled for an instant, but Ramirez only struck harder, pouring every shred of himself into the cadence. The drums answered, alive with a will of their own, drowning out the fury of gods and monsters.

Your sacrifice will save them all.

Ramirez looked once more toward the group, huddled behind the curtain of his rhythm. Terracotta clutched the recorder like scripture. A faint smirk tugged at his lips, but his eyes told the truth... he knew.

"Yeah," he said, voice swallowed by the beat. "Guess it's up to me to finish the show."

The chaos of the arena thundered around them, drumbeats still reverberating, the Architect's rage echoing like a storm. Amid the noise, a figure emerged, striding with quiet authority. The man in the purple robes raised the Staff of Enoch, its carvings glowing gold, pushing back the tide of shadow with a veil of golden light.

Madison and Savannah clung to Davidson's body, sobbing.

"We can't leave him!" Madison's cry tore through the arena.

Ash and grief streaked Roo's face. He steadied Madison with a hand. "We're not leaving him. I swear it."

481

The robed man's voice cut through, calm but commanding. "Move. Now. The light will hold, but not for long."

Roo heaved Davidson's body over his shoulders, grunting with effort. Lizzie stepped in to help steady the load, but Roo shook his head and adjusted Davidson's weight.

"This is my burden. Keep the others safe."

The group ran beneath the veil of golden light, their footsteps disappearing into the sand. Behind them, the Architect's fury cracked like thunder.

"You dare defy me?! You think you can steal my prize? I will show you the futility of defiance!"

He leaped from his throne, landing on the arena floor, the impact causing a tremor that freed some hounds from Ramirez's control.

Ramirez stayed by the warped drums, mallets loose in his grip. He stood tall as the Architect advanced, his grin still sharp.

"You're going to miss me when I'm gone, big guy."

The Architect's shadow fell over him, vast and consuming. His hand wrapped around Ramirez's throat, lifting him into the air like a broken doll.

Ramirez smirked, his lips twisting as his eyes darted from Terracotta at the gates to the girls around Roo, and then to Roo himself, struggling under Davidson's weight. For a moment, his face softened. Then, with a sharp grin, he turned back to his killer.

"You've got anger issues, you know that?"

The Architect's snarl was answer enough. With a sickening crack, Ramirez's neck gave way. His body crumpled to the ground.

Death wasn't enough. The Architect lifted the Staff of Eden, and it pulsed with dark energy. Shadows swarmed like starving insects, stripping flesh from bone until nothing remained but gleaming ivory.

The Architect bent and lifted the skull, holding it aloft with something almost reverent, but twisted. He fixed it to the staff alongside the others, its hollow sockets burning like a warning.

"I will always remember your defiance," he said, his voice cold as eternity.

At the arena gates, Dr. Terracotta turned just in time to see Ramirez's bones claimed. A sound ripped loose—his scream, jagged and desperate, burning through the chaos. Lizzie seized his arms, dragging him, while Roo shouted for him to move, but he fought against them, eyes wild, shattered at the sight of his fallen friend.

Behind them, the man in the purple robes lowered his head. For one fleeting second, the golden glow of the Staff of Enoch dimmed, as though even the heavens mourned.

The group charged through the gates into the desolate landscape, gasping for air but maintaining their speed. Roo staggered under Davidson's weight, but his legs didn't fail him. The air outside was cooler, sharp with the bitter scent of ash and ruin.

Before they could catch their breath, two figures emerged from the shadows. Purple robes billowed, staffs striking the ground in unison. A radiant barrier flared upward, sealing the arena gates in a wall of shimmering light.

The group froze, their eyes wide. Lizzie's whisper carried across the air.

"There's... three of them?"

The first robed figure stepped forward, deliberate and steady. He approached Roo, who had laid Davidson's body down to rest, his face pale and streaked with sweat. The figure placed a hand on his shoulder, his voice calm and resolute. "You have done well. The trials ahead will demand the same strength. Their sacrifices have given you time. Use it."

Roo met the man's eyes, grief softening for a heartbeat. He nodded, then lifted Davidson's body once more.

"This is mine to carry," he said, refusing the man's hand. "Keep the others safe."

The group pressed on until the arena was a fading silhouette on the horizon, its glow distorted by the veil of light. At last, Roo lowered Davidson's body, collapsing to his knees beside it. His chest heaved as he clutched the scroll given to him like a lifeline, its edges biting into his palm.

They gathered in a circle—pale, ash-streaked, and broken. Madison and Savannah leaned against Lizzie, their small shoulders trembling.

Terracotta stood apart, his gaze fixed on the shimmering barrier behind them. His hands shook as they touched the golden drumsticks Ramirez had given him. The faintest trace of rhythm seemed to thrum in the metal, echoing against his pulse.

When he turned, his voice was quiet, but it cut the silence clean.

"I spent my life hiding. Surviving by staying in the shadows. Doing whatever it took not to be noticed." He shook his head, a bitter laugh catching in his throat.

"But Ramirez... Ramirez was never like that. He didn't just survive. He threw himself into the fire every time with that damn grin on his face, like he knew something the rest of us didn't."

He stepped closer, fingers tightening on the drumsticks.

"In the Hall of Silence, he told me I'd make it through. That I was the one who saw good in people, who would figure out the why. I didn't believe him. Not until right now." His voice cracked, but he steadied himself. "Ramirez wasn't just a fighter. He was a friend. He found humor in everything—in madness, in chaos, even in defiance. Today... he sacrificed his life for us."

Terracotta's eyes swept the group, lingering on Roo, who bowed his head over Davidson's body.

"They built the Terracotta Army to guard an emperor in death, but Ramirez wasn't a guard. He wasn't stone. He was flesh, blood, and spirit—and he fought for life... for ours." Terracotta's voice dropped to a whisper. "Now we are his army. We carry his rhythm forward. He was my Terracotta Drummer, and we will remember his legacy."

He put a hand on Roo's shoulder. "He gave us time. Let's not waste it."

The circle fell silent, the weight of his words pressing into their bones. Roo tightened his grip on the scroll, his eyes burning with new resolve.

"We will. For Ramirez, President Davidson, and all of us."

The words hung in the air, carried off by the wind. Behind them, the Architect's enraged roar echoed, promising no mercy. Ahead lay only silence. The group pressed on, into the wasteland, each step heavier, the kind that lingered like grief.

CHAPTER THIRTY-SIX

Lamentations

The group trudged forward, the weight of their escape pressing on their shoulders. Their clothes hung heavy with sweat and dust. No one spoke. Each stride felt like a betrayal of those left.

The purple robes moved ahead, their pace unhurried but deliberate. A gust of cool, damp air met them at the mouth of an intricate cave system, brushing against sweat-streaked faces like the whisper of a ghost.

One of the purple-robed men looked back and raised his hand.

"This way," he said, his voice echoing in the hollow quiet.

The overwhelming heat and disorder of the arena shifted to a more frigid atmosphere, a stillness unlike any other. The cave walls shimmered with ancient runes carved deep into the stone, their shapes twitching and shifting like something alive just beneath the surface. A hum pulsed through the air, low and constant, like a heartbeat or a warning.

Dr. Terracotta's fingertips danced over the symbols, illuminating a faint glow. His face was a mask, eyes wide and fixed, jaw clenched tight. A flicker, like a hidden flame, danced behind his lenses.

"This energy..." he said, "it's like nothing I've seen before."

Lizzie glanced over her shoulder, her voice more than a whisper.

"Is that good or bad?"

Before he could answer, the purple-robed guide spoke again, in a measured tone, but something in it felt... heavy. "The Architect cannot reach us here, but his eyes are everywhere. A beacon shields us... for now."

The group exchanged glances, and nobody dared to ask what would happen if the beacon failed.

At the heart of the cave, the group found a towering structure of luminous stone. Its jagged edges clawed upward at erratic angles—chaotic yet deliberate. A dense, protective energy pressed on their skin like unseen hands. The air crackled, heavy with static and the smell of something ancient.

Dr. Terracotta stepped forward, drawn as if pulled by gravity. "This..."

His voice caught in his throat, the words dying before they could form. He adjusted his glasses, his fingers trembling as he felt the cool metal frames against his skin. "This is like what Heliosa said about Stonehenge... but more intense."

One of the purple-robed figures gave a slow nod. "Its purpose is the same. To block the Architect's reach, but even this cannot hold forever."

Lizzie folded her arms, chin lifting in defiance. "So, what? We're just buying time?"

The purple-robed figure turned toward her. His face remained cloaked in shadow, but his voice carried a strange blend of sorrow and certainty. "Time is what you need. I have given you time."

The hum of the beacon deepened, as though reacting to his words.

A sudden bark shattered the heavy silence, followed by the rapid clatter of claws against stone.

Brutus burst into the chamber like a cannonball of joy, his knobby tail wagging in broad, erratic sweeps as he darted from one stunned face to the next.

Roo was the first to react. "Brutus?!"

The dog froze mid-step at the sound of his name, ears perked. He pivoted, eyes locked on Roo, and then bolted into his arms.

Roo dropped to his knees, wrapping his arms around the dog's thick neck. "Good to see you, buddy."

Brutus responded with a happy whine and his tongue lolling.

Lizzie smiled, arms crossed, voice softening. "Looks like you've got yourself a shadow."

Roo gave a faint laugh, the first since they'd escaped. "Best I've ever had."

Behind them, Dr. Terracotta let out a brief chuckle. For a moment, the tension in his shoulders eased. "Of all the things to survive that chaos... of course it's him."

As his gaze lingered on the joyful reunion, something flickered behind his glasses, a shadow of grief trying to claw its way forward.

A quiet rustle stirred the silence as one of the purple robes stepped forward. He lowered his hood, revealing a weathered yet composed face. His skin was dark and sun-worn, his eyes piercing, an impossible blue—ancient as the ages themselves. They glimmered in the runic glow, resembling one that had witnessed much and held faith.

He said nothing at first. He waited until everyone faced him, their grief heavy in the air, before speaking. "I am Enoch... Enoch the Last."

The name settled over them like a forgotten hymn remembered. None of them understood its weight, but they felt it all the same—ancient, inevitable, and heavy with prophecy.

Enoch's gaze moved across their faces, then settled on the necklace still clutched in Dr. Terracotta's hand. "He gave that to you."

Terracotta didn't look up. He stared at the metallic drumstick charm, his knuckles white from gripping it so tight. "He said it was for luck," Terracotta said. "But it didn't save him."

Enoch knelt, not before the group but beside Terracotta. His gaze carried only understanding, the kind that bore weight without the stain of pity. "No. It didn't, but it gave you something far greater than luck. It gave you a piece of him."

Terracotta turned away, his shoulders shaking.

Enoch stood upright, observing the group. "Grief rings with love's unsaid words. Let it speak. Let it ache." His eyes swept the group once more. "You are hurting and have every right to." He paused, letting the silence settle before he continued. "Understand this... your survival holds a purpose."

The words floated in the air like delicate petals, waiting to be carried away by a gentle breeze.

"The prophecy... still breathes."

He stepped back without another word, his figure folding once again into the shadows cast by the flickering cave walls.

Brutus nudged Roo, his warm, furry presence grounding him. Roo reached down, fingers threading through the coarse fur, trying to find stillness in the storm of his thoughts. The simple gesture brought a flicker of calm.

Lizzie broke the silence first, her voice small and hollow. "So... we just keep moving forward? Is that it?" Her words floated in the air like ash.

Enoch stepped forward from the shadows. "Forward is the only way," he said. "But not without honoring those who lit the path first."

Lizzie's jaw tightened, her voice sharper than the silence around them. "If you were guiding this the whole time... why did you let so many die? Why Davidson and Ramirez?"

Dr. Solomon glanced at her, his expression caught between agreement and caution. The question hung like a blade in the air.

Enoch didn't flinch. His voice was steady, threaded with sorrow but unshaken. "Because it was not time for you to rise. You had to see the cost and to bleed, to lose and to break... only then would you understand what must come next." His eyes swept across them, ancient and unyielding. "You were not ready before. You are now."

Roo looked up. He knew what Enoch meant. The fire inside him, the one Davidson had sparked in those last moments, was still burning. Underneath it, terrible grief churned.

Enoch gestured deeper into the cave, toward a domed chamber bathed in the runic light. At the center stood a raised platform of smooth stone, surrounded by jagged, ancient monoliths, like watchers of a forgotten age.

"Prepare the pyre," Enoch said. "Let this place bear witness to the end of the Eagle's flight... and the burden he passed on."

They worked in silence. There were no rituals or hymns. Just hands placing kindling and stones arranged with reverence. A body wrapped in cloth and carried with the care of unspoken gratitude.

President Davidson lay at the center of the pyre, his hands crossed, the faded seal of the United States stitched over his chest.

Only the memory of Ramirez remained. There might not have been a body, but that didn't stop the grieving.

One by one, they came forward.

Lizzie placed a butterfly pin the girls had given her onto Davidson's chest, then whispered so only the fire could hear, "You gave us hope when we had none. Thank you."

Savannah and Madison stepped forward together, each holding a small wildflower they had gathered from the sparse weeds near the cave's edge. Their hands trembled.

They knelt beside the pyre.

Savannah placed her flower first, her lips quivering as she stared down at the cloth-wrapped figure. "You told us to be brave," she said. "Even when you were scared." Her voice broke. She bit her lip hard, trying to keep it together.

Madison set her flower down beside her sister's hand and then clutched Savannah's hand tightly. Her eyes brimmed with tears but didn't fall. "We miss you," Madison said. "We miss both of you."

A heavy, suffocating silence hung in the air. And then, softer than a gentle breeze, almost inaudible, "It's not fair."

Savannah nodded, her voice cracking into sobs. "It's not fair at all..."

Madison leaned her head against her sister's. They knelt together like that; grief and love wrapped around each other.

Just then, two butterflies emerged from the shadows above.

They drifted downward from the mouth of a narrow crack in the cave ceiling, wings glowing in the flickering firelight. They circled once above the girls' heads... then rose and vanished into the runes etched into the stone above.

No one spoke, but everyone saw, even Enoch.

His piercing blue eyes followed their ascent, the faintest smile tugging at the corner of his mouth. His silence was accompanied by a physical change, his posture softening with a lowered chin and relaxed shoulders, as though recognizing an undeniable revelation.

For a fleeting heartbeat, he looked not at the fire nor the pyre but at Madison and Savannah.

It wasn't a smile of comfort but of recognition. He knew.

Dr. Terracotta approached, eyes red-rimmed and breath shallow. In one hand, he held a small, polished American flag lapel pin. In the other, he clenched the drumstick necklace Ramirez had given him, clutching it like breath.

He stopped beside Davidson's body, staring down for a long time before speaking. "You were the first leader I ever trusted," he said. He swallowed hard and placed the lapel pin on Davidson's chest. "You gave us purpose and hope. You were a good man." His hand lingered on the pin for a moment longer before his body tensed. He turned away from the pyre but didn't leave. He took a few steps back, then dropped to his knees, clutching the necklace tight against his chest.

That's when it hit him. "Ramirez..." The name fell from his lips like both a prayer and a wound. "I hated him at first. He made my life a living hell." Terracotta's voice trembled, his chest rising and falling with each word. "In the end... I saw who he was. We shared a love of music. He apologized and meant it. Somehow... we became friends."

His voice cracked, unraveling into something raw and splintered. "He didn't care about the facade, about who I presented myself to be. He saw right through it all, and he gave me this..." The necklace was clutched to his heart. "... said it would bring me luck." His breath hitched. "I did nothing, though, when he needed me."

His face twisted as sobs overtook him, deep, gut-wrenching sobs that echoed through the chamber like thunder in a tomb.

"He's gone. I didn't even get to say goodbye." He dropped further into his knees, curling in on himself, the necklace clenched in his hand, the metal biting into his skin.

Roo moved first, kneeling beside him, arms wrapping around his friend.

Madison and Savannah followed. One took his hand. The other rested her forehead against his back.

They said nothing. They didn't need to.

Roo tightened his hold on Terracotta's shoulder, his voice low and steady. "We were wrong about Ramirez," Roo said. "He was tough on us, no doubt... but when it mattered, he was on our side. He saved us. We're alive because of him. He will be remembered as a hero, not the bully we thought he was."

Terracotta's sobs quieted, the storm easing into ragged breaths. His grip on the necklace loosened just enough for the pain in his hand to fade. He gave a small nod, though his eyes stayed shut tight.

When the silence returned, Roo rose to his feet and stepped forward. He knelt beside Davidson's body; the scroll he gave him clutched in his hands. He unrolled it, not to read but to feel the weight of what it represented. The firelight danced across the parchment, casting strange shadows across his face.

"You believed in me," he said. "Even when I didn't."

He traced the edge of the scroll with his fingers, then looked down at the man who had pulled him out of darkness and handed him purpose. "I don't know if I can be the man you hoped for, but I'll try. I'll carry this... for as long as it takes."

He turned toward Madison and Savannah, standing together, their eyes red and swollen. Roo's voice dropped, solemn but resolute. "They're your daughters. Your legacy. I swear to you I'll protect them. Whatever it takes. No matter the cost."

493

His eyes lingered on the girls, their small hands clutching each other for strength. A shadow flickered across his face as another child and another memory gathered in his thoughts.

Jefferson.

The laughter on the playground and the sickening fall. His brother's lifeless body, and the guilt that had stalked him ever since.

Roo's throat tightened. He turned back to Davidson, his voice breaking but fierce. "They won't meet the same fate as Jefferson. I won't let that happen again. They will never fall like he did." His hand pressed firmly against the butterfly pin on Davidson's chest. "I couldn't save you... but I'll keep them safe. I swear it."

He tucked the scroll back into his pocket. "We'll finish this. I promise."

Dr. Solomon lingered near the edge of the pyre, hands clasped, eyes reflecting the firelight. The loss cut deeper than rank or duty — Davidson had been his charge, his friend, and the soul he'd sworn to keep steady when the burden of the world grew too heavy.

He drew in a slow, trembling breath and spoke softly — delivering his farewell to a friend and a brother in faith.

"You came to me with questions, not orders, sought faith when others sought power, and carried the weight of a nation and never let it break you."

The flames flickered in his eyes as he lifted his gaze toward the smoke rising through the runes above.

"May the Creator remember your mercy and forgive your doubt. And may He find you now — free of fear and a man of unwavering faith."

He lowered his head, letting silence finish what his words could not.

494

The pyre was lit.

Flames rose in silence. There were no sounds from the group. Just Brutus, sitting beside Roo, ears low, eyes fixed on the fire like he understood everything.

The wood cracked and hissed. The smoke climbed high into the cavern above, curling into the runes like ancient prayers being awakened.

And as the last sparks rose into the air, Enoch stepped forward once more, his voice rising above the dying flames.

"Many lives were taken." He took a moment to look at the group. "But many more... will rise."

CHAPTER THIRTY-SEVEN

Gospel of Enoch

The fire from Davidson's pyre still crackled in their ears, even as its light faded behind them. The cave dimmed, and with it, the sounds of grief settled into silence.

Enoch stepped forward, his robes catching the flicker of the dying fire. "You three," he said as he pointed to Roo, Lizzie, and Dr. Solomon, his voice low but unwavering, "come with me. The climb is long... but you must make it to understand."

Roo, Lizzie, and Dr. Solomon shared a look. The feeling hung in the air, a foot in the past, the other venturing forward.

Enoch turned without another word and walked toward a narrow passage hidden behind the shimmer of a rune-marked wall. As he moved, the markings glowed, revealing a steep stone path that twisted upward into darkness. A stiff wind funneled from above, carrying with it a faint but ancient hum.

Roo stepped forward, but then he paused. He turned back, eyes locking onto Madison and Savannah, who sat quietly near Brutus, their small hands still clasped together in the fading light.

"I'm not leaving them," Roo said, voice firm.

Enoch didn't hesitate. He looked over his shoulder and offered a calm nod. "My brothers will remain. No one will harm the butterflies. Not here."

The other two purple robes stepped forward silently, their heads slightly bowed as if they had already heard this exchange before it happened.

Reassured but still wary, Roo exhaled and turned back to the rising path. "Alright," he said, "let's climb."

As their footsteps faded into the stone, the cavern behind them became silent. Roo, Lizzie, and Dr. Solomon disappeared into the twisting climb behind Enoch, the stone swallowing the last flickers of light. The air was still. The weight of what lay ahead pressed down—unseen but undeniable.

*　*　*

Far beyond the cave, across the scorched wastelands of a fractured Earth, the Architect stood alone in the black heart of his throne room.

The silence was absolute.

The Staff of Eden pulsed faintly in his grasp, casting jagged, angular shadows across the walls etched with dying light. Suspended before him, a fractured holographic map flickered and groaned—a broken echo of the world as it once was. Cities throbbed red like open wounds. Vast regions blinked with static; entire nations reduced to memory. Borders had vanished. Empires had crumbled. Civilization now teetered on the brink of final collapse.

Four new symbols ignited on the map. Dim... but steady.

The Architect's eyes narrowed. "Let them gather their Nine and find their weapons. It changes nothing."

Behind him, his four hands stood in reverent silence, heads bowed.

"They rise. Believers who serve the past. Raiders who feed on fear. The loyal still hear the Herald, and the hollow ones..." The Architect's lips curled into a smile. "Let them rise. All of them. The more paths they walk, the more they splinter. They splinter because they still believe they have a choice, but all paths lead back to Eden—and to me."

He turned from the map and raised the Staff of Eden. The runes on the walls dimmed as the staff drank the room's light.

"In the end... they will kneel."

*   *   *

The wind howled through the jagged teeth of the mountain pass, biting at their clothes as Roo, Lizzie, and Dr. Solomon followed Enoch up a winding, rocky trail. Each step away from the others felt heavier than the last. Behind them, the warmth of the funeral pyre still smoldered in memory, and Brutus's quiet whine echoed in Roo's ears.

Enoch led without a word, his purple robes trailing like a ghost behind him.

The trail curved sharply, revealing a massive stone arch jutting from the mountainside. The markings seemed to be a natural part of the stone, as if they'd always been there.

Beyond the arch, a vast cavern yawned open, its mouth cloaked in shadows.

Enoch stopped and turned to them. "The Cavern of the Comets," he said. "Where the sky once touched the earth and Enoch first heard the voice of the stars."

A low hum stirred beneath their feet.

Dr. Solomon narrowed his eyes. "What exactly are we meant to find inside?"

Enoch stepped into the dark. "Understanding."

Roo didn't speak. He watched the entrance, his heart thudding strangely in his chest. Something about this place pulled at him, piquing his curiosity.

As Enoch vanished into the mouth of the cavern, the group followed.

The air grew warmer as they stepped deeper in. A soft glow radiated from the walls themselves—etched in swirling patterns that pulsed faintly with violet light. The air tasted metallic and old, like the inside of a forgotten tomb.

Enoch walked ahead in silence, torchlight catching the curve of his hood. At the end of the corridor, the space widened dramatically into a vaulted chamber.

The group stepped in... and stopped.

The far wall rose at least fifty feet high, a sheer face of smooth, dark stone. Etched into it were twelve names—stacked vertically in a single winding column. Each name glowed softly, its light pulsing in rhythm like the beat of a cosmic heart. Between the names were symbols: stars, comets, suns, and eyes, each one telling a part of their journey.

Lizzie exhaled, breath fogging in the air. "What... is this?"

Enoch approached the base of the wall. "The Lineage of the Robe. Every one of us, from the first to the final three."

He reached out and touched the lowest name, his own. It gleamed softly under his fingers.

"We do not choose this path. The comet chooses us."

He began tracing upward, name by name, as he recited them aloud. "Enoch the First. The one who walked with the Creator."

"Echon, scribe of the prophecy."

"Noche, the voice in the wilderness."

"Cheno. Honec. Onche..."

With each name, the glow on the wall flickered and danced, as if stirred by the sound of their lineage being remembered.

Dr. Solomon stepped closer, captivated. "They're all anagrams."

Enoch nodded. "All but the first and the last. Enoch was the beginning, and I am the last. The rest of them... echoes."

Roo glanced sideways at Lizzie. "If this is real... then this line goes back thousands of years."

Enoch didn't look at him. "It goes back to the beginning, and it will end with us."

That thought settled like dust.

Lizzie walked up beside the wall, eyes following the trail of light as Enoch's finger rose higher.

"You've all just... waited? For what?"

Enoch turned to her. "For the Nine to rise and the prophecy to begin. Each of us had a part to play. Most knew they would never live to see the prophecy fulfilled." He stepped back and looked up at the wall—at the twelve names, some glowing, others dim, all part of a single unbroken chain. "Now," he said, "the comet no longer chooses."

Dr. Solomon frowned. "What do you mean?"

Enoch's voice, now softer, barely a whisper, hung in the air. "There will be no more purple robes after us."

A chamber opened before them—circular and wide, with smooth stone walls that echoed the slightest breath—in the center stood a pedestal of violet crystal, its surface pulsing with a slow, ancient heartbeat. Upon it sat a massive tome, its cover wrapped in preserved violet cloth, so dark it was nearly black.

Enoch approached with reverence, his footsteps echoing as if the chamber itself were listening. He looked at Dr. Solomon. "You have questions," he said. "The answers are there." Enoch pointed to the tome sitting on the pedestal.

With slow, deliberate hands, Enoch unwrapped the cloth, revealing the tome. Its cover shimmered with an otherworldly luminescence, like polished obsidian and pearl, reflecting an ethereal light. Inlaid on the surface was a symbol of three comets arcing in parallel over a tree with twelve branches.

"The Gospel of Enoch," he said. "Our truth."

Solomon stepped forward, his hands trembling as he opened the book. Illuminated with shifting cosmic maps, sacred diagrams, and celestial charts, the pages were thick and textured, their inks rich, almost glowing. The language was ancient... but somehow, he understood.

"I can read this," he said. "But I don't know how."

Enoch gave a knowing nod. "Because they intended it for you."

Solomon turned the pages slowly. On one, a great comet blazed through the sky, arcing above a fractured world. A name was written beneath it in a bold golden script.

ENΩKH'S COMET

The next page showed a more ominous sight: three comets, side by side, trailing fire across a night sky filled with weeping stars. Beneath it, the words: THE TRINITY COMET–THE LAST SIGNAL.

His voice broke the silence as he read aloud. "Once every two thousand years, the Trinity Comet returns. Between those ages, a single comet—Enoch's Comet—appears in the heavens to mark the rise of each new Purple Robe. One light for one keeper, nine in all. But when three comets burn together, it is no mere birth; it is the reckoning. The Trinity Comet ends the line and awakens the final three robes—and the Trinity."

He paused, then looked up at Enoch.

"That's how you knew... When to set everything in motion? To find us... Why we're important?"

Enoch answered only with a slow, solemn nod.

Lizzie leaned over his shoulder, her eyes wide. "It's beautiful," she said.

Solomon flipped further. The Gospel spoke of the Nine Trials, Remnants of the First Genesis, and the forging of an ultimate weapon to pierce the veil and defeat the Architect.

The last section caught his eye—far more cryptic than the rest. The image was of a man standing between three great doors. A phrase written in starlight appeared overhead.

The Conduit shall rise... He who hears the Whispers of Zion.

Solomon looked up, his voice hushed. "This was written long before any of us were born."

Enoch stepped beside him. "It was written when time still answered to the Creator."

Solomon closed the book carefully, his eyes still wide with wonder. "How much of it is true?"

Enoch looked toward the glowing crystal beneath the pedestal, its light reflecting off the walls like trapped starlight. "All of it."

Solomon's hands trembled as he rested the Gospel of Enoch on the pedestal, fingers lingering on its cover as though anchoring himself to the weight of its revelations. His breath came shallow, as if the air itself had thickened. He stepped back from the pedestal, clutching the edge to steady himself.

"This isn't just prophecy," he said. "It's divine blueprints. Scripture before scripture."

Lizzie placed a hand on his back, steadying him.

Dr. Solomon looked at Enoch, his voice cracking. "I've studied the Word my entire life, given sermons and written essays. I thought I knew the story... but this rewrites the foundation."

Enoch stepped forward, his voice low and resolute. "It does not rewrite it, Solomon. It exposes what was hidden. What the world wasn't ready to see."

Solomon stared into the torchlight, eyes unfocused. "All this time... I believed faith was the root of strength. What if it's always been memory?"

Enoch placed a hand on the pedestal beside the Gospel. "The Architect seeks to sever that memory. To erase the line from Eden to this moment."

He stepped to the side of the chamber and gestured toward a sealed alcove. With a slow movement of his hand, the stone parted, revealing a raised slab of onyx. Upon it rested a sword unlike any forged by man.

It shimmered like flowing metal, shifting between silver and shadow, its blade etched with divine symbols that danced like starlight on water.

Lizzie's breath caught. "What... is that?"

Enoch's voice, ancient and echoing, spoke words that seemed older than time itself. "The blade of Goliath—the First Nephilim. It was not hubris that forged it but divine hands. The Creator Himself shaped its form from the breath of the stars. It has been waiting... for this hour."

Dr. Solomon stepped closer, awe carved into his features. "David never used this. He defeated Goliath with a stone."

503

Enoch nodded. "A stone unlike any other. The Rock of Ages. Perfect, whole, and untouched by time or darkness. David gave it to Enoch the First before he vanished from history. He said, 'Keep it hidden. It will find its hand when the time is right.' So, it waits, even now."

Solomon turned to look at Roo, who appeared visibly shaken, and then he looked back at Enoch. "What about this prophecy? It speaks of Nine and of Trials and remnants."

Enoch nodded solemnly. "There are trials ahead meant to awaken the truth within each bloodline. To stand against the Architect's final veil, you will need more than courage. You will need the Remnants of the First Genesis."

Lizzie raised an eyebrow. "Remnants?"

Enoch gestured toward the sword again. "This is but one. Scattered across the world are the others; artifacts infused with the Creator's essence. They must be reunited. Only then can the Spear of Genesis be forged. The only weapon capable of piercing the heart of the Architect."

"What about the scroll that was given to me?" Roo asked, almost afraid to speak.

Enoch turned to him, his eyes piercing. "The Scrolls of Destiny are the map to these remnants. There are nine. You carry the first."

Roo instinctively reached into his pocket, pulling out the scroll President Davidson had entrusted him with. The edges were worn; the surface covered in swirling etchings that refused to stay still.

"It hasn't shown me anything."

Enoch smiled faintly. "The scroll reveals itself when the bearer is ready. The path cannot be forced."

Roo stared down at the scroll, a flicker of something ancient whispering in the back of his mind.

The chamber seemed to tighten around them as the Gospel of Enoch lay closed upon the pedestal. The flickering torchlight danced across the stone walls, casting long shadows that mirrored the storm now stirring inside each of them.

Enoch let the silence settle, letting the weight of centuries hang between every breath. In a voice laced with both reverence and finality, he spoke. "When the Trinity Comet blazes across the night sky, three bloodlines shall rise to face the dark: One born of the slayer. One born of the song. One born of the fall."

Roo exchanged a look with Lizzie. Dr. Solomon's brow furrowed. The words pressed into them like a blade.

Enoch didn't let the mystery linger. He lifted his hand, pointing first to Roo.

"A father to the butterflies. The bloodline of Cain."

His hand shifted to Solomon. "The son of Goliath. The bloodline of the Nephilim."

His eyes locked on Lizzie, and his voice deepened with reverence. "The spirit of David. The bloodline of the king."

He lowered his hand, the firelight catching his impossible blue eyes.

"The Father, the Son, and the Spirit. The Trinity was reborn in flesh, and with you, the prophecy still breathes."

The cavern fell into stunned silence. Roo's pulse thundered in his ears. Lizzie's lips parted, but no words came. Solomon staggered back a step, the truth cutting deeper than any blade.

Nothing would ever be the same again.

"You are three of the Nine. Marked by your destiny," he said. "Chosen by inheritance, circumstance... and purpose. The Nine are not complete. Six remain, scattered across a broken world."

He stepped away from the pedestal and walked toward the torchlit edge of the cavern, where the shadows seemed to listen.

"The Architect knows. He hunts them even now. That is why we must move swiftly. The trials await; ancient crucibles meant to reveal and refine those who carry the blood. Only through the trials will the Nine be awakened."

Dr. Solomon swallowed hard. "What if we cannot find them?"

Enoch turned, his expression unreadable. "Then the Nine will remain broken, the Remnants will remain lost, and the Architect will not fall." His hand lifted slightly, gesturing toward the scroll in Roo's pocket. "You already carry the first key. A scroll passed down by the eagle. One scroll of Destiny. Its map will reveal nothing until it is the right time."

Roo's fingers unconsciously tightened around the worn scroll, a quiet resolve beginning to rise within him.

Enoch's gaze shifted between them, the gravity of his mission fully landing on their shoulders. "When the Nine are gathered... and the Remnants reclaimed... they must be forged together. Only then can the veil be pierced. Only then can the Spear of Genesis be born."

The phrase echoed off the cavern walls, ancient and absolute.

Enoch's voice softened. "Know this: the Nine will not walk alone. There are others untouched by prophecy but bound to destiny. The butterflies, the scientist, and the conduit."

Roo glanced toward the cavern entrance, as if sensing them even now.

"They will gather what is broken and carry what is too heavy. When all falls to ruin... They will decide what rises from the ashes."

For a moment, no one moved. The prophecy had shifted from myth to mandate.

Nine to be found, remnants to recover, a veil to tear down and two young girls, once symbols of innocence, would reshape the world.

The mountain wind whispered as they descended the rocky pass, leaving behind the Chamber of the Comets and the truths it unveiled. Roo gripped the scroll tightly, his thoughts still spiraling with prophecy, lineage, and the burden that now lived in his chest.

As they neared the mouth of the cave, the place they had left Madison and Savannah with the two silent robes, an unfamiliar voice broke the silence.

"Well, took you long enough."

The group froze.

A man stood near the fire, arms crossed, a smirk playing on his face. His leather jacket was torn, his boots caked with dried mud, and his eyes were sharp and calculating; they tracked every move. Behind him, a second figure emerged.

"Heliosa?" Lizzie stepped forward in disbelief.

Heliosa looked exhausted but alive. In her arms, she clutched two worn books bound in cloth that shimmered faintly in the firelight: the Testament of Eden and the Journal of Goliath.

"How did you get here?" Lizzie asked.

The man beside her raised his hand in mock surrender. "Relax. I'm the reason she's not dead. You're welcome."

Dr. Solomon stepped protectively in front of Lizzie. "And you?"

"Call me Gus," he said, glancing around. "Though I get the sense that name means nothing to you... yet."

Roo moved closer to the girls. Brutus growled low in his throat, his fur bristling.

Enoch stepped forward, his voice calm but commanding. "He is not what he seems," Enoch said. "But he is where he is meant to be."

Gus raised an eyebrow. "Is that supposed to be comforting?"

507

Enoch gave him a slow nod. "You have a part to play, Gustavo. Even if you do not yet see the stage."

The tension in the cave thinned but didn't vanish. Lizzie kept her eyes on Gus, still uncertain. Roo stepped back toward Madison and Savannah, who watched everything in silence.

"You two alright?" he asked.

They nodded. Roo looked back at the fire, then at Heliosa, and finally at the books. Something was happening. Fate had sent new pieces to the board.

Enoch turned to the group. "Rest now, as the first trial approaches, and with it, the world will shift."

A gust of wind swept through the cave, stirring the ashes from Davidson's funeral pyre into the chilly night air. Roo stood in the center, watching as the flames dwindle, his promise to the girls still echoing in his heart.

Above them, the comet no longer burned, but the fire left behind burned in them all.

So, it began... not with triumph but with fire, ashes, and the trinity—and the weight of nine bloodlines waiting to rise.

The Prophecy will continue in
Bloodlines of Eden: Trials of the Nine

About the Author

M. Bryan Haggard is a U.S. Air Force veteran and lifelong storyteller whose imagination was forged in the cold winds of Alaska. What began as a personal way to confront loss and faith grew into *Bloodlines of Eden*—an epic saga exploring creation, sacrifice, and the battle between light and darkness.

Blending myth, science, and raw emotion, his writing reflects a journey of redemption and resilience.

When he isn't writing, Bryan enjoys spending time with his daughter, traveling the world, and reflecting on the companions—both human and four-legged—who helped shape his story.

He lives in Tennessee, where he continues to expand the *Bloodlines of Eden* universe and the worlds that live beyond it.

Follow his journey on social media @MBryanHaggardAuthor

www.ingramcontent.com/pod-product-compliance
Lightning Source LLC
Chambersburg PA
CBHW061506020726
47502CB00006B/1955